IN THE COURTS OF THE CRIMSON KINGS

Tor Books by S. M. Stirling

The Sky People
In the Courts of the Crimson Kings

IN THE COURTS OF THE
CRIMSON KINGS

S. M. Stirling

 A Tom Doherty Associates Book
New York

This is a work of fiction. All of the characters, organizations, and events portrayed in this novel are either products of the author's imagination or are used fictitiously.

IN THE COURTS OF THE CRIMSON KINGS

Copyright © 2008 by S. M. Stirling

A Tor Book
Published by Tom Doherty Associates, LLC
175 Fifth Avenue
New York, NY 10010

www.tor.com

Tor® is a registered trademark of Tom Doherty Associates, LLC.

Library of Congress Cataloging-in-Publication Data

Stirling, S. M.
    In the courts of the crimson kings / S.M. Stirling.—1st ed.
        p. cm.
    "A Tom Doherty Associates book."
    ISBN-13: 978-0-7653-1489-5
    ISBN-10: 0-7653-1489-4
    1. Mars (Planet)—Fiction. 2. Life on other planets—Fiction. I. Title.
PS3569.T543I6 2008
813'.54—dc22

                                                            2007042151

First Edition: March 2008

Printed in the United States of America

0 9 8 7 6 5 4 3 2 1

TO JAN, MY EMERALD-EYED MUSE

ACKNOWLEDGMENTS

To Melinda Snodgrass, Daniel Abraham, Sage Walker, Emily Mah, Terry England, George R. R. Martin, Walter Jon Williams, Yvonne Coats, Sally Gwylan, Laura Mixon-Gould and Ian Tregillis of Critical Mass, for constant help and advice as the book was under construction, which enabled me to avoid some of the faults I couldn't see. A fish can't see water!

Thanks to Jerry Pournelle for some inside information on matters fannish . . . but he's not to blame for the things I got wrong! And to Mike Ralls Jr. for a suggestion about the prologue.

To the Pulpsters and Golden Age writers, from the author of *Phra the Phoenician* on down, to the creators of Northwest Smith and John Carter; and to P. J. Farmer. For inspiration!

All mistakes, infelicities and errors are, of course, my own.

IN THE COURTS OF THE CRIMSON KINGS

PROLOGUE

World Science Fiction Convention
Chicago, Earth
Labor Day, 1962

Fred sat in the suite's bedroom and sipped his beer. A hot, muggy Midwestern early autumn day was dying outside, but he didn't think he'd gone more than a block from the hotel since he'd arrived. It had been a wild ride of a con: Nobody wanted to talk about anything but the pictures from the Russian probe on Venus, of course. Dinosaurs and Neandertals and beautiful blond cave-princesses in fur bikinis . . . although excitement was building about what the American lander would find on Mars.

He hadn't wanted to talk about anything but the Russian probe on Venus—except what the American probe was going to find on Mars. Orbiters and telescopes over the last few years had seen what looked like structures and cities. There had been evidence as far back as Lowell's investigations in the nineteenth century, and spectroscopes had hinted at free oxygen in the air as far back as the 1920s, but it was all a whole lot more credible after what had been found on Venus. The entire world was holding its breath and waiting, when it wasn't babbling.

Nineteen sixty-two: the year everything changed.

But as his agent had told him, the publishers weren't going to pay *him* to burble, and he had his rent to pay and groceries to buy regardless of whether or not Mars turned out to have intelligent life. Plus, fiction of his sort was going to get a lot more difficult; it had already, in fact. Extrasolar stuff, that was the ticket . . . From now on, books set on Mars and Venus were going to be a variety of . . .

Westerns, he thought. *They'll be like Westerns—like the penny dreadfuls they wrote while the Old West was still going on.*

He'd heard somewhere that Kit Carson had read dime novels about his own supposed adventures while he was *really* a scout and Indian fighter out in the Rockies. And Buffalo Bill had been taking his Wild West show around Europe before the last Indian wars had been fought.

And our astronauts—no, our planetary explorers—will be reading about themselves while they do it; probably watching movies and TV about themselves while they do it. Louis L'Amour and James Michener will horn in on our territory. I don't think the president meant "New Frontier" quite so literally, but that's the way it's turning out.

"Come on, Fred, Carol! They're about to switch from the talking heads to the real pictures!"

He picked up his Tuborg—Poul had brought in a case, saying that the occasion required actual beer, rather than Schlitz—and they walked through into the lounge of the suite. It was crowded, but virtually none of the fans were there. Not today, though that young friend of Beam's was off in a corner, the one doing surveys of the writers for Boeing and the Pentagon.

Someone kicked over a footstool, and he sank his long, lanky frame down on it; Ted had the seat in the middle, right in front, but then he was Guest of Honor. There was an awesome amount of talent in the room now, all the way from Jack—who'd sold his first story to Gernsback in the '20s, for God's sake!—through the Big Bull Gorillas like Bob and Arthur to the postwar crowd of Young Turks like him and Poul and first-timers like young Larry from L.A.

"Amazing we've gone from the first satellite to this in only a little over ten years," Isaac said, looking like a balding Jewish leprechaun as he grinned and rubbed his hands.

"We had the incentive, once they proved Mars had an oxygen atmosphere back in 'forty-seven," Bob replied. "That's why we had von Braun hard at work from the day we caught him, and the Russkis were slave-driving *their* Krauts, too. Without that to push us, we might still be waiting for the first manned mission to orbit, or even the first satellite."

Then, softly: "But we do have the motive. A whole *world*."

"Two," his redheaded wife said sharply. "We're not going to let the Reds have Venus all to themselves, even if they did get the first probe there."

"What's really bloody amazing is that we're going to watch it on TV. In color, worldwide, no less," another writer said, in excruciatingly British tones. "Which is like Ferdinand and Isabella watching Columbus land in a newsreel at the cinema."

"Hell, Arthur, you predicted it fifteen years ago," Poul replied, and they all chuckled. "Or at least you predicted transmission satellites for TV."

"Prediction is becoming less and less attractive, with actual reports from other planets expected daily. I think I'll stick to writing historicals and time-travel from now on and leave the solar system alone," one tall distinguished-looking man with a goatee quipped.

"You lie, Spreggie," Catherine said crisply. "You won't be able to resist it."

Then all sound died; even breathing seemed hushed. The little crackle as someone sucked on a cigarette and added to the blue haze of smoke under the ceiling sounded loud. Walter Cronkite was pontificating on the screen; for once, his solemnly portentous tones matched the occasion, probably for the first time since D-day. Werner von Braun was beside him, looking like a cat with little yellow feathers stuck to his lips . . . well, a man might, when the U.S. government was giving him ten percent of its budget to play with on a lifetime basis. It might be twenty percent, after this, or more.

Fighting over Berlin is starting to look a lot less important. To both sides.

Behind him, a model of the Mars Viking Lander dropped down a hypothetical trajectory and settled on long spidery legs. Half the fans at this convention were wearing Viking helmets with horns. Poul grumbled that the horns weren't historical. A lot of them had added little propellers on top, too.

Bob began: "You know, I had this idea for another Mars book a couple of years ago, about an orphan adopted by Martians, but then the preliminary orbital telescope reports came in and I didn't dare—"

"*Now!*" someone else said. "Everyone shut up!"

The color screen flickered, showed snow. A groan started, then cut off abruptly as the picture cleared save for a few rastor lines; smoke faded away, blown by a stiff wind. Someone swore softly. The ground in front of the lander was a plain covered in low-growing reddish-green plants.

"Mars, Commie-Colored Cabbage Planet," someone said.

That brought a brief nervous chuckle. The ground cover *did* look a little like splayed-open cabbages with thick waxy leaves the color of dirty rust. Here and there was a reddish-gray shrub covered in white flowers. Neither seemed to want to burn; the circular fire set by the rockets died quickly.

The vegetation rippled in the wind, and there was a haze like dust on a horizon that shaded up to a sky that was pink as much as blue. Low rocky hills showed in the distance. Between the lander and them was . . .

"It's a canal! If only Edgar could be here!"

"Hell with Burroughs, if only *Lowell*—"

"Shut *up!*"

It *was* a canal; about fifteen yards wide, sweeping from left to right and then turning so that it dwindled out of sight like in a perspective drawing, curving to follow the contour of the land, for all the world like a canal in California or Arizona, except that it was covered in an arched roof of some transparent stuff so clear it was barely visible at all. The banks were reddish, man-high stone or concrete, sloping away from the interior and covered in abstract figures something like hieroglyphics, ancient and crumbling and faded.

A low black shape like a flattened turtle, about the size of a Volkswagen, crawled over the crystal roof without visible means of support, unless there was something like a snail's foot beneath the carapace.

"Guess that settles the question of whether those structures we saw from orbit were the product of intelligence or not," Isaac said dryly.

"That . . . turtle, beetle, whatever it is . . . could be something like a giant social insect," Frank said stubbornly. "Beavers build dams. That . . . whatever it is could be doing it."

"Beavers don't carve hieroglyphs on them and neither do ants. The hominids—well, some of them—on Venus looked awfully damned human, which means we're not reasoning from a sample of one any more. Panspermia and parallel evolution—"

"Shut *up!*"

The audio pickups were transmitting a soft whistling of wind, accompanied by a murmur of commentary from the technicians at Cape Canaveral. There was something in the sky, distant and moving slowly—but too quick for the pickup to track it, given the time-lag factor, so they didn't try. They waited, and not much happened. A shout went up as a small and fuzzy animal hopped by, but it was gone too quickly to see details except that it precisely matched the color of the leafy ground cover and jumped on its hind legs.

"Camouflage," Beam noted; he'd come into the field in the '50s, but looked older than he must be. "When you're small and at the bottom of the food chain, you want to be invisible."

More of the whatevers hopped around, and turned out to look like desert rats with tufted tails and squashed-in faces; some of them had miniature versions of themselves clinging to their backs. A reading of temperature and atmospheric density came up in the lower right-hand corner of the screen.

"So at Martian sea level the air's a little thinner than Denver," Poul commented, taking a pull on his beer. "The interior highlands must be like Tibet or the Bolivian Altiplano."

"Yeah, but with lower gravity—"

"The dropoff will be slower, yes. Where Viking came down it's chilly and very dry, but you or I could be comfortable there with a good warm coat."

"So much for wearing oxygen masks and skating on the canals," Bob said, and chuckled ruefully.

That was probably because of the Mars book he *had* written back in the early '50s.

"It's northern-hemisphere summer there now, though. Betcha

winter is a sockeldanger," Ray put in. "And twice as long as ours, don't forget."

"Wait, what's that?"

People jostled toward the screen, then sat back with self-conscious control. A dot was coming up the long stretch beside the canal, growing until details could be seen . . .

A *landyacht*, he thought as a wordless cheer rang out, then corrected himself when the scale snapped into his perception. *No, a landship.*

Six long outriggers with giant wheels supported it; they dipped and returned as they rode over irregularities in the terrain, keeping the boxy hull nearly level.

"Good suspension system," Sprague said. "Pneumatic? Or efficient springs. Even in one-third gravity. The sails look transparent. I'd love to know what they're made of; it doesn't really look like cloth."

Two masts and yards supported huge gossamer sails that looked like lanteens but weren't. Galleries and windows ran around the hull; if the builders were sized anything like human beings, that meant the landship was at least a hundred and fifty feet long. As it grew closer they saw a figurehead at the front below the bowsprit, some sort of gruesomely fanged beast . . .

"Now we know something about the local wildlife. Something bad," Jack quipped.

"Either that, or they've been reading Clark Ashton Smith, Jack."

It might be mythological, Fred thought, over the hammering of his heart. *Don't jump to conclusions.*

Closer still, and there was writing behind the figurehead—symbols at least, with a generic family resemblance to the ones on the canal banks. Figures moved on the decks, bending to incomprehensible tasks.

"It's heading toward the lander!"

It did, the front pair of outriggers turning, then the hull foreshortening as the prow swung toward the camera. The sails twisted and did something; Poul liked messing about in boats, and he murmured about pointing into the wind.

"Beat-up old . . . whatever-it-is," Fred heard himself say.

Closer to, they could see that most of the structure was made out of some dense close-grained reddish wood, intricately carved but worn and patched and replaced in places. But other sections like the outriggers were strange, glossy and looking like metal or crystal or some unearthly—*Watch it!* he told himself—alloy.

The sails came down neatly as the craft coasted to a halt. They couldn't see all of it, for it was too close now; they could observe how the big wheel at the end of one of the outriggers effortlessly climbed over a boulder, the tire deforming and springing back as it did so.

"That wheel looks as if it were *spun* somehow, out of resilient crystalline wire," Bob commented. "Nice engineering. It must grip like fingers. Do we have anything that could do that? They may be ahead of us in some fields."

"But they're using *sails* for propulsion," the editor of *Astounding* said.

His head pushed forward pugnaciously, and he crushed out a cigarette. "I refuse to believe we're not the most advanced species in the solar system. We're going to them, after all, not them to us."

"Mars is smaller than Earth," Bob replied. "There may not be any fossil fuels or fissionables. Our rockets burn hydrogen cracked with power from burning coal, or oil, or more and more from nuclear power. We're testing atomic-powered rockets for deep-space work, for the manned missions, to get us out there in person—" he nodded at the screen— "but lack of power sources would push Martian development into other paths."

Beam drew thoughtfully on his pipe, a minor affectation. "Or they may have come to us first . . . but a very long time ago, and then they had a Dark Age or two. And to Venus. That would account for—"

"Lookatthat!" Larry cried joyfully.

A ramp dropped from under the snarling figurehead, and a dozen figures descended.

"Martians," someone said reverently. "Men from Mars."

"Humanoids from Mars, at least," someone else murmured with the abstracted air of a man taking mental notes. "Bilaterally symmetrical bipeds . . . hard to tell more with the way they're muffled up. There might be tails under those robes . . . their joints bend the same way as ours . . . look, four fingers and a thumb on the inside! *Definitely* hominid, like the ones on Venus!"

"And those are weapons," Beam said. "Rifles, pistols . . ."

"And they're all wearing swords," Sprague commented. "And one of them has a bow. Unless they're very primitive firearms, muzzle-loaders, you'd expect edged weapons to go out of use fairly quickly."

"Could be some sort of honor code. Maybe Burroughs got that right, too! Gentlemen don't use a gun if the other guy draws a sword."

"Nobody's *that* honorable," Sprague said. "Not in the real world . . . worlds. Not for long; the cheaters win too often. This place the probe's in could be the equivalent of, oh, nineteenth-century India or Africa, and the weapons are imported from elsewhere—a transitional phase."

"Hey, look, the one with the bow doesn't have a nose—or at least it's a real stub under that headdress. Look, he's turning his head again—you can see it when he's in profile."

"They're not primitive guns," Beam said flatly; he was an expert, and a crack shot himself. "I can't make out the mechanisms but the barrels are too slender and too precisely formed for that."

Fred peered more closely. The figures cautiously approaching the lander were swathed in clothing. The basic garment seemed to be a loose wide-sleeved and calf-length robe a bit like an Arab burnoose with an attached headdress that hid everything but a slit over the eyes . . . or what were presumably eyes. Beneath that he could see baggy pants and boots, and gloves that covered quite humanlike hands. Broad belts and body harnesses of worked leather carried tools and weapons—long curved knives with carved hilts, swords whose guards were intricately worked cages of some glossy stuff, holsters with slender-barreled pistols and fanciful grips.

One had a bandolier of rope and a grappling tool looped over one shoulder. All of them had something like a cargo hook clipped to their body harness. Another bore something that looked roughly like a rifle as well, with a long thin barrel, a short bulbous body, and a skeletal stock. The archer had a quiver over the shoulder and a strung bow, a complex-looking recurved thing that reminded him a little of pictures he'd seen of Chinese archery.

The robe of the figure in the lead was a dusty rose color edged with black, and there were jewels and goldwork on the harness. The ones behind ranged from someone nearly as gorgeous to plain brown patched cloth.

"The captain and officers and crew," someone murmured. "Or something like that."

They came closer and closer, until eyes showed through the slits in their headdresses—humanlike, but detail was frustratingly absent. All were tall and slim despite the muffling cloth; Fred estimated the leader as most of the way to seven feet. The leader . . . *might as well call him the captain* . . . drew his sword. Light shimmered off the metal; it was double-edged and looked disconcertingly sharp, but not exactly like steel.

"Cut-and-thrust blade," Sprague said. "More thrust than cut. A good deal like some seventeenth-century European types."

Everyone caught their breath as the captain turned and spoke to his . . . men? The voice sounded human, perhaps a little high-pitched, but the language was wholly unfamiliar. It sounded ripplingly musical with an occasional staccato burst.

"Tonal and monosyllabic, I think, like Chinese," Sprague went on, as two of the robed humanoids turned and trotted back toward the ship. "Maybe. Difficult to learn, if it is. I'll bet the grammar is analytic, too."

The captain turned back and prodded the lander, reaching up; they could all hear the *tunk . . . tunk . . .* as the point of the blade prodded the light metal hull.

The television spoke: "We are attempting to communicate. The message shall be, *We come in peace for all mankind*."

"Some advertising man thought *that* up," Fred said, and there was a nervous chuckle; everyone knew how he felt about *them*.

Minutes passed, and the English words sounded tinny and strange through the pickup in the thin Martian atmosphere. The Martians jumped back; the one with the bow turned and ran. A rifle came up and fired—there was no bang, no flash or smoke, just a slight *hsssst* sound, but the lander rang under an impact.

The captain didn't run. Instead he shouted something in his musical language and waved the long blade at his followers. One hurried back up the ramp and returned with a folded tarpaulin; the

Martians threw it over the lander, and then the screen went dark. Creaking noises followed.

Poul broke the long silence with a guffaw. "They're putting it on board, by God! They swung a yard over and tied it up in a sack and they're hoisting it on deck!"

Walter and Werner came back on, both looking sandbagged and starting to stammer explanations that couldn't possibly have anything behind them.

"I knew it!" Leigh shouted, punching her fist into the air. "I told you sons of . . . sons what it would be like years ago!"

A rebel yell cut loose, and suddenly the room was a babble of voices.

Several years later, the captain's words were determined to be in the Tradeship dialect of Demotic Modern, and were tentatively translated:

"It's alive! Those fools at the Scholarium will pay a fortune for this!"

CHAPTER ONE

Encyclopedia Britannica, 20th edition
University of Chicago Press, 1998

MARS—Parameters

ORBIT: 1.5237 AU

ORBITAL PERIOD: 668.6 Martian solar days

ROTATION: 24 hrs. 34 min.

MASS: 0.1075 x Earth

AVERAGE DENSITY: 3.93 g/cc

SURFACE GRAVITY: 0.377 x Earth

DIAMETER: 4,217 miles (equatorial; 53.3% that of Earth)

SURFACE: 75% land, 25% water (incl. pack ice)

ATMOSPHERIC COMPOSITION:

NITROGEN	76.51%
OXYGEN	20.23%
CARBON DIOXIDE	0.11%

TRACE ELEMENTS: Argon, neon, krypton

ATMOSPHERIC PRESSURE: 10.7 psi average at northern sea level

The third life-bearing world of the solar system, Mars is less Earthlike than Venus, although like Earth and unlike Venus its rotation is counterclockwise, and the length of the Martian day is nearly identical to that of Earth's. The atmosphere is thinner than Earth's, and is apparently growing thinner still; though it remains easily breathable for Terran humanity at the lower levels, uplands tolerable for Martians require oxygen masks of the type used by mountaineers on Earth. More significant is the fact that Mars has a thick, rigid crust that prevents the plate tectonics characteristic of the other two worlds.

Average temperatures on Mars are roughly 10 degrees Celsius lower than those on Earth, due to the lower solar energy input. This effect is moderated by the higher percentage of carbon dioxide in the Martian atmosphere, a phenomenon puzzling to scientists because the planet lacks the plate tectonics needed to recirculate carbon compounds and, presumably, has less vulcanism. The year, twice the Terrestrial, and the greater eccentricity of the Martian orbit render seasonal contrasts greater than the Terran norm even at the equator.

Temperatures on Earth may have been in a similar range, however, at some periods of geologic time (see "Snowball Earth"). It is believed that the gradual thinning of the Martian atmosphere and hence its reduced ability to hold heat has been offset to some degree by the gradual increase in the Sun's energy output over time.

The proportions of land and water on Mars are almost a precise reversal of those on Earth. Mars has seas surrounded by land, rather than land surrounded by oceans, and so the total land area is not dissimilar to that of Earth. The bulk of the water area is concentrated in the Great Northern Sea in the northern polar zone, with a smaller equivalent in the Antarctic Sea. Smaller bodies of water are present in parts of the main equator-girdling land mass . . .

Mars, City of Zar-tu-Kan
Tau-il-Zhi (Tower of Truth)
May 1, 2000 AD

"How can you work for the vaz-Terranan? They're rich and they have some curious and powerful *tembst*, but by the First Principle, they're ugly!" Jelzhau said, considering the board.

He moved his Chief Coercive diagonally two squares and threatened her Despot.

The woman who called herself Teyud za-Zhalt sipped at her flask of essence through the glass straw, savoring the musky tartness of the liquid, and then moved her Flier Transport onto the same square.

The mild euphoric was doubly pleasurable since Jelzhau would be buying if she won the game, and he had never toppled her Despot in a bout of *atanj* yet, unless she lost deliberately.

I am glad to have found alternate employment, she thought, studying the board. *He never grasped that I was occasionally throwing the game, either.*

Guarding the life of someone you'd rather see dead was a means of earning your water too heavily spiced with irony for inner peace. Besides that, he was a cheapskate. Occasionally his *atanj* play was good enough to be entertaining, but usually . . .

Ah, yes. Once again, excessive conservatism in his employment of the Coercives and Clandestines. He relies too much on his Blockade and Boycott pieces, as might be expected of a spice merchant.

If you didn't exercise your Coercives, you increased the odds of their defection.

"You deal with the *vaz-Terranan,* too," she pointed out, as he threw the dice to determine whose piece would win the battle for the square. "Extensively."

"That is a series of expeditious meetings. You have to *associate* with the hideous things. Ah, randomness falls out in your favor."

The dice showed three threes; that gave the paratroops in her Flier Transport time to emerge and capture his Chief Coercive.

"Oh, not necessarily so very hideous," she said, taking the dice. "Some are grotesque—like a squashed-down caricature of humanity—but some are just stocky and perhaps a bit irregular of feature and extremely muscular. The ones I've met are all rather clever, too, if naïve."

Jelzhau shuddered. "And they *ooze*. They're positively *slick* with water and mucus most of the time. You can feel it on their breath. An extra three on whether my Chief Coercive will defect?"

"Oozing would be unaesthetic," Teyud admitted. "Three, agreed."

She threw; three ones, a low-probability result. In the game, that meant her paratroopers had bribed or threatened his Chief Co-ercive to turn against his Despot. She moved the pieces, now both hers, into another square.

"Your Despot is now confronted," she said formally. "He must restore *Sh'u Maz*, or abdicate."

Jelzhau sighed and tipped over the tower-shaped piece. "He abdicates; your Despot proves superior fitness to perpetuate his lin-eage and establish Sustained Harmony. And as for the *vaz-Terranan*, they have a distinct and unpleasant odor, as well."

Her nostrils flared in irony; Jelzhau was given to excessive use of *odwa*-scent, himself.

"I can't detect any untoward odor most of the time. In essential respects, they resemble us. For example, they have their own inter-nal disputes and differences."

"They all seem much alike to me."

Privately she thought the spice-factor was being a little bigoted, even if there was some truth to the physical description. The travel-ers from the Wet World couldn't help their semblance, and the ones from Kennedy Base usually dressed in local garb, and *tried* to behave in seemly fashion. Which was more than you could say of some of her own race, such as that clutch of deep-chested highlander carava-neers who were singing—they probably thought it was song—over in one corner, and pawing at one of the De'ming servitors.

If you couldn't integrate an essence without losing harmony, you shouldn't partake in public.

Mind you, the *Blue-tinted Time Considered As A Regressing Series* was that sort of canal-side dive. It had seen better days, but those had probably been when the Crimson Dynasty still ruled. Someone was neglecting the glow-globes set in the fluid-stone of the ceiling fifteen feet overhead; badly fed, they gave off less light than they should, and it had an unpleasant greenish cast that made the figures of scholars and warriors on the wall look decayed.

And there was a grease mark on the smooth pearl granite behind her head; the taverner claimed that it had been made by the famous unbound hair of Zowej-ar-Lakrid in the Conqueror's student days, fifteen hundred years ago, when he was conspiring to overthrow the city's despot while playing *atanj* in this very spot, and that it would be sacrilege to remove it. Some deep layer of it might indeed be that old.

For the rest, the stopping-place looked depressingly like a thousand others she'd seen, from one end of the Real World to another: a circular room on the ground floor of a tower more than half abandoned. In the more-traveled places near the exits the hard green stones of the floor were worn into troughs that menaced the balance of the patrons. Deepest of all were the spots before the entrance to the spiral staircase in the center of the room.

The floor was set with circular tables of *tkem* wood that had been polished blackness once and were nicked and dark grey now.

Hers held a tiny fretted-copper brazier with a stick of cheap incense burning, and a bowl of tart dipping sauce for the small platter that had held raw *rooz* meat cut into strips. She took the last strip between a mannerly thumb and forefinger, touched it to the sauce and ate.

Too hot, she thought. *Cheap* narwak *badly ground, or steeped too long.*

The meat at least was decently fresh, pleasant, lightly marbled, deep red, richly salted, and slightly moist; the animal had not lost its flaps in vain.

Just then the clock over the entrance to the staircase opened its mouth, gave a sad, piercing cry and sang:

Hours like sand
On the shores of a bitter sea
Flow on waves of time;
Seven hours have passed
Since last the Sun
Rose in blind majesty;
It shall yield heedless to night
In ten more.
One . . . two . . . three . . . four . . . five . . . six . . . seven.

That meant the flier would be arriving soon. Teyud packed her board and set, folding them into a palm-sized rectangle and slipping it into its pouch at her belt as they rose; Jelzhau would have taken the lead if Teyud had not adopted a hipshot pose of astonished sorrow. He flushed darkly and made his bow excessive.

"True, you are no longer in my employ, Most Refined of Breeding," he said.

"Indeed," she replied tranquilly, neglecting to add an honorific.

I wonder what the Wet Worlders truly think of us she wondered idly, as they began to trot upward.

It was still hard to have a conversation with them beyond the obvious, and they were less than frank about some things. That was probably wise of them—everyone loved flattery, and criticism was rarely popular—but a pity nonetheless. They were the first new things to come into the Real World for a very long time.

Even as her father's lineage reckoned such things. And they had ruled this world for twice ten thousand years.

But they do so no longer; now they hide in ruins and brood, she reminded herself. *Do not waste life span in reverie on things past, as your father did . . . does. For each being, the time from birth to death is as that of the universe itself. You are not in the Tollamune Emperor's court at Dvor Il-Adazar now . . . and if you were within sight of the Tower of Harmonic Unity, you would die slowly.*

"This trip is the first time I've seen this many Martian faces uncovered," Jeremy Wainman said as the *Zhoming Dael* slowed on its approach to the tall slimness of the tower. "Here on Zho'da, that is, not in videos back Earthside."

Martians called their planet Zho'da; that meant "The Real World," or possibly "The Only Significant Place." It was all a matter of perspective, he supposed.

"It makes sense to muffle up outside on this planet," said Captain Sally Yamashita of the United States Aerospace Force Astronaut Corps. "Dry, cold, windy, lots of acrid dust. Plus—"

The Martian airship had made several stops on its way from Kennedy Base, but those had been at caravanserais and isolated trading posts. He and his superior were the only Earthlings—*vaz-Terranan* in demotic Martian—in the curved forward lounge with its transparent outward-sloping wall. The dozen or so locals mostly remained seated in their nests of cushions and traveling silks and furs, many with a board between them and the eternal Martian *atanj* game under way; it was routine for them. Jeremy leaned eagerly over the railing, looking as the long bright line of the canal opened out into the glittering shapes of the half-ruined city ahead.

"Plus, *it's the custom*," he said, grinning and quoting the most common phrase in the orientation lectures that had started back on Earth right after the summons he'd dreamed of but not seriously expected, and had continued at short intervals while the *Brackett* made its long passage out and then at Kennedy Base too.

"I *am* an anthropologist, you know," Jeremy added. "With a secondary degree in archaeology, to boot, and one in Martian history."

Sally nodded. She was tall by Terran standards—everyone assigned to Mars was, though like her, most were below the Martian average. But even at five-eleven, she gave an impression of close-coupled energy, and her slanted hazel eyes were very keen. Her father had been California-Japanese, richer than God and a marine biologist with a hobby in martial arts; her mother was from a long line of Napa Valley winemakers but had broken the mold by going into modern dance. Sally's own specialty was the study of Martian technology; she had degrees in molecular biology and paleontology. But she was also a general fixer and contact person, helping Kennedy Base interface with the Martians. And, at thirty, she was several years older than Jeremy, with the weathered skin of an Old Mars Hand.

And . . . I think she's a spook. Not all the time, we're all multitasking here, but I think that's what she is if you dig down through all the layers. Why are they sending a spook on an archaeological scouting mission? Granted, this can be a very hairy planet, and she looks like she can clip hair with the best of them, but . . .

"You're an anthropologist . . . a very *inexperienced* anthropologist," she said.

It *was* his first trip outside Kennedy Base. He'd seen pictures of the these towers with their time-faded colors and the lacy crystalline bridges that joined them, the transparent domes below full of an astonishing flowering lushness, the narrow serpentine streets between blank-faced buildings of rose-red stone . . . but now he could see them for himself. They reminded him a little of Indian Mughal architecture done by someone on opium and freed from the limits of stone and the constraints of gravity, but there was a soft-edged quality to them unlike anything his world had ever bred, as if they had *grown* here.

In the distance loomed jagged heights that had been the edge of a continent when the site of this city was below the waves of a vanished sea . . .

Sally snorted; he had a sudden uncomfortable feeling she knew just what sort of greenhorn romantic twaddle he was thinking. Her words confirmed it.

"Even the experienced are just scratching the surface here. Venus may be full of hunter-gatherers or Bronze Age types like the Kartahownians, but this isn't Venus—the Martians were doing calligraphy and building cities forty thousand years ago. The Crimson Dynasty ruled before the Cro-Magnons painted mammoths on those caves in France, and it *fell* about the time we invented writing."

"We came to them, not vice versa," Jeremy pointed out. *And I'm teasing you. Do you have to be so* solemn *about everything?*

Apparently she did. Even her nod was grave as she went on.

"We have a technological edge. Sort of, or so we like to think. But Earth's a long way away and there aren't many of us here. We can't push these people around and we don't impress them much, either. I repeat: This isn't Venus. We can't play Gods-from-the-sky here. We're on sufferance. And never forget we don't know dick about this place, really."

"Yes, teacher," he said good-humoredly. "I'll try to make us a little *less* abysmally ignorant, hmm? We *do* need to start learning more about Martian history. Besides what their chronicles tell us. They don't always ask the same questions we want answered and it's always a good idea to check words against the stones and bones anyway."

"Yeah, so you talked them into sending us to do a dig at Rema-Dza. Which may or may not actually exist."

"The satellite photos show *something* large is there. And according to the chronicles, it could only be the city of Rema-Dza."

"Now who's relying on words? Those are chronicles after fifteen thousand years of recopying, sometimes by people who thought it was a good idea to goof on their descendants, as interpreted by contemporary Martians who sometimes like to play see-what-the-Terran-barbarians-will-swallow. I'm still not sure it was a cost-effective decision."

It was hard *not* to be good-humored. He'd finally *made* it here. He'd dreamed about it since he was old enough to distinguish the stuff on the news from the fairy tales his mother had read him. He'd worked and planned and sweated and competed, but tens or hundreds of millions had shared that dream. Now he'd *done* it, while they went on dreaming and reading bad novels about people like him, and watching even worse movies and video shows and breathless documentaries on the *National Geographic* channel.

"Why are you along, then?" he asked. "We're all *supposed* to be able to handle stuff on our own. We have to, with only a hundred-odd people to study an entire world."

Three years of lobbying, and suddenly they found the funds for me and for a survey of the lost cities of the Imperial era. God, I thought it would stay tied up in the USASF bureaucracy forever.

She snorted again. "We're not supposed to be self-sufficient on our first time out! And you're a civilian."

"Yes, ma'am," he said tolerantly, with a good-natured mock salute.

If it weren't for the planetary exploration program, the Pentagon would be an afterthought these days—there hadn't been a significant international conflict since the Laotian incident in the '60s, unless you counted occasional scuffles in backwaters like the Near East and Africa, which nobody in the real centers of civilization had spare time or energy to get involved with. The competition with the East-bloc and Eurobloc was real enough, but on a more rarefied level—civilization seemed to have outgrown direct confrontations. Most people of his university-and-sciences background thought that was an inevitable product of technological and economic progress.

"Mars and Venus are probably the *reasons* things are peaceful back home," Sally pointed out dryly. "But out here, things get a bit more hairy."

He nodded, not exactly *in* agreement but unwillingness to argue with someone senior over a minor point. *He* was the one in a traveling robe woven from the exudation of jeweled moths—cloth that was Kevlar-like armor as well as clothing—with a sword by his side and a minicam and blank data chips in the haversack slung over his back. When he got back to base, the chips would have enough on them to keep Earth's scholars working for a generation. Plus, there was the sense of bouncy, dreamlike enjoyment that you felt under one-third gravity; he still had to remind himself now and then not to go bounding everywhere like a slow-mo grasshopper.

The Tower of Truth rose eight hundred feet above the glassine roof of the Canal Named Liquid Abundance, growing from a tiny, asparagus-stalk shape to its full immensity as the airship approached. Most of that height was a fluted smoothness of stone striated in dusky green and dark rose, broken only by tall narrow windows. The top flared out into a shape like an elongated teardrop set on its base, ringed about with circular doors large enough to take the pointed nose of an airship; the wall between each door was transparent.

One of the doors irised open as the *Zhoming Dael* drifted to a near stop three thousand yards away, hanging as weightless as did the dandelionlike seeds for which it was named. From above the passenger deck one of the crew sent an *orok* out a hatchway, a sort of domesticated eagle with a body the size of a big dog, a crest of bronze-gold feathers on its cruel raptor head and a twenty-foot wingspan. It beat its great pinions twice and then glided to the open portal with a cable in its claws, folding its wings as it stooped through the entranceway and hopped toward the ground crew.

"You might say birds do well on Mars," Sally said.

That surprised him into a chuckle at the understatement. The lower gravity more than made up for the thinner air, and being able to migrate was a big plus here.

The long fabric of the *Drifting Frozen-white Thistle Seeds* jerked as hands within took the line and reeved it through geared windlasses. The ship's engines stopped; Jeremy could hear them panting for breath in the propeller pods above and behind him as the whirring hum died away. In utter silence, the huge craft slid forward until the smooth hull mated with the collar of the portal. Before him, the front of the gondola folded down to make a ramp, and the yellow-red light of Martian glow-globes shone brightly through.

The passengers stood, slung their bundles over their backs, and walked forward to pay the entry toll. Zar-tu-Kan's officialdom was represented by a robed figure standing by the exit next to a pillar with a slot in the top. He had a small animallike a dark furry cylinder clutched in his right hand; there was a little red rosebud mouth—or anus or, possibly, both—at one end, but no eyes or limbs. The customs agent held it out from his side so that the six feet of thin, pink, slowly curling naked tail was well away from his body.

You didn't want to make accidental contact with a shockwhip, even if the wielder wasn't squeezing it to turn on the current. Everyone was allergic to the proteins on its surface.

Each passenger reached into the slot and dropped something as they went by; Sally Yamashita added two inch-long pieces of silver wire.

"*One tenth* shem," a voice in accented Martian said, through a grill on the side of the stone post.

"Correct weight for two foreigners and up to fifteen *zka-kem* of noncommercial baggage," the functionary added. "You may pass."

"Doesn't anyone ever try to stiff the tax man?" he murmured to her. "Slipping in copper for silver?"

"There's a mouth with teeth below that slot," she said. "It can taste the purity of metals with its tongue. And if the weight or composition's wrong, it bites down and holds you for Mr. Revenue Service to beat on with his Amazingly Itchy Electro-Rat."

Ouch, Jeremy thought. *There are times when Martian technology is just plain . . . icky. And they could use a Martian Civil Liberties Union. Admittedly they don't have really* bad *tyrants, but they have far too many fair-to-middling ones.*

A crowd was waiting to greet the airship. Quietly animated bargaining started as soon as the passengers disembarked, with raised eyebrows and the occasional spare gesture doing service for shouts, insults, and windmilling arms. Ground crew brought hoses forward to clip to sockets in the *Floating Thistle*'s nose and pump sludge aboard to feed the engines and the bacterial solution that produced hydrogen for the lifting cells. Fine sand ballast vented from the keel to compensate.

The interior of the tower here was a huge circular room with a groin-vaulted ceiling; bales and sacks and containers of cargo stood about in it, but not enough of them to prevent a feeling of dusty emptiness. The faded, half abstract, half pictorial frescos above the entry portals showed a traffic far thicker and more bustling . . . but they might be older than Western civilization, beneath their coating of impenetrable glassine. There was a faint smell in the air of things like burnt cinnamon and something halfway between hibiscus and clove, of acrid smoke, of sweat that was harsher and more concentrated than that of his breed because it wasted less water.

And somehow the scent of *time*, like faded memories piled in an infinite attic, layer upon layer until the present seemed no more than an image seen in a dream.

"Our contact?" he said.

"Jelzhau Zhau-nor. He's a big wheel in the Zhau-na, the spice merchants' guild."

"It's not really a—" Jeremy began automatically.

"Guild. Or clan. Kin group, corporation, thingie, whatever—"

" 'Thingie' won't do for the *Journal of Martian Cultural Studies*."

"Don't the younger generation have any respect for their elders these days?"

"Did you, mother dear?"

"No, but I had an excuse—I was rebelling against my Japanese heritage. Anyway, we buy from him."

Jeremy nodded. Martian spices and drugs—they didn't distinguish the concepts in Demotic—did things to the taste buds, metabolism, and nerves that Terrestrial science was having problems understanding. They were the only things besides information that could really show a profit after interplanetary shipping costs; gold and gems didn't even come close.

One of them was a genuine anti-agathic, slowing down aging for Martians and *probably* for Terrans too, though that would take time to prove. Particularly since Martians had about twice the Terran life span anyway, and the metabolisms of the two species were similar but not identical.

"And he's got contacts everywhere. He's the one who hires our guides for us."

Two Martians came forward and took greeting stances ten yards away—which meant, between those of roughly equal status, something that looked like shaking hands with yourself. Martians certainly didn't shake hands with each other; this culture put a premium on social distance.

And the gesture was the local equivalent of waving, whistling between your teeth, and shouting, *Hey, Mac!*

He and Sally returned the signal. One of the Martians was a man who looked middle-aged—which probably meant he was pushing a hundred, in Earth years—and whose height equaled Jeremy's own six-six. That was average for standard Martians, though they varied less than humans in that way. His smooth, beardless skin was pale olive, and the oiled hair dressed in elaborate curls was raven black, also common. His robe was striped white and dark green, and the leather of his belt and curl-toed boots nearly shimmered with enameled inlay work.

The woman beside him made Jeremy's eyes go a little wider. *She* was over seven feet tall, with even more of the big-eyed aquiline delicacy of features than most Martians, but looking more *solid*, somehow.

Less as if she'd blow away in a stiff wind, he thought.

The color of those huge eyes was distinctly odd, yellow as fire, and so was the almost bronze sheen of hair caught back in a fine metallic net. There was an eerie loveliness to the alien face . . .

"Hey," he whispered in English. "You didn't tell me our guide was—"

"Of the old Thoughtful Grace caste. They were—"

"The Crimson Dynasty's military elite, yes," Jeremy said. "The caste just below the top."

For God's sake! he thought. *I'm not an ignoramus because I arrived on the* Brackett *six months ago and this is my first off-base field trip. I've been studying Mars since I was twelve!*

But he didn't say it. There were too few Terrans on Mars to start quarrels, even with the selection for stable types. And you were stuck with the same people for the rest of your life; only two people had returned to Earth from Mars in nearly twenty years. Tiny Kennedy Base, off on the shores of the Bitter Sea, wasn't a real frontier settlement like growing Jamestown on Venus, but it would be his home for a very long time to come. He'd made *that* decision when he'd walked through the suddenly open door.

Sally shrugged apologetically for the same reasons. "I didn't know it would be her this time; there are a couple who we use regularly. Mostly hunters and caravan guards."

"*I* didn't know there were any purebred Thoughtful Grace left, at least not outside the Wai Zang towns," he said, professional interest growing in his face. "And that's a *long* way away."

"Hell, my specialty is Martian technology."

"Just that," Jeremy said dryly.

Biotech from this planet was revolutionizing a dozen industries on Earth, from waste disposal to fuel production. The powers-that-were viewed archaeology and cultural studies mainly as a means to get the Martians to cough up their knowledge, and to figure out ways of keeping them from lynching or poisoning or *infecting* the irritatingly inquisitive Wet Worlders.

"I know just enough of the cultural ins and outs not to get killed—yet," Sally said with a wry twist to her mouth. "At least they're more likely to *listen* to you on short acquaintance, you God-damned beanpole."

The labor gang squatting on the many-footed cargo pallets trotting forward to the flier's freight ramp were the reason for her complaint. They were *De'ming*, bred for menial labor by the geneticists—or possibly wizards—of the Crimson Dynasty era. They didn't exactly look like Earth-humans—they were thick-bodied and short by this planet's standards—but enough so that they were well within the Terran bell-curve. That was enough to get anyone below six feet perceived as inherently stupid and servile here.

And I don't like their eyes. There's nobody "at home" there.

Their kind had been working with that same placid, witless docility for the last thirty thousand earth-years or so, just smart enough to take simple directions . . .

Icky. Really, really icky.

Jelzhau Zhau-Nor tucked his hands into the sleeves of his robe and came to about twice the conversational distance a North American considered comfortable, and cocked his ears forward; they were a bit larger and a bit more elongated than a Terran's, and a whole lot more mobile. That was a let's-get-down-to-business signal.

"I profess amiable greetings, Respectably Wealthy Jelzhau Zhau-Nor," Sally said politely in Demotic. "Intent and event produced timely arrival. Mutual delight and profit will probably follow."

"Hello, my friend Jawen Yama-shita!" he replied, in English.

With only a few hundred personnel on the planet, the U.S.–Commonwealth Organization of American States base could afford to be *very* selective, but it was still difficult to find people who met all the other qualifications and were *that* tall. Not only was Jeremy Wainman six-six, he had a fencer's physique, long limbed and with a wiry muscularity; his face was handsome in a beak-nosed fashion that would last well after he passed his thirtieth year next April. His blue eyes and close-cropped dark brown hair would be accepted as merely exotic.

Make that sort of *in English,* Jeremy thought.

The sounds were difficult for Martians. At least for speakers of Modern Demotic—the only spoken language on the planet, as far as they'd been able to discover, though there were different dialects. Which simplified things considerably, as learning it made Japanese look easy and Chinese a walk in the park.

Christ, it's fun to get out and really use all that language training.

Then the factor went on in his own tongue: "You have met the highly bred Professional Practitioner of Coercive Violence, Teyud za-Zhalt."

And "highly bred" means exactly the same thing as describing highly bred about a racehorse, and it's a compliment in this language. The title Professional Practitioner of Coercive Violence covers cops, soldiers and bandits.

Minds with a profound understanding of linguistics had been at work shaping Martian for a very long time.

All that in a hand gesture and three words, one of them a proper name. It's a bitch to learn, but I love this language! It's so . . . smooth.

The woman inclined her head slightly and laid her ears back, a gesture of respect to an employer or patron from someone equal in eugenic rank, which was a courteous assumption. Her breed had been lords once.

"My blades are ready, my guns are fully fed and loaded, other necessary equipment and personnel have been procured, and I command the directional template for our journey of exploration, employer," Teyud said to Sally, adding the last in Deferential Mode.

Her voice was beautifully modulated, a little deeper than the normal Martian soprano; if a bronze bell had been precisely machined by computer-directed lasers, it would sound like that. And her accent was noticeably different from that of the spice merchant.

Perhaps her diction is a bit . . . crisper? And there's something about the way she handles sibilants, too. Wait a minute—it's like the way the pillar-with-teeth spoke . . . archaic, maybe? A dialect from some out of the way place that hasn't changed much? I've got to get to know her well enough to ask questions!

Then she turned to him. "Identity? Skill? Status?"

"Jeremy Wainman," he said. "Scholar, of variation in custom through time; a partner to Sally, of lesser seniority."

She moved her lips slowly, then surprised him by pronouncing his name nearly as he had.

"Jeremy Wainman, my subsidiary employer, I profess amiable greetings. May randomness produce positive outcomes for you in this period of endeavor, and malice be absent."

Mars, City of Dvor Il-Adazar (Olympus Mons)
Ringing Depths Reservoir Control
January 1, 2000 AD

"What do you see?" Sajir-sa-Tomond said to the Terran named Franziskus Binkis. "What amuses you?"

He had held the shrunken dominions of the Ruby Throne for two hundred Martian years; in Terran terms, he had been born in the year Elizabeth the First was crowned at Westminster. Those centuries of experience and the Crimson Dynasty's inheritance gave him composure with Binkis, despite the extremely odd way the *vas-Terranan* and his companion had arrived here in the depths of the City That Is A Mountain.

On balance, I am content that I did not kill him when I found him in the Shrine.

Binkis chuckled again. The pumps throbbed in the icy dimness of the great cavern; it had begun as a volcanic bubble, and been shaped to other purposes very long ago. The sound of Binkis's amusement was lost among the harsh raw power of the sound, and there was a disturbing flicker to his lightly colored eyes. He was six feet tall and lanky for his breed, which made him a little shorter than average and squat to Martian eyes. The Emperor was a foot taller, and mantis-gaunt by comparison.

"Incongruity," Franziskus said. "I appreciate the incongruities."

His hand moved slightly to indicate the brute angularity of the Earth-made reactor amid the flowing organic machinery that Martians built—or more usually, *grew*.

"And yet," the Terran—

Who is no longer entirely a Terran, or even entirely a man, Sajir sa-Tomond reminded himself. *He has been touched by the things of the Most Ancient, and carried across space and time by them.*

—went on, "I also see in my mind devices that are not machines at all but *relations*, contiguities of time and space as complex as the dance of neurons in a brain and as abstract as a mathematical theorem. Both these technologies are as crude as a wooden spear hardened in a campfire by comparison."

Sajir heard the clearing of a throat behind him. He turned; it was one of the EastBloc diplomats, throughout Lin Yu-Pei.

He had arrived in conventional wise; by what the *vas-Terranan* called a nuclear rocket to orbit around Mars, and then by lander dropping on a tail of fire to the field at the Mountain's foot, where Sajir sa-Tomond had allowed the Eastbloc base to be erected. The diplomat was as diminutive as a *De'ming* and interestingly different from Binkis in physical type, but Sajir had found him clever enough despite first appearances.

Though now he is modified. His mind now edits reality and does not perceive Binkis at all.

And there were the guards in their insectile black armor, drifting like ghosts as they moved to keep the Tollamune, Sajir sa-Tomond the Two Hundredth and Twenty-Fifth, from any risk.

A little farther back, a knot of officials stood with their hands in their sleeves of robes gorgeous in red and purple, precious metals and jewels like banked embers, but cunningly patched and repaired, great-eyed faces blank beneath round caps worked in filigree. The golden traceries of their headgear were rotten and blackened with age, the emblems of vanished provinces, of services that had once spanned the planet. The air of the great, arched chamber was cold and faintly damp—sopping, to the Martians.

Sajir sa-Tomond adopted a posture of permission, turning the palms of his hands forward and then back, and the functionaries glided forward, moving in the formal pacing that made their robes seem to slide across the pavement without a hint that legs and feet moved them rather than wheels.

Lin Yu-Pei was sweating; probably because of the incongruity between what his eyes were seeing and what the script implanted within his brain would let him perceive. But then, Terrans sweated so readily . . .

And the elderly of the Real World let their minds lose focus. Attention to the present, Sajir sa-Tomond!

Even with the Tollamune genes and the finest anti-agathics he was *old*, slimness turned gaunt, raven hair gone white, hawk face deeply seamed with a mesh of wrinkles that moved and interlaced like cracks in spring ice among the northern seas. The bleak golden eyes were hooded and pouched but keen.

"Yes, the water of the Great Lower Reservoir once more flows to the distribution chambers," he said. "This is a highly desirable occurrence both in contemplation and accomplishment. *Sh'u Maz!* Let harmony be sustained!"

The room echoed with the response to his command: *"Sh'u Maz!"*

The ritual was comforting. Sajir sa-Tomond used it to calm himself as he considered:

My reaction to Binkis is odd. Any of my people who addressed me so would be infected immediately with larvae of the most malignant breed. Yet I do not even resent the fact that I may not order it in his case. There is . . . something else present, with this one. In the legends of the most ancient beginnings . . . and yes, he arrived here in a most *extraordinary manner. A fortunate randomness. Through him I may hope to recover the Ancient tembst. And even if I do not, his advice has enabled me to reverse the intent of the Eastbloc Terrans that I be their puppet.*

At his nod, High Minister Chinta sa-Rokis moved in a smooth arc and touched a finger cased in metal fretwork to a spot on one of the great crystal pipes that ran from floor to ceiling like pillars, a spot where a flow-gauge circled the clear tube. Her cap proclaimed her Supervisor of Planetary Water Control; in ancient days, that had been a post second only to the Commander of the Sword of the Dynasty in the planet's government.

Currently, it meant managing the municipal works and the stretch of canals immediately adjacent to the Mountain. Unlike most of the High Council, she still had *some* actual function.

"*Three hundred* ska-*flow per second*," the monitor said, in a dialect of Demotic so ancient it was almost the High Tongue; it had been a *long* time since this reservoir was active.

"*Purity is within acceptable limits for all standard use. Flow has been steady for one hour, seven minutes, twenty-two seconds at the—*"

The words stopped and a brief pure tone rang out.

"A remarkable display of power," Sajir said. "To raise fluid from such depths."

Chinta sa-Rokis hissed slightly; or that might have been the long slender black-furred symbiant coiled around neck and shoulder, whose lips whispered next to her ear. Then the bureaucrat spoke, while the creature stared at the Emperor with what might have been curiosity . . . or a predator judging distance.

"Yet how long will this"—she made a mangled attempt at pronouncing *pebble-bed reactor*—"continue to function? A mere five or six decades without more fuel than that store which our *allies* of the Wet World have supplied; and the machinery itself is not self-reproducing or self-repairing, as our accustomed *tembst* is. As the one tasked with maintaining the long-term supplies of water, I must"—deferential mode—"caution of the disruption which will arise among those dependent on the additional flow when it ceases in so brief a time."

"We have the water *now*," Sajir said. "Water to bring life and wealth, to pay Professional Coercives, to overcome irksome limitations."

"Even so, Supremacy"—extreme deferential mode, with emphasis on nonironic intent—"problems of management present themselves."

"Death presents one with few managerial dilemmas, yet it is generally believed to be less desirable than the wearisome complications of continued existence," Sajir remarked dryly.

"I will implement the Tollamune will," Chinta said, adopting a pose of submissive obedience.

"This is generally considered a corollary of high office beneath the Tollamune Emperors," Sajir said, his tone even more pawky.

"And we shall, of course, put a program in motion to duplicate the *reactor* and its fuel."

Chinta sa-Rokis blinked in astonishment. Nor was she the only one. Sajir saw some of the others casting dumfounded glances at each other, and sighed inwardly. The idea might well never have occurred to *him* if Binkis had not suggested it, along with making the delivery of reactor and spare fuel pellets a condition of East-bloc access to Dvor Il-Adazar's anti-agathics and antivirals.

Aloud, he continued, "The *vaz-Terranan* have only *had* this tembst a matter of fifty or sixty of their years, which are half the length of the Real World's. Prior to a similar number of *our* years, they were unaware of even the basic principles upon which this device functions. Surely we, with the principles in our minds, can expect our savants to duplicate the accomplishments of the Wet World?"

And surely Chinta will not publicly denigrate our capabilities, he thought with satisfaction. *In fact, I am not entirely confident. Our savants have merely recirculated known data for a very long time.*

The High Minister was capable, once prodded into action, but no more inclined to act on her own than a sessile-stage canal shrimp was to swim. Usually this was convenient; he could simply set her in motion in a chosen direction and then turn his attention elsewhere while she ran on rails like a cargo cart in a mine. When innovation was required, on the other hand . . .

And I myself am most unlikely to survive such a period at this point in my probable life span. Odd, to foresee personal extinction from natural causes in so brief a time as a few decades. I must learn to hurry, as if I were once again heedless with youth. This is an inconvenience. So many problems resolve themselves spontaneously with a mere twenty or thirty years of patience. On the other hand, I must keep in mind that death from another's volition is possible at any point on one's personal world-line.

"Such is the Tollamune will!" he stated in the imperative-condescentive tense.

There was only one possible public response to *that*. The officials lifted fingertips to their temples, bowed their heads, and chanted in chorus:

"*King Beneath the Mountain! Crimson King, holding and swaying the Real World!*"

They would draw the small sharp knives in their sleeves and slit their throats in ritual Apology if he commanded. But just as the portion of the Real World he in fact commanded was much smaller than theory suggested, so would they still conspire and intrigue with every breath they drew to bend *his* will to *theirs*. The more so as he aged toward the ultimate limits and had no immediate heir. That, too, was a situation without precedent, but not one they seemed to find difficult to factor into their calculations.

No heir save for her. *And some of them realize with horror that if my plans succeed, they will have functional duties once more. A balance is required.*

He was tempted to give the order for a mass apology in any case, but their probable successors would be no more reliable, and far more energetic and hungry. Best to keep these for the present. Their underlings had had many years of waiting, which would keep the ministers looking both upward and downward. Younger replacements would be positioned securely enough with their subordinates to look only toward *him*.

The most advantageous circumstance of being at the summit is the added velocity of the downward kick; next, the fact that there is nobody above one to do the same.

"I am glad that Your Supremacy is pleased with our fraternal aid," Lin Yu-Pei said, eyes flickering as he struggled to follow the conversation in Court Demotic.

He was rather obviously translating too literally from his native speech; he had been ambassador for only a few years. The attrition rate from incompatible proteins made the implantation risky with *vaz-Terranan*. The courtiers tensed very slightly, adopting postures of disassociation, implying that they were not present. The guards reacted in a more unambiguous fashion, touching weapons.

"That is not the most appropriate of phrasing," Sajir said gently.

"Your Supremacy?"

Sajir sa-Tomond fell into the Terran language called Russian; they had a ridiculous number of languages, and used them all simultaneously, but it was an ability he had thought sufficiently useful to cultivate. Communication beyond the basics required more than translation of words; modes of thought and perception embodied in the underlying syntax must be understood.

"You implied a genetic relationship with myself, the Tolla-mune," he explained gently. "This is a serious breach of protocol and may not be done even as a matter of metaphor. Further, you did not use the metaphorical mode."

"My apologies, Your Supremacy."

"While not forgotten, the offense is allowed to pass without repercussion, due to your ignorance of the Real World's usages," Sajir said formally.

Unnoticed by the Terran diplomat, the Expediter of Painful Transitions lowered the grub-implanter.

"Concerning the treaty—"

Binkis giggled and uttered two command code words. Lin jerked and stood stock still. Just below where his spine met his skull something glistened for a moment as it moved.

"Thank you, Your Supremacy," Lin continued. "I request permission to return to my quarters. I . . . I have matters to consider."

"Permission is granted with formal expressions of amiable goodwill. Let harmony be sustained!"

Binkis giggled again as the Terran walked away, shaking his head as if bothered by some annoying parasite . . . which, considering the ancestry of the implant, was not too far from the truth. Sajir sa-Tomond gestured in a manner that meant *anticipated reaction*. As Binkis was possibly possessed by the ancient entities, but was certainly a Terran with limited appreciation of the High Speech, he added aloud:

"How long before they begin to suspect? Eventually the knowledge that a Terran who did not arrive by spaceship is at my court will reach them. Not all are suitably infected by the neural controller. The high rate of fatalities is an inconvenience; the new model is still prone to prompting severe allergic reactions."

"They already suspect something. It will not matter if we can interface your ancestors' devices fully with the Terran power plant, their numerically driven controllers, and also with their weapons."

"Ah, yes, the explosives dependent on deconstruction of nuclei in a feedback cycle and the expanding-combustion-gas propulsive missiles," Savir said. "I am still somewhat dubious. Reducing territory to toxic dust seems . . . excessive if one wishes to control it."

"A few examples will produce submission."

"A good point. Force is always more effectively employed as threat than actuality; the greater the raw strength, the more this is so."

"And they will give you leverage against the Eastbloc and against Terra as a whole. They were designed to counter possible USASF action; they have that capacity against Eastbloc ships as well. You will effectively dominate space near Mars."

"True. There remains the problem of the interface, though. New devices are required. Mere selective breeding, or even enzymatic recombinant splicing of the cellular mechanisms of existing machinery is not sufficient; my savants are definite and unanimous, and my own judgment is the same. The very mathematics are different, and require neural devices of novel types, incorporating the target algorithms. The theory needed to produce such is known; practical implementation of such ceased very long ago."

"You have the original cell-mechanism modification devices. The Tollamune genome will activate them."

Ah, Sajir thought, *he still longs for the repair of his consort, who arrived with him.*

The Terran woman was quite mad; only a form of synthetic hibernation had preserved her life this long. The Ancient-derived devices probably *would* suffice, if only it were possible to use them.

He frowned thoughtfully before he spoke. "There is a reason they have not been employed for so very long. They are quite old, they have been used intensively without maintenance, and as a result, *they* are . . . distressed. My genes are correct; my endurance, however, has diminished to the point where further contact would endanger my life."

And that is all you need to know. The true secret, you do not know, nor shall you.

He turned and left; etiquette did not require anything further for the Emperor, of course. His back still crawled slightly, as if in anticipation of the knife or the needle.

Yet that is one of my most familiar sensations, he thought. *I cannot recall a time beyond infancy when it was not chronic. We have preserved the consensual myth of the absolute authority of the Tollamune Throne for so long, yet was it ever more than literalized metaphor? Not in the opinion of my ancestors, certainly. And most certainly, not since the loss of the Invisible Crown.*

The elevator was a bubble of warmth and color and light after the dank dimness of the pumping chamber. It had been repaired and resurfaced for his visit, and the murals were pleasantly pastoral; they showed small, four-legged creatures with silky fur and overlapping rows of teeth gamboling through reeds beside a lake while the tentacles of predatory invertebrates prepared attack. Idly, he wondered if the place still existed; probably not. The small creatures were extinct save for their preserved genetic data, and so were the invertebrates, except in derived weapon- and execution-forms.

"Rise to the Imperial Quarters level," the captain of his bodyguards said, though this shaft was a dedicated one.

The elevator began to hum quietly as it rose through the Tower of Harmonic Unity. The tune was soothing but a little banal, though it covered the quick panting of the engine as it worked the winch on the traveling chamber's roof. The ride was water-smooth otherwise; the engine had been replaced with a fresh budding as well, and the rails and wheels greased by lubricant crawler. The smooth efficiency was bitterly pleasant, as if he had fallen back through the ages, as if all Dvor Il-Adazar were so, drawing on the resources of a world. When it stopped, he pressed a hand to a plate that was warm and slightly moist; it pulsed as it tasted him and identified the Imperial genome.

When the door dilated and he walked through into his sanctum, the present returned on padding feet; murals ever so slightly faded . . .

One wall was glassine, as clear as ever and at the three-thousand-foot level. It showed the slopes of the western cliffs tumbling away below, carved into tower and dome, bridge and roadway, as far north and south as vision could reach. They had been wrought from living rock black and tawny and golden, but always framed in the blood red that had given his lineage its name. Beyond stretched the Grand Canal that circled the huge volcanic cone and collected the water its height raked from the sky. On either side of the canal lay the greenish red and blue-green of life, with here and there the soaring white pride of a magnate's villa.

Fliers drifted past, lean, crimson patrolcraft, diminutive yachts with fanciful paint, plain, fat-bodied freighters; riders mounted on *Paiteng* swooped and soared among them. Landships by the hundred waited by the docks, or sailed the ochre-colored turf of the passageways that led through the croplands to the deserts beyond. Behind him rose the Mountain itself, towering near seventy thousand feet above, through layers of garden and forest and glacier, and then on to the thin verges of space.

If Dvor Il-Adazar was only a city-state now, it was at least the greatest that yet remained in the Real World . . . though from here you could not see how many towers and courts sheltered only dust and silence and fading legends. If the empty ones were fewer than they had been in the year of his accession, then the credit was his, the long struggle against entropy.

"Attend me," he said to the guard-commander, and led the way into the Chamber of Memories.

A flick of a finger brought attendants who left essences and a bowl of smoldering stimulative and then withdrew. Sajir sa-Tomond sat in a lounger that adjusted to his frail length and began to administer warmth and massage. The room was neither very large nor very grand, except for the single block of red crystal shaped into a seat against the far wall; there was only one other like that in all existence, in the Hall of Received Submission.

He stared moodily at it as he sipped. The essence gave him the semblance of strength, and he closed his eyes for a moment to settle his mind. A game of *atanj* lay on a board before him, each piece carved from a single thumb-sized jewel or shaped from precious metal: ruby and jet for the Despots, black jade for the Clandestines, tourmaline for the Coercives, gold fretwork and diamond for the Boycotts.

"Sit," he said to the Coercive. "Unmask. Refresh yourself. You have not made a move today."

The commander did, raising the visor of his parade helm with its faceted eyes and golden mandibles. When the Tollamune opened his own eyes once more, sorrow pierced him to the heart at the sight of the face beneath, the steady golden eyes and the bronze hair in its jeweled war-net. So like, so like . . .

The Thoughtful Grace moved immediately; a Transport leaping a Boycott to deliver a cargo.

Ah! Sajir thought, *daring, yet clever. I will not win this game in less than twenty-three moves now.*

"I have a task for you, Notaj sa-Soj," he said softly.

"Command me, Tollamune," the man said.

The voice was different from *hers*, a little deeper, a little older—Vowin sa-Soj had been only fifty at the beginning of her long and bitter death. Notaj sa-Soj was her sire's youngest brother by another breeding partner, and at a century young for his post. His eugenic qualifications were impeccable, and his record of action matched it.

"To recapitulate that which is universally known but rarely expressed: I have no heir," Sajir said. "None of more than one-eighth consanguinity, and none of sufficient genetic congruity to be accounted of the Lineage or to operate the Devices. With me, the Crimson Dynasty ends, after eighteen thousand years of the Real World, and all hope of restoring *Sh'u Maz* in its true form."

"This is true, Supremacy. With you will perish the significance of our existence and such meaning as sentience has imposed on mere event. There is little consolation in it, but the line of the Kings Beneath the Mountain will at least end with a superior individual."

The nicating membranes swept over Notaj's eyes, leaving them glistening. "I will preserve your life as long as event and randomness permit, your Supremacy," he added, his voice firm.

Despite everything, Sajir sa-Tomond felt himself smile at the harmonics that underlay the flat statement. The voice of a Thoughtful Grace purebred could rarely be read for undertone by anyone but a Tollamune.

"At least, the official perception of matters is that I have no heir of closer than one-eighth consanguinity," Sajir said, and saw the other's pupils flare and ears cock forward.

Their breed had been selected for wit, not merely deadliness. They had been generals and commanders once, as well as matchless Coercives on a personal level. The implications and possibilities needed little restating.

"Vowin's offspring survives?"

"Correct, Captain. Concealed here until relatively recently. When she matured, traces of the Tollamune inheritance became unmistakable."

They shared a glance that said: *And then she must be hidden and exiled, for what crime is more reprobated than the theft of the Tollamune genome? But now, perhaps, the balance of forces allows . . .*

"The knowledge is no longer so closely held as would best suit my purposes," Sajir went on. "You will understand that multiple factions wish the official and perceived reality to be made objective truth, lest the pleasantly empty field left after my long-anticipated departure should prove not so empty after all."

"But you do not so wish, Supremacy?" the guard captain said, his voice neutral as the cool water in the fountain.

"I never did." Sajir's eyes closed again, this time against remembered pain. "As evidence, she lives."

"But Vowin does not—interrogative-hypothetical?"

"Certain courses of action were . . . necessary. If she had waited longer to make herself receptive to fertilization, as I instructed . . . But you of the Thoughtful Grace are headlong. And there was doubt as to my own survival at the time. The arrival of the *vas-Terranan* machines disturbed a most delicate balance."

Notaj blinked, integrating the information. "She must have been willing to undertake death by infestation in order to secure the Lineage," he said; there was a hard pride in his tone. "She was, as you say, youthful and headlong, but a fine strategic analyst, and ruthless. And genetically ambitious. To bear the first outcross of the Tollamune line in ten millennia . . ."

Sajir sa-Tomond let his shoulders and head fall into a pose of acceptance. "So she said. Such pride was worthy of eugenic elevation. We of the Dynasty have hugged our seed too close, to the detriment of *Sh'u Maz.*"

The guardsman gestured agreement-with-reservations; unspoken was the reason for that—the tools of power responded to the genome, not the individual. Too many Emperors had died at the hands of their own close kin for any to forget it. So their numbers had dwindled across the millennia and their own long life spans.

As have the water and atmosphere of the Real World itself, Sajir thought. *This is a congruity far too apt for comfort.*

"There are many factors to be considered," Notaj said. "Your demise would, with a high degree of probability, be expedited if an heir were anticipated, but not yet in place and aligned with effective power. Those disaffected elements content to wait now for their chance would act precipitately in that hypothesis."

"True. Therefore the heir must be found, brought to Dvor Il-Adazar, and put in an unassailable position. Those who wish to kill or capture her—"

"Capture her?"

Both words were separately in Interrogative; the guardsman raised two fingers to his brow in apology. Sajir sa-Tomond moved a hand in a gentle curve that covered his words in a glow of affection:

"The offspring was female. And there is the *vas-Terranan* to be considered. There are implications of possession of the Tollamune genome that you do not know; suffice it to say that the Terran requires access to the genome. Prince Heltaw sa-Veynau, for example, wishing to rule through a puppet and gain access to the Tollamune genome. Possibly others, but certainly him."

"The Terran?"

"Him. Unfortunately, he is necessary to my purposes. And I very much depreciate the high-probability consequences of his no longer needing *me*."

"I will begin contingency planning immediately," Notaj said. "The necessary information, Supremacy—identity and location?"

He gave the data—keys to the files, rather—and watched the brisk efficiency of the commander's stride out of the entrance with wry amusement.

Then the man halted and turned in the doorway, his eyes going to the *atanj* board.

"Twenty-*five* moves, Supremacy."

That also reminded him of a woman dead many years.

His loyalty is absolute, though intelligent and independent, the Tollamune thought. *And now I have activated his own Lineage ambitions. He will operate at maximum efficiency. To promote this is to sustain harmony.*

With a sigh he rose from the recliner and walked to the crystal throne. Eddies moved within the dense redness of it, like wings of gauze. He gave a complex shiver as he sat, resting his head against the recess behind it and feeling the featherlight pressure against the scar on his neck, then a slight sting. Exterior reality vanished. A murmur as of distant hive insects seemed to fill his skull, but it was no mere vibration of the air. An inexpressible sensation of draining, as his recent memories joined those of all his life, and of the Lineage of the Crimson Dynasty and their consorts since the beginning.

Visions: death, birth, love, hate, accomplishment and cruelty, glory and despair. The bowed heads of ancient kings kneeling before the First Emperor; the feel of his own blood pouring out over the crystal, and the knives in the hands of kin. The temptation to lose himself in that endless sea was strong and bitter, as strong as the taste of *tokmar*; he knew that, for a memory of it was here—not his, many generations removed, but as real as the weary weight of his own bones.

"For a moment," he whispered. "Only for a moment I will see you again, my Vowin, so beautiful and so fierce. Then I will fight for the child of our union, until we are united once more."

CHAPTER TWO

Encyclopedia Britannica, 20th Edition
University of Chicago Press, 1998

MARS—History of Observation

The lack of the consistent layer of high cloud which rendered earth-based telescopic investigation of Venus so difficult was partially offset by the smaller size of Mars and the rarity of close approaches. By the early nineteenth century, astronomers such as Herschel and Schroeter had determined the size, axial inclination, and seasons of the red planet. The presence of polar icecaps and the distinct yearly changes in their dimensions argued for a basically Earthlike world. However, the small size and poor definition of available refractors long delayed further definitive conclusions as to the surface features of Mars, although in the 1830s Beer and Mädler accurately located the *Sinus Meridiani* and determined a rotational period close to the true one.

Over the next two generations, several other features were discovered, among them the Hourglass Sea, and the seasonal fluctuations in ice cover on the North Polar Sea. The Jesuit scholar Angelo Secchi, director of the observatory of the Collegio Romano in Rome, conclusively proved the existence of continents and seas during the opposition of 1858, a result confirmed by the British astronomer William Rutter Davies in 1864. The investigations of Giovanni Schiaparelli in the next thirty years discovered and began the mapping of the Martian canals.

These were extended and refined by the American Percival Lowell, beginning with his Arizona expedition for the opposition of 1894, and confirmed by E. M. Antoniadi in the same period. Lowell also made the first relatively accurate calculation of the density of the Martian atmosphere; the first positive though still ambiguous and disputed evidence of oxygen and water vapor was discovered by Walter S. Adams and Theodore Dunham, who attached a spectroscope to the 100-inch reflector at Mt. Wilson Observatory in the 1930s.

Conclusive proof that Mars had an oxygen-nitrogen atmosphere similar to Earth's, though somewhat less massive, was produced by Gerard Peter Kuiper at the McDonald Observatory in Texas in 1947. Since it was now widely appreciated that free oxygen can only be a by-product of biological action, this evidence removed the last serious objections to Lowell's theory that the canals were a product of intelligent design, and created intense worldwide interest . . .

Mars, City of Zar-tu-Kan
May 1, 2000 AD

Jeremy Wainman grinned to himself as they followed the two Martians toward the Alliance consulate. Most people his age knew what a Martian city looked like, but . . .

Or they think they do. They haven't lived it. I hadn't, until now. They haven't felt it or smelled it.

He'd been born near Los Alamos, New Mexico, and raised there and points south before being selected for the Academy in Colorado Springs. Zar-tu-Kan reminded him of Sedona, down in Arizona—if you could imagine the colored buttes and cliffs as made by hands and minds, rather than by eroding wind and sand. Those forces had smoothed and rounded here too, until every sharp edge had blurred; the streets of Zar-tu-Kan felt like random alleyways laid out by the wanderings of ancient Martian burros through a maze of low cliffs stippled in a faded rainbow of colors.

They weren't; computer analysis had shown subtle planning, something like the deep patterns you got in a fractal . . . or it might be the result of constant minor adjustments over inconceivable lengths of time. The tall, blank walls of melted-looking stone on either side were mostly close, but they waved and curved like frozen water, usually giving you a place to step aside when a caravan of tall, spindly, hairy beasts laden with huge packsaddles went by, or a rider mounted on a *rakza,* an animal that might have been a big ostrich, except for the thick neck and massive hooked beak.

The *rakza* screeched and shook its head as a wagon blocked its path for a moment, flicking up the crest of green-gold feathers on its long skull, until the rider gave a sharp tug on the reins. A pair of patrollers paused at the sound; they rode on self-propelled unicycles, with dart-rifles slung over their backs and helmets with eyes on stalks peering rearward, ready to warn their masters of attack. When they saw the incident would die of its own accord, they leaned forward, swaying and turning to weave through the traffic.

Now and then they passed a doorway, which might be blank or elaborately carved wood with the sinuous glyphs the Crimson Dynasty had made the planet's standard script, or cast with designs in imperishable frosted crystal, sometimes in styles so old that the Martians themselves had forgotten what they meant. Zar-tu-Kan had been a city before the Kings Beneath the Mountains began their rise half a world away. Fine lines showed against the sky, where anti-bird nets strung between the upper stories made sure no migrating predators would drop in for a snack.

Most of the passers-by were natives of the city or its dependent territories, with their hair in elaborate coils to denote occupation and status, and vertical stripes on their robes—farmer, smith, artisan, soldier, clerk, or occupations that had no precise Terran equivalent.

A scattering were from much farther away: Highlanders even more eerily elongated than the standard Martians and barrel-chested, goggles over their eyes, *Wai Zang* mercenaries in glittering black armor and visors with the faceted eyes of insects, and students in carved masks abstract or whimsical or bestial, come to study at the Scholarium.

Sometimes the alleys opened out into an oblong space surrounded by shops and service trades, their clear glassine windows showing their wares. *Atanj* players looked up from their boards and spheres of essence as the Terrans walked by—and it wasn't easy to pry a Martian loose from their equivalent of chess. Shoppers looked up, too.

And I wouldn't mind shopping here, Jeremy thought. Usually he was bored stiff by it, but that was in the hypermarkets back home.

Flaps of artfully arranged *rooz* meat looked a little like beef; red-purple canal shrimp swam in globular bowls and huddled back in tight knots when a storekeeper dipped a net in their tank; there were piles of mysterious vegetables and others of breads like fluffy pancakes. And there were other merchants with fabrics, weapons, tools, jewelry, animals of scores of specialized uses, the Martian books with their narrow pages bound at the tops . . .

Fliers passed by overhead; towers reared impossible heights into the pink-blue sky like skyscrapers in Manhattan, and above it all, the two small moons passed like rapid stars. It was nearly twenty years since the first Terrans had come out of the desert to the city, but they still attracted a fair bit of attention, though only the children showed it openly. They ranged from knee-high to almost grown, and the younger ones gaped and pointed and gave peals of shrill laughter.

"Cute little tykes," Jeremy said as they passed a knot of them where two of the narrow streets intersected.

They were playing a game much like *atanj*, but with themselves for pieces. When the commander of one team maneuvered two of his pieces onto a single one of the other side, they gleefully pummeled each other. *Atanj* was supposed to be an analogue of war, like chess, but they took that more literally here.

"Don't let the big eyes fool you," Sally said, and then shouted in Martian, *"Don't even think about it!"* as one of a slightly older group bent to pick up something unpleasant.

He—probably he, it was hard to tell when everyone was muffled up, and anyway Martians were less sexually dimorphic than Terrans—continued to bend for ammunition. Teyud wheeled to face him and flicked her right hand. Something like a small disk with curled spikes along its edge appeared between finger and thumb, and her hand cocked back with lazy grace. The *atanj* teams dove out of the way, squealing.

Whoa! Jeremy thought. *Let's not let things get out of hand!*

He tensed his leg muscles and jumped. The results sent the little almost-mob of near adolescents scattering, as he soared through the air as if launched by a hydraulic catapult. Twisting, he landed in front of the fleeing would-be dung-thrower, forcing him to backpedal furiously and nearly drop on his butt to stop. The boy's eyes were bulging with surprise through the slit in his headdress. Jeremy didn't give him any time to recover, or to go for any of the various unpleasant devices undoubtedly concealed under his ragged robe. One hand gripped the back of his neck, the other at his belt, and the Terran pivoted and *threw*.

He'd had six months' practice with Martian gravity. The boy flew ten yards, arms and legs kicking, to land neatly in a two-wheeled cart filled with the droppings of various draught-beasts. Those were a lot drier and fluffier than their earthly equivalents; a big cloud of pungent brownish dust shot skyward. The boy tumbled out of it a few moments later, coughing and retching and beating at his garments. He stopped a moment to make three comprehensively obscene gestures at Jeremy, then took to his heels.

"Suboptimal random breeding," Teyud said, insulting the fleeing boy more than an avalanche of scatology could have done. "It would be public-spirited to cull him before he reproduces."

"Please do not kill anyone unless it is necessary to protect us," Sally said. "That is a categorical instruction."

"Reluctant agreement," Teyud said, then shrugged and slid the spiked throwing disk back to its place in her sleeve.

For the rest, the crowds' reaction was sidelong glances and low murmurs—and they were low indeed, pitched for the more efficient ears evolved in this thin air.

You know, Jeremy thought, watching as Teyud za-Zhalt swayed along ahead of them, *she really moves beautifully. Different from most Martians—she doesn't give you that sense she'd fly away in a high breeze, even though she* does *look like someone took her by the neck and ankles and stretched her by about twenty percent.*

They came to a larger open space. One side of it was a semicircular border, a smooth olive green wall twenty feet high that vanished behind buildings on either side which, he knew, made a circle more than a mile around. Above that rose a glassine dome, and through it, he could see the tops of trees. A central tower reared gigantic in its center, but the fliers clustered around its thousand-foot peak were all warcraft in the red and black markings of the Despotate, the local government. Traffic was brisk over the russet-colored pavement, save where they swerved around a crew at work repairing a worn section.

Several *De'ming* shoveled crushed rock from a wagon into the maws of creatures like twelve-foot furry bricks with stubby legs and flat paddlelike scaly tails. A third of their length was mouth, studded with dozens of thick square black teeth around a muscular purple tongue. They caught the gravel and began to crunch it down with every sign of enjoyment; the sound recalled that of a man eating celery, but a thousand times louder and with a metallic overtone.

Some had already been fed, and lay on their bellies with an occasional contented belch. A circle of children crouched to watch and giggled with disgusted delight as the animals turned and projectile-vomited into the hole in the pavement in unison. A thick, vile, sour-smelling yellow sludge filled the hole, and the beasts turned at the foreman's urging and smoothed it flat with their tails. By the time the Terrans and their guides walked by, the surface was already hardening and turning a slightly lighter shade of reddish-brown than the rest. The crew then moved on to the next gap.

"Did you ever hear the expression 'tough enough to eat iron and shit nails'?" Sally asked.

"Yeah," Jeremy began. Then he looked at her. "You don't mean—"

"Near enough," she said. "Near enough."

Ahead of them, gold-robed warriors wearing masks like the faces of mantises and long ceremonial spears of translucent crystal stood before the huge circular gate of the fastness, graven with the solar disk. Above it was a symbol that looked like a figure eight laid on its side, surrounded by a glyph in the High Speech of ancient times: SH'U MAZ. Sustained Harmony, from time out of mind the motto of anyone who wished to claim the status of Acknowledged Ruler.

A much smaller portal accommodated the real traffic. The guards beside it carried swords and dart pistols, and one of them held a beast on a leash. It looked a little like a dog, perhaps a starved, elongated greyhound with teeth like a shark, a high forehead, and disturbingly versatile paws. All four of the party stood while it approached and sniffed them over.

"Ssssstrannnngeee, master," it whined to its handler, growling a little. "Ssmmmeelll sssstrannngeee."

"Are they on the list?" the bored trooper asked, giving the leash a jerk and waving a collection of strips of cloth bearing the scents of those authorized to enter the central dome.

"Yesss."

"Pass, then."

The door rolled aside as the beast flattened itself on the ground beside the guard, watching them walk by with slitted eyes. Sally and Jeremy turned and shook hands.

"Tomorrow at the docks," Sally said.

"Tomorrow," Teyud said. "I anticipate our joint labors."

Mars, City of Dvor Il-Adazar (Olympus Mons)
Palace of Restful Contemplation
February 1, 2000 AD

Genomic Prince Heltaw sa-Veynau watched the children running silently through the gardens beneath the dome, weaving in among tall, slender trees whose trunks bore masses of flowering vines, their blooms trumpets of orange and crimson and purple-striped white. The thick, dense mat of vegetation beneath their feet was composed of soft ochre fibers, a strain that had once been nearly as common as atmosphere plant, but which in these times was rare far from the Mountain. The mountainside bowl that cupped the palace gardens rose beyond and all around, parts left rough in the native reddish tufa veined with black and gold, others carved in the fanciful elongated animal style common in the Orchid Consort Period, eight thousand years ago.

A small fountain burbled within a column of glassine, and birds like flying jewels trilled the songs for which his remote ancestors had designed them. He had followed his customary program before

making important decisions: a light breakfast, a bout of sword practice with his trainer, parareproductive coitus with his partner, and
a period of nonreflective contemplation.

Now it was very restful to lie here as the recliner gently mas-
saged his back, smell the *wadar* incense, and watch the children at
play under the careful eye of their nannydog; they were his sister's
offspring, and he had none of his own . . . not yet . . . despite being
well into middle age, sixty years this spring.

Or a hundred and twenty, as the Wet Worlders reckon it, he thought;
they had been much on his mind of late. *Reproduction, in my position,
would have been evidence of unseemly presumption, or, to phrase the matter
more bluntly, suicidal.*

The captain of his guards waited—*taking knee* as court slang had
it—on his right knee, with the scabbard of his sword in his gloved
left hand, and the right on his left thigh. His personal Coercives
wore black robes and hoods, and unmarked harnesses; he believed
their attire conveyed a sense of disciplined seriousness, in contrast
to the ironic detachment or frivolous archaism so common here in
the City That Was A Mountain.

"Competitive patience is a trying form of contest in this regres-
sive era," he remarked.

"Query, Prince Heltaw?" the soldier said.

"I characterize my contest with the Supremacy. The Emperor is
among the most skillful practitioners of *waiting* the Crimson Dynasty
has ever produced. So skillful that it is never entirely certain that he
is, in fact, waiting and not merely mired in sloth and resignation."

"Prince, I would not care to wager anything with which I would
grieve to part on the latter hypothesis."

"Neither would I," Heltaw said dryly. "Especially not after the
little display with the Terrans earlier this year."

"The pumps, Prince?"

"Correct," he said. To himself, *You are perceptive. Perhaps trou-
blingly so? No, merely competent.*

"No other of the Tollamunes has actually increased the available water resources for a very long time indeed," he went on. "And
to do so with the *tembst* of the *vaz-Terranan,* which is accessible only
through him . . . and to exhibit the anomalous Terran who did not
arrive as the others . . . yes, that was quite skillful. It will give those

who might otherwise hasten the succession pause for thought, and give credence to his claim to restore Sustained Harmony."

"Yet in a contest of patience, you possess the matchless advantage of comparative youth, Prince," the guardsman pointed out. "Since neither you nor the Supremacy have close and immediate heirs, this would appear to be a balance which can only tilt in your favor. *Sh'u Maz* is impossible where succession is not clear."

"Unless one of us were to have an heir," Heltaw said. "If I had done so prior to this date, my demise would have been unfortunate, widely received with grief, accidental . . . and entirely certain."

The guardsman's hand moved in a spare ironic gesture, an acknowledgement of the humor. "Given the length of time in which the demise of the Supremacy has been anticipated, the same might be said of him. Leaving aside capacity, surely he would not be in a position to socialize an heir to maturity."

"I have obtained news from my sources in Zar-tu-Kan," Heltaw said quietly. "A Thoughtful Grace mercenary by the name of Teyud za-Zhalt has been engaged to command the landship and escort of two *vaz-Terranan* savants seeking the lost city of Rema-Dza. This person is not at all as she appears."

In the narrow slit of the headdress, the Coercive's eyes widened slightly. Heltaw approved; the man would be useless if he required long explanations.

"Kill, capture, or incapacitate?" he said.

"Capture, if possible. Kill only if essential to prevent escape. Keep a full sustainment kit ready to prolong the life of a reproductive sump of the body if killing is necessary, or at the very least to preserve viable ova. This is a formidable individual; take all precautions. Also, at least two other groups will be seeking to preempt you."

"I will begin the necessary research immediately, Prince," the guardsman said.

"A unit of *Paiteng* will be made available," Heltaw said. "You will, to a high degree of probability, have a very narrow window of opportunity. When you strike, strike swiftly. You are, of course, not the only resource tasked with this mission."

An eyebrow went up. "You have made an open offer, Superior, rather than entrusting the task solely to your permanently affiliated Coercives?"

"There are several offers concerning this individual, at least one other of which I know simply for delivery of the detached head. It is the reproductive organs that are my optimum target, preferably attached to a living body. Hence, I have let it be known that a larger reward is available for a capture in order to present disincentives for entrepreneurial activity contrary to my interests. I cannot, of course, prevent freelance individuals and groups from contesting the matter."

"This is a straightforward and sensible course, Superior."

"I will, of course, pay a substantial bonus above the stated open reward if the personnel you lead accomplish this task to my satisfaction," Heltaw said. "My personally affiliated Coercives justly anticipate treatment more favorable than temporary employees."

"As always, you optimize incentives, Superior. As you order, we will endeavor most earnestly to accomplish—subject to event and randomness."

When the Coercive had left, Heltaw reached out and took a biscuit from the table with the incense burner, warming and scenting it briefly over the flame before nibbling at it. The time for patience would soon end, but until then . . .

The Prince smiled slightly to himself as one of his nieces stood, laughing at the half dozen birds that perched on her slender arms and sang counterpoint to each other.

Until then I must be patient. Or my Lineage will die to the seventh degree.

That was as far as the Expeditors could push a purge; he was in the eighth degree from the Ruby Throne himself. Officially, there was none closer.

Mars, City of Zar-tu-Kan
May 1, 2000 AD

"Do you know anyone who wishes to inflict harm on the Terrans?" Teyud asked as she and the spice merchant turned away from the portal to the inner city.

"No," Jelzhau said.

His ears cocked forward as he turned his head toward her. "Do you suspect malicious conspiracy?"

She frowned slightly, scanning the crowd in the plaza. It could be compulsive suspicion . . . but then, compulsive suspicion was a survival characteristic in the greater world as well as in Dvor Il-Adazar.

"I suspect that we were followed. By relays of very skilled operatives."

Jelzhau pursed his lips. "I will have enquiries made. Losing the profits of their trade would grieve me to the point of melancholy."

Or perhaps they *are on my trail again,* Teyud thought.

It was an unpleasant and surprising speculation, but not one that could be disregarded.

Randomness has a fortunate configuration in that case; I will be voyaging to the Deep Beyond with the vaz-*Terranan. One can see a menace more clearly when away from a city's crowds.*

"Though," he went on, "I anticipate with gladness the end of close association with the hideous things."

Teyud absently adopted a pose that acknowledged the remark without commenting on it. Sally Yamashita was indeed *very* strange-looking, at one moment like a dwarf, at another like an aged child. Jeremy Wainman, on the other hand . . .

One could very nearly call him handsome. And he has a pleasantly effervescent personality.

The U.S. Consulate had once been a local notable's city palace. It did duty for the Commonwealth and OAS countries and Japan as well; their flags flew over its front entrance. It wasn't particularly *large*, about the size of the White House, and like most buildings under the dome it was built in a light, airy style in total contrast to the blank massiveness of most of Zar-tu-Kan outside, all tall slender columns and translucent window-doors and balconies.

Robert Holmegard and his wife Dolores, who was also his assistant and a biologist of note, gave a dinner for the explorers on a balcony of clear crystal supported by two curving braces of the same material shaped like slender snakes, a structure that seemed nerve-wrackingly fragile if you didn't know the strength of the stuff.

To the stomach it was *still* nerve-wracking, particularly as it was sixty feet to the tough reddish-green sward that made up the roadway below. Even in one-third gravity that was a *long* way.

"God, it's good to see some Terran faces," Holmgard said.

"Yeah," Dolores said. "I knew I'd been here too long when I read the latest *Newsweek* and wondered which candidate for president was going to establish the most *Sh'u Maz*."

Her husband chuckled and shuddered at the same time. "It's been months! I know there were storms, but . . ."

Jeremy shuddered a little in turn. "Storms" didn't begin to describe what the Martian polar winter was like—and seasons lasted twice as long on this planet. Sometimes more, if you were unlucky enough to be in the hemisphere that got the downside of the eccentric orbit that time around. It gave you a lot of time to brush up on your research and perfect your game of *atanj*, though no Terran had yet become more than mediocre at it.

"Bob, we came as soon as we could," Sally said soothingly. "And we've got that disk from Susie and Joyce."

The Holmgards brightened and stuck the disk into the reader on the table; it was a bit of incongruously homey Texas Instruments bluntness amid the stretched elegance of Martian glassware. The screen came alive and showed two children of twelve and ten, their looks halfway between Robert's hulking Minnesota-Swede blondness and his wife's dark Peruvian-Spanish delicacy.

Jeremy paid attention to the entertainment while they listened to the message: Not far away a bird the size of a six-year-old sat on a perch and sang a song with a haunting minor-key melody, now and then making sounds like wind chimes to accompany itself, and moving wings like living Tiffany glass in time to the music it made.

"Dammit, we should have a fiber-optic cable between here and the base by now," Holmgard said, turning off the message and sighing. "Given what the weather does to radio."

Jeremy nodded. That had been tried once, and had failed at hideous expense—there were limits to what the USASF budget could bear, especially now that the first flush of wonder had worn off and the voters weren't quite so enchanted with pouring tens of billions yearly into space. And the peculiarities of the Martian atmosphere limited wireless bandwidth.

The Holmgards tore themselves away from their children's disk with commendable speed and devoted themselves to their hostly duties. Jeremy speared a strip of grilled *rooz* and nibbled it; despite the fact that it came from a bird—more or less—it didn't taste at all like chicken. A bit like beef, a bit like pork with a soupçon of shrimp, meltingly tender and spiced with something that tasted like a cross between garlic and chili with a hint of flowers. There was a heat to it that hit you after a moment of hesitation, like slow-motion napalm.

Although it's better not to remember it's cooked over dung fires, he thought, taking a drink of water that had a slightly metallic taste.

Granted, the animal in question essentially shat thumb-sized pieces of pure charcoal, but the thought was still a bit off-putting if you dwelt on it.

"Okay, let's go over your mission," Bob said.

He touched the screen with fingers that were thick, muscular, and nimble. A map of Mars sprang up, then narrowed down to the section around Zar-tu-Kan; it was the product of satellite photography combined with local knowledge.

"If your interpretation of the chronicles is right, there's not much doubt that the lost city of Rema-Dza is around *here*," he said. "Out where the dead canal runs. But that's bad country—dust storms, nomads, God knows what. Keep in close touch. Even the atmosphere plant dies out there sometimes."

Jeremy and Sally nodded soberly. That low-growing, waxy-leaved plant was the Martian equivalent of grass . . . and also, ecologically, of oceanic plankton; it kept the oxygen content of the air. It had a fantastically efficient version of photosynthesis, flourished nearly everywhere, and stood at the bottom of nearly every food chain. An area too hostile for it was likely to be bleak indeed, even by this dying planet's standards.

Holmgard poured essence into their cups. The purple liquid glowed faintly as it made a graceful low-gravity arc, with motes moving within it. Stars shone many and very bright through the dome above, making the mild springlike temperature—tropical warmth to Martians—seem like the small bubble of life it was, in a universe coldly inimical. The gasbags of floatlights shone as well, a light cooler than electrics and tinged with red, circling the building as they sculled themselves along with feathered limbs. Things rustled and clicked in the dense groves and gardens that separated the mansions and palaces of Zar-tu-Kan's inner zone.

"And on that cheerful note . . ."

————

Teyud za-Zhalt finished her last inspection of the *Intrepid Traveler* as the sun rose eastward behind the highlands. The air was slightly cool, just enough to leave a rime of frost on exposed stone, and the din and clatter of the port sounded sharp through it.

The landship was a sixty-footer with a central hold and two internal decks fore and aft; a hundred fifty tons burden, which made her medium sized. Old but sound, with a single hundred-foot mast and an auxiliary engine that could supply enough hydraulic pressure to the rear axle motors to move the craft at better than walking pace in a pinch. The layout was standard for a vessel of her size, with one fixed axle at the rear, another amidships, and a longer pivoting one forward. Axles, mast, and spars were single-crystal growths; unfortunately there was no way of telling how old they were—the slight yellowish tinge to the clear flexible material meant only that they weren't new.

They could be a hundred years from the plantations and good for another thousand, or a thousand and likely to go to dust at any moment. Bearings, cables, and sails all looked reliable, and there was a good ring-mounted darter on the quarterdeck.

The crew . . .

She grimaced very slightly at the score of them: a collection of scar-faced toughs, *tokmar* addicts with a faint quiver to their hands, and obvious lowbreeds. One was nearly noseless, with nasal slits that closed and opened nervously, and he had a russet brown hue to his skin—some sort of hybrid from the deep deserts. They stood waiting, a few working on their personal gear or playing *atanj*, while *De'ming* trotted from the stone wharf across the boarding rams to stow bundles of dried meat and *asu*-fruit, ceramic casks of pickled eggs, ammunition and gun-food, spare cable, and stores of a dozen kinds, down to glow-rods and blood-builders. Half a dozen of the little subsapient laborers went and squatted on the foredeck when the loading was finished; she'd bought those for the usual tasks. Ordinary workers attached a hose to fill the tanks; this district had a water tower and pressure in the mains.

Several of the crew came more erect as they felt her gaze. She knew that a yellow-eyed stare was disconcerting. Old legends

spoke of it. Others remained dully indifferent, and one kept chewing on a *kevaut* on a stick he'd bought from a vendor with a portable
grill, spitting out bits of carapace as he sucked out the last shreds of
flesh.

"What do you think of the engine?" she said to the hireling
who had an engineer's hairdo.

"Middle-aged, and the temperature is just a little higher than
I'd like, so I would advise not straining it," the hatchet-faced
woman said. She was short, a full foot shorter than Teyud's seven-
two. Shaking her head, she went on, "But it's of a good local budding strain, it doesn't cough or have the runs, the tentacles are
well-bonded to the sleeves of the cranks, and it's been adequately
fed and the sludge-tanks are full. As long as we eat and our bowels
function, it won't starve. I'd rather replace the drive-train gearing
and put new bearing-races on all axles before starting a long trip,
but all should function for the next few months."

*Exactly my own analysis. Jelzhau didn't try to cheat us. Extraordi-
nary. Even more extraordinary, this* Baid tu-Or *seems to know her work.
I wonder why she wants to get out of Zar-tu-Kan badly enough to sign with
us. At least she will probably play an acceptable game; I have yet to meet
one of the* vaz-Terranan *worth setting up the board for.*

A little reassured, she checked that all six of the addicts had sufficient *tokmar* to last out the trip; of all the fates available, being
trapped in the wilds with a *tokmar* sniffer deprived of his or her
daily dose was one of the least attractive.

One of them *didn't* have enough, and asked for an advance to
buy; she simply let her hand fall to the hilt of her dart pistol and
looked at him until he shuffled off. That one didn't have much
longer to live. The tremor was turning into jerks, and the mental effects of his habit had obviously gotten beyond the point of mere
recklessness—nobody but the reckless would have signed up for
this cruise—to outright loss of survival instinct.

"Now listen to me, you fodder for the recycling vats," she said,
pitching her voice to carry and using the Imperative-Condescentative
tense. "I have no interest in how you feel about the *vaz-Terranan*, as
long as you fear *me* as you do personal extinction. Do you?"

"We fear you exceedingly, even to the relaxation of sphincters!"
they chorused, in the convictive-metaphorical tense; and spoke

honestly, she thought, except possibly for the hybrid with the nostril slits and the long bow over his shoulder. "You are pain and death in sapient form!"

"Good. Maintain an attitude of terrified submission and harmony will be sustained. Suddri, Xax, Taldus, crew the darter. The rest of you, on board and to your stations, make ready to depart. Show speed!"

She turned to survey the docks as the *De'ming* finished their load and trooped back toward the warehouses under the touch of the supervisor's rod. The *Traveler* was at the last of the docks that still saw regular use; beyond to the south was a tumble of wharfs half buried in drifted soil with a sparse cover of atmosphere plant, and a wilderness of broken-roofed buildings eroded to snags by wind and abraiding sand. The tops of actual trees showed there—the ruins would concentrate stray moisture.

Northward, every second slip was occupied, and a big three-master was in the graving dock, with the planking off its hull and artificers crawling about within. A crane extended a tentacle as she watched, hoisting some massive fabrication out of the structure and onto a repair platform.

She kept an ear cocked backward; the sounds indicated the scratch crew had some idea of what they were doing. Her eyes narrowed to focus on two craft that had stayed at anchor out on the plain. They were long and low, a bit bigger than the *Traveler*, and lay quietly with furled sails. The hulls had few openings and no walkways or balconies, and all the hatches were closed.

Not local, by the lines, she thought, then shrugged. Trade from all around the planet found its way here.

The *vaz-Terranan* arrived, with their surprisingly scanty baggage.

This voyage will be both profitable and an interlude of respite from boredom, she told herself. *The life of an exile is irritatingly lacking in long-term goals.*

She had dreams enough: what she would do if she sat on the Ruby Throne, for example. That was about as likely as a trip to the Wet World. Though with her broader experience of how the Real World fared . . .

The taller Terran smiled. His face was rough, as if hewn from rock by a not very skilled sculptor who used a percussive method, but oddly engaging, even intriguing in its open mobility.

Teyud allowed her lips to turn up very slightly.

Mars, City of Dvor Il-Adazar (Olympus Mons)
Ministry of Hydraulic Management
February 1, 2000 AD

High Minister Chinta sa-Rokis sighed in exasperation.

"No," she said. "I do *not* consider the reactivation of that reservoir by the Supremacy's Terran *tembst* a positive development."

She waited patiently while her three carefully selected listeners blinked at the blunt contradiction of the Tollamune will.

The listeners were all members of the High Council. They sat in recliners around a black jade table, their postures of informal communication, as one did with social equals. If you looked very closely, you realized that the seemingly solid block of the tabletop had been carved until it was as insubstantial as lace in a pattern of repeating fractals that could hypnotize the unwary. The essence in the globes each held was of an antique pungency and swam with a living culture that guaranteed vividly entertaining—or terrifying— dreams to the user. The floor was a slab of living honey-colored wood whose rippling grain responded to body warmth by exuding a pleasant scent. Rugs crawled to envelop the feet of the four officials, warming and gently caressing.

By contrast, the heroic murals on seven of the eight walls were boringly antique, depicting the semilegendary construction of the Grand Canal in the early years of the Dynasty. Their very age guaranteed that the Minster must endure them, however, and since they celebrated a notable Imperial accomplishment, modification might be taken as a gesture of disrespect. Nobody else was present, except for a brace of her personal *De'ming*, and they were of a special subspecies with no sense of hearing. The glassine eighth wall looked over nothing but empty courts until the farmlands at the city's foot, and her personal Coercives manned the towers between.

The silence stretched. All of the other High Councilors she had invited for private consultation were, in Chinta's opinion, nitwits, though not in any technical sense. Their minds had rotted from dis-use. One was obsessed with collating an encyclopedia of the poetry of the Terminal Lilly Period; another spent nearly every waking hour on the records of *atanj* tournaments although she was no more than a mediocre player herself; the third provided an essential source of *valuata* for the city's more expert commercial specialists in parareproductive entertainment.

I despise them all, she thought. *Ironic, that this makes them the most suitable to my purposes. I may take consolation that I also further Prince Heltaw's purposes . . . at least to a certain degree . . . and he is a man to respect. And hence to fear.*

The three High Ministers' accumulated resources and the influence of their Lineages, however, were far from contemptible. And besides that, they all shared genetic linkages with her, common among the bloodlines of the upper bureaucracy. Competitive examination for office had been the rule since earliest Imperial times, but you could breed for success in that capacity no less than for any other. If you did so and hoarded your genome strictly, you could expect a practical monopoly.

"It seems to be of long-term benefit that our water resources be increased," one said cautiously, sipping at his essence. "Water is life."

"'Benefit' is a relational term, not an absolute," Chinta said, wincing slightly at the ancient cliché about the fluid. "The question is, how do *we* benefit—or the reverse."

"How do *you* benefit, or the reverse," another pointed out, which, if obvious, was at least not sententious.

"We will *all* suffer losses," Chinta said forcefully. "A ten per-cent addition to the flow will profoundly disrupt the productive pat-terns of this area—patterns from which we derive our incomes. True, there will be benefits, but the benefits will accrue to individ-uals either not yet born or to those presented with new opportuni-ties. The costs will be immediate and to established interests, which is to say, to us and our client lineages. First and foremost, the value of the water allocations to our properties will be depressed *at once* as prices decline."

"While painful, a decline of ten percent—"

It is a crime against your lineage and what remains to us of Sh'u Maz that you have been allowed to reproduce, Chinta thought.

Aloud, she said, "Since the water will be available *now*, and the added plantations, manufacturing facilities, biomass, and population will take some time to appear, the fall in prices will be extreme. Perhaps as much as a third; at least one quarter within ten years of this date. Because we are not likely to command all the eventual increase in production—it will accrue to the Ruby Throne's chosen clients, of course—the ripple effects will be similar even when the price of allocations stabilizes with higher net use. Overall equilibrium will not be reestablished for generations and when it is, we and our offspring will be at a relatively lower position in the economic hierarchy."

Their faces fell as she presented the figures and graphs. Chinta went on, "And you all heard the Tollamune's will: We must begin a program to copy the *tembst* of the Wet Worlders."

She pointed at a chart. "Which means increased activity for the Ministry of Savantiere,"—her finger moved—"the Ministry of Tembst Refinement,"—and a third move—"and the Ministry of Mineral Supervision."

All three Councilors adopted postures of concern, the response as involuntary as willed; she had just pointed out that they would have to finance and oversee the very changes that would threaten their steady incomes and relative status.

"Surely you are not proposing a Dynastic Intervention?" one said, a slight quaver in his voice.

Chinta spread her arms out to either side with fingers spread, and widened her gaze for a moment as she stared upward: *horrified negation.*

"No. It is the tragedy of our age that there is no heir to the King Beneath the Mountain . . ."

Which meant, without any offense that could call for an Apology or the services of the Expediter, *The Emperor will die soon and then all options are open.*

". . . save Genomic Prince Heltaw . . ."

Who was known to be notably conservative, apart from the matter of *his* relative status.

". . . and only in this age of declension would one who shares so slightly in the Tollamune Genome be considered at all. Even if he were to use one of the stored ova."

They all nodded. Considering Heltaw's own age—which promised a reign of at least a century, given the probable maximum life span of the current Emperor—and then the likely disposition of an heir socialized under that very conservative Genomic Prince's supervision . . . and there was doubt about the viability of the stored ova. Subtle sabotage had been one of the weapons in the last Dynastic Intervention, and they had been in storage for more than two hundred years of the Real World in any case. Entropy could not be defeated forever. The sperm were viable, yes: the more complex ova, very probably not.

This made Heltaw's gender a factor, unless he was prepared to merely keep the Ruby Throne warm for his siblings' potential grandchildren.

Chinta was pleased to see the calculation behind the three pairs of eyes that met hers. She relaxed into an informal Communicative posture. At least they had *that* much survival instinct left intact.

"But why have you called us for this consultation, if all we need do to avoid the unpleasant alternatives you have sketched is to exercise patience?"

And drag our feet in implementing inconvenient decrees, went unspoken. The bureaucracies they headed had a great deal of practice at that.

"Because the current Tollamune may not be as bereft of offspring as we have assumed," she said grimly. "And sustained pressure from the Ruby Throne by a young, energetic, and potentially very long-lived Emperor is"—metaphorical mode—"another kettle of *to'a* altogether."

That brought them all sitting erect, hands flashing to press palms to either side of their faces: aghast concentration.

When Chinta had finished, she stroked her symbiant. It raised its head and whistled; the ears of the intercom system opened their tympani. "Let the Professional Practitioner of Coercive Violence Faran sa-Yaji enter," she said.

The door dilated. The other three High Ministers bristled a little when the mercenary adopted an insolently undeferential posture, each hand clasping the opposite elbow and golden eyes level. That he was obviously of pure or nearly pure Thoughtful Grace strain made the hostility stronger, not less; the rivalry between them and the Imperial Administrator lineages was as ancient as the Mountain.

Chinta ignored it. "We have a contract for you," she said.

The Thoughtful Grace raised one eyebrow. "One attractive relative to that offered by Genomic Prince Heltaw, Superiors?" he said smoothly.

Chinta restrained herself from grinding her teeth. She had *hoped* that the news hadn't spread that far. Still . . .

"One comparable, and easier of accomplishment," she said. "You have contacts in Zar-tu-Kan?"

"Disreputable ones," Faran said whimsically.

"Excellent. One does not engage a savant of *Sh'u Maz* for illegal lethality. Then—"

Mars, Approaching the Deep Beyond
Southeast of Zar-tu-Kan
May 2, 2000 AD

"Ahoy, matey! Avast the cross-forgainsails and clew up the lower buttock shrouds!" Jeremy said, holding on to a line of the standing rigging with a foot on the leeward rail.

"Oh, stop being cheerful!" Sally snarled, still looking slightly green.

The *Traveler* was heading out into what the Martians called the Deep Beyond now, spanking along at nearly twenty miles an hour before a following breeze, with each low rise in the undulating plain making the hull heel and then roll back slowly against the suspension system's muscles. The result wasn't much like a watercraft's motion, but it could produce the equivalent of carsickness. The Martians had watched in horrified fascination as Sally gave back breakfast to the ground cover; *they* didn't throw up unless they'd swallowed poison or were very ill indeed.

"You're the one who's traveled all over on these things," Jeremy pointed out.

"Retching most of the time," she answered grimly. "There, I think the pill's finally working, thank the Buddha."

The *Traveler* had passed the end of the active part of the canal last evening. The mountains that marked the edge of the old continental shelf had gradually fallen out of sight to the left as they headed north-east. Gritty reddish soil showed through the thinning mat of atmosphere plant, individual specimens growing too far apart for their leaves to overlap, and the air had a haze of fine, dark pink dust. It smelled intensely dry, with less of the sharp medicinal scent of the crushed leaf. Sand of the same reddish color had piled up against the abandoned wall of the canal in a series of long drifts on the western side, sending tendrils out across the glassine of the covering and burying it in places.

They hadn't seen anything much bigger than the ubiquitous little kangaroo-ratlike things for hours, though just after dawn they'd passed a herd—or flock—of four-footed flightless humpbacked birds that scampered off with black-and-white tails spread, caroling fright with a sound like a mob of terrified bassoons.

"What are those?" he'd asked.

"Wild *zharba*," Sally had said. "They live off atmosphere plant and anything else that comes along and they manufacture their own water from their food—in fact, they store a couple of gallons in that sack on their backs, and you can tap it without hurting them if you know how and don't mind the taste: Sort of a cross between cold, salty chicken soup and bird pee; it's actually a fairly complete diet. The tame variety of *zharba* is what the nomads live off, mainly."

"*Tembst?*" Jeremy had asked.

"*Tembst,*" she'd replied. "Very, very old *tembst.*"

Tembst meant something like "technology," but not quite. *Perhaps "matter shaped by intent for utility,"* Jeremy thought. *They use the word for a knife or for something living like these . . . well, you expect another planet to be alien.*

The *Intrepid Traveler* was following the line of the abandoned waterway. The section beyond Zar-tu-Kan was lined with fortified farmhouses and an occasional small town built around a tower for airships, but those had long since dwindled to ruins.

I need to examine the dead canal here as a base for comparison, Jeremy thought. *The way to Rema-Dza probably wasn't abandoned all at the same time.*

"Let's take a look at it," he said aloud.

"Okay, might as well. It's not as if we're in a hurry," Sally said.

She walked forward to where Teyud stood near the wheel; a landship was steered from on top of the forecastle. The Martian was standing motionless except for an automatic flexing that kept her upright despite the motion of the *Traveler*. Unlike most of the crew she had pulled back the headdress of her robe. She nodded at Yamashita's order and called in a voice that cut through the soughing blur of wind in the rigging and the creaking and groaning of the ship's fabric:

"Strike sail, full rolling stop!"

The huge lugsail came down with a rush and a whine of gearing as the lower yard rolled it up like a sliding blind; the wheel-crews tapped at controls built into the base of each outrigger and great skeins of muscle flexed to close the brake-drums in a gradual surge of power.

Jeremy grabbed a line against the forward pressure as the landship glided to a halt with a whine and pant of brakes. It bobbed back and forth with a rolling, sideways motion for a moment, and the top of the yard and mast flexed like bows. Sally swallowed again, then sighed with relief as the motion steadied, though there was still a little, from the wind and from the crew shifting position, but not nearly as much as before.

Like most landships, *Traveler* had a ramp that let down at the bows, leading from the interior of the hull to the surface. Jeremy didn't bother with it; he sprang from the deck and landed with flexed knees on the ground below. To his surprise, Teyud vaulted over the rail and landed likewise; it was an athletic feat equivalent to a Terran jumping out of a second-story window but she didn't even grunt as her feet struck the soil of Mars.

Sally and the four crewfolk followed more sedately, down ropes; it wasn't necessary for the Terran, but she'd told Jeremy she'd never been able to make her gut believe it was safe to drop distances like that.

"Maintain vigilance for *dharz*," Teyud said to her crew.

The word meant "predators" and usually referred to the huge hunting birds that stood at the top of the food chain here; some of them were flightless, half the size of a cow, and bad.

The flying ones ranged up to twice that size and were much worse.

Several of the Martians set up a watch, standing in a triangle with their backs to each other and their rifles cradled in their arms, scanning the skies. That left the Terrans free to focus on their work; Jeremy's minicam whirred as they approached the ancient canal.

Ancient even by Martian standards, he thought.

The glyphs were slightly different from those on the sections nearer Zar-tu-Kan, less sinuous and more blocky. And worn, worn until sections were smoothed to blank obscurity and he had to use the thermal imaging to trace where they'd been.

His lips moved as he translated the stiff archaic dialect of the repeated message:

"Tollamune Shel-tor-vu, 'am Zho'da nekka mar ha, tol—"

Another voice spoke, reading the glyphs more fluently than he could despite his years of study. Teyud's voice. "The Emperor Shel-tor-vu, fifty-second of the Tollamune line and the eighth of that name to sit the Ruby Throne, ordered the reconstruction of this canal in the four-thousandth year of the Crimson Dynasty. Look upon my works, all ye who pass by, and know that the Kings Beneath the Mountain shall hold the Real World fast while the Mountain stands. *Sh'u Maz*—Sustained Harmony!"

Astonished, Jeremy looked at Teyud. Her face had the usual hieratic Martian calm, but something flickered in the lion-yellow eyes as she read. The accent he'd noted in her voice grew stronger as well, staccato and clipped, with a harsh tone that made the little hairs along his neck stir and a sound-shift that turned the usual Demotic *z* into an *s*.

"But they did not sustain Harmony," she went on, almost in a whisper, her voice soft once more. "Though for long and long it seemed to be so. Cycle upon cycle of years passed, and with each, the Deep Beyond grew more and water and life grew less, little by little but steady and very sure. Sibling fought sibling for the Ruby Throne, and canals died, and cities fell, and generals rebelled, and the nomads pressed inward from the deserts and down from the heights, until nothing was left but the shards of a broken world. A world where winter comes, and will not yield again to spring."

She shook herself very slightly, and resumed that feline alertness; the nicating membranes swept sideways across her lion eyes for an instant.

"You wished to examine?" she asked calmly.

Jeremy looked at Sally. *She* looked surprised as well, and the crewfolk were exchanging glances, too. He cleared his throat.

"Yes," he said.

It would be easy to jump up onto the top of the canal's covering, only twenty feet from the surface; easy and dangerous, since glassine was near frictionless as no matter. Instead, he walked until there was a drift of sand up the side, and then went up that with infinite caution.

"Or is it frictionless?" he said aloud, kneeling and touching the surface of the glassine.

Normally it would be so clear you could only see it by the way it refracted light a little more than air did. This was like very fine glass instead, and the surface . . .

He stripped off a glove and felt it. Cold and very, very slightly granular.

"I've never seen glassine do that," Sally said when she'd joined him. "Show abrasion like this. What could have done it?"

"Time," Teyud said.

This time they both looked up, startled. They'd been speaking English.

I suspected she understood more of it than she let on, Jeremy thought. *Very bright lady.*

"Enough time," she amplified. "A very, very long time. The—"

She used a couple of Martian words he didn't know. Sally whispered: "That means 'molecular bonds,' I think."

"They cannot resist the entropy embodied in sand and wind forever if they are not renewed. When this happens, be cautious. Loss of structural strength follows, to degrees unpredictable and which can be ascertained only by experiment."

She drew her pistol and fired northward; the sound was a sharp *ffftht* as methane mixed with air and exploded. Fifty yards in that direction, a spot of canal covering gave a musical *ting* with a shattering undertone, and then a ragged section fell into the emptiness below. Sand poured downward for a while.

"I express enthusiastic appreciation," Sally said. "The information is of substantial use."

She was making notes with a little pod recorder hitched to her belt. Then she bent and flipped up a big hemispherical shell, like a perfectly symmetrical turtle the size of a small car. The underside was empty, save for parts of a skeleton attached to the inside; the foot that had secreted fresh glassine was long gone.

"Canal roof repair bug," she said to Jeremy. "It's a variant of the standard construction type. Must have died when this section was abandoned."

He nodded. The bottom of the canal lay about twenty feet below his perch. This section had only a foot or so of sand on the floor, and he could see the skeletons of endless rows of canal shrimp—the human-sized adult phase, when they attached themselves to the bottom like barnacles and waved their tails in unison to create a current and drive the water where the builders wanted it. The canals had their own ecology, and he was looking at the ruins of it.

There was something scratched on the opposite wall of the canal, on the inside just above where the old water level would have been. He knelt, feeling the gritty sand moving beneath his knees through the robe and pants, and aimed the minicam, his thumb dialing up more magnification. The glyphs were a bit irregular, as if someone had scratched them into the hard quasiorganic concrete in a hurry. Jeremy spoke into the microphone as he read:

"I *told* the fools this section couldn't maintain flow if they didn't extend the catchments!" He almost laughed. But the laughter died. That was a cry of despair across millennia, and one that presaged the death of cities, migration and flight and death.

He seemed to hear the keening. Then he *did* hear something, and whirled awkwardly at Teyud's shout of warning.

That saved his life. His feet shot out from beneath him as the sand moved on the glassine, and talons flashed through the space he'd toppled through rather than into his throat. A fluting scream followed, bloodlust and frustration set to music but loud enough to nearly deafen him, and there was a dry carrion stink.

The hilt of the still unfamiliar sword thumped him under the ribs as he fell, leaving him wheezing with pain. A snake-slim figure poised over him; he had a confused impression of gaping jaws edged with sawlike points, a long, whipping tail, and a flaring mane of red-bronze feathers—and long arms tipped with claws reaching for him.

Then there was a sharp wet smack and one of the slit-pupil eyes gushed out in a miniature volcano of matter and blood. The creature pitched backward, convulsing as the neurotoxin in the needle sent every muscle into spasm, head arching back to its heels with a crackle of snapping spine.

Jeremy forced himself to breathe, and his mind to function. Back on his feet, he saw a wave of the *things* swarming around the *Traveler's* crew in a maelstrom of flashing blades, warbling jaws where purple tongues showed, and snapping dart pistols. One Martian had gone down and three of the things savaged the body. Some of the attackers had sticks or crudely formed stone hand axes in their clawed hands. Their motions had the darting quickness of snakes, or great predatory birds, which they resembled even more.

Teyud tossed her dart pistol to her left hand to let it recover and drew her sword, lunging with blurring swiftness; a narrow body tried to dance aside and instead took the point through its torso, collapsing limply as she withdrew the blade. Without pause, she reversed her grip and thrust backward into another that was raising a rock over her head. Then the pistol gave the *pip* sound that meant there was enough methane for another shot.

Baid tu-Or was holding off a pair, their heads lunging out in snaps that ended in *clomp* sounds as she swept her sword back and forth; Teyud shot one of them in the base of the skull, and the engineer cut the other's legs out from under it as it turned. Sally was backed up against the canal's wall, her Terran automatic pistol in her hand, trying to get a clear sight at one of the darting, quicksilver shapes without shooting a Martian by mistake.

Time to get involved, Jeremy thought.

He jumped. A dozen saw-beaked faces and twelve pairs of crimson eyes pivoted upward as he soared and then fell, his robe billowing against the restraint of his harness. His pistol was in his hand as he touched down on the sparsely vegetated surface—and his was no Martian dart gun, but a good alloy-steel .40 Colt Magnum shipped from Earth by solar-sail cargo pod.

One of the things had a fire-hardened spear, and it ran past him at Teyud's flank. He fired at point-blank range and the thing's head broke apart in a spray of bone fragments, feathers, and blood. Sally shot a moment later. The bullet punched into a snaky torso and knocked the beast down; it beat its head and tail on the ground in blind agony, screaming like a laserdisc of a Wagnerian soprano turned to maximum volume, then went limp.

Then Teyud's pistol was pointing straight at *him*. He threw himself down and rolled as it snapped, just in time to see an attacker behind him spasm backward with a dart in the paler short fuzz of its throat. He shot the one following it from the ground, holding the pistol two-handed.

The smashing roars of the Terran weapons broke the attack where more familiar dangers hadn't. Suddenly all the creatures were fleeing in a mob, scattering northeastward, crying out in oddly melodious fluting voices that sounded like short, sad tunes played on a saxophone. Teyud called sharply to one of her subordinates, and the man tossed her a dart rifle. She went down on one knee, brought the long slim barrel up and aimed carefully, firing as quickly as the chamber could regenerate and the beasts were in range.

Phhttt. Phhttt. Phhttt. Phhttt.

Four of the . . . mob or pack or flock . . . went down. Then she handed the weapon back to the crewman.

"Everyone feed your guns!" she called. "*Dharz* are prone to unanticipated actions and they may return."

Feeding the gun meant pushing a syringe of sludge into a port on the weapon's top, as well as reloading the ammunition.

At least my Colt doesn't wheeze or smack its lips, Jeremy thought as he snapped in a new magazine.

And it didn't depend on igniting organic methane to push its projectiles out. The sharp scent of nitro powder mingled with the faint sulfurous burnt swamp-gas reek of the Martian weapons in the thin, cold dry air; beneath it ran the smell of Martian blood, saltier and more metallic than that of the creatures Earth bred. Teyud watched Jeremy's hands as he reloaded and holstered the automatic.

"Interesting," she said. "How does it operate?"

"Explosive combustion of nitrogenous compounds driving a heavy metal slug through spiral stabilizing grooves on the inside of the barrel," he said, which took five words in Demotic.

Her brows went up. "Extravagant, but effective. Could I use one?"

He shook his head. "The recoil would break your wrists, I'm afraid," he said.

Which was true enough, at least for standard-breed Martians, although he didn't know about Thoughtful Grace, who were a lot stronger. But it was also policy not to let the locals have Terran weapons.

Though theirs are nearly as effective, he thought. *Unless the gas generator part dies of old age or gets indigestion. And they're difficult to replace.*

"What *are* these creatures?" he asked, turning one over with his toe.

It still looked like an eight-foot feathered snake with long legs and arms. The head had a scaly flesh-covered beak that came to a point, but formed interlocking saw-edged blades behind. The skulls were narrow too, but long, and must hold a fair-sized brain. His toe moved on and forced a hand axe out of a grip that clenched in death.

"*Dharz*," Teyud said. "In origin, small, social carnivores of the Deep Beyond, *tembst*-modified for the hunt in ancient times."

"Modified for the hunt? It was far too much as if they were hunting *us*."

"Feral now." Her mouth quirked very slightly. "Perhaps my . . . our ancestors should not have made them so clever, or so large, or so indiscriminate in their search for edible protein."

A slight inclination of the head and a spare gesture of one blood-spattered hand; it meant, more or less, *insincere apologies are tendered for the sake of form*, and in this context it was an ironic joke.

Another Martian came up, the ship's engineer; she had a bleeding wound down one cheek, clotting with an alien swiftness as he watched.

"They were not so many, or so bold, in the Conqueror's day," she said. "Nor did they come so far out of the Deep Beyond. We have one dead, Expeditionary Supervisor Teyud; and three wounded, one seriously. All will recover but the worst will not be fit for duty for a twentieth of a year."

"The Beyond is dangerous," Teyud said, as she carefully wiped her sword clean and sheathed it. "And the casualty was a *tokmar* sniffer. That is a seriously self-destructive habit."

As she spoke, the crew bandaged injuries, carried the wounded—which by local notions included only those too badly hurt to walk or work—back to the *Traveler*. Several returned with a rack of poles that they erected, snapping the members together; the rest had gathered the bodies of the *dharz* and were preparing what looked unpleasantly like butchering tools. Sally Yamashita had gathered the crudely shaped weapons the beasts had used and was examining them thoughtfully.

"Ah . . . those things are a bit too intelligent for me to feel comfortable eating them," Jeremy said, as the crew drained the beasts' blood into containers.

Teyud and the engineer looked at him in puzzlement; their nicating membranes swept over their eyes and they blinked, a disconcerting double sideways-and-vertical gesture.

"*Dharz* are not humans," said the engineer. He remembered her name was Baid tu-Or.

The phrase she used meant specifically "not of the lineages of those present" and implied the capacity to interbreed.

As far as he knew, Terrans and Martians couldn't interbreed, being nearly as different from each other genetically as humans and chimps, but evidently Baid was being generous.

"And we are preparing them to feed to the engine," Teyud reassured him. "Higher-quality feed will increase its range and intensity of effort. Our own supplies are ample at present and *dharz* are reputed to be very rank in taste. Note that we intend to dedicate the remains of our dead fellow employee to the same function."

"Oh," he said. Then, "Thank you for saving my life."

She quirked a small smile and said gravely, "It would be detrimental to my reputation if my employers were eaten by wild *dharz* only ten days out from Zar-tu-Kan. In any case, you have performed the same with respect to me, so the balance of debit and credit is neutral."

"Well . . . let's get going, then," he said. "The Lost City awaits!"

That made him feel better for a moment, until Teyud gave one of her disturbing not-quite-smiles.

"The *dharz* are heading in the same direction," she pointed out. "They evidently feel it will be safe for them. This is not a favorable indicator."

CHAPTER THREE

Encyclopedia Britannica, 20th Edition
University of Chicago Press, 1998

Mars: Biology

Martian biology at first glimpse appears much more distinctive than that of Venus; hominids apart, there are few or no species with a close resemblance to extant or extinct Terran forms. And although *homo sapiens Martensis* is unquestionably a close relation of *homo sapiens sapiens*, it is not a type historically attested on Earth. It is therefore not surprising that the "alien transplantation of earthly forms" theory of the origins of life on Venus and Mars was first definitively proven on Venus.

Close examination of modern and fossil records and recent genetic analysis shows two reasons for the distinct developmental paths of Martian and Terran life since their point of divergence some two hundred million years ago. The first is that the Martian environment is less Earthlike, and much harsher, than that of Venus. It is, on average, far harsher than that of Earth itself, with the most favored zones corresponding to Earth's high, dry deserts and much land comparable to the fringes of Antarctica or the Tibetan plateau. Other observers have called it "Australia in an icebox."

To simplify, one may say that the ecology of Venus is higher-energy than that of Earth and contains a greater scope for diversity. The ratio of ocean to land on Venus further amplifies the number of separate niches and species. Mars has less solar energy to drive the food chain, and a single world-girdling equatorial continent that has endured in roughly its present form from earliest times; hence the Martian land ecologies are more uniform, with a smaller number of more universally distributed species. The large number of migratory species and the high significance of fliers exaggerate this tendency.

Humanoid action seems to have at first further simplified matters. Fossil evidence shows that the first hominids were introduced by the still-mysterious "Lords of Creation" some two hundred thousand years ago; if earlier hominids had been planted, they died out before becoming common enough to enter the fossil record. These Old Stone Age archaic sapiens were dropped into an ecology dominated by a stable postdinosaurian fauna composed largely of rough analogues of birds, and like birds descended from Cretaceous therapods, and by the large and complex invertebrates of marine origin made possible by the lower gravity.

In this setting, repeated transplants of Terran mammals had had more failures than successes. The hominid strain flourished, however, and the extinction of most large land animals—never common on this life-sparse world—followed rapidly within the next twenty thousand years in a manner analogous to the late-Pleistocene extinctions on Earth. The Martian hominids became fully behaviorally modern long before our own ancestors, perhaps pushed rapidly into full sapience by the challenge of the alien environment . . .

It was after the emergence of the third wave of Martian civilizations in the Mons Olympus area that the next burst of speciation occurred. Since this was simultaneous with the abrupt development of the modern Martian humanoid type and of the beginnings of the distinctive Martian biotechnology, conscious intervention is the most probable cause.

Mars, The Deep Beyond
Southeast of Zar-tu-Kan
May 3, 2000 AD

Jeremy Wainman could see the air smoking with his breath as the *Traveler* lay at anchor, creaking slightly when a gust of icy wind made the boxy hull sway on the outriggers. Both the moons were up, small and bright, and stars larger than any he had seen from Earth were like the contents of a jewel box flung across the sky, but the Martian night was still very dark and cold, but the robe and the clothes beneath were very good insulation.

They'd anchored in the lee of a hill half as high as the mast—or perhaps a stabilized sand dune was a better description—but in any case big enough to give some shelter to the landship's hull. A faint mist of fine dust blew from it and gritted on the planks under Jeremy's feet as he walked; the taste of it on his lips was bitter and alkaline. There was nobody about, other than the lookout in the crow's-nest atop the mast, and a tall figure leaning on the compass binnacle by the wheel on the forward deckhouse. He walked forward and saw her uncoil with leopard grace as he approached.

"I express amiable greetings, Jeremy Wainman," she said.

"I reciprocate, Teyud za-Zhalt," he replied. "What keeps you awake this diurnal cycle?"

He sat on a hatch combing. Teyud leaned back against the lashed-down wheel, looking upward again; despite the cold her face was bare, though her hands were tucked into the sleeves of her robe.

"I originally began a single-hand game," she said, indicating the *atanj* board and pieces set on the deck. "But that palled, and now I examine the stars and speculate," she said. "Look, there is . . . Earth."

He followed her nod, toward the bright white star. She continued, "I speculate as to the nature of life on a world that does not die."

Was that an ever so slight wistfulness? He answered, "All things die. In the end, hundreds of millions of years from now, the sun will expand to consume all the life-bearing worlds of this solar system, and then shrink itself to an ember. Or so our philosophical savants who study natural patterns deduce."

He thought she smiled slightly; it was difficult to say, with starlight and moonlight casting shadows across her aquiline face.

"Truly? That is interesting; but the Real World will perish far sooner than that. The Tollamune savants deduced long ago that in as little as twenty-five thousand years from the present—"

Fifty thousand Earth years, he translated to himself. *Roughly.*

"—this globe will no longer be capable of supporting higher forms of life. Long before then, civilization and its arts will die. In the end, not even the microbes far beneath the surface will survive. And this despite all the efforts of the Crimson Dynasty and its servants to promote *Sh'u Maz*."

She did smile then. "But tell me something of Earth. What is your natal area like?"

He chuckled, though he kept it quiet. Martians underplayed expression.

"Oddly enough, it is not so very different from parts of Mars, apart from the biota, fauna, and the gravity, of course. I come from northern New Mexico"—he said those words in English—"and it is an elevated plateau with many mountains, low air pressure, and by Terran standards it is quite dry and, in the winter, cool. Hence, its winter has similarities to the lower, warmer, and more humid parts of Mars in summer."

"An amusing expression of randomness," she said. "Those of your lineage are savants?"

"My father studied atomic interactions. My mother managed machines that process information."

He didn't know whether his translation of "systems analyst" was accurate, but Martians didn't have computers . . . or at least, they weren't supposed to. Some of the documents he'd studied had suggested otherwise.

"I have four siblings."

"So many!" Teyud exclaimed. "Your lineage must command enormous resources."

"Well, it's a little more affluent than most, yes."

This is *a dying world. Fewer people every generation, and of course they can control conception by thinking about it. And they space their kids out over a long, long life span.*

Being able to plan your births was a survival trait on this world of steadily dwindling resources. And even if something did slip up, they could also shed a fetus by willing it. It was a major reason for the more or less equal status the sexes had always had here, as far back as records stretched.

"You mentioned this place, Los Alamos. It is a Scholarium of sorts?"

"A place for investigations, many sponsored by our government."

She looked at him for a moment. "What was the subjective experience of socialization in the company of so many siblings? I had none. It would be rare here to have more than one preadult, in any case."

Well, I was the youngest and they pushed me around a lot, he thought.

"Hmmm. Well, we were at the beach once, and my sisters started to bury me in the sand upside down . . ."

For once a joke came across well, and she gave a silent, breathy Martian laugh.

"You mentioned that you were an only child," he said.

"Yes; neither my sire nor my mother reproduced otherwise . . . there were complications. I was socialized as a Coercive by maternal relatives; I learned *atanj*, tactics, dance, the history and nature of *tembst*, logistics, calligraphy, intrigue, and weapons skills."

"I fence myself," Jeremy told her. What he actually said was, "I have studied formalized long-blade methods."

"Ah!" she said approvingly. "We must engage in a trial of skills. This would be instructive."

Then she stretched and yawned, catlike. "Regenerative slumber becomes appealing. I profess amiable temporary farewells, Jeremy Wainman."

Faran sa-Yaji nodded as he examined the tracks of the landship they pursued, clear in the chill night's starlight. You could tell how recently a craft had passed by how much sand had drifted into the mesh patterns its wheels left, and these showed the target maintaining a steady speed. The problem here was unusual; he did *not* want to overtake the *Intrepid Traveler* as fast as possible, but he *did* want to follow as closely as he could without alerting the prey.

Chinta sa-Rokis had presented him with an intriguing task

when he took her contract, and his own intentions added an enjoyably complex additional set of factors. Stretching one's skills was as exhilarating as assimilating much fine essence, without the subsequent pain of dehydration and toxicity.

"Excellent," he said. "The *Intrepid Traveler* maintains exactly the lead I wish, given the terrain ahead. I assume that they will rest at anchor in the darkness, since they have no reason for haste."

The captains of the *Robbery With Armed Violence* and the *Insensately Vicious Plunderer* looked at him with bewilderment. One was male, the other female; one favored a dull gold robe obviously seized from a wealthy merchant, and the other a plain gray robe of double thickness; the female had a missing eye covered by a patch, and the male scars just short of that. One smelled of *odwa* and dried blood soaked into cloth; the other of neglected personal sanitation. Other than that they might have been siblings from the same ova.

The female with the eye patch glanced back at the low-slung black hulls of the two pirate landships.

"My overhead and running expenses increase with each passing day of delayed pursuit, eroding my ultimate margin of profit," she rasped—the harsh tone a legacy of some throat injury, judging from the puncture scar over her larynx. "My *Robbery* has more sail area relative to its mass and greater speed than that lumbering freight hauler. Even the *Plunderer* does, despite an inefficient rig and suboptimal maintenance. We could have caught them long before this."

The other captain adopted a posture of indignant refutation slanted toward his colleague, but nodded and continued. "We might already be reveling in our seizure of a valuable ship and cargo, celebrating by absorbing costly essences and engaging in brutally nonconsensual erotic entertainments of a type I find deeply gratifying but which are difficult to arrange on a commercial basis. Why this delay?"

"My additional payments more than compensate for your costs," Faran drawled. "If you wish to satisfy your curiosity and repellently deviant urges as well as your larcenous greed, a reduction in the commission could be arranged."

The captain of the *Robbery With Armed Violence* shook her head, and the silver-and-turquoise tassels attached to the tips of her ears chimed softly.

"By no means!" she said, and glared at her counterpart with her single eye. "Larcenous greed wholly typifies my interests and those of my crew! I am earnestly businesslike in my lack of conventional ethics; my concern is solely with efficient implementation of our predatory intentions, not with frivolous amusements."

"Anticipation adds spice to depravity," the other captain said grudgingly. "And I am second to none in this profession where insatiable and ruthless greed is concerned. Otherwise I would have continued in my initial, parentally sponsored choice of career as a pediatric physician."

"Then return to your vessels," he said. "We will resume pursuit in no more than three hours."

They did, bickering as they went. Faran's partner snorted softly, but only when they had gone out of earshot; pirate captains were notorious for lapses into whimsical and impulsive excess.

"I would not try their patience excessively, comrade," he said.

"They must suffer the agonies of frustration for some time," Faran said. "Also, they are aware that we have the fungus-grenade launcher. And that all six of us are Thoughtful Grace."

"And that their bonus waits in a banker's safe-deposit vault and can be opened only by our *living* genetic signature," the other Thoughtful Grace replied. "Yet the *Intrepid Traveler* is now beyond the Despotate of Zar-tu-Kan's patrols, and a financial instrument a thousand miles away may not unduly restrain individuals so lacking in patience."

Faran shook his head. "There is still a chance that Teyud za-Zhalt might turn the landship and evade us in broken ground. We pursue one of us . . . one who is of at least half Thoughtful Grace genome, and of a most select lineage at that. Also, consider the other half of her inheritance. It is best to eliminate all possible extraneous factors she might use against us. A flat plain of *twom* will maximize the numbers we can bring to bear and minimize possible ingenious countermeasures."

"Her formidable talents are why we agreed to simply kill her, rather than attempt the more lucrative live capture," his partner grumbled; *he* had argued in the Lineage council for an attempt at capture and the startlingly generous offer from Prince Heltaw. "You need not recapitulate incessantly."

"There is still a chance of harvesting her ova, collecting Chinta sa-Rokis's fee for her death, and then selling the contents of the victim's uterus to Prince Heltaw," Faran said. "But that also requires the privacy of the Deep Beyond—and to eliminate all the pirates will take some time. Space and time are interchangeable; this is a profound truth."

"And the data known to the dead are lost to entropy. But I admit apprehension at the prospect of then attempting to defraud the High Minister by selling the Tollamune genome to Prince Heltaw."

"Once we have the Prince's patronage—and he stands to gain the Ruby Throne—her annoyance will be a negligible factor. And of course there is the possibility that the *vaz-Terranan* will find the treasures they are reputed to seek in the lost city. In that case we may kill them and rob them of the hypothetical treasures, then kill the pirates and so remove the necessity of sharing with or paying them," Faran said consolingly.

"*That* might even be construed as furthering *Sh'u Maz*, since we would then be wealthy enough to become law-abiding, while the pirates never would."

"That is one construction of our intent, and one that I intend to contemplate at length in my future prosperous, peaceful years. In the course of plundering the *Intrepid Traveler* and killing Teyud za-Zhalt she and her followers will doubtless kill many of the pirates, sparing us the effort; we can sell her head to Chinta sa-Rokis, and then her ova to the Prince. This is an elegant optimization of an admittedly brutal and unscrupulous course of action. Still, we are impoverished freelance contractors and cannot afford extreme scrupulosity."

"*Four* payments for one violent attack—that *is* an elegant least-effort path, thus one deeply satisfying to professional vanity as well as gratifying the Lineage's need for assets. I admit this, Faran, yet in principle I depreciate your tendency to make overly complex plans. And even without suffering fatalities of our own in the course of killing all the others, the six of us are not enough to helm even a small landship. Walking across the Deep Beyond does is not practical . . . even assuming randomness brings no nomads across our vector."

Faran chuckled softly. "I have made other arrangements for our subsequent transport, and at modest cost."

"Made arrangements on a need-to-know basis?"

"Of course; some of our younger Lineage-mates are deplorably given to boasting after assimilating essence. All three craft will vanish, and we six will be speedily transported to Dvor Il-Adazar in an inconspicuous manner, possibly with *valuata* of immense worth."

His partner bowed in a posture of ironic exaggeration. "You are more attached to your own cleverness than to me."

"You indulge in an implausible rhetorical flourish. Let us return to our cabin and demonstrate its falsity."

Mars, The Deep Beyond
Southeast of Zar-tu-Kan
May 4, 2000 AD

"Again," Teyud said as they disengaged.

Jeremy puffed out his cheeks and stepped back into the "ready" position, bringing his sword up to put himself en garde.

"Here's where I get my ass kicked again," he said cheerfully.

He was about used to working with the slow roll and pitch of the landship now, and to ignoring the landscape of low ochre hills and endless plain as it sped by in a long plume of dust. And the thin air didn't bother him; he'd grown up at around seven thousand feet in the Jemez mountains, which was pretty similar to the density at Martian sea level. Pressure dropped off more slowly with altitude here, too.

Teyud's relentless perfectionism with the blade and the fact that she seemed to be constructed out of monofilament cables— now, *that* bothered him a little. And the fact that he'd lost six for six so far.

Be a good sport, Jeremy, he told himself. *There are Neandertals on Venus but you helped get the ERA passed. This is your recreation but it's her job. And the Thoughtful Grace were bred for it.*

"Your speed of reflex is acceptable if not outstanding and you are very strong," Teyud said. "And you have been taught with some skill."

The clear glassine face mask of her practice helmet showed a slight frown of disapproval. She took up the Martian version of the en guard position, slightly more face-forward than he was used to, front knee bent sharply and free hand tucked into the small of the back.

"But you are treating this exercise as an entertainment," she went on. "That is not a survival trait."

That translated as "deplorable," more or less. "Entertainment" could also mean "game." Or "pseudoconflict under constrained parameters." *Atanj* was a game, although it was also called the "Game of Life."

"The sword is for death, and nothing else," she pointed out. "As there is no constraint in combat, so there should be as little as possible in training in preparation for it. *Now.*"

He let the part of his mind that controlled his body slip into the ready state, empty of thought and ready to react out of pure reflex, eye, and nerve, balance and hand and limbs all as one. The practice sword flickered at him, a synthetic without point or edge but exactly the same weight and aerodynamically identical to the real thing. It was about a yard long, and was of enough mass that it would have weighed a bit over two pounds on Earth. No knitting-needle-like Olympic brands *here*. To muscles bred under three times the gravity, the weapon was still feather-light, but you had to remember that the inertia didn't go away with the weight.

And I'm not used to fencing with someone taller than I am, either.

He beat her blade out of line with a simple parry and then cut at her neck from the wrist, forehand and backhand, the blade a blur of motion. Working with a Martian longsword was more like saber fencing than anything else; perhaps a combination of saber and épée styles came closest.

She parried in prime and turned it into a circular cut, a *moulinade*, likewise minimally and from the wrist, then thrust with beautiful extension; when he parried in turn she came in foot and hand with hard insistence.

The sound of the practice blades meeting was a sharp *clack-clack*, more like hard plastic than steel. Their feet shuffled back and forth on the grit-surfaced boards of the deck; his breath showed in quick puffs in the cold air, unlike her drier, cooler exhalations.

He kept his focus on a spot halfway between the point of her blade and her eyes, seeing everything without narrowing in on any one spot. So easy to move, when you could flick yourself back with just a flexing of the ankle; he needed the advantage to break contact and recover.

Christ, she's fast, he thought, as a high-line thrust came at his eyes.

He parried in tierce, blade moving up and to the outside with the point higher than the hand, then around in a circle to control her blade, parry counter-six.

Gotta remember that every part of the body's valid on Mars. And she's got damned long arms.

The blades slid along each other in a glide, maintaining constant contact as he turned his wrist, scraping until the guards locked. He sprang in to punch at her hilt, the bully swordsman's trick, trying to use weight and the greater strength of his grip and arm to tear the weapon out of her hand. The instructors who'd tried to turn a fencer into a real sword fighter recommended it, and it would have worked on most Martians . . .

Her arm resisted his for a moment; they were corps-à-corps. Then he was doubled over as her knee smacked into the light cup he was wearing, backing away frantically in a crippled attempt at a *passé arrier* as her sword came for him again.

He could call it off, but he didn't; instead he let himself collapse and dove under the point, down on his left hand with his body parallel to the deck and his sword flung out, the showy Italian Passata-sotto. That surprised her, and the parry was a little slow; she would have taken a nasty wound to the thigh if it had been for real . . . before she pinned him to the deck through the lungs.

This time her smile curled up both sides of her mouth, the equivalent of a wide grin, as she tapped her blade on his back to signal the lethal hit. Martian fencing bouts didn't stop until someone "died."

"Excellent!" she said. "Commendable motivation! And that was a move not in our repertoire. This time you wounded me before I killed you. Let us try again."

CHAPTER FOUR

Encyclopedia Britannica, 20th Edition
University of Chicago Press, 1998

MARS: Atanj

Atanj, or Martian chess, is like Terran chess in that it is a competitive game analogous to wargaming and strategy contests, although unlike chess, it encompasses economic and cultural weapons as well as direct confrontation; there is no Bishop, but there are Merchants, Savants, Boycotters and others. The standard mode is played from the viewpoint of the Despot, but variations involve using another piece as the principal, sometimes the Consort, more often a Savant or Merchant, or the Chief Coercive.

It can be played by up to eight individuals at one time, though two is most common for casual entertainment, and the board is octagonal with sixty-two squares on each side. Each piece has its own set of permitted moves, which, however, may vary according to the place the piece occupies on the board. When one piece is moved onto a square occupied by another, the result depends on the relative importance of the pieces, the course of action the moving player calls, and often by the use of three tetrahedral dice.

"Taking" pieces does not necessarily remove them from the board, as they may be turned against the original holder. In fact, perhaps the most notable feature of the Game of Life, as it is often called on Mars, is that any of a player's pieces may "defect" to another player at any time, and that certain strategies—allowing oneself to be "boycotted," for instance—increase the probability of defection sharply.

Mars, the Deep Beyond
Southeast of Zar-tu-Kan
May 5, 2000 AD

The topnest of the *Intrepid Traveler*'s mast swayed in long, looping ovals as the landship sped before a following wind. Teyud clipped her harness to a ring and raised the far-viewers to her eyes. The device was a rare and precious heirloom of Imperial *tembst*, one of the few inheritances she still had from her mother. It wrapped its tentacles around her face, and there was a slight sting at one temple as it tapped her blood supply, and another sensation as it plugged its bundle of filaments into her nerves, as if tendrils inside her head had been stretched out and scraped with knives, fading to blackness.

Once in place the device supported itself, and adjusted for movement; light returned. A push of the will brought a flexing of the muscles that controlled the liquid-filled lenses, and the stretch of ancient seabed to the south sprang into focus. Her breath hissed between her teeth.

I cannot be certain, but . . .

"Strike sail!" she called without turning her head.

The order was unexpected, but it was obeyed promptly; two weeks in the Beyond had knit twenty dockside loafers desperate enough to take any berth into something of a crew. Below her, the translucent surface of the big sail scrolled down onto the spinning yard with a *slapslapslapslap* sound, and the balloon spinnaker billowing out between mast and jib was hauled in as well.

The landship's motion changed at once, swaying back upright

as the pressure of the wind ceased to press through the mast and against the muscles of the suspension. The mast flexed and then steadied. Momentum kept the landship going for a few moments, until it halted on the crest of a low rise.

Teyud focused the binoculars again. *Now* she was sure; the tips of four masts showed over the ridge behind them for an instant, then disappeared as the two ships following them braked and let themselves slide backward. An estimate of the range insinuated itself into her mind, a scratchy ghost-thought from the instrument. She commanded, and the landscape turned into a mottled palimpsest of colors, in which the yellow heat plumes from the two hidden vehicles were plain.

And . . . they are not closely spaced. Indeed, they are probably not visible from each other's positions.

"Yes," she said. Then downward, "Make sail, resume course!"

She peeled the far-viewers off her face with a series of *plock* sounds and normal sight returned, along with a momentary fierce itch that reached into her brain stem and then faded to a dying tingle. The instrument crawled obediently down to her wrist and then into its container on her waist belt. She unclipped from the mast, transferred to a stayline, and slid downward toward the deck. Her feet swayed out over the rail and the ground starting to move below as the landship heeled again, and then she jumped lightly free.

"What's the problem?" Sally Yamashita asked sharply, looking up from the screen of her curious device for recording and manipulating information.

"We are being followed," Teyud replied. "By two other landships. I saw the tips of their masts; they are taking pains to be unobserved. Probably they are using an *orok* as a scout. They may be acting in concert, or in rivalry."

Sally looked upward for an instant, trying to spot the flying observer. Jeremy came up, frowning. It made his face look a little contorted, like a drama-dancer's mask for *concern* at a popular comic burlesque.

I am coming to believe that their emotions are not much *stronger than ours,* Teyud thought. *But their faces are more mobile, so that I assume that they are. This is a problem in communication and probably works in reverse as well. I must remember to exaggerate my expressions and discount theirs.*

"Why would they be following us?" he asked.

Teyud looked at him in mild astonishment; Sally gave him something of the same stare. There were a very limited number of plausible reasons for two ships to track another well into the deserts.

"Since they have followed us into the Deep Beyond, and endeavor to conceal their presence, voluntary exchange of *valuata*, a game of *atanj*, or parareproductive mutual pleasure are unlikely motives."

"What does *that* mean?" Sally asked, exasperated.

"My apologies. I should not attempt humor across linguistic boundaries. Let me rephrase my remarks: They are to a high degree of probability pirates and wish to rob and kill us."

Teyud frowned before she went on, calculating distances and sailing time. "Though this is barren hunting ground for pirates. We are far from the usual routes for either landship trade, or fliers. Only nomads pass through this area, and they make it unsafe for routine travel."

"Perhaps they followed us from Zar-tu-Kan?" Jeremy said. "Not wanting the illegal deed to be observed."

"It is possible. I cannot be certain, but they might be the two ships I had noticed anchored some distance from the docks there. If so, why have they not caught us? The *Traveler* is not exceptionally swift, and we have been making frequent stops to examine artifacts. One week would be ample to be beyond the Despotate's patrols, and prolonging the journey they must make to fence the plunder would cut into their profits."

"We can find out," Sally said.

She went below, then came up with their satellite hookup; it had a curved dish mounted on a tripod. As she snapped a headset into the open port she said, "We can get an aircraft diverted . . . one of the Despotate of Zar-tu-Kan's through the consulate there, if not one of ours from Kennedy Base."

Her fingers touched the controls. Teyud watched in fascination; she found Terran technology as outré as Earthlings found the Martian variety.

Most are not interested in Terran tembst if it is not immediately profitable. This is a failure of imagination. For a beginning, they can consistently make more of their devices whenever they please. For another, some of it has capacities we lack. They are chaotic, yet perhaps they may be the means of restoring true Sh'u Maz.

Sally repeated the sequence, then went through it again.

"Nothing," she said quietly. "The pickup is fully functional as far as I can tell, but we're being jammed."

Jeremy sucked in his breath. Teyud looked keenly from one Terran to the other.

"Significance?" she said sharply, after a silence that stretched.

"That means that other Terrans are interfering," Jeremy explained.

"Ah, the Eastbloc," the Martian said.

Now both of them stared at *her*. Martians who had any grasp of Earth's internal divisions were few and far between. Most were utterly uninterested.

"I have had some contact with them," Teyud explained, then turned away. "It was not of an amiable nature."

I hope that this interference is aimed at you, my employers. Otherwise half a world was not far enough to run . . . and if I run farther, I approach the source of peril once again.

Mars, Near the lost city of Rema-Dza
May 10, 2000 AD

The dead plantations began to line the canal a day's sail out of the lost city of Rema-Dza. Crystal stumps showed through the red sands, some still jagged where they were recently uncovered, most worn to smooth nubs. Pieces of glassine pipe showed where distribution systems had curled around the low hillsides along the contour lines to fruit trees in their individual pits. Eroded shards of wall stood out of the sand now and then, with thin scatterings of atmosphere plant on their leeward sides, protected for a while by their stabilizing effect on the moving dust. When the city itself came into sight, there was more of the green-red vegetation clustering around the bases of the towers still intact.

The pitiful hint of life was doubly welcome as the dryness of the cool air clawed at their mouths and sinuses. Both the Terrans had special masks with water-soaked linings that they used every so often to stave off nosebleeds, and they were also using double portions of lotion on their hands and faces to minimize chapping and cracking. Even the Martians found it uncomfortable here, except for the weird one with the odd tint to his skin who didn't seem to *have* a nose.

"Why's the growth concentrated around the towers?" Jeremy asked Sally. "Though that's pretty sparse to call *concentrated*. More of a 'very thin' as opposed to 'nothing'."

"The towers have—evidently did have even back when this place was built—systems that suck what water there is out of the air. It's a supplement to canals and reservoirs. That would keep some life going."

Winds cracked the sail taut and wailed mournfully through the thin lines of the rigging; beneath that was the hiss of sand like abrasive talc, and beneath that, the deeper, irregular sounds the air made as it wove through the ruins and hooted through their twisted passages. The quiet hum of the wheels faded as they slowed and the buildings loomed larger, turning from a model in the distance to immensities like a long-lost New York.

Teyud slid down from her perch high on the mast. Jeremy hid a slight shudder as she peeled the vision device from her face; it looked like she was being hugged at eye level by a semitransparent octopus with waxy skin and an unpleasant pinkish tinge spreading through its veins and capillaries.

The thing scuttled into its container at her belt, filling it like a viscous fluid, then darted a tentacle back out, grabbed a handle on the underside of the lid and slapped it shut with a sharp *click*.

Damned if I'll ever like equipment that drinks your blood, he thought. *Even if that does make it . . . loyal. Give me plain old electronics and optics any day.*

He was getting better at reading Martian expressions, though, or at least those of Teyud za-Zhalt. He'd spent thousands of hours looking at video, but there was a gestalt you could only pick up at first-hand.

She's not just a collection of traits, he told himself. *I think I'm actually getting to know her a little as a human . . . that is, a sentient being.*

She was looking worried but not alarmed; evidently there was still no immediate sign of the possible pirates. Which he heartily approved of—pirates sounded much more romantic in a book about the Spanish Main than they did out here in the thoroughly modern

Deep Beyond, and when Martians decided to be nasty, they could be *very* nasty indeed. This culture wasn't long on empathy at the best of times; he suspected that the emphasis on genetics tended to make them indifferent to individuals. Perhaps the fact that, as far as anyone could tell, they'd never had anything resembling a religion or a belief in an afterlife had something to do with it as well.

"There is no sign of pursuit," she said. "The weather will probably turn bad now. Possibly very bad; seasonal wind and sandstorms are common now in this location. However, this has positive features in our situation. We will have shelter and pursuers will not."

The dunes that surrounded and half buried the lost city were higher than any which could stand under Earth's gravity even in the Erg, the sand seas of the Sahara; so were the structures that towered out of them. Rema-Dza's buildings didn't have the candy-striped colors of Zar-tu-Kan as they jutted from the red-pink dunes. The towers still standing were reddish brown from base to tip, and they looked more like tall spindly mushrooms with buttressed bases than asparagus stalks. Some were stumps; a few had been ground open to show the honeycomb of passages and halls within but hadn't fallen yet. Life showed there, wheeling dots that coasted between the great ruins. It wasn't until you realized how far away they were that they stopped looking small . . .

"Wild *dhwar* and *paiteng*," Teyud said.

Those were the Martian birds that held the top predator niches wolves and tigers did on Earth. Dhwar had thirty-five-foot wingspans, paiteng more like fifty or fifty-five; and their claws and beaks were of uncomfortable size. Dhwar hunted in packs or flocks and had a nasty habit of squabbling over their prey in midair, letting bits and pieces drop as they did. Paiteng had smaller groups, usually parents and subadult offspring. Around here it helped to be able to patrol a hunting territory of a couple of thousand square miles.

She went on, "This would be a good nesting site and they do not need to feed locally; nor do they need liquid water. We must be cautious."

The buildings and broken domes that clustered around the feet of the towers were a little different too, structured as if they'd been put together from LEGO blocks and blunt wedges, staring out with more windows than the exterior of a Martian building would have these days. Even the Deep Beyond hadn't been quite so hostile, when this place was built.

"A very long time since it was inhabited," Teyud said. "Since the days when it seemed *Sh'u Maz* would indeed endure."

"One of the last cities to be built in the Imperial era, but also one of the first to be abandoned," Jeremy said cheerfully.

He'd studied the chronicles from Earthside long enough to be sure of that, and he was feeling more than a little smug at having his— not guess, estimate . . . confirmed. There had been quite a few skeptics. Martians usually had a pretty blasé attitude toward history, as they had so much of it, and it was refreshing to have Teyud showing curiosity; most of the crew had given the place one glance and then gone back to work, except the lookouts who kept watch for anything dangerous.

"Well, lookitthat," Sally murmured as they coasted closer.

The winds were backing and filling; the sail boomed and thuttered above them. Teyud made a gesture and it was brought down; at another, the engine gave a grunt and began working its cranks to turn the wheels of the stern axle. The motion of the *Traveler* became steadier as she swayed upright, more like the powered vehicles the Terrans were used to at home. A circular domed building at least as large as the central part of Zar-tu-Kan slid by, and half draped across the other side of it was the ruin of an airship. Teyud's brows went up slightly, the equivalent of whistling, swearing, and slapping her knee.

"That is very large," she said. "And from its lines, a warcraft."

"Thousand feet, easy," Sally said. "Maybe fifteen hundred. They don't build them that large anymore."

The skeleton reared four hundred feet into the air, the thin flexible covering gone except for scraps. That showed the geodesic mesh of the structure below, except for large patches that had fallen in, either burned when the craft fell or simply eroded away since. If it was similar to what the Martians used now, it was made of a composite, long fibers of single-molecule chains in a resin matrix. On Earth they'd call the material synthetic, though here it was secreted by animals rather than made in a high-pressure vat.

"To a high probability, this city was evacuated in haste," Teyud said, looking at it. "With some fighting."

Jeremy nodded. "The redaction I saw was a commentary on a list of abandonments, done rather later—more than two thousand years later for the list, and another two thousand for the commentary. Two thousand of our years, one thousand of yours. The implication was that the canal was cut off upstream in some sort of disturbance—"a violent agitation of resistant elements," the commentary said—and everyone had to get out fast when the water stopped flowing, and go somewhere where the resistants weren't waiting for them."

"Ah," Teyud said—that was a conversational placeholder in Demotic, rather like "well" or "so" or "um." "You hope that the ruins were not thoroughly stripped of Imperial *tembst*?"

Teyud went on, "The nomads will have been visiting for some time. Possibly beginning not long after the city fell. There were always some of them in the Beyond, if not so many or so dangerous as now. In any case, only the shells of the *tembst* would remain."

Jeremy looked at her and nodded. There were drawbacks to using organics, one of the most obvious being that they died if you didn't feed and water them.

"Yeah, it wouldn't be useable, but the remains will tell us things. We're hoping that the nomads won't have taken everything that civilized people would, if they'd had time to strip it during a gradual decline or a planned evacuation. Of course, that was a long time ago. There might have been an expedition afterward that never got recorded. But we can hope, and even if there was, we'll learn."

The desire of it overwhelmed him. To *know* . . .

Teyud gave him an odd look, shrugged, and turned to the helm. Sally smiled at him.

"Abstract curiosity isn't something this culture encourages," she said.

He was getting good at interpreting *her* expressions, too—being cooped up with someone did that. There was a hint of something she wasn't saying in the narrow dark eyes.

"They must have had it once, or they'd never have developed the . . . hey, let's call it *tembst* in the first place."

That look was there again. "The usual explanation is that modern Martian culture is decadent," she pointed out.

He snorted. "Yeah, but that's insufficient even if 'decadent' means anything besides 'I don't like your sex life.' You're a biologist, Sally. Hasn't it occurred to you that these people are awfully backward in things like physics to have gotten so far with the biological sciences? How did they get the equivalent of electron microscopes?"

"They've got things that will do the equivalent. Those tailored enzymes they still use to splice genes, for example. And they used to have more in the Imperial era," she said neutrally.

"But they're biological, too. How did they get from here to there? Their physics is pre-Einsteinian, barely Newtonian, and their mathematics are early-twentieth-century equivalents, and largely an intellectual game to them anyway. They'd never thought about atomic structures or quantum mechanics before we arrived, so how the hell did they get molecular biology? And don't tell me they knew more once and forgot it all later. It's a long time since the Early Imperial era, yes, and their technology literally manufactures itself, but they never lost literacy and there are *some* documents that old. They've never had better physics than they do now and they should have had something much better to develop the *tembst* they've got."

She hesitated. He saw it and went on, "Come clean. Does this have anything to do with my project getting approved?"

Another hesitation, and then a shrug before she spoke. "Okay, there's need-to-know now. We . . . the big brains back home, actually—think that there may have been an Ancient intervention here, way back when."

"Of course there was. Mars was a dead rock before the Lords of Creation—"

She winced slightly at the lurid name science fiction writers had placed on the aliens who'd terraformed Mars and Venus two hundred million years ago. Half the thud-and-blunder fiction on the market today involved them.

"—stuck their oar in."

"Not just the initial terraforming or the transplanting of Terran life-forms," she said. "We know they were active on Venus fairly recently, historically speaking."

Jeremy nodded. Some languages on Venus were related to ones on Earth, to Proto-Indo-European specifically. That had been demonstrated back in the late '80s. Humans had been taken from Earth and dropped there recently . . . relatively recently. Plus, there was the Diadem of the Eye . . .

"But all we've got on Venus is one enigmatic artifact and a native legend about what it did before it became totally inactive," he said. "Yes, there's been a theory around ever since then that the Lords gave the early Martians a kick-start in biotech as part of their big experiment. But what's changed?"

Reluctantly, she went on, "The Eastbloc base is at Dvor Il-Adazar; that's where the Kings Beneath the Mountain started from and it was the capital throughout the Imperial period. If any place on Mars has preserved the records of the very earliest era of the Tollamunes, it's under Mons Olympus."

Jeremy's brows went up. "You think the rulers there are telling the truth when they claim to be the lineal descendants of the Crimson Dynasty?"

She nodded. "The Eastbloc investigators think so. What's more, they're worried about what's happened to their mission. They've stopped obeying all their orders, and our sources say that it's stranger than that, that it's as if they don't *know* that they're not obeying all their orders."

"And they haven't done anything about it?"

"At the end of a hundred-and-eighty-day round trip, with a ship twice a year? Even laser messages take hours. And every new guy they send out starts doing the same shit. That thing on Venus, the Diadem of the Eye . . . it apparently could do things to your mind, or so Marc Vitrac always swore, and he had some evidence for it. It was working when he found it."

Jeremy felt his brows trying to climb up into his hairline, and his lips shaped a silent whistle.

"The Diadem of the Eye doesn't do anything these days but sit there and baffle analysis. They think there are functioning artifacts from two hundred million years ago at Dvor Il-Adazar?"

She shook her head. "From thirty or forty thousand years ago, at least. Jeremy, the Diadem of the Eye *was* something like what the natives and Vitrac said it was. And we've been studying it for twelve years and we still can't even tell definitely whether it's made of matter or just looks like it does. But it was functional for a long time, and the Ancients showed the locals how to use it."

He nodded. "And the USASF—"

"The president and the NSC and the commonwealth people and the OAS," she amplified grimly.

"The president and the National Security Council and our wonderful allies think that there may be Ancient artifacts *here*? That the Lords of Creation gave the Tollamunes . . . things . . . and showed them how to use them?"

"Yup. And there's as good a chance of finding that stuff here as anywhere outside Dvor Il-Adazar, and if there are Ancient artifacts they won't be affected by the passage of time. That's what suddenly rang bells on your research grant proposal. It crosschecked with a lot of what our historical research people said. Something *happened* here, back toward the end of the Imperial period, just before the era of the Civil Wars."

"The Dissonance, the Martians call it. There's not much chance of finding functioning stuff," he warned.

Lay people keep forgetting that what archaeologists find is usually junk. Informative junk, but still junk.

"It's a chance we can't take. If the Eastbloc were ever to get control of ancient technology, we'd be . . . how shall I put it delicately . . . totally ass-fucked. Those people, or whatever the hell they were, could alter *planets* like Play-Doh. If they weren't gods, they were close enough for government work. I wouldn't want *our* government to get that much power—and I work for them! The Eastbloc . . ."

She shuddered, and Jeremy nodded thoughtfully. "But right now, it looks like the technology, if it's there, has control of *them*."

"There is that."

He went on, "And according to *my* specialty, the Crimson Dynasty's experts could do a lot of mind tricks too, even more than modern Martian drugs can—and those are scary enough. Maybe the rulers of Dvor Il-Adazar have some of that . . . *tembst* . . . of their own still handy, and they've been using it on the Eastblockers. Just what they deserve, too."

"Which could be nearly as bad. Remember what the Eastbloc base has on hand in the way of weapons systems."

"We do, too."

"Right, but we—and they—just use it for deterrent purposes, like the subs and silos and orbital lasers back home. Imagine Martians getting their hands on it. We don't sell them weapons, and being careful about that was a big reason we put our base here, way out in the boonies."

"Then why did the Eastbloc put *theirs* right next to Mons Olympus?"

"Hubris, we think. I told you back in Zar-tu-Kan we couldn't do the beads-booze-and-blank-treaty-form thing here. Our best bet is that the Eastblockers thought they *could*, and now it's biting them in the butt."

"That's a pretty unpalatable pair of alternatives you've got there, Captain Yamashita," Jeremy said. "Either the Eastblockers have found the powers of gods and are planning on using them—"

"Which means we have to discover the equivalent here. This is our best bet."

Jeremy nodded. "Or if we're lucky, the rulers of Dvor Il-Adazar have messed with the Eastblockers' heads enough to take control of their weaponry." He chuckled. "At least that wouldn't be my responsibility, no?"

"No, just the government's. And they would have to try to deter whoever's running Dvor Il-Adazar . . . or watch them nuke and burn their way back to a planetary empire, in which case they'd have a planetary government with access to our technologies, *including space travel*. Or to stop that, we'd have to give equivalent weapons to their enemies."

"That's assuming they'd go right ahead and use what they took."

"Have you ever met a Martian who'd hesitate for a second?"

"Hey, that's a stereotype. Like the unemotional half-Martian Science Officer on the Federation Starship *New Frontier* . . ."

His peace offering was ignored, even though they'd happily discussed favorite episodes over the winter at Kennedy Base. Sally went on doggedly: "Stereotypes get to be stereotypical because they've usually got a big kernel of truth. The only reason Martians don't fight more wars between their city-states is that they've learned that it isn't likely to produce results."

"That wouldn't stop *us*, judging by Earth's history."

"Yes, they're more sensible than us."

He smiled. "Hell, they're so sensible sometimes they decide wars by having the leaders play a game of chess instead!"

"*Atanj*, not chess. And only when the force on both sides is about equal. Then the rulers or generals play with living pieces."

"Yeah, but the losing side actually *accepts* the result when they do that. And only a few die, instead of thousands. That's strength of character!"

"No, it's just being cold-bloodedly smart—it's a war game, after all, and the result probably would be the same if they actually fought the war. And the leaders accept the result because the *followers* are smart, too."

Jeremy frowned in puzzlement. "How so?"

"They don't have more geniuses than we do, because they don't deviate from the mean as much, but their average IQ is about 125, which means they've got a hell of a lot fewer hopeless sub-one-hundred chuckleheads. If they ever get a really scientific worldview and a technology that isn't limited to biological sources of energy—"

"We might have some very useful friends," Jeremy said. "There's something to be said for *Sh'u Maz*, you know. It gave them peace for a long time

Sally laughed. "Oh, you *are* a round-eye, aren't you?"

"What's that got to do with it?" he asked, baffled. "And hell, you're half round-eye yourself."

"More than half, but I'm East Asian enough to know that what *Sustained Harmony* actually means is everyone doing what they're told, and filling out the forms and standing in line and then doing it all over again . . . over and over and over . . . with Grandfather as official Tin God . . . which is the sort of Confucian claptrap my ancestors left Hiroshima Prefecture to get away from. And we didn't have it as bad as the Chinese, and even the Chinese didn't have as bad a case as the Martians."

Jeremy went on, "They're smart enough not to fight much, anyway. *That* sort of Sustained Harmony doesn't sound so bad."

"No, they're smart enough not to fight if it doesn't look like a good idea. If they had weapons that gave an overwhelming advantage, they'd—sensibly and intelligently—use 'em. These are the people who think infecting criminals with parasitic grubs is model penology and funny as hell to watch, too, and who use the same word for 'cop' and 'bandit' and 'soldier.' And the same words for 'ruler' and 'despot.' And the closest you can come to saying 'liberty' in Demotic is 'not subject to official sanction.'"

Jeremy winced. "Well, Teyud's a good sort; I like her. Quite a bit, in fact."

"Teyud's an honest mercenary. She stays bought. And she's got more of a sense of humor than any other Martian I've met, and she's interested in things. That doesn't mean she'd be safe with a hundred-megawatt orbital laser or a thermonuke. Hell, *we're* not safe with that stuff and Terrans average a lot higher on the milk-of-human-kindness quotient than Martians do; we just got too obsessed with space travel to kill each other off. So far. If the ancients hadn't given us an interesting couple of planets to explore and squabble over—"

"And the ancients themselves to worry about," he put in.

"—and that, odds are we'd have destroyed Earth by now."

Jeremy looked back toward the ruins. Suddenly his abstract love of knowledge looked as if it had unpleasantly practical applications.

Mars, the lost city of Rema-Dza
May 11, 2000 AD

Teyud watched as the winch groaned, hauling the *Traveler* stern-first through the gap in the great russet wall. It had taken some searching to find a suitable building with a break big enough to take the landship without being enlarged, but this was perfect; the interior was large enough that they didn't have to dismount the mast, and the street outside was broad and aligned with the prevailing east-west winds, so they could scoot away quickly at need. The intact roof made it easy to exclude predators.

At a guess it had been a gas storage tank; the simple building was similar to those used for that purpose even today, a square exterior with a hollow cylinder inside, topped by a movable dome, and the interior was utterly bare except for a layer of drifted sand. Probably an explosion after it was abandoned had broken a wall, one of which was usually left a little weaker than the others, to focus the effects of any such accident.

And there was an intact thousand-foot tower nearby, one that didn't have a *dhwar* rookery; that would do for a lookout. She wished for a moment that she could hand her viewer over for the scouts she planned to keep on duty up there every hour of the night and day, but it would take far too long to familiarize it with a new user of a distinct genetic pattern, and be too stressful for the recipient.

Possibly fatal, in fact, and they had already had annoying crew losses; more would depress morale. This was similar to an *atanj* game, where you had to reach the Victory Conditions without driving your pieces to defection . . . but then, it *was* known as the Game of Life. They would have to make do with the cheaper, less capable commercial systems.

When the landship was well within, the crew trotted back out, carrying a heavy cable over their shoulders. Baid tu-Or oversaw its anchoring to a thick stub of solid wall across the abandoned boulevard, and its covering with sand. With that in place they could use the engine-driven winch to pull the ship out into the street in a matter of moments.

That done, Teyud personally supervised those assigned to mask the tracks of the *Traveler*'s wheels, easy enough with sand as fine and friable as that of the Deep Beyond. It would be impossible to conceal that the landship had headed into the ruined city, but they could mask which streets and turns it had taken.

I do not believe those two ships abandoned the chase. Not unless they destroyed each other over the prospect of seizing our possessions, and randomness seldom falls out so conveniently.

Jeremy came up to her, still sweating from the effort he'd put into helping, even though the temperature was mild—quite close to the freezing point of water. He sank down on a piece of wall, and she squatted on her haunches; that put their heads near enough on a level for easy conversation.

Her nostrils twitched. His scent was strong, yes, but also oddly mild in a musky sort of way—less salty than that of a Real Worlder. He swigged thirstily from a vessel, and offered it to her. She accepted and sipped politely though the water was bland, of low mineral content as Terrans preferred. But water was, after all, water; to despise it was to despise life, and that was to welcome death. When she returned the flask, she looked at his face and blinked; they had seldom approached this closely.

"Permission for contact?" she said.

Granted, he replied with a side-flick of his gaze; execution of the gesture was flawless, save for the twitch that his small immobile ears could not perform.

Teyud reached out and touched the side of his cheek briefly;

there was a bristly sensation, not quite like anything she'd felt before. Not exactly unpleasant, but . . . strange.

"Fascinating," she said. "I had heard that this was so, but never observed it. There is *hair* growing on your *face*. Hair of easily perceptible size, nearly equivalent to your scalp."

He nodded. "It's common to Terrans." He gave a wry grimace that she couldn't quite place. "And similar hair grows on other parts of our bodies, as well."

"Fascinating," she repeated for emphasis.

And slightly grotesque, she thought: Her own people had only the finest down anywhere but the head. *Grotesque but interesting. So is his manner of speech. His Demotic is fluent, but this English influences his usage, as the High Tongue does mine.*

She went on, "But why has it not been noticeable before on you or Sally Yamashita?" She peered more closely. "The individual hairs are of considerable diameter but they were not nearly so apparent yesterday."

Amusement glinted in his eyes. "Facial hair is limited largely to males. We use . . . males in my culture often use . . . a blade or depilatory cream to remove facial hair; otherwise it would grow nearly as long as that on our heads. I didn't have time to depilate this morning."

"Is the hair for insulation?" she asked. "There seems to be too little for that purpose, and it is said that . . . Earth . . . is on average considerably warmer than the Real World. Or is it some sort of secondary sexual characteristic, like a *nokor* male's ruff?"

She used "Earth" instead of "the Wet World," which could also be translated as "the Big Muddy Bog" or "the Swamp-Planet." Terrans seemed very sensitive to slights.

"Ah . . . we're not sure. It's called a beard."

She nodded thoughtfully. "Your people are so intriguingly . . . rough-hewn."

He laughed at that. "Our favored hypothesis is that your ancestors employed *tembst* to suit yourselves to this environment . . . or to make yourselves more aesthetically pleasing according to the canons then prevalent. To us you look neotenous and . . . very refined."

Teyud nodded thoughtfully. "Yes, I have heard your theory that we are descended from . . . Earth . . . life. Certainly your world seems, by all reports, to be more suited to life in general. And there have always been puzzling inconsistencies in the records of presapient life here on the Real World."

He shook his head and threw up his hands in an unfamiliar gesture; she judged it to be one of exasperation.

"That is what educated Martians usually say."

She frowned. "It is the reasonable response."

"But you don't seem very concerned by it."

"Why should we be? Origins one hundred million years ago—two hundred million of your years—do not affect our lives today directly, after all. For each sapient, as the proverb runs, its own existence spans the life of the universe."

He laughed aloud. "Now, on Earth it caused . . . is still causing no end of trouble!"

Killing trouble, sometimes, he didn't add aloud.

She cocked her ears forward. "Intriguing. Well, to judge from the Terrans I have encountered, scholarship seems very important to you. It is surprising that with your brief history, you have theorized on the origins of life so deeply."

"Fossils . . . mineralized remains . . . are much more common on Earth, and there's a very complete sequence. I suppose that's why our theory of evolution appeared so early and why everyone—nearly everyone—has accepted it."

"Ah," she said thoughtfully. "Although of course you have no evidence that your planet also was not seeded with life rather than developing it."

"Well, we do have fossil records that go back long before life was present on either Mars or Venus," he said. "And both planets were definitely altered to be habitable and seeded with Earth life. A hundred million of your years ago."

She nodded, emphatically to imitate the Terran version of the gesture.

"Yes, but that says nothing of how life originally arrived on your Earth. It merely demonstrates that it was not at an advanced level when introduced."

She concentrated, calling up lectures from her clandestine tutors; those had included information from Terra, as well as geology and Imperial *tembst*-lore and investigations of non-directed-development . . . what Terrans called "evolution."

"Your savants say that Earth had a thick reducing atmosphere at an early period? Then very primitive forms could have been dropped there at a remote time, multiplied explosively, and then evolved into the present species. Including those later introduced to the Real World."

He started to speak, stopped, and gave her an odd look. "That is . . . I don't think I could refute it."

"The hypothesis is inherently nonfalsifiable, unless one had access to artifacts or records from the aliens of your hypothesis," she said. "Still, an interesting thought-construct."

She reached out again and touched the beard, then pushed gently sideways. There was an immense solidity to the feel, more so than even a Thoughtful Grace, a feeling of huge strength. It contrasted so oddly with his scholar's enthusiasm for details—

A shout interrupted her train of thought.

The ruins of the airship loomed above Jeremy as they followed the messenger, fading into the hazy air at the extremities.

It takes a lot of getting used to, how tall things can be here, he thought. *Looking back, Earth seems . . . squished down somehow.*

When they clambered up a dune and slid down inside, it was a little like being in the decaying carcass of a whale millennia dead. The wind had risen, flicking red dust everywhere that even *smelled* dry, and though it felt as soft as talc when you rubbed your fingers lightly together, it was actually like an industrial abrasive under pressure. That made it maddening if it got in your underwear and worse beneath an eyelid. He was beginning to appreciate why Martians kept their faces covered, and to envy them that nicating membrane, and the natural oils in their skins that slowed chapping and cracking, and a whole bunch of other things.

"The control cabin must have been plated in flame-retardant armor," Jeremy said as they climbed down a drift half disassembled by shovel work.

Teyud nodded beside him. The hard and supernally strong

stringers of the hull couldn't burn. They *had* melted and slumped in grayish dribbles and pools against the black of the cabin armor as the blazing hydrogen overcame the fireproofing anticatalyst and blazed like a blast furnace; there had been better than twelve million square feet of it, after all. The lines of the cabin were still clean and sharp, though they had the smooth curved edges of most Martian artifacts, where right angles were rare. The control cabin was about twenty-five feet by fifteen, judging from the section that had been cleared. In the middle of the roof was a two-foot circle marked by a thin white line.

Jeremy shaped a soundless whistle as a thought struck him. The structure of the airship had not only survived that fire, it had lain here since before men built the Great Pyramid.

Objectively he knew that these compounds simply didn't oxidize or decay—they made glassine look about as lasting as potato peelings by contrast—but it still made his archaeologist's reflexes boggle. When you considered what most digs on Earth looked like after a few centuries . . .

Of course, Earth wears harder on things, he thought. *Hotter, and it's heat that drives weather; more gravity, more water, more oxygen. And this was under sand for almost all that time.*

"The cabin was armored and the stringers and ribs are of reinforced dimensions," Teyud said. "This *was* an Imperial warcraft; I would postulate that it is . . . was . . . of the *Rampant Intimidator* class. The *tembst* of making that armor has been lost, except perhaps in Dvor Il-Adazar . . . a place of which I know little."

Her voice always had more modulation than that of most Martians, who commonly had a rather flat, low-affect tone. He thought he *might* be hearing something a little strained in that last phrase.

The sky had vanished in a pink haze since the morning, swallowing the tops of the towers, and everyone had his or her head-dresses on; the two Terrans wore goggles, and the Martians' nicating membranes flicked constantly back and forth sideways across their eyes, getting the grit out. The six *De'ming* who'd done the actual digging squatted and leaned on their shovels with their backs to the main force of the wind, one of them nibbling on a cake of *asu*-flour, the others swaying and humming in some sort of collective passing-the-time ritual that might be religious or social or their equivalent of flatlining.

Baid tu-Or slid down beside the two Terrans and the Thought-ful Grace, to stand atop the long black rectangle where it emerged from the sand. A trickle of the pinkish stuff ran around her feet as she did; digging it was only a little more permanent than shoveling water. In a day it would be ten feet deep here again, unless they did a *lot* more work.

"The chitin along the seams is still smoothly fused," she said. "Even after so long. This is impressive work. Still, let us begin around this circular line, which I think is probably a hatchway."

She had a tank on her back, and a long hose and nozzle con-nected to it in her hands. Everyone scrambled back a little on the loose, shifting sands as she sprayed a thin clear liquid. The cutter enzyme and its carrier had a sharp smell, something like winter-green and mint; the jet settled on the area around the inner edge of the hatchway and immediately began to form a thin ring of bub-bling white foam. When that turned green and began emitting ten-drils of vapor even more livid, everyone scrambled back more than a little, a few coughing at the acid-chemical-and-decay reek, and one of the crew motioned the *De'ming* to retreat as well. They didn't have much sense of self-preservation about anything but the most obvious threats.

They waited; most of the Martians with their slightly disturbing patience, Teyud with the relaxed alertness of a tiger in the brush beside a water hole, and the two Terrans with tense eagerness.

Jeremy looked aside at Yamashita. *I wonder why she's quite that eager,* he thought. *I know why I am. If there's really untouched material from the Imperial period in there, my name's made and I'll have a lifetime's work ahead of me. But she's a biotech specialist, not an archaeologist, and anything biological in there is going to be very tough jerky, if that. Or maybe she knows more about that ancient stuff than she was telling . . .*

The hatchway sagged, and then dropped in. Teyud drew a nar-row rod from her harness and tapped it sharply against a buckle. There was a click as barriers broke and the internal ingredients mingled, and then the rod began to glow with a bright bluish light. She dropped it in through the hatchway and fell prone beside the hole, peering through with her pistol in her hand.

"No immediate danger," she said. "But the glow-rod has devel-oped a yellow tinge; we should wait for breathable air to penetrate."

Then she turned to Baid to-Or. "Secure the ground against inward collapse, and erect an air-scoop to ventilate this. We may need to cover it and then dig again, if the storm is as bad as probability and evidence indicate."

The engineer nodded and turned to the crew. "You two, frames and sailcloth for wind-screens, in a wedge pointing *so*. You, get the *De'ming* working on shoveling the crest lines along there—"her finger traveled three-quarters of a circle around them—"down on the exterior side. And the crew will shovel as well, in relays by watches. Six *De'ming* are not enough to move the necessary cubic footage without imposing undue wear."

There was a rising grumble from the standard-Martian crewfolk present; Baid tu-Or glanced at Teyud and she twitched an ear in Sally Yamashita's direction. The Eurasian woman nodded.

"Double payment for the duration of such work," Teyud added . . . but she put it in the Imperative-Condescentative tense, which conveyed a blunt threat.

The grumbling died down and the Martians scattered to their tasks. Teyud swung through the hole and down an accommodation-way ladder. The two Terrans followed suit; the twelve-foot drop to the floor was nothing, but it was dim within and they didn't know what the surface below would be like. While they climbed down, the Martian picked up her glow-rod and peeled a cap off one end, using the sticky surface underneath to attach it to the roof; when you were as tall as she, and long-limbed, that was easy enough. The minicam whirred as Jeremy scanned the interior methodically. It was reassuring to look through its sights and see the interior slightly grainy, more like a training video.

The decking turned out to be some substance that looked like dark reddish brown linoleum but felt like concrete beneath their boots, giving excellent footing despite the thin scatter of dust that had drained in when the hatchway failed. The control chamber was like a box with the floor smaller than the ceiling, connected by inward-sloping walls. By the light of the glow-rod they could just see that there were portholes in the walls, shut with circles made of the same black armor. A horseshoe of control positions stood around the forward end of the chamber, with chairs fixed to the floor and with the infinity-symbol of *Sh'u Maz* over the central station.

Each control position had instruments before it, though most of them were simply holes in the curved panels before them. They would have been mostly organic . . .

And nothing organic could survive this long, not even in a hermetically sealed chamber, he thought. *Nothing that could rot or rust.*

The battle armor the crew had been wearing *had* endured, a matte black, chitinous stuff much like the fabric of the control cabin itself, though the weird-looking helmets had slumped forward as the spines disintegrated over the eons. The suits were eerily elongated, made for slender forms easily matching Teyud's seven-foot-plus.

One set was crimson, not black. Teyud started at the sight of it, visibly surprised for a moment.

"That is Imperial armor!" she said. "Only a member of the Tollamune line could wear it!"

The breastplate bore a device like two spirals interlinked, crimson on black, and encircled by an ancient ideographic glyph that seemed to be inscribed in sinuous strokes of flame.

It was the sigil of the Tollamune emperors of Dvor Il-Adazar, the Kings Beneath the Mountain.

The glyphs were a script used only to write the High Tongue, the ancient court language of the Crimson Dynasty and the distant ancestor of modern Demotic. Jeremy's lips moved as he silently translated it to himself, reading the elements one by one:

Knowledge-completeness-returning-recurrence-rebirth.

"A Designated Successor's badge," Teyud said, shaken.

Jeremy mentally translated what the Martian had said: *The Crown Prince's regalia . . . or the Crown Princess, same thing with Martians. Oooooh, something important* did *happen here.*

The black breastplates bore the same symbol, but enclosed in a white circle; it was the livery badge, worn only by the Ruby Throne's closest servitors. Teyud made a slow complex gesture with her pistol and holstered it.

"These were of the Thoughtful Grace," she said, in that bronze-bell voice. "They died at their posts, attempting with complete commitment to accomplish their assigned mission. Since dissolution is ultimately inescapable, there are far worse manners in which to complete the track of one's world-line."

She placed two more glow-rods on the roof, which gave a good reading-level light. That made the long-lost compartment a bit more strange, not less. He was uneasily conscious of the odd smell, a neutrality with only the faintest memory of must, and the way he had to breathe deeply to get enough air, and of how the distant hooting of the wind was muffled by the thick chitin armor and the sand piled against the walls. It had been a long, quiet wait.

And Teyud is the only Martian in here. The others are avoiding the place. That could be lack of curiosity . . . or something else. A superstition? Rare, then. Martians generally don't have 'em.

A scattering of objects lay about each of the chairs, where they'd fallen when the crew's leather harness disintegrated. Some were merely rust smears on the floor, where the steel of weapons and tools had disintegrated. Others remained.

Sally bent to touch a pile of bloodred sheets beside the central chair; a faint discoloration around them was probably the remains of a box.

"Careful!" Jeremy said hastily. "That looks like writing and they could disintegrate."

He had his minicam going as he stooped closer. "It *is* writing!"

Teyud knelt on the other side of the documents, drew her dagger and pointed, then used the tip to delicately tease apart the stack. The individual pieces were about the size of legal paper back on Earth, and were made of something that had the consistency of slightly stiff parchment stained a reddish color, overprinted in black and gold and blood crimson. It couldn't be paper of any sort, of course, not after the span of years.

The Thoughtful Grace said, "It is a Vermillion Rescript, swaying the Real World. Instructions from the Emperor of the day . . . yes, there is his name: Timrud sa-Rogol, who reigned in the beginnings of the Age of Dissonance. A Vermillion Rescript was . . . is . . . always written on imperishable material for future storage and reference. This will not disintegrate; the conditions here have been as stable as the Vaults of Remembrance beneath the Mountain. It could have lain here waiting until the Real World died and the sun swallowed it."

They carefully moved the sheets until they lay side by side; Jeremy recorded every step of the process. Fortunately, they were only inscribed on one side. He tried to decipher them and then shrugged and looked at Teyud. "Got any idea what they say?"

She frowned slightly; he could see the little crease between her eyes in the slit of her headdress, and then she pulled it back suddenly for better vision.

"Yes, but the glyphs are in the High Speech, and a somewhat strange form at that, when it was a spoken language, before it became sharply distinguished from the ancestral form of Demotic. This is the Rescript proper, the original instruction."

She looked at it for a long moment. "It is an order to the Designated Successor to seek out this city and remove the Imperial *tembst* to Dvor Il-Adazar. More than a dozen devices are listed; that is more than in most cities, even in the High Imperial period. But—"

"But?"

He thought he saw what she meant; the devices were listed, and then an entirely separate glyph was touched by the modifier that meant "maximum importance" . . . or something like it.

Teyud added slowly, "And one in particular is encircled by 'numinous-significance,' qualified with 'treacherous-departure.' We speak here of secrets which were always very closely held. Evidently this city was founded to be a center for—"

She used a word neither of the Terrans knew; it was an archaic term, she explained, meaning something like "research."

"Yes, research into the Deep Beyond and possible ways of controlling its spread. See, here is the glyph-element 'Tollamune beginning,' with the paired helix symbol encased in a constellation. That is the original Imperial designator, which fell out of use a few thousand years thereafter. According to this, several bearers of the Tollamune genome—"

The Imperial family, Jeremy translated to himself.

"—including the reigning Emperor and his Successor, visited here regularly. Then . . . it gives no specifics. It refers to the 'unfortunate event' or 'failure to Sustain Harmony.' That might be any event, including a usurpation or assassination, or other failure of propriety."

Sally stiffened slightly; Teyud flicked an ear at her and went on, "These surrounds modify the central glyph; the helix interrupted by wedges is *tembst*-origin, or 'source,' which is the Ruby Throne. And this qualifier is 'returning-to-beginnings' . . . return to the Mountain, combined with 'commanded-required'; that is equivalent to the imperative tense of the modern tongue."

She looked at the other sheets. "This is simpler: It is the authority of the bearer to commandeer and command in pursuit of the Rescript. Here is a list of the equipment and personnel."

Teyud frowned. "This last is the Successor's Statement of Apology, written even as the warcraft was destroyed by those attempting to commandeer it for evacuation."

"You read the High Speech very well," Sally said neutrally.

Teyud shrugged. "I am Thoughtful Grace. For ten thousand years and more we were bred to guard the Ruby Throne. Even scattered among the caravan towns and the *Wai Zang* cities, even today, we remember."

"So they *didn't* get the materials they came for," Jeremy said. "Especially the *numinously-significant* whatever. Wait—this is a map, is it not?"

He pointed the minicam toward the last page. It had schematic drawings as well as glyphs; not precisely in the style of modern Martian maps, but it had something of their look, more like a circuit diagram than the bird's-eye-view style of their Terran equivalents. Or perhaps more like a flow-diagram, of the sort you got as guides in the London Underground. It had the advantage of giving relationships precisely, but you needed to know the key, and the distances weren't proportional.

"It is a map. Of the underground ways between the principal buildings. And these mark the locations of the Imperial *tembst.*"

She picked it up; his cautious archaeologist's soul cried out in protest, but the tough flexible material seemed to suffer no harm.

"The key would be the location of this"—she pointed to an elongated symbol—"which would represent the centrum of Imperial power in this city. I estimate that the most efficient approach would be—"

CHAPTER FIVE

Encyclopedia Britannica, 20th Edition
University of Chicago Press, 1998

THE SPACE RACE: The Second Phase, 1988–

Knowledge that the solar system contained two more life-bearing planets besides Earth, and that they had intelligent humanoid inhabitants, was enough to fuel the first two decades of the space race. Both the great blocs devoted enormous resources to establish bases on Mars and Venus, and to the huge infrastructure of space stations, orbital power and manufacturing plant, and lunar bases and mines necessary to support the expeditions to our sister planets.

However, by the 1980s it was becoming apparent that while Venus and Mars were treasure houses of scientific knowledge, they were not *economic* frontiers. There would be no equivalent of the sugar and tobacco, the silk and gold and silver, which had rewarded the pioneers who sailed Earth's oceans during the Renaissance. Virtually nothing could bear the costs of interplanetary travel at a profit; the whole enterprise was dependent on vast and continuous subsidies. Voices were heard arguing that to devote a fifth of the gross national product to merely scientific ventures, despite the many valuable spin-offs of space-based enterprises, was a waste of resources that could be better used on earth.

However, research on Venus and Mars had already begun to raise disturbing questions as to the origins of life on those worlds. Paleontology and geology conducted at the U.S. and Eastbloc bases increasingly indicated that prior to approximately 200 mya, both globes had been sterile: Venus a hell of sulphuric acid and superdense atmosphere, Mars a cold frozen globe with only a wisp of carbon dioxide. *Something* had happened to turn both into passable analogues of Earth, and it had happened in a geological eye blink of no more than a few million years, possibly as little as a few thousand. Only intelligent action could account for it—and action on a scale and level of technological prowess that made Earth's vaunted sciences seem like tools of chipped flint.

Advances in the life sciences reinforced the conclusions of the planetologists. Naïvely, the first explorers had been unsurprised at the exceedingly Earthlike forms life on Venus and Mars took, which fitted in with generations of imaginative extrapolations (see *science fiction*). But detailed examination showed that many species on both planets were not just similar to their Terran counterparts, but similar in ways that made common origins almost certain. Molecular biology and DNA analysis, then entering their period of rapid growth and practical application, showed the same. The clinching proof was the discovery on Venus in the late 1980s of groups speaking an Indo-European language, and possessing an artifact—albeit nonfunctioning and extremely enigmatic—that they insisted had been given to their ancestors by "gods" who brought them to their new home.

The shock of discovering that the ancients—sometimes more colorfully called the Lords of Creation—had been modifying the solar system, and continuing their actions into the era of recorded history, was fully as great as that of finding humanoid life on other planets. In the 1970s, the first large space telescopes had confirmed the existence of life-bearing planets with oxygen atmospheres orbiting other suns. Now humanity had conclusive proof that at least one alien species was vastly more advanced than our-selves, and that it had been intervening in our history for its own enigmatic purposes since the time of the dinosaurs.

As space-based telescopes and other sensors grew in power and refinement in the 1980s and 1990s, disturbing hints of engi-neering on a *stellar* scale were observed in the heavens, a scale that made the terraforming and seeding of two planets minor by comparison. These discoveries unleashed an ever-growing scien-tific, philosophical, and religious turmoil. They also provided the impetus for maintaining and expanding the scope of human activ-ity in space. If the universe contained aliens of such inscrutable power, humanity had no choice but to expand its own knowledge and capacities as rapidly as possible.

Mars, the lost city of Rema-Dza
May 15, 2000 AD

Outside, the windstorm had brought visibility down to nothing and was doing its best to rearrange the landscape; at this time of year, it might be covering half the northern hemisphere. The Martians had rigged cables to connect the *Traveler*'s hiding place with the nearest buildings, and you had to slog through the sandy dust with an elbow around the line, blind as a bat.

Every time Jeremy Wainman did it, he remembered that the *dhwar* had headed this way and that their lair might well be in the square miles of abandoned tower and building and tunnel around them. The memory of those saw-edged beaks was uncomfortably vivid. At least the wind would keep the aerial predators pinned to their rookeries.

"I don't see why the hell they sent an archaeologist here," he said cheerfully to Yamashita as he rolled a door shut behind him and stamped and shook his robes to get as much of the dust out as pos-sible. "I mean, you're a troubleshooter and you know more about the tech stuff, so why didn't they just send *you?*"

"It's a ruined lost city, isn't it?" she replied sourly, looking up from her portable computer. "With a goddamned lost treasure in it somewhere. All that's lacking are pygmy natives with blowguns. Classic archaeological stuff, like those movies back in the seventies with the temples and the big rolling stone balls and giant snakes and the idols with emeralds in their eyes. We need you to find the stuff and me to keep you alive and working *and* possibly to figure out what the stuff you find does."

"You're showing your age, and those movies were set on Venus anyway. And real archaeologists don't do ruined cities and treasures. That's for tomb robbers, not archaeologists. *Archaeologists* spend years excavating antique latrines and rubbish dumps with toothbrushes and whisk brooms, like when I worked on Anasazi digs. And didn't you notice? I'm completely bullwhip-free."

She smiled, which was good to see again; she'd been a bit glum since they had their last little chat.

"You *do* have a sword and a pistol," she pointed out.

He cleared his throat. "Anyway, what have you got?"

The chamber they were in had once been the entranceway to a block of living quarters; akin to an apartment building's vestibule, though it might just as easily have been a palace, or a block of offices, or something with no exact Terran equivalent. It had a knee-high bench all around the oval interior, and it was lined with polished hematite, green and blue and red. He sat down on the bench beside her; they'd padded it with silks and furs from the landship, spare bedding, glow-globes and boxes and sacks of supplies. The light vanished in the smooth curves of the vaulting above; you didn't need much to imagine lost banners stirring in the drafts.

They'd put the portapotty in another room. Even now it took a certain amount of willpower for Jeremy to use it. The damned thing was *alive* . . .

"Here's the latest on the tunnels," Sally said. "Teyud's been sending reports by runner as they find stuff."

A spider web sprang into existence on the screen, with sections color-coded in blue, red, and gray.

"These are clear; those are filled; these are collapsed; and these are partially choked but clearable."

"Why on earth . . . well, you know what I mean . . . do Martians burrow like ants? Every place they've been around for a while, you find these warrens underneath."

"Storage and insulation. And they just seem to like it. At least they build tunnels big enough to get around in without knocking your head, mostly; and it's convenient during weather like this."

"Plus, you're safe from flocks of giant flesh-eating birds."

"That, too." Her voice lost its bantering tone. "You have any luck getting through to base, or Zar-tu-Kan?"

"None. But this crappy weather is bad enough that that might be natural, now."

"Yeah," she said flatly. "It could be. But it isn't."

He shrugged uneasily and took a swig from his canteen; Sally reached out a hand, took a drink herself, poured a little into a mask, and clipped it across her face.

Being pursued by Boris and Natasha who want to steal the treasure of the lost city really isn't what an archaeologist is trained for, Jeremy thought.

Granted, he was an Olympic-level fencer and a rock-climber of note; you didn't get to go off planet unless you had physical *and* academic qualifications. Intrigue and possible violence, though . . . not his style. He would have thought it had gone out of fashion even for the Eastblockers, now that they were ravenously successful capitalists. At least the eastern part of the Eastbloc were, and they ran the show nowadays.

Pardon me, now that they're employing "socialism with special characteristics." Which mostly means exporting areaphones and videoplayers and thinscreens and replacing beautiful old pagodas with the butt-ugliest skyscrapers outside Chicago—only twice as big—and building mansions outfitted with gold-plated bathtubs and squads of big-titted blond Russian housemaids in skimpy uniforms. But I guess when the stakes are high enough, atavistic instincts come to the fore.

Luckily, if there *were* Eastbloc agents out there shadowing them, they'd have to use locals for transport, probably those ones Teyud had spotted. And this weather would ground local aircraft and send landships into buttoned-down mode, bare poles and noses anchored into the wind and everyone waiting it out belowdecks. Martians didn't try to fight a sandstorm. There weren't that many in a season—this planet had fewer active weather systems than Earth—but a bad one could strip the flesh off your bones and then grind your bones to meal. They were the cutting edge of the Deep Beyond, claiming a little more of the Real World each year.

"I'd better go have a look in person," he said.

He was smiling as he left. Teyud seemed to have caught some of his passion for ancient relics; or at least she was very enthusiastic about *this* set of them.

He could see the glow-sticks that illuminated the Thoughtful Grace's improvised command post long before he got there. The oval walls of the ancient tunnel were slick enough to reflect light, still held by the chemical saliva-mortar of the beast that had drilled them. Mica glittered in the glassy rock; at closer range, he could see the light shining in the Martians' great eyes, as luminous as those of cats.

Teyud looked up at him with a slight, enigmatic smile, made a gesture of greeting-acknowledgment, and then went on to her second in command as she made a mark with her ink-stick on the wall of the junction. "Anything of significance?"

They were in a Y-fork of what had been the waste recirculation system that was linked to all the larger buildings and lined with reconfigured rock. A foot-deep layer of surface dust had accumulated here; the problem was that in some places it had filled the tunnels completely, and in a few, the fall of the towers above them had ruptured the passageways. Approaching their goal in the former centrum of power would not simply be a matter of following the airship's map. They would have to draw a map of their own, testing which ways were open.

"We have cleared a passage to the large chamber *here*," Baid said. "There are promising exits which may lead to that which we seek, as of yet still blocked by accumulated sand. There are also many cockroaches and a large variety of small, burrowing insects in these areas, particularly the large chamber."

She indicated them with a finger. "Once or twice there is a brief glimpse of very fast mammalian vermin, possibly rodents of unusual size."

"Interesting," Teyud replied, and the engineer nodded. "Very interesting."

"Why is that interesting?" Jeremy asked as he came up. "It is what I would anticipate in such an environment."

Baid looked at him and took a pose of comically exaggerated

surprise, which meant widening her eyes slightly and touching the fingers of one hand to her chin.

"Incredulous disbelief," she said.

Teyud realized the problem. "Life requires water," she explained. "We are in the Deep Beyond, and this city has been abandoned for a considerable period."

"Oh," he said.

Yeah, the Deep Beyond isn't a place, really, it's a condition. The deadest spots on a dying planet, where even evolution can't keep up with the freeze-drying process anymore. This makes the Sahara look like the Everglades.

"The towers?" he said.

"They would provide a little moisture, but not enough, I think, for the observed activity, particularly of late. Even the Mountain does not reap as much water from the atmosphere as it once did. The flying predators would be a source of organics, but in the towers where they nest, not here. *Something* dwells here below. This may complicate our search and produce delay. Baid, relieve the watch on the *Traveler*. Jeremy, come; we should investigate."

She turned on her heel and led the way, which was perfectly polite in Martian terms, if a little imperious.

She's worried, he thought. *Which means I should be worried. But I'm not. We're so close!*

They went through the tunnels the crew of the *Traveler* had explored. The way was faintly lit by glow-globes—the original ones, cleaned out and given fresh cultures of algae and feeding sludge. *But not very many. Granted, Martians see in the dark better than we do, but not* that *much better.*

"Why so little light?" Jeremy said.

"Hibernation," Teyud said.

"Explicative-Interrogative?" Jeremy replied—actually an expressive sound that meant "expand on your last statement." In Martian, even the equivalent of "huh?" was precise. You could communicate the same with an inclination of the shoulder and an ear-flick, but they weren't face to face.

"Carnivorous and parasitic organisms in hibernation will be stimulated to full activity by heat, light, the increased moisture brought by our exhalations, and the scent of our flesh," she said succinctly without turning around. "It is unwise to give them more stimulation than strictly necessary."

Which was exactly what you wanted to hear when you were struggling through sand soft as talc, in a dimly lit warren of tunnels in a lost city in the Deep Beyond, with a blasting sandstorm raging above and possible pirates, assassins, and spies waiting for you. Most Martian land animals did hibernate, too—even the hominids could do it if they had to, by a sheer act of will, something that still had the biologists a bit puzzled. Hibernation was logical on a planet with winters longer and colder than anything Earth had ever seen.

"Screw logic," he muttered to himself in English, with his hand on his automatic.

They climbed up a sand drift that half filled the tunnel, then down a spiral staircase that had been shoveled open and from there upward into a great chamber, circular and about a hundred yards across, with a floor covered in waist-high dunes; the walls were of the native ironstone bedrock for fifteen feet, and the smooth synthetic—or *digested*—stone above that. The roof was intact, a low, seamless dome of the poured-stone material reinforced with organic glass fiber. That had been the staple of Martian buildings since early in the Imperial era. It was deep in shadow; pools of light were scattered here and there where the crew had set up globes on portable stands.

There was a faint odor, too. Nothing you could really call a smell; it was more of an absence of the utter *lack* of smells that most of the tunnels had.

"This was a manufacturing facility," Teyud said. "I think the repair shops for the warships were located here; possibly a hospital or budding-plant for engines."

Jeremy nodded, then gestured agreement. There were glassine pipes along the wall for distributing the noxious waste-sludge that engines ate. Places on the floor where the slow accumulation of sand had mixed with rust and odd eroded shapes marked the location of machinery.

The leathery faced hybrid with the nose slits came up to them; he had an arrow on the string of his bow, and he was glaring around.

"Too much," he said, in gutturally accented Demotic. "Bugs in the sand. All dark here."

It took a moment for his remark to register with Jeremy; how could you have a food chain without light? The answer was straightforward; you had to have a rain of nutrients from someplace that *did* have light, the way life of the abyssal depths of Earth's oceans survived. Something had to be bringing organic matter to this lifeless place, even if that only meant crapping on the floor.

The thought seemed to strike Teyud, the noseless one, and Jeremy at the same time. Their heads snapped upward, and Teyud shouted:

"Elevate the lights!"

You did that by using a reflective collar. One of the crew rose and used the thin flexible length of mirror to throw a beam upward. At first Jeremy thought the ceiling was merely blotched. Then it began to move, rippling. Eyes blinked open, huge and crimson.

"Feral engines!" the hybrid shouted, and the string of his bow went *snap* on his bracer as he shot upward and snatched for another arrow.

A moment later the shout turned into a gargling scream. A tentacle lashed downward, growing thinner and thinner until it was like a wire loop, hooked around the man's body and reeled up like a bungee cord recoiling. Only this one didn't stop until it hit a mouth. The thing had no vocal cords, but the crunching noise the man made as he was smashed in past the circle of horn plates that surrounded the orifice was loud enough. So was the moment of silence that followed the scream's sudden end.

And underneath that, you could hear the endless waxy *puckapuckapuckapucka* as the beasts' tentacles slapped their suckers on the polished stone and tore them loose while they moved; and the harsh panting as their lungs swelled like veined sacks on either side of their bodies.

Jeremy threw himself backward onto the sand with his pistol up. "Christ, how many—there must be hundreds of them!" he shouted.

"Forty-two," Teyud answered calmly, and opened fire with the dart gun in her left hand, the sword ready in her right. "Doubtless they lair here and climb to the towers above to prey on the birds and their leavings." In a ringing shout like a brass trumpet: "We must kill them all *expeditiously!*"

Everyone started shooting, the sharp echoing *brak-brak-brak* of

Jeremy's automatic overriding the slower *phffft* of the dart pistols and rifles, the sharp upward stab of orange-white flame as he emptied the magazine, the smell of the cordite choking-strong in the cold dry air. A huge limp shape fell to the sand next to him with a thud he could feel along his whole body, ripped open and leaking blood that smelled like copper. Its tentacles raised a fog of dust as they thrashed the ground like whips of boiled leather.

One struck him across the upper thighs with paralyzing force; Jeremy screamed, but forced himself to keep shooting with an effort of will that left his face gray and running with sweat. His eyes stung in the darkness, half blinded by the muzzle flashes, and he wasn't sure if he hit anything. Then the slide locked back as the last cartridge flicked out, and he fumbled at his waist-belt for the spare magazine, ejected the spent one, fumbled a little again as he strove to click home the next. It finally snicked into place and he started shooting again.

Another robed figure rose sprattling toward the ceiling, with a shriek that ended in that grisly crunch. Chewing and sucking sounds followed, and bits and pieces rained down. More of the beasts fell dead as the neurotoxin in the Martian dart guns struck; unfortunately one of them fell directly on top of a glow-globe, cutting the light in half. Now there was only one island of visibility in the middle of the great room, and all around it shadows where monsters walked.

"They are coming down the walls!" a voice shouted.

"Twenty remain," Teyud said; somehow her voice cut cleanly through the brabble of shouts and screams. "To the light, but do not look closely at it. Back to back, stand!"

The pain in his groin had subsided a bit; the tentacle hadn't struck squarely—he'd be dead or puking and screaming if it had—and the adrenaline washed a bit of the agony out. Harder was standing up when one of those organic whips might crack down out of the darkness above and carry him toward the waiting maw.

Christ, what a place for an archaeologist to end up! he thought, sweat sending raw pain through his chapped lips. *And I asked for it! Goddamn Mars and Goddamn me, too!*

For an instant he felt a paralyzing longing for the sight of green grass and trees and the smell of barbecue cooking.

It didn't stop him moving. The seven remaining Martians and Jeremy stood in a circle around the glow-globe, blades and guns pointing outward. Ripping and crushing sounds came from the night's blackness as the bodies of the dead beasts were eaten by their pack mates. Hibernation didn't shut down the metabolism completely, just immensely slowed it, and they were probably very hungry indeed. He could hear their wheezing breath, not much different from the engine that ran *Traveler*'s auxiliary. But louder, quite a bit louder.

"Report the status of your ammunition," Teyud said again, in that living-bell voice.

They did; most were low, and he was nearly dry.

"Blades in hand, then," she said. "Be ready."

He tossed his pistol into his left hand and drew his sword. It would be more awkward for him than for the Martians; they were all fully ambidextrous from birth, and he'd only practiced at it. He heard Teyud mutter something under her breath:

"This situation is of excessive difficulty. Exasperation, frustration, annoyance!"

That gave him time for just one snort of incredulous laughter before the darkness came alive with waving tentacles, and behind them, scuttling forms the size of lions. Plate-sized crimson eyes shone like lamps, with pupils like S-shaped slits. A crash of shots, the automatic bucking in his hand and knocking a half-seen shape backward, a wild swipe that took the tip off a reaching limb and jarred him from wrist to shoulder. The muzzle flashes were like strobes of lightning, giving him a flicker of nightmare shapes and then plunging his dazzled eyes into a worse darkness.

Outside the circle of light, feral engines reared, beating at the circle of humans like a storm of whips, the plates of their mouths clacking eagerly as the dust cloud cut visibility to arm's length. The tentacle that struck the side of his head came out of nowhere. There was a flash of light inside his head, and then something was around his ankles, dragging him over the sand. Huge, unblinking eyes stared at him, growing larger and larger as the robe bunched up around his waist and he slid toward the snapping mouth.

Teyud leapt, moving with a long-striding grace that made her blurring speed seem deliberate. The blade of her sword punched into one of the scarlet eyes, and the circle around his ankles tightened to just short of bone-crushing pressure and then relaxed. He kicked frantically at the twitching thing and staggered backward onto his feet, wheezing thanks, then collapsed again into a squat, gripping his sword convulsively and panting as the hunting engines had.

Silence fell. The Martians danced in to stab at the nerve-ganglions of the dead or dying beasts, making sure on general principles. Teyud gazed around keenly, greenish blood dripping from the long blade of her sword, looking almost dark enough to be black in the dim, dust-ridden air. A smell like metal and acid filled the air.

"Forty-one," she said. "Furthermore—"

The *shhhsshsh* of cloven air as the tentacle came down in a long looping swing was the only warning; Jeremy could feel his own throat tightening to shout, but the cry didn't have time to begin. Teyud had already begun to leap backward and twist before it struck; the air went out of her lungs in a single agonized whoosh as it slammed across her stomach. Then she disappeared upward, the sword dropping from her hand as the thigh-thick length of muscle twisted around her torso, locking her right arm to her side.

Jeremy acted before his conscious mind had recovered from the shock. He came up out of his crouch with all the power of his long legs and of well-trained muscles bred in a gravity three times this. The ceiling where the feral engine hung was thirty feet above his head. He was more than three-quarters of the way there when he passed Teyud and threw his left arm around the tentacle above the point where it gripped her. It felt like hugging a thigh-thick length of living cable wrapped in suede; the muscle surged with daunting power as it jerked them both toward the ceiling, and he barely had time to extend the blade in a *Flying flèche,* some remote fencer's corner of his mind insisted.

The great eyes were his target, or rather the patch of darkness between them. If the others had been the size of lions, this was a grizzly bear, and it stank with a hard dry scent that was still stunningly intense. The impact as they struck was like being thrown into a stone wall by a catapult with a large de-boned ox for padding. Pain shot up his arm at the slamming impact of the point in thick muscle and cartilage, and then a harder one as the point struck stone, forcing his fingers to open in reflex. The glowing eyes vanished, and suddenly he was falling with the dreamy slowness of low gravity.

Even so he barely had time to get his feet beneath him before he landed again, staggering with an *ooff* as his feet sank ankle-deep in the soft sandy dust on the floor. His head craned upward. Two seconds later Teyud fell downward toward him; he snatched at her and caught her, with another *ooff* as her solid weight came into his arms—the equivalent of catching fifty pounds on Earth.

Her arm had gone around his shoulder as they nearly collapsed to the ground. One of his stayed around her torso as she came to her feet again. She didn't have the fragile, birdlike lightness of most Martians, instead feeling slim but supple-strong inside the curve of his arm. Their faces were close; before he was aware of what he intended, he brought their lips together.

Teyud's eyes went wide in surprise for an instant. Then she put a hand behind his head and pressed it firmly closer. Her tongue flicked at his lips—

Whomp!

They both sprang backward in reflex at the flash of motion and the heavy impact on the floor not a yard's distance from him. Teyud landed crouching, her long curved dagger in her hand. Jeremy shot ten feet into the air, fell and hit the sand with his buttocks and one hand, bounded erect and staggered backward, his other hand clawing at the empty pistol holster at his belt.

They both straightened, looking at the dead creature that lay twitching on the floor of the chamber with the hilt of Jeremy's sword jammed between its eyes. Its remote ancestor had been a sea creature, a distant relation of ammonites and squid. This looked more like a naked bluish cuttlefish flanked by two purple-red-blue sacs, flaccid now that it wasn't breathing, but with a body that came to a blunt point and then flared out into a single large sucker.

"Excessive excitement," Teyud said. "I feel a strong desire for uneventful days, even unto tedium."

"*Amen!*" Jeremy said, conscious of how his body wanted to shake and overcoming it with an effort of will.

In Demotic he went on, "Agreement!" together with a posture that added *emphatic mode*, and a posture that said the same thing. That wasn't good grammar, but it got across what he felt.

They looked at each other for a long moment and began to laugh; Jeremy stopped because some of the surviving crew of the *Traveler* were wounded, and Teyud went forward to nudge the dead creature.

"This is a breeder," she said. "There are immature buds. At least one must have been abandoned while not bonded to a crankshaft. The others would have been its offspring. They are parthenogenic and enter the reproductive stage if fed high-quality protein. Very strong, and adaptable—the original form was a small, semisessile predator of caves and cliffs. Fortunately they are not very intelligent."

"Why not?" Jeremy said, unable to keep a slight edge of sarcasm out of his voice. "Everything *else* you people make seems to be."

Teyud frowned for a moment, then smiled slightly, more a droop of the eyelids than anything else. Her cool voice went on: "That was found to be counterproductive. There is little environmental stimulation in the existence of an engine with its tentacles bonded to a crankshaft."

"So?"

"They would attempt to escape. Boredom causes engine failure."

Sally had given him the hairy eyeball and looked like she could barely stop herself from quoting regulations when Teyud matter-of-factly took him by the hand and led him to the captain's cabin of the *Traveler*, under the prow. He'd given *her* the finger and a big shit-eating grin as he passed.

Damn regulations, and damn Sally, too. She can go find her own fun, he thought several hours later.

He stretched contentedly, pulling one of the furs up around his neck and watching Teyud as she bent and twisted just an arm's length away. It felt a little cold to be naked, now that things were cooling down in both senses of the word.

Besides, I like Teyud. A lot.

Teyud wasn't bothered by the mid-fifties temperature of the room. She was still cleaning herself with handfuls of a soft, absorbent dust that collected liquid, and then something like a damp sponge; not, thank God, a *living* sponge, which he'd been afraid of before he used it himself. Things were evidently messier with a Terran, but she didn't seem to mind that, either.

He admired the sight of her. Naked she looked a bit less like *h. sapiens sapiens* than she did with her robes on; the differences in proportion were more apparent, the longer limbs and deeper chest, and the near-total absence of body hair. What little there was showed like fine bronze down against the natural pale olive of her skin, and the muscle moved beneath it like skeins of steel wire. There were interesting marks on the insides of her forearms, too. He'd thought they were tattoos, but apparently Thoughtful Grace had natural birthmarks there, like elongated swirling red-and-black signs.

Martian women didn't really have much breast, either, just a slight curve like the base of a turned goblet, which made the nipple stand out more.

Odd, he thought. *You'd expect them to look like Eskimos, short and stocky and padded, with the cold here, in spite of the lower gravity. But they stay warm by other means than subcutaneous fat. And I do like slim. Yeah.*

He'd noticed the coolness of her body, one more point of intriguing difference. He grinned; there were other intraspecies distinctions, some of which had been fun to work around.

She grinned back at him for an instant; not precisely a natural expression, but not forced, either. It seemed more as if she was trying it on for size.

"Aesthetic-sexual appreciation," he said in Demotic.

"Desire for further intromission?" she said, raising one eyebrow. "If so, I express a favorable response."

The posture that went with *that* was a rather graphic movement of the hips.

"Regretful inability!" he said.

"Ah. Who knows the powers of the *vaz-Terranan*?"

She chuckled soundlessly as she walked back to the oval bed and raised the sleeping fur and gave him a frank examination. Then she slid back under it herself.

"Pleasant warmth," she said, sliding into contact and resting her head on his shoulder. "Feelings: repletion, exhaustion, very slight soreness, a surprising degree of affection."

"Me too."

She touched his ribs and thigh. "Your pleasantly agreeable personality contrasts in an intriguing manner with the brutish power of your appearance."

"Ah . . . thanks," he said.

His mental gears shifted as he made himself hear the real meaning: *You look macho but you're really sweet and gentle.*

She went on: "You are as strong and resistant to damage as a Thoughtful Grace; stronger, in fact. This is novel to me but agreeable."

"Agreement-apprehension of inflicting involuntary injury during parareproductive exchange minimizes anticipatory stimulation."

There was a weird sexiness to talking Demotic in bed, he found. You *couldn't* talk dirty in it, really. Cursing involved scatology or comments on someone's inadequate genome—saying "unequal to the environment" was *seriously* insulting. But talking about the body parts and their functions had the same vocabulary whether you were calling out in the middle of things or writing a medical textbook; *I request more energetic intromission, emphatic tense!* was the sort of passionate murmur you could expect.

"Tell me more of your reproductive in-group," she said.

"Only if you tell me about *your* family," he replied.

Wish I had a cigarette, he thought dreamily; the habit had come back since they learned how to deactivate the carcinogens, but nobody was shipping it to Mars.

She remained silent for a while. The *Traveler* was intensely quiet, with only a deck watch; the rest of the crew were in the building they'd selected as base. But he could hear the faint screech of the wind as it scoured around the building that held the landship, and even fainter creaks and metallic noises as the ship shifted slightly on its axles.

"I was born . . . in a remote city," she said, very softly; he could feel the slight flutter of her breath against the skin where his shoulder met his neck.

"Long ago and far away?" he said, stroking the hard, resilient curve of her back.

"Very far away and thirty years ago," she said; mentally he translated it as sixty earth years.

Which gave him pause for a moment, but actually, given their respective potential lifespans, they were about the same age.

"Near the Mountain?" he said.

That was the only place she was likely to have met Eastblockers.

She nodded, and continued, "My mother was of the Thoughtful Grace. An officer of some rank and of excellent lineage."

"Your father *wasn't* Thoughtful Grace?" he said, surprised.

She certainly had all the canons of the breed, as far as he could tell, and he'd just had a chance for a *very* close examination.

"No, he was her employer; a male of very high caste and rank in the city-state where she was employed; of the pure Imperial Administrator genome. They had an erotic and emotional bond of some duration and intense commitment, and would have formally contracted for reproductive partnership if that had been practical."

Were in love as well as being lovers, he silently translated. There were some things that Demotic did not express compactly. *And would have married if it were allowed.*

"But her fertilization was unauthorized."

Jeremy's brows went up again. *That* was rare. Martian women didn't get pregnant unless they wanted to; in fact, they usually had to concentrate for a while to start the menstrual cycle and become receptive.

"Accidental?"

"Not on her part," she said. "On the insistence of my father's kin-group and political associates, she was punished by infestation for theft of his genome. Questions of access to power were involved. And the *vaz-Terranan*, the Eastbloc, were involved in the intrigues."

Ouch, he thought, with a wash of sympathy.

Infestation was a memorably gruesome way to die, being put in a glass bottle and eaten alive from the inside out, like a digger wasp's prey, and it could last *years*; watching a couple of still photos of an advanced case had made him think twice—three times—about wanting to go to Mars, back when he was a teenager.

"My father had wished to meld genomes, but not at that time, and could not protect her," she went on. "But he was able to conceal my birth and have me socialized and taught by other of his

Thoughtful Grace retainers, until it became apparent that I was of mixed origin."

He nodded. Genetic testing was trivially easy here, and had been for untold millennia. Who your father was wasn't a matter of opinion on Mars, and never had been.

"That was eleven years ago. One of my tutors, who had a para-parental bond with me and a close genetic link with my mother, accompanied me for a time, but was killed when Coercives in the pay of my father's enemies discovered us."

She fell silent again with a sigh, then added, "My father still lives but, to a high degree of probability, I can never return. I wander, seek employment for my talents, and the avoidance of ennui until dissolution."

"That's too bad," he said.

Tragic, in fact. This is one hell of a woman. She could do anything, but she's stuck being a low-level mercenary.

Teyud shrugged. "This mission has been an interruption in a long period of low-level discomfort and tedium. As for the trajectory of my world-line, it is an analogue of that of the Real World in this age without even the illusion of *Sh'u Maz*," she said. "A declension from imagined security toward the maximization of entropy."

Her hand moved, touching feather-soft and then rhythmically. She rolled over and grinned down at him.

"The *vaz-Terranan* do have powers!"

CHAPTER SIX

Encyclopedia Britannica, 20th Edition
University of Chicago Press, 1998

MARS: Impact of Martian Tembst on Earth

Science has learned much from Venus, particularly about the history of life on Earth. It was studies of Venusian life and the remarkable adventures of Ranger Marc Vitrac (see *Cloud Mountain People, Lords of Creation/Ancients*) that established beyond doubt that both Mars and Venus were originally terraformed and seeded with Terran life, including various hominid species and our own, by aliens with a technology advanced beyond our comprehension. The one alien artifact recovered by Ranger Vitrac has been endlessly analyzed with absolutely no result. (see *Diadem of the Eye*).

However, it was on Mars that we found a biological science surpassing our own but enough like it to be readily accessible to us. Although much Martian knowledge had been lost in the fall of the planetary empire of the Crimson Dynasty, many of their creations remained, including biological tools that used tailored enzymes and forced-evolutionary mechanisms for producing new microorganisms of astonishing capabilities on demand. This technology—which could be easily shipped interplanetary distances, as it bred of its own accord—has provided us with the genetically engineered organisms which in the past decade have had a profound impact on Terran economies and societies.

The earliest and most significant of these were the ability to quickly and inexpensively transform any biomass into hydrocarbon products such as petroleum, as well as similar products that concentrate and sort wastes (even heavy metals) into easily processed raw materials, and the engineered yeasts that cheaply desalinate water. Further developments . . .

Mars, The Lost City of Rema-Dza
May 18, 2000 AD

The sandstorm that had peeled back a little more of the fabric of life on Mars had blown itself out at last, or mostly, retreating into the vast, empty deserts to the east. You couldn't say the air was fresh, exactly; it was dry and cold and that was all, but it did have a lot less finely divided dust in it, and didn't make you feel as though you were suffering from black lung by the end of the day. Jeremy whistled happily as he ducked out of the *Traveler* and slogged through the dust to the building that was their access to the tunnels. The *De'ming* had cleared a fair space around the door, and he could open it without a torrent of reddish powder pouring in along with him.

Sally was sitting in front of her portable, eating *to'a* from a bowl with a spoon while she studied the screen. The dish was flaming-hot, a sort of curry of meat and nuts and dried fruit over groats made from *asu*, which tasted like nuggets of sweet potato. The spice was all to the good, since the meat was from the feral engines they'd killed, made edible with a tenderizer that was one of the staples of Martian cooking. When you cooked it enough, engine-meat just tasted gristly-tough and a little fishy, sort of like badly overdone calamari. The pots simmered on a heating element on the stone bench, filling the room with the spicy rich scent.

Jeremy was still whistling as he went over and ladled himself a bowl and took a round of flatbread. His bowl was one of a pair, twice the size of the ones the crewfolk used; Martians found the scale of Terran appetites for food and water astounding, amusing, and sometimes revolting.

"Looks like they've found something," he said.

"You think this was the sanctum sanctorum?" Sally said.

She pointed to the screen, which showed a stretch of corridor two hundred yards beyond the chamber where they'd fought the feral engines.

"Very probably," he said, then blew on a spoonful of *to'a* and put it in his mouth.

"*Errrrk!*" he said, though he'd been raised on jalapeños. "Who made this today?"

"I did," Sally said dryly. "I was trying to fool my tastebuds into forgetting what's in it, like lots of wasabi on not-too-fresh sushi."

Even a native New Mexican would consider *this* hot—by comparison, the most potent carne asada was like peach yogurt. Still, that *did* hide the taste of the other ingredients. A *to'a* could be a noble dish, but you didn't expect to eat like an epicure on a dig, and he really didn't like remembering those organic whips coming down out of the dark.

He tapped the screen, bringing up his own research studies. "See, it's to the right of the axial spine of the tower—"

"Right facing which way?"

"Facing the Mountain—Mons Olympus, Dvor Il-Adazar. They used that as their orientation point until nearly the end of the Imperial era, before they shifted to a north-south-east-west, I think because of some political dispute. You can tell from the layout of this place they were still using the old system when it was built. And there's a nice, short connecting tunnel through here. That would be the proper orientation for a treasure vault. If you think Martians today are fanatics about doing things in proper form, the old Imperials—"

She made a sympathetic noise and he rolled his eyes. "What you'd expect for a bureaucracy dating back to the Paleolithic."

"I think you may be right," Sally said meditatively, "despite the way you're making a complete idiot of yourself."

He felt himself bristle and then forced a smile. "Yes, Mother."

"It's not you walking away with a broken heart I'm afraid of— fuck your heart, Wainman, and your overactive dick, too."

She sighed, and exhaled in a long, exasperated sound. "Look, I shouldn't have said that. I'm sorry. I *do* care that you're letting yourself in for a world of hurt. But I care about the mission even more."

Jeremy felt his indignant bristle gave way to a flush. "I'm doing my job. And I appreciate your concern, but it isn't your job to be my keeper."

"Yes, it is. Why do you think they sent me? *Get the stuff.* That's *your* job."

"Why do you think I'm not doing it properly?"

"Because you're introducing unpredictable emotions into the mix. Martians act about the same way we do when it comes to profits and bargains—some of them are more honest than others, but that's true in San Jose, too. They *don't* act the way we do all the time in their personal lives, and I've been here long enough to see that's not just doctrine, it's the Buddha's own truth."

"There have been plenty of relationships—marriages, too, like Vitrac and his cave princess—with locals on Venus."

"With *human* locals on Venus, not the other varieties. Coming into a relationship from a different culture is bad enough—ask my grandmother—but Martians are not *h. sap. sap.* even if Tab A fits. Not quite. They don't have exactly the same instincts we do."

"So?" Jeremy said with heavy patience.

"So you don't know when you're suddenly going to be hitting some landmine. Keep it simple, keep it at the level of conscious explicit thought and formal communication, and you're safe . . . well, safer. Getting in this deep—"

He thought she used the phrase with malice aforethought and shot her a pained look.

"—is an invitation to a sudden explosion." More gently, she added, "Why do you think they usually insist on married couples at Kennedy Base?"

"Why, Sally, I didn't know you cared," he said, batting his eyes. She'd been a widow since a week after the arrival of the First Fleet.

Sally rolled her eyes toward the ceiling. "I give up," she said in an obvious lie.

"And I'd better get to work."

He finished the bowl, scoured it out with sand, tapped the screen again, and waited while the little machine spat out three pages of diagrams. Then he rolled them up, took a biscuit from an open box near the camp stove, bit into it—quite nice, dusted with something that resembled cinnamon and filled with a nut that tasted like coconut and cream, and unlike most Martian baked goods, not too salty—before he passed through into the tunnels.

There were more lights now, and in each long section stood one of the crewfolk with a dart-rifle. A slight tang of coppery molluscan blood remained in the chamber where they'd fought, and a slighter one of decay, but as they'd noted there were bugs in the sand, and they were efficient scavengers. They'd gotten almost every scrap of blood and flesh left over from the fight.

You *really* wouldn't want to lie down here for a long nap.

Beyond that, the newly excavated section of passageway was half filled with sand and he had to walk crouching past a staircase whose entrance had been covered with a section of sailcloth tacked to the wall with glue to keep the dust that filled it from getting ahead of the diggers; past it, he slid downward until he was only ankle-deep in the powdery stuff. A glow-globe gave bright light in the confined space and the six *De'ming* were busy there, stolidly shoveling dust into a box on a sled and then hauling loads back to be distributed in the big chamber. He coughed as he breathed in a little of the finely divided material.

Teyud, her headdress back in place, turned from the door and gave him a smile. One that actually parted the lips. He felt as if there was a breath of warmth in the constant chill of the dead city. He returned it, deliberately turning down the wattage so it wouldn't look impossibly exaggerated to her—she was making the same effort for him, from the other side of the teeter-totter.

If we're both willing to work at it, I think we can make a go of this.

Baid ignored the byplay—one nice thing about Martians was that the respectable ones considered showing open inquisitiveness bad form—and continued an inch-by-inch examination of the door, shooing the magnifying glass she was using around with a finger.

The portal was a hard, fiber-bound black synthetic with the Tol-lamune sigil in the middle, and oval in shape—twelve feet tall by six feet across at the widest point, which meant it was designed to swing on a hinge, rather than roll sideways. The handles molded into the surface meant that it was designed to open outward; probably the door itself was beveled to mate with its surround, so that pushing on it merely transferred the strain to the frame and then to the solid poured stone of the foundations.

He touched it, and it *felt* massive, with that underlying solidity you felt only from big blocks of masonry and things like bank vaults. The seal with the edges was good enough that there probably wasn't any sand in the chamber beyond.

"Yes," the engineer said, completing her examination. "The sensor is centrally located, below the Imperial symbol. Contemporary practice would put it to one side, near the hinge."

She took a small, heavy, edged tool from her harness and struck the surface three times. A plate swung down, hanging open from interior hinges at the bottom; it still swung freely after all this time.

Within was a shallow depression; examining it closely, Jeremy saw that it was lined with some shiny, dark brown substance.

"This would have been the identity sensor," she said.

Back home on Earth, they'd been talking about using DNA for identification for a while—they called it biometric ID—but apart from some forensics work they hadn't gotten around to developing it. It wasn't as if there were many places you had to check people's ID, after all. Not in the Free World, at least, where even passports were falling out of use; in the paranoid Eastbloc you even had to show an identity card to get on a domestic flight. But this was the equivalent of a bank vault—or a secret lab at Los Alamos—so he supposed it made sense.

Hmmm. Or perhaps it was just their equivalent of a key and lock system.

"What's the actual locking mechanism?" he asked.

Baid shrugged. "This is quite old, and so might be nonstandard. In a modern system, it would be cylindrical bolts working by air pressure in matching holes in the door and in the jamb opposite the hinge. If it was a very redundant system, there would also be bolts in the wall above and below the door. It might be an active system, with the rods retraced when the mechanism was not activated. In that case—"

She tugged hard on the door, with as much effect as pulling at a fifty-ton boulder.

"—it would open. If a passive system, the sensor would open a valve to retract the locking rods. In that case, they are still in place, and cannot be moved because the pressure system is long decayed.

I confess bafflement. This material is too refractory to be dissolved easily, and even a highly powered adamantium-tipped drill would require prolonged effort."

"Is there likely to be anything immediately behind the door?" Jeremy asked.

He was already wincing inside; this was tomb robbing with a vengeance.

"No," Baid said. "Typically, there would be a section of corridor beyond the door."

She looked at Teyud, and the Thoughtful Grace nodded. "That was the usual pattern in the Imperial era as well."

"I have something that might . . . that with a reasonable degree of probability might . . . solve this problem," Jeremy said.

The Martians looked at him, doing that disconcerting double blink. He found it a bit less eerie after waking up for a while with an example beside him on the pillow.

"It's called plastique."

The Martians all shook their heads and then twitched their ears rapidly, despite taking his warning and covering them while keeping their mouths open. Further back, the *De'ming* called out in thin-voiced distress until their handler gentled them down. Dust roiled against the lights, making it nearly as dark in here as it had been when they fought the feral engines. The others had the cloth of their headdresses pressed tight against mouth and nose; Jeremy and Sally had their masks and goggles on.

The slightly moistened air through the protective mask was a blessed benediction for Jeremy's tortured mucus membranes. Excitement made his mouth dry anyway, the way it would get as a kid when he stayed up late on Christmas Eve, watching the candles of the Farolitos burn down in their brown paper bags on the eaves outside. Bit by bit, the dust drifted downward, more slowly than it would have on Earth, and the air cleared until it was less of a bloody mist. Teyud managed to slide in ahead of him as they went into the tunnel.

Mindful of her duty, he thought, smiling a little before he snapped back into a hunter's alertness.

He was used to hunting things long dead.

The tunnel was still and silent, with only eddies in the dust, but it still seemed to ring with the force of the explosion, as if it had shattered not only the armored door but an unthinkable weight of time.

"Well, let's be sure it actually shattered the door, before we wax poetic," he muttered to himself in English.

It had, and into six or seven pieces, at that. The bioceramics Martians used were strong up to a very high breaking point. But when they failed, they *failed*. The man-thick door lay in ruins like a broken dish, with the remains of the wrist-thick locking bars strewn among it like shattered sticks of candy cane.

Teyud stopped and touched the fallen door where the symbol of the Kings Beneath the Mountain was cracked in half. Her touch had a gentleness that surprised Jeremy. To herself, she murmured, "You held your post as long as you could, sentinel, and yielded only to entropy at the last, as we all must."

Then to Jeremy, in the imperative tense: "Assistance."

That made sense; they were far and away the strongest pair in the party. Careful of their hands despite the gloves, they gripped a chunk and pitched it backward into the tunnel. The *De'ming* chattered softly for passage, loaded it onto their sled and dragged it away, as contented to do that as shovel sand, or to sit doing nothing. The rest followed, and then Teyud tossed a glow-stick in; the light didn't turn yellow, so the air inside must have been exchanged by the explosion.

She went ahead down a short stretch of corridor, then sheathed her sword and holstered her pistol. "This was the only entrance. The contents are undisturbed."

He thought he heard a little stress in her voice, a catch; he'd gotten better at reading it.

Well, so I should, no? And it's a beautiful voice.

He shivered a little. There hadn't been many digs like this one in his brief career, though he'd been working on them since high school.

Well, there was that weird one in Arizona, he thought. *That was . . . startling.*

He followed her even as he mused, scooping up the glow-stick and holding it up like a torch. It was faintly warm to his touch, like gripping something made of flesh.

"*Madre de Dios!*" he blurted. It wasn't often he fell back into his mother's language without intending to, but . . .

But this is justification in full!

It was another circular room, about thirty feet across. The light seemed almost painfully bright because the interior was lined with some white stone, almost crystalline in its purity and polished to a high gloss but faintly laced with streaks of crimson. It sparkled, too, from the gems set in intricate patterns in the ceiling, blue and crimson, diamond white and tourmaline yellow. In the walls were a spiraling row of niches; some held to nothing but dust, or a scattering of rust-colored debris. Others held—

An enigmatic sculpture of some hard green stone, like a face and yet abstract as a snowflake; a diamond carved in the likeness of a striking *Paiteng*, its beak open in a scream. A sheet of crystal marked with the constellations, but arranged across a sky quite different from the ones that looked down on Mars today, and almost as different as the stars that had shone on the coronation of the First Emperor. There was also an *atanj* set in black jade and platinum, carved with a whimsical realism that made him long to pick it up, and a stack of the parchmentlike material that the Vermillion Rescript had been painted on; his fingers itched at the thought of the lost knowledge that might be on it. More items, and more . . .

And one thing that didn't seem to fit with the others at all. It was a helmet, but an openwork one, of slim rods that might have been silver if silver could have lasted so long without collapsing into tarnish. This still shone brilliantly, and it had a red jewel over the middle of what would be the forehead if anyone wore it.

"Uh-oh!" he muttered, taking a step backward. "That's like the Diadem of the Eye from Venus. That's far too much like it. Oh, Jesus. Sally was right. There *is* an ancient artifact here."

As he watched, the jewel began to glow; when he lowered the stick of illumination, the light more than made up for the loss, but its glow seemed to paint the chamber with crimson. The outline of the helm was too sharp, as if its existence cut into the world all around it, tearing slips in the fabric of things themselves. Time and space fractured along lines of weakness, like the slippage planes of a crystal breaking under stress.

Teyud took a step forward. The jewel flared more brightly yet.

"No!" Jeremy called. "Teyud, darling, don't!"

She moved like a sleepwalker, yet with all the light, powerful Thoughtful Grace precision. Then she took the helmet in her hands and raised it, lowering it over her head. The silver ran and moved, until the thing was a perfect fit, and then it seemed to blur, as if it were sinking into her flesh and bone.

The world vanished.

Mars, City of Dvor Il-Adazar (Olympus Mons)
Hall of Received Submission
May 18, 2000 AD

In the Hall of Received Submissions, the two hundred twenty-fifth of the Tollamune Emperors rose screaming from the Ruby Throne, drawing free from the connection before it could obey his will. The thin, keening sound echoed from the vast hall's ceiling as blood ran from his nose and the small lesion on his neck. Within the depths of the crystal throne, shapes moved, not with their usual slow drift but with sharp, darting distress.

Then he collapsed backward. The Thoughtful Grace caught him before the frail bones could strike the uncushioned parts of the Throne; strong, gentle hands bore him backward. Others applied bandages of living skin that bonded with instant strength and wrapped him in a blanket that clung and hugged as it radiated warmth.

Before the Ruby Throne, a score more took stance, their black-armored bodies blocking the view of petitioner and courtier and bureaucrat.

"This audience is at an end!" their commander cried. "Go! Suppress speculation ungrounded in secure data! *Go!*"

As she spoke, the guards were in the antechamber behind the Throne, closing the door and laying Sajir down on the couch there; it purred and began to vibrate beneath him.

The physician in attendance withdrew a handful of colored segmented worms from his work chest, selected the ones he wanted, and applied them. One tapped into the Emperor's jugular and began to pulse as it injected drugs. Another crept up a nostril, sipping thirstily at the blood and rippling with colored bands. A helmet of smooth glassine filled with a pink, faintly pulsing jellylike substance went over the Emperor's head; the jelly spread, oozing into a thin, translucent film that settled over the monarch's skull and then showed patterns coded in blue, red, and green.

"Disorganized neural function but no stroke," the healer said after a moment. "The Supremacy is suffering from severe shock, in synergistic interaction with longstanding general debility. The organism approaches its failure limits."

The guard captain came through the door in time to hear that. "Cardiac arrest?" she asked.

"Heart function is thready and faint but regular, Superior Adwa sa-Soj, and improving. No known synthetic toxins present. Core temperature is depressed and there was a severe surge in blood pressure. I will administer stimulants and blood cultured from the Supremacy's banked stem cells. Recovery is highly likely, but a period of rest and freedom from stress is necessary."

Just then, the Emperor's eyes fluttered open. "Supremacy!" Adwa said anxiously. "Can you inform us? Is this enemy action?"

"Water," Sajir said.

He remained silent as he sipped, then stared upward; the pupils of his yellow eyes were distended, and the nicating membrane flicked across them half a dozen times. Then the guard captain repeated his question.

"What has happened, Supremacy?"

"The foundations of existence shook," Sajir whispered.

Washington D.C., Earth
Smithsonian Institute, Living Planets Exhibition
May 18, 2000 AD

In the Smithsonian Institute's Venusian room the Diadem of the Eye sat in its place of honor. The USASF guard—technically he was a corporal assigned to Base Security—yawned as he walked by it with his assault rifle over his shoulder; the spotlight above kept it brightly illuminated even at night when the rest of the lights were dimmed. Invisible beams protected it, and the guard was careful not to approach too closely; the alarm system was alarming in itself, and like his own presence was part of the price the USASF had demanded for turning over the device that had baffled Earth's best scientists for more than a decade.

Best scientists outside the Eastbloc, he thought sardonically. *Probably they'd like to give it a shot.*

Having the only authenticated artifact from the Lords of Creation had been a big boost for the United States and its allies. Not being able to tell Thing One about it hadn't helped, though. The big-domes weren't even sure if it was made of atoms. Nothing they could do to it affected it at all, short of strapping it to a nuclear weapon or throwing it into the Sun . . . and he'd heard that they weren't sure that would do anything either.

He looked through the glass of the case; there were pictures of lean, dark Marc Vitrac, the ranger from Jamestown Base, and Teesa of the Cloud Mountain People, the Venusian hottie who'd originally held the Diadem as her people's high priestess-cum-princess. She was smiling, her snub-nosed, amber-skinned face surrounded by a long fall of sunlit blond hair against a background of huge Venusian flowers and a bee the size of his thumb. A whitewashed adobe wall was behind her, and a great, mottled, doglike creature lay at her feet and looked suspiciously at whoever was taking the picture. Its teeth were of finger-long, and bared in a warning snarl.

Unfortunately the picture showed her in a Terran-style house-dress, not in the fur halter and g-string loincloth that were supposed to be her native costume, and she was carrying a young child—doing her Mrs. Vitrac thing, which interfered with the guard's fantasizing a bit. Unless one fantasized about being Vitrac himself, adventurer on the High Frontier and husband of a beautiful princess he'd rescued from dinosaurs, Neandertals, Eastbloc conspirators, and the ancients themselves.

And it was a cute kid, too. The guard grinned to himself. He had three daughters.

"Guess *that* settled whether the Venusians were human or not," he murmured to himself.

Then he sighed. Like millions of others, he'd applied for the space program himself back in high school, and like all but a tiny percentage, he'd been turned down, despite being tall enough for Mars. All it had gotten him was a career in the USASF that was probably less interesting than his original intention to graduate from Cal Tech.

He took a turn through the rooms, which were dim and smelled faintly of ozone, disinfectant, and floor polish, past blowguns and stone-headed spears and flint hatchets and crude hand axes, feather cloaks and bronze rapiers. The whole exhibit was devoted to the history of the exploration of Venus; one case held a seven-foot stuffed raptor portrayed in mid-leap, its sickle-clawed hind foot lashing out. Screens showed video of ceratopsians hauling logs and wagons around a building site, with humans seated on their necks and the little plastic hemispheres of the ICE machines on their foreheads showing how they were controlled by electrodes implanted in their brains.

Pictures showed more: street scenes in Kartahown, the Bronze Age city-state that was home to the planet's highest civilization; plesiosaurs attacking a sailing ship on an azure sea, their long necks looping down toward the deck; a sabertooth caught in mid-leap as it pounced upon a mastodon mired in a swamp . . .

That gave him an idea for a scene; he was trying to break into the adventure-fiction market. He shook his head as his belt-com beeped and the thought vanished; when he flicked it open he saw the face and voice of his counterpart in the Martian section next door. Oddly enough, the other man was an aspiring teller of tales as well.

"Anything new, Harry?" the Aussie rasp said.

"Not a thing, John. Just walking and thinking."

He turned back as he spoke. Then the little comm unit dropped out of his hand, shattering on the hard marble of the floor, bits of plastic and microchip scattering. A pillar of silvery light stood where the Diadem had been. And it . . . sang.

Slowly he dropped to his knees, and his rifle clattered to the stone as well. The sound echoed inside his head, and he could feel the column expand—feel it passing through his face and body, like the breath of a cool wind *inside* him. The sound rose to a piercing note and vanished.

So did the lights. He fumbled at his belt and clicked on his flashlight. *That* worked. Unfortunately what it showed was an empty case—oh, the pictures were still there, and the little display screen with the background story running on a video loop.

"Shit!"

But the *Diadem* was gone. The single most unique and valuable artifact on Earth, and it was gone. On *his* watch.

He was cursing when he noticed the perfectly cylindrical hole that had been drilled through the ceiling, the floor above, and all the way through to the roof.

"Shit!"

Venus, Gagarin Continent
Jamestown Extraterritorial Zone
May 18, 2000 AD

"Dad! *Dad!*"

Marc Vitrac looked up from his papers. For a moment he frowned, and then the desperation in his son's voice turned the father's expression to a questioning one. It was late afternoon, with the sun sinking in the east across the walled garden outside the French doors, and the scents of the late-blooming roses drifted in along with cut grass and warm, unbaked brick. He'd been thinking of knocking off and making some jambalaya and dirty rice.

"What is it, eh, p'tit?"

Marc Vitrac Junior was twelve, shooting up taller than his father had been at that age and still all hands and feet and gawky limbs, bowl-cut hair a tawny sun-streaked mane.

"It's Mom."

Young Marc was trying to control his fear. His father didn't bother; he just dashed down the corridor to the nursery. Baby Jeanette was lying in her crib, chuckling at the mobile of dinosaurs and flying things above it, but her mother was lying on the floor beside the crib, and her eyes had rolled up until only the whites could be seen, and she shook as if with palsy.

"Calisse!" he swore as fear went through his gut like ice water, dropping to his knees beside her.

Then she sighed, blinked, and shook her head, and when she opened her eyes again, the woman he loved was there again. But the look on her face wasn't one he was used to: It was one of raw fear.

"Teesa!" he cried, snatching her up.

The strong, slender arms went around him, tight enough to make him gasp a little. Then she drew back.

"It was the Cave Master," she said. "But . . . Marc . . ."

"*Weh?*"

"It wasn't as it was when I wore the Diadem and talked with It. It was . . . *bigger*. And it was angry."

CHAPTER SEVEN

Encyclopedia Britannica, 20th Edition
University of Chicago Press, 1998

MARS: Biology

Although Mars was sterile until terraformed by the ancients two hundred million years ago, life on the Red Planet is, in a very real sense, "older" than that on Earth. It lacks the catastrophic mass extinction that followed the Yucatan asteroid impact of 65,000,000 mya, which marks the Cretaceous-Tertiary boundary on Earth. There is considerable support among paleontologists for the proposition that the asteroid was the result of ancient intervention, as neither Mars nor Venus shows an equivalent.

As a result of the uninterrupted evolutionary history, apart from a few subsequently introduced mammals, the lineages of most Martian species run back without interruption to the most successful of the late-Cretaceous introductions, birds, and the closely related birdlike therapod dinosaurs. All are warm-blooded, all exhibit cooperative care for eggs and young, and many are social. While few are large—the largest terrestrial species is comparable to a bison in body mass—the brain-to-body ratio is, on average, comparable or superior to modern Terran mammals. This, however, may be in part due to the widespread biological engineering of the Crimson Dynasty period, which "uplifted" many species to make them more useful as domesticates. Subsequently many escaped and spread their genes.

Mars, City of Dvor Il-Adazar (Olympus Mons)
Chamber of Memory
May 19, 2000 AD

If the Thoughtful Grace on duty outside the personal chambers could have seen him now, Sajir sa-Tomond knew they would have dragged him bodily back to his bed and drugged him to keep him as quiet as the physicians wished . . . and then taken the Knife of Apology to their throats. Particularly their commander Adwa sa-Soj; she was young and zealous, sometimes beyond reason.

The thought made him smile a little as he sat back and let the tendrils grope toward the entry point on the back of his neck. Usually that contact was soothing; now he could feel the agitation that swept through the great protein machines that stored and manipulated data. He groped backward through layers of memory, the minds of predecessor after predecessor, until he reached the earliest days of the Age of Dissonance, the beginnings of the long decline.

Images flickered through his mind; the silverlike filigree of the Invisible Crown, and the experience of wearing it.

I feel intense pride in being her progenitor, he thought. *To survive that without training, without assistance . . . this represents a degree of eugenic fitness unprecedented for hundreds of generations!*

He had spent little time on the matter of the Crown. Even as his Lineage reckoned time, it had been lost for a very long while. But now . . .

Now I must know. Show me!

Mars, the lost city of Rema-Dza
May 19, 2000 AD

"God, is she going to be okay?" Jeremy asked anxiously.

They'd all recovered from that weird momentary blackout, not even headaches or anything else beyond a few bumps and scrapes from falling. His watch said it had been a few seconds, though somehow it *felt* longer.

All except Teyud. *She* was still unconscious, resting on a nest of silks and furs in the antechamber. Baid knelt on her other side, applying the contents of the *Traveler*'s first-aid kit, much of it alive and wriggling. If you didn't have a doctor on Mars, an engineer was the next best thing; they were the closest thing to vets anyway. The largest single item was a weird little creature with vestigial gripping paws and a bottle implanted in its back; it plugged into Teyud's jugular and dripped fluids into her system. Every once in a while, you had to top up the bottle with water mixed with nutrient powder.

Jeremy found that even the squirming bait-box look of the Martian medical devices didn't bother him now; he was simply too afraid. It wasn't like fearing danger to himself, and to his surprise it was worse because of the added helplessness.

Does her face look better? A little less waxy? Or am I fooling myself?

Baid withdrew a worm from one of Teyud's nostrils and looked at it. "Her temperature is rising, although still a percentile below normal. I would speculate that blood flow to the extremities returns."

She peeled back an eyelid. "And pupil reaction is better, but only slightly; there may be neurological damage. There is little we can do but wait and apply hydration."

"I . . ." Jeremy groped for the words in Demotic. "I anticipate improvement with intense desire for favorable outcomes."

Baid nodded as she stowed the devices in the box and rose, dusting off the knees of her robe.

"I also entertain emotions of affectionate respect for this Thoughtful Grace," Baid replied. "Even beyond the necessary terrified awe one feels at the display of Imperial *tembst* thought to be fictional or long-lost, and its response to her genome. Teyud za-Zhalt has repaired my economic status beyond reasonable anticipation—I will purchase the *Traveler* myself and enjoy sufficient security of income to breed and perpetuate my lineage."

A group of *De'ming* pulled a sled through the chamber, with a crewman following behind. They'd stash the loot in the *Traveler*'s holds. Baid looked at it with a small, satisfied nod: Imperial-era artwork and records would fetch impressive prices.

Even then Jeremy felt an impulse to wince: This was a reversion to nineteenth-century tomb robbing with a vengeance, like Belzoni rampaging through the Valley of the Kings with a pickax and flogging the results to collectors. Then Teyud moved slightly, and his attention snapped back into focus.

He held her hand in his; long fingers slightly rough with callus, cooler than it should be—cooler than the lower Martian body temperature could account for. Her eyes had a slightly sunken look, too. Jeremy wondered what he'd do if she didn't wake up, or woke up a drooling idiot, and swallowed convulsively at the sudden bleakness of the world that the thought laid before him.

"Damn, woman, don't you die on me now," he murmured softly. "I was just getting to know you. Yeah, we have absolutely nothing in common. That's the point."

Time passed. Jeremy remained, refilling the bottle of nutrient fluid as the slow drip emptied it and doing the ongoing nursing tasks; when he had to rest, he napped curled up in silks and furs of his own. Sometimes Sally came and spelled him, long enough to let him clean himself and change his clothes.

When he was alone with Teyud, he found himself telling Teyud about his family—she'd been fascinated by it—including his two sisters, his brother the jock, his father the physicist, and how his mother had played the cello. And about his life; high school in Los Alamos, studying archaeology at the University of New Mexico; the fencing team; the weird cave he'd found on that dig in Arizona, with the rows of skeletons hanging from the ceiling and the mummified body of the little old woman and her copper pot.

At last Sally came and put a gentle hand on his shoulder; Baid tu-Or was with her.

"Jeremy, we've got to get back to Zar-tu-Kan," she said. "We have to move her. The *Traveler* is ready."

He started violently, and his murmuring broke off. He coughed, shook his head. "Yes, of course, you're right. Let's—"

Teyud's hand clenched on his, powerful enough to hurt. Her eyes fluttered open and sought his.

"I heard you," she said, her voice dry and hoarse. "I heard you in my darkness and the darkness did not consume me, though it hungered." Then: "Water."

He held her head up and dribbled a little between her lips. She sipped, coughed again, drank a little more.

"Strange," she whispered, when he'd laid her head back. "This has been a very strange experience. I express astonishment, wonder, a sensation of psychological displacement."

"Are you all right?" he asked desperately.

"I am . . . physically undamaged beyond the effects of stress," she said, her voice a thread. "I apparently retain continuity of experience—"

I'm still me, he translated to himself.

"—but I feel . . . extremely strange. Aspects of my . . . mind . . . have expanded. As if empty chambers were always there but are now unlocked, yet still bare and unfilled, in which I wander as a stranger to myself."

"What *was* that thing?" he blurted.

Beside him, Sally tensed. Teyud looked at them both, and did the Martian double blink. Then her great yellow eyes looked elsewhere, as if they saw beyond the confines of the room. Her voice was stronger but pitched to a wondering softness as she answered:

"It was the Crown."

"A crown?" Jeremy said.

"*The* Crown. The Invisible Crown of the Tollamune Emperors. *S-smau 'i Taksim*. That Which Compels. The Crown of the First Emperor, Timrud sa-Enntar."

"But that's a myth!" he blurted.

Sally cursed antiphonally in English and Japanese. Baid tu-Or made a choked-off sound and went down on one knee, bowing over a hand pressed to the sand until her forehead touched the ground.

Teyud smiled at Jeremy, and with that, he felt she had actually returned; it was the same ironic tilt of the lips he'd seen the first day they met.

"Not a myth, although I had strongly suspected the same, despite . . . privileged access to information concerning it. It was not a literalized metaphor after all. It is an objective truth; simply one that has been missing for a very long time."

She touched a finger to her brow, tracing the line where the lower rim of the net of silvery metal had lain, or where what had seemed to be metal had rested.

"It has been missing since the beginning of the Age of Dissonance and the reign of Timrud sa-Rogol. The Supremacy whose identifying glyph rested in that wrecked airship."

"Nobody ever saw it!"

"Hence the name," Teyud pointed out. "It is visible only when removed . . . and only rarely was it removed except by the death of the bearer."

She took his hand and touched it to her forehead; there was nothing there to feel, except smooth skin and dense, silky hair the color of bronze.

"Missing since the *beginning* of the Age of Dissonance," Sally said.

"Exactly," Teyud said.

She gave Jeremy's hand a gentle, careful squeeze and released it. He flogged a brain that felt stupid with fatigue, and drugged with the endorphins of relief that had flooded him like a bath of warm water. Then something clicked.

"And which began when they lost it. Wait a minute! Wasn't . . . wasn't the Invisible Crown linked to the Imperial bloodline? Wasn't it supposed to kill anyone who touched it without the right?"

"Without the genome of the Kings Beneath the Mountain, yes," Teyud said.

Her breathing quickened, and she sat up; he leaned forward quickly to put an arm behind her, and she rested against it.

"There's something you haven't been telling us, Teyud za-Zhalt," Sally said grimly.

Teyud turned her head until her cheek touched Jeremy's for an instant.

"Which I have not informed *you*, Sally Yamashita," she said, her voice proud as a sky full of eagles. "I told Jeremy Wainman that my mother was of the Thoughtful Grace, and this statement was truth.

I told him that my father was of the highest caste and ruler of a city . . . and that statement was also truth, though incomplete. He was Sajir sa-Tomond, and the city he rules is Dvor Il-Adazar."

"Ooohhh, *shit*," Sally said, almost reverently.

Jeremy simply stared. She smiled again.

"I am of the Tollamune line, to an acceptable degree . . . acceptable to the Invisible Crown, and since I bear it, I am rightfully Emperor and King Beneath the Mountain, holding and swaying the Real World. Or at very least, the Designated Successor."

"You find the Crown, that makes you Emperor?" Jeremy asked.

Uh-oh, you meet a nice girl and suddenly she's a planetary princess. Life just sucks sometimes.

"The Invisible Crown is not found. It finds *you*," she said. "And chooses its own moment to depart. Often, if ancient records are accurate, at the most inconvenient of moments for the bearer. It has its own purposes."

Then her eyes snapped wide and she leapt to her feet; she staggered and would have fallen if he had not jumped up as well, and caught her by the arm.

"Danger!" she said. "We are in great danger. We must depart *now*."

Teyud allowed Jeremy to support her as they shambled back toward the *Intrepid Traveler*, even though strength flowed back into her with every pace. His touch seemed to bring strength of another sort, of a kind that defied easy definition. Sally Yamashita snatched up her portable as they left the antechamber; nothing else remained except the bedding—even the portapotty had gone back to the landship.

They were halfway down the sand-choked avenue toward the ship's hiding place when the alarm wailed from the tower where she had set the lookout. It went on wailing in the lookout's arms—they did, once you'd twisted their tails sharply—as the scout herself dove off the window and into space. The parachute blossomed out above her, a rectangular thing of boxes of fabric fastened side by side, swooping and circling down toward the street. One of the *Paiteng* swooped over itself to examine the strange thing that invaded the air, then sheered off at the high-decibel wail that hurt its sensitive ears.

By the time they reached the shattered wall of the gas storage plant, Teyud felt strong—stronger than she ever had in her life, as if her brain was moving like a mechanism of jewels and steel precisely formed. The *conviction* that the two hostile ships were close was strong; for now, she simply accepted that. With Jeremy at her side, she halted until the parachutist landed; as they did, the cable came taunt and the stern of the *Traveler* began to emerge.

Activity boiled on deck as the fifteen remaining crewfolk made ready to depart, but the crew took a brief moment to do obeisance—going to one knee and bowing with right hand on the ground. They had heard, and even the most ignorant knew what the Invisible Crown meant.

"Two landships approaching from the northwest, Supremacy, currently approximately eight miles in that direction," the lookout said, pointing. "Two-masters, large and low-built, apparently fast."

They must have waited out the storm, Teyud thought. *Probably in a hollow, and then had to dig their hulls and outriggers free of accumulated dust. They are between us and Zar-tu-Kan.*

"What is your command, Supremacy?" Baid said.

"We run," she said succinctly.

The engine gasped as the landship came free of the building, then subsided into a shuddering, panting wheeze beneath their feet as they vaulted over the rail.

"Get my harness and weapons," Teyud said to the scout.

It was not factually of much importance, but she felt more *natural* as she buckled the straps around herself and settled the sword and pistol. The quarterdeck gun was crewed and charged.

"Set all sail," she said, and looked up; the sun was a little past noon, and the wind was out of the northeast, about seventeen knots, she estimated.

The hands bent to the winches, sending the long, triangular sail up the mast and the V-fork the upper boom formed with it. The sail thuttered and then snapped taut as the impermeable sheet caught the breeze, wasting nothing. There was a burring sound of sealed bearings turning in their races as the ship leaned against its suspension and began to move.

I earnestly hope that no dust penetrated the suspension, she thought. *Spontaneous combustion at this point would be a very negative factor.*

Jeremy was beside her—not touching, but close enough to feel the odd, comforting warmth radiating from his warmer than natural body.

"What is your plan?" he said, offering her something.

She took it, and peeled back the odd metallic foil that covered it. Most Terran foods were either boringly bland or disgusting, but *chocolate* . . . well, that was a different matter.

"We run," she repeated, as she bit into the bittersweet, nutty stuff. "Anticipation: that we run until full dark, and then elude them by a cunning maneuver in which you will be of great assistance."

A sudden enormous hunger made her want to gobble, and she suppressed it with an effort of will. Her digestive system was probably in partial shutdown mode.

"What happens if they catch us first?"

"My custody of the Invisible Crown becomes the briefest in all the annals of the Real World," she said, and looked at him with her face blank.

He stared back, and then slowly began to grin. "You have quite the sneaky sense of humor," he said.

She smiled back. *I am not excessively apprehensive*, she thought. *Remarkable. Is that caused by the Invisible Crown . . . or Jeremy?*

Jeremy looked back at the four black sails behind them, holding on to a stay and shielding his eyes as the cold, desiccating torrent of the wind blew into them. Rema-Dza's towers had dropped out of sight, and the enemy landships were as far away as you could be on Mars and not drop below the horizon, which wasn't as distant as it would be on Earth. They were spread far apart—forty-five degrees if you used the *Traveler* as the central point of a circle.

And they were catching up. Slowly, but surely; a stern chase was a long chase, but this would be barely long enough.

"What, exactly, are they trying to do?" he asked.

"They are forcing us out into the plains of Tharsis, farther into the Deep Beyond," Teyud said. "Rather as in the *atanj* move known as "isolate-to-destroy.""

"Dvor Il-Adazar is that way, isn't it?"

"Yes. Unfortunately, it is three weeks sailing *that way*. Between here and the edge of the civilized zone is the most desolate portion of the Deep Beyond in this hemisphere."

"Oh."

"Their disposition makes it very difficult for us to turn back, because if we do—"

She held her hands out, palms vertical and one pointing to each of the pursuers. Then she brought them together with a slap. The gesture had an unpleasant finality.

Sally glared at the Martian. Jeremy suspected she had the same feeling that he did, that events were spinning out of control, but reacted to it more strongly, mainly because she was more used to making things happen than he was.

"What are you going to do about it?" she asked.

"Options are limited. No hills are immediately available. We might try to get past them in the dark, but our heat will be very conspicuous at night. Once we are in the *twom*, the flatlands, their superior speed will enable them to close with us. However, steep dunes would do, and after the storm there probably will be mobile dune fields sufficiently near."

"I don't think they're pirates, somehow," Sally said.

Teyud sighed slightly. "Perhaps not; though the ships are such as one would expect in that trade. There is a high probability that they are commanded by Coercives in the employ of political opponents of my father. I would leave the ship, but it would probably do very little to alter the fate of ship and passengers. If those opponents have pierced the deceptions surrounding my identity, they will leave no associate of mine alive."

"Isn't that . . . Invisible Crown . . . supposed to *do* things?"

Teyud nodded. "Unfortunately, from our immediate perspective, few of the things which it does are presently useful. I felt it . . . touch . . . my father, and some others. There is some chance that he will attempt to aid us. But it cannot control shiploads of those determined to be hostile."

"You're taking it very calmly!" Sally said.

"Displays of agitation would not increase the probability of a favorable outcome to this situation. The reverse, in fact."

Sally made an inarticulate sound and stamped away. Teyud shrugged, but Jeremy had a strong suspicion that the Martian had been teasing.

"You *don't* seem very concerned," Jeremy said.

"I am moderately apprehensive," Teyud said. "However, I find that the Crown tends to reduce this emotion. Also it has opened up—what was that Terran expression you told me? Ah, yes: an itch I cannot scratch. I have a distinct impression that there are great powers just beyond my reach. This is frustrating and distracting. It holds out the possibility of restoring *Sh'u Maz*, but my information is incomplete."

"I suggest concentration," Jeremy said, and then chuckled. "I also feel surprisingly little apprehension. I attribute this to feelings of relief that you were not injured."

She looked at him quickly, and then smiled—broadly, for her. "I find that one thing the Crown *can* do is determine the veracity of statements," she said. "Therefore I am certain of your sincerity. Your feelings of emotional bonding and commitment are reciprocated."

Even though he'd been thinking in Demotic for weeks now, it took him a moment to realize that she'd said something like *I love you, too.*

"What can we do?" he said after a moment of just reveling in that thought.

"For eight hours until sunset, we—interpreting "we" in the sense of this ship and crew—can do nothing except flee before the wind. There are no convenient terrain features here and we need darkness. Further east, perhaps. In the interim—"

"Yes?"

"In personal terms I suggest we go below and—what was your English expression?—fuck like bunnies."

Her voice lost that tinge of playfulness. "We may not have another opportunity."

CHAPTER EIGHT

Encyclopedia Britannica, 20th Edition
University of Chicago Press, 1998

MARS: Tharsis

The Plains of Tharsis (Martian Demotic: *Ferwarh*) are an elevated lava plateau on the Martian equator, the upper portions of which are primary examples of the Martian highland ecotone (qv) and possess the only remaining continental glaciers on Mars; the lower and middle portions, however, are among the most productive life zones on the planet, and have long been among the primary centers of civilized life. The closest analogue in Terran geology would be the highlands on either side of the Great Rift Valley of East Africa; and the long fissure of the Valles Marineris (Martian Demotic: *Tomek'a*, the Long Sea) has riftlike characteristics.

The rain-shadow effect of the giant volcanoes and the highland mass in general, however, also produces an unusually abrupt drop-off into extreme aridity, the condition known on Mars as the Deep Beyond. In earlier periods of Martian history, a unified global authority and slightly more humid conditions allowed irrigation to push back the fringes of the deserts.

Notable features of eastern Tharsis are the great volcanoes of which the largest is Olympus Mons.

Mars, the Deep Beyond
Tharsis Plain, west of Dvor Il-Adazar
May 22, 2000 AD

The land had been tending upward all the long day of pursuit as they skimmed eastward before a twenty-knot wind; now the terrain rose in high, steep dunes, sand that had walked when the storm came. The temperature had dropped with the rising altitude, and the air had thinned. Not as much as it would have on Earth for a similar rise, because of the weaker gravity, but enough to notice and to make Jeremy feel a little short of breath; they were up to a level equivalent to the Tibetan plateau, or the Bolivian altiplano.

Now that the sun had vanished behind the heights ahead, it was very cold; he estimated it at about forty below without the wind-chill, and still dropping fast. The occasional atmosphere plant was curled up into a tight, tennis-ball shape, like a man hugging himself to keep warm. Even the multicolored glitter of stars added to the chill, in a way he remembered from winter nights at home. Teyud stepped up onto the rail and looked east, toward their pursuers. Jeremy couldn't see anything except perhaps moonlight on an occasional plume of dust, but she was wearing those disturbing-looking octopus goggles. When she spoke, her voice was flat.

"They are not carrying their running lights. This is a severe violation of navigational regulations, for which a substantial fine may be levied."

Jeremy laughed; so did a few of the crew within earshot, if a bit nervously. They'd taken the revelation of the Crown more calmly than he expected—it was, the equivalent of being present when someone pulled the Sword out of the Stone and proclaimed themselves Pendragon, after all. On the other hand, Martians *were* generally calmer than Terrans, and they had thoughts of pursuit and probable death to occupy their minds anyway.

After a moment, Sally got the joke as well. "Send them a summons to the Harbor Court in Zar-tu-Kan," she said dryly.

The Martians all had their headdresses pulled tight; the two Terrans wore face masks and goggles, and Teyud her biological equivalent of binoculars. Jeremy could swear that he saw it shiver, despite the way it tapped warmth as well as blood from its bearer's veins. The wind was like liquid nitrogen whenever it managed to worm its way into contact with his skin, despite the thermal long johns he wore underneath his Martian desert togs, and his fingers were a little numb in their astronaut-style gloves.

Plumes of fine dust shot up in rooster-shaped trails on either side of the *Traveler*'s wheels as they ran along the narrow crests of the west-tending dunes; the talc-fine sand floated silver and black in the light of stars and moons, falling with dreamlike, low-gravity slowness. When the landship had to dip into the hollow between two of the great sand hills, the long swoop downward made his feet feel as if they would come free of the deck. Then there was a gentle rising-elevator sensation as they bottomed out and coasted upward, the sail going limp and then filling with a crack as they came out of the wind-shadow of the last crest.

It would have been fun if black-hulled death weren't following close behind, like surfing or abseiling down a rock face.

"They still there?" he said.

"Yes," Teyud said. Her gaze was locked on their trail, monstrous behind the organic bulge of the binoculars. "Their heat plumes are clearly visible through this device. They are approximately one mile behind us, and a quarter-mile from each other. If the wind holds, interception will be in . . . twenty-two minutes; by that time they will have converged to hailing distance from each other."

Baid tu-Or was beside the wheel. "They plan to come up on either side of us and board. I express intense hope that randomness and event move in ways favorable to your plan and your person, Supremacy."

"I also," Teyud said, dryly. Then her stance shifted to courteous-departure. "If I come into my own, rest assured that our association shall not be dismissed as insignificant. We shall yet play *atanj* in the Court of the Crimson Kings while the musicians serenade us."

She turned to the two Terrans: They might not be used to the desert, but their extra strength more than compensated. As did their gear.

"On my signal," she said. "It has been an honor to journey in your company, Sally Yamashita."

A smile at him, visible in the movement of hands and shoulders. "And from you, Jeremy, enlightenment and oneness."

He nodded, wishing that didn't sound so much like *goodbye*. Actually it was a Thoughtful Grace way of making sure the necessary was said, just in case.

But I'm not the result of a twenty-thousand-year eugenics program to produce the perfect warrior or ruler, Jeremy thought. *I'm a nice, peaceful scholar and I've just met this great girl . . .*

The thoughts made his teeth bare themselves in a snarl behind his mask. *Damned* if he was going to die, not *now*. Not with the salt of her kisses on his lips. Not with the greatest mystery of all time just beyond his reach.

"Ten minutes," Teyud said. She pointed ahead, marking a spot for Baid. "We shall disembark at that crest. Halt after the next."

"As you instruct, Supremacy."

The minutes ticked by. Sally spent them checking and rechecking her gear; Teyud swayed slightly, probably doing isometrics to keep limber. Jeremy concentrated on controlling his breathing, which had a distressing tendency to escalate to panic-inducing panting.

"Ten seconds," Teyud said.

Baid pointed, and the two crewfolk beside the wheel spun it sharply. The *Traveler* cut left, swaying and then heeling over until the hull's edge hit the stops on the outriggers there; the suspension squealed in protest as its tendons were stretched. The prow cut the crest of the dune with a shuddering thud, more felt through the feet than heard, and a huge V-shaped plume of dust shot skyward from either side of the landship's bow, silver with the slightest touch of pink as it boiled upward to conceal the jeweled sky.

"*Now!*" the Thoughtful Grace barked.

They vaulted over the rail into the dust cloud. With the tilt of the landship, the distance to the surface was only ten feet. They landed, let their legs work as springs to cushion the impact, then dashed into position, to flatten and lie still, spaced twenty yards apart. Dust fell down around them, covering the black over-robes they wore for concealment and protection.

"They will veer sharply to follow," Teyud said conversationally—the enemy would still be too far away to hear. "Three minutes."

She was right almost to the second; they could hear the heavy whirring hum of the bearings, the *sssssss* of the woven-fiber wheels riding over the sand, the creak of hulls, and the sharp commands of the helmsmen to the deck crews as they adjusted sails to catch every breath of the wind.

And just like she said, they've closed in to take the Traveler *on either side. Maybe we can take them both out—*

"*Attack!*" Teyud shouted.

The word seemed to kick him somewhere in the stem at the back of his brain without passing through his ears or mind, and he found himself reacting with an efficiency no amount of practice could have produced. A huge prow rose over the dune above him, the long bowsprit first, below it the fanged horror of the figurehead. The great arch of the forward axle spread out to either side; the black hull suspended above it had a rime of frost that gave off a low glitter like the dust of stars. It was an immense thing, more than twice the size of the *Intrepid Traveler*, looming like a black cliff in the Martian night.

They were each to strike at the closest enemy landship. Jeremy whipped up the grapnel, whirled it around his head once, and let fly with all his strength. It flew upward and struck on the forward mast of the landship with a glutinous splat, gripping frantically with all eight tentacles. The long cord paid out behind it, and then the satchel charge was ripped out of his hand, pulling the fuse cord free as it did. A low hiss added itself to the screams and shouts; he leapt skyward, over the swift menace of the second axle and out in an astonishing leap that must have carried him forty feet.

Teyud had waited an instant longer; her grapnel struck the railing three-quarters of the way along the rushing length of the ship. She dodged a wheel taller than she was and raced past him; he followed with a bounding run that would have done credit to a kangaroo on Earth.

Behind them—a huge *crack!* And then another.

The harsh hot orange-white flash of the plastique exploding lit the desert ahead of him like a bolt of lightning; he risked a glance over his shoulder. That cost him his balance and his leap turned into a sprawl, landing him on his back with a bruising force that sent the air out of his lungs in an agonizing whoop and put the iron-salt taste of blood into his mouth. The sight was worth it: the great black hull pitching as the foremast snapped and dropped, and the second explosion ripping the third axle's connection loose from the hull.

The other outriggers tried to compensate and couldn't, as the great mass of the landship careened down the slope of the dune, over further and further . . . and then past the tipping point, the bowsprit digging in, the whole three-hundred-ton bulk flipping forward and breaking up at the same time. The massive inertia of the mass tried to decelerate from thirty miles an hour to zero, plank and beam and bodies and bits of equipment spinning up against the sky. Then fire flickered in the wreckage.

Crack!

Teyud's hand gripped his harness with bruising strength and hauled him erect. They ran on toward the other landship, to the figure of the other Terran where it lay motionless. Sally's grapnel had landed on one of the outriggers and the cord wound tight around it before the charge exploded. The single-crystal growth was immensely strong, but fifteen pounds of plastique was as much explosive as a six-inch howitzer shell carried. The spar of the axle shattered like glass under a hammer, and the wheel went bounding free to disappear into the night.

The results weren't as spectacular as the other landship's destruction. The vessel heeled sharply as the broken tip of the axle dug in, and the next two came loose with a scream as the hull scraped ground; blood fountained in a huge black spray as the suspension broke and ripped open its wrist-thick arteries. Then the landship pinwheeled in a huge cloud of dust, rigging thrumming and snapping in turn, masts swaying like whips and cracking under the strain.

But it didn't flip, and someone on it had the time to trigger a weapon, one that fired with a hollow *shoonk . . . shoonk . . . shoonk.* That showed impressive reflexes and even more impressive determination.

Barely visible black dots soared in their direction and landed around Sally, bursting with subdued *ptack* sounds.

"Fungus grenades!" Teyud shouted.

When he didn't stop, she tackled him and threw herself across his body, drawing her dart pistol and firing at the wrecked landship. Sally's body convulsed as he watched, then settled to a steady twitching that wasn't like any motion he'd ever seen a human body make.

He tried to rise and go to her. Teyud slapped the pistol back into its holster and swung him around westward.

"Sally!" he cried. "We have to—"

"She is dead. A spore must have hit moist tissue."

"She's still moving!"

"That is the fungus consuming her body mass, rapidly. When it bursts and sporulates, everything within a thousand square feet will die—everyone on that ship, too, unless they flee rapidly. *Now! Go!*"

The last was an astonishing husky roar of command. Again, it somehow seemed to bypass the horror-frozen surface of his mind. They turned and ran; after a moment he seized Teyud and slung her over his shoulder. It barely slowed his fifteen-foot bounds, up the other side of the dune and down into the hollow below where the *Traveler* waited.

He was barely conscious of reaching the deck, or of much else, until suddenly they were under sail once more, heading westward into night, with a band of purple across the sky behind. Teyud held him to her breast as he wept.

"She was my friend," he said at last. "She was trying to protect me . . ."

"She did her duty," Teyud said softly.

A drop of moisture fell on his face. He looked up, startled into alertness; Martians didn't weep. She had not; instead she had nicked her cheek with her dagger, and a single drop of blood fell before the tiny wound clotted.

"I too shed the water of my life for her, Jeremy. We were not friends, but we worked and fought together. I am grieved."

"We must reduce speed," Baid tu-Or said, after she climbed back aboard from a perilous trip down one of the outriggers. "Left-three and right-two are definitely overheating. Dust has penetrated the sealing of the bearing-races. Ideally they should be removed and rebuilt, but we are some distance from a graving dock."

They were on a stretch of what the Martians called *twom*—what the Tuareg of the Sahara knew as *reg*, a flat, gravelly plain of rocks stuck in a matrix of sand and dust. The plumes from under the wheels were lower here, and flew ahead of them with the brisk, cool noonday wind; the sound of the woven-wire wheels on the rock had a grating, crunching undertone, and occasionally a stone would split with a crack and ricochet off the planks of the hull.

With full robes and the head cloth drawn across the face the *twom* was almost comfortable, except for the dryness. Here and there in the shadow of a rock was a miniature atmosphere plant, the size of a golf ball when unfurled. Nothing else showed signs of life, and even the sky was empty of it.

"This is an unfortunate randomness," Teyud said—which was awfully close to whining for her.

Baid shrugged elaborately. "It is an old ship more suited to routine voyages, and we have stressed it to ten-tenths of capacity, Supremacy," she said.

"What is the probability of failure within the next fifteen hundred miles at current speed?"

"It approaches unity."

"And at reduced speed?"

"As closely as I can calculate . . . even odds. Erosion rates increase geometrically with the speed of revolutions. But they might fail at any time."

"Reduce speed, then. Our dice have given us a low number in this Maintenance Round."

Forty-eight hours after the brief battle, Jeremy felt the cold numbness begin to lift a little.

I wonder how professionals manage it, he thought. *Sally . . . she wasn't my favorite person in all the world, and I didn't know her that long, but she was someone I knew, and now she's gone. Just . . . snuffed out, so many millions of miles from home.*

Then, *Dead is dead, it doesn't matter where*, he told himself.

He flogged his mind back into alertness as the sail rattled down and the *Traveler* swayed upright again. Teyud unfastened the button of her headdress and pulled it back until it lay like a hood on the shoulders of her robe.

"Do you . . . feel something?" Jeremy asked quietly.

Her ears twitched. "Yes. But nothing definite. Frustration! I have a mechanism of matchless power, and I cannot use it effectively for want of sufficient information. I am like—metaphorical mode—some nomad confronted with a dart rifle for the first time, and reduced to using it as a club."

They stood together near the prow of the landship. Baked reddish desolation lay all around them. The *Traveler* crested over the height of a slight rise and down into a depression. Widely scattered over it were little cones of dirt with holes in the center. A thin stalk with an eye on the top protruded from each; as the landship passed they whipped out of sight into the darkness, rising slowly and cautiously back out as they passed.

"Why are we heading east?" he said after a moment. "I haven't been . . . focusing. But surely we could return to Zar-tu-Kan now?"

She looked at him, surprised. "It is essential that we push east. Dvor Il-Adazar is in that direction."

He blinked. "Uh . . . you're going to claim the Ruby Throne?" he said, almost squeaked, in fact.

"The Succession, at least: The piece must reach the end of the board to be doubled. Now that my identity is known, the alternative is running until I am caught, and then dying. There are more Coercives on the Real World available for my Lineage's enemies to hire than there are places for me to conceal myself as a fugitive without resources. Also, I now wear the Invisible Crown. In Dvor Il-Adazar that is a potentially decisive advantage; and the information on its proper use is there. Elsewhere, it will merely astonish the individual who at last succeeds in decapitating me."

"Aren't your—our—*enemies* also there in Dvor Il-Adazar?"

"I concede the point. But bear in mind that there I will know where they are."

"Urrrkkk!" Jeremy said.

Mother of God, I'm in the middle of a faction fight for the Imperial throne!

And Martians played politics for *keeps*; he'd had a sample of that already. But Teyud was right—this was the sort of game where you could survive only by winning it all. And their fates were linked; he couldn't run away even if he wanted to . . . which, he found, he didn't.

And if she wins, there's the archives of the Mountain, and all those early sites . . . God, you could spend a working lifetime there . . .

"What are our chances?" he said, surprising himself with his calm.

"Impossible to quantify," Teyud replied, putting one foot up on the railing. "Information is insufficient. But I do think that more searchers are abroad looking for me than those we dealt with. Zar-tu-Kan is a major hub; I remained there too long . . . no, just long enough."

She smiled at him when she said that, and they touched hands.

Then her head came up. "Something approaches."

Something turned out to be several dozen giant birds, eight feet at the shoulder, with long legs, thick necks, and viciously curved hawklike beaks. The crystal lances of their riders sparkled unmercifully in the bright sunlight of noon, visible for miles in the clear thin air, and the jewels on saddles and reins and the complicated-looking arrangement of bars and levers that did duty for the bits their mouths weren't shaped to take. They paced along with a quick, elastic stride, as fast as the *Traveler* or a little better.

"Nomads," Teyud said. Then she applied her binoculars. "Annoyance! Severe annoyance! Not all of them are nomads!"

She willed focus; the instrument responded with a speed and clarity it had never shown before. Most of the riders were in the dull maroon robes of the tribes of the Deep Beyond, equipped with sword, lance, and bow, their faces flat and noseless behind the cover of their headdresses, their feet in splayed moccasins. Many carried tufts of hair or strings of finger-bones slung from their lances; one had a skull on the pommel of his saddle, the polished bone set with turquoise and silver.

Ostentatious and primitive, she thought. *But the others . . .*

Five wore robes of civilized weave and had dart rifles slung over their backs; one looked as if he had torso armor under the fabric. They lacked the fantastic mantis elongation of the Deep Beyond dwellers, and she could see where the cloth covering their faces tented out over normal aquiline noses.

Jeremy looked at them through his own inanimate viewfinders. "That's significant, that they aren't all nomads?"

"The Deep Beyond dwellers are generally hostile to other breeds, but can be hired or bribed into temporary cooperation. I speculate that these are the survivors of the landships we wrecked, and that they have promised extravagant rewards to secure the assistance we see. The nomads are all warriors—no vehicles or children, only a few pack-birds and remounts. It is configured as a raiding party, able to travel quickly and far."

"Can they catch us?"

"If we were able to proceed at full speed, there would be a high probability of our escape; even if not much faster, the ship will not tire as the *rakza* do. Limited as we are, yes, they will overtake us before their mounts are exhausted."

She looked over at Baid tu-Or. "If they catch us, the consequences will be negative."

"Painfully and with decisive fatality," the engineer said with a sigh and nodded. "We must risk damage to the bearings, and see how randomness dictates our roll of the dice."

"Make all sail!" Teyud called.

The sail slatted up to expose its full surface as the crew spun the cranks on the deck winches. The *Traveler* heeled, and began to accelerate again, and the blunt wedge of riders fell farther behind. She cocked an ear toward the outriggers; Teyud did so too, but she could detect no change in the hum of the bearing-races. Of course, they would only begin to whine sharply just before they failed.

Something itched at the back of Teyud's mind, like a scab or the way your gums felt when a new tooth was coming in to replace one knocked out. Instead of commanding the binoculars back into their container, she turned her gaze skyward, careful to avoid the sun. After a long moment she sighed in vexation.

"It is fortunate that I have not played the Game of Life for large stakes of late," she said.

"Why?" Jeremy said.

"I would undoubtedly have lost heavily," she said, and pointed upward.

"Uh-oh!"

A flier was hanging in the sun at high altitude to stay invisible from the ground, and could be glimpsed only from the corner of the eye, but it was unmistakable. She looked at her lover; he was feeling fear, she could sense, but controlling it tightly—and without the re-signed fatalism she felt from the rest of the crew, who had mostly de-cided that they were effectively dead. They were muted colors, but the strength of will *blazed* from Jeremy. She warmed her self at it for a moment.

"What else could go wrong?" he said, with a wry smile.

The bearings began to whine.

I had to ask, Jeremy thought, a half-hour later. *I really had to ask, didn't I? Oh, hell, at least being threatened with death's got me out of my funk.*

He glanced sideways at Teyud, who was supervising the crew as they put up spiked mesh antiboarding panels all along the bul-warks. The smell of frying lubrication was still strong, although there weren't any more flames, just a trickle of acrid smoke from the joints where the wheels joined the axles. The Thoughtful Grace checked the fastenings, nodded in satisfaction, and spoke:

"We have a superior position and better weapons. The nomads will not press an attack in the face of heavy losses. Resist strongly and fight for your lives; much depends on the combat rolls for each move."

To Jeremy's surprise, the Martians gave a brief cheer—not something he'd heard very often on this planet. Baid tu-Or went down on one knee, placing the palm of one hand on the deck and bending her head. The others followed suit.

"Guide us according to *Sh'u Maz*, Supremacy!" they chorused, and then rose and waited.

The nomads and their employers were at their ease a thousand yards or so away from the stranded landship. Teyud looked at them, frowned, and went to the dart caster on the quarterdeck.

"Give them two rounds," she said. "Miss, but not by an exces-sive amount."

The crewman nodded and inserted a magazine into the lips of the feed tray; it sucked the ammunition in with a wet, smacking sound. The long barrel swung around and he squeezed the handles to ignite the methane in the combustion chamber.

Ptank!

One of the nomads' *rakza* screeched like a calliope and danced backward as the metallic crystal slug slammed into the sand between its clawed feet and raised a head-high plume of red dust.

Ptank!

Another nomad pitched out of the saddle with a screech as the lance shattered in her hand, scattering jagged fragments for yards around; another of the Deep Beyond dwellers ran screaming with a six-inch splinter pinning his robe to his meager buttocks. The rest of them retired; many seemed to be laughing.

"That was an excellent shot," Teyud said.

The gunner shrugged, with a slight smile. "Random," he said.

"Aiming to miss?" Jeremy said softly.

Mind you, I'm glad, he thought. *If there's one thing about Teyud I'm not in love with, it's that she's sorta-kinda casual about killing people.*

"Nomads can be deterred by casualties," she said quietly. "Alternatively, they can be enraged by the loss of lineage members, and moved to irrational frenzies as they attempt revenge. It is—what did you say the English expression was for difficult-to-calculate aspects of randomness?"

"A toss-up?" he said. Then in English: "The way our luck breaks."

There wasn't really any word in Demotic that exactly corresponded to "luck," whether good or bad; Martians didn't anthropomorphize impersonal forces at all, not even as a metaphor. That made a surprising amount of difference, when you started thinking in this language; and if your native tongue was from Earth, it made for an occasional mental stutter, like stubbing your toe.

"A useful idiom. Now let us attempt to communicate."

One of the hands ran a flag up the mast—a rectangle colored like a candy-cane in red, white, and purple. Unlike Earth, they didn't use the same visual signal for "I surrender" and "let's talk," which also said something about Martians.

That started an argument over in the enemy camp, nomads against employers. At last the standard-form Martians adopted the spread-armed pose with head turned away that meant "reluctant acquiescence." One of the nomads put an equivalent pennant on his lance, and he and a standard-form rode forward, the quick pacing step of their *rakza* covering the ground faster than a horse could move on Earth.

Teyud vaulted over the rail of the *Traveler*, and Jeremy followed, after a sip at his canteen to wet a mouth that felt as if it had been stuffed with cotton wool. Half the crewfolk covered them with dart rifles, and the three who manned the heavy darter did the same from behind their weapon's shield; the other six kept a careful lookout all around, with Baid tu-Or watching both.

Checking for nomads crawling up with knives between their teeth, Jeremy thought. *Mother of God, this is far too much like those damned movies about the so-called archaeologist.*

Sally had said that, too. *And look what happened to her,* he thought grimly. *We didn't have the scriptwriter on our side.*

"Won't these guys respect a flag of truce?" he said to Teyud.

"They will, unless they see a substantial advantage in doing otherwise. They are not noted for taking the long view of such matters. And they *are* known for their whimsical sense of humor."

"Christ, that's reassuring," Jeremy muttered in English.

The two *rakza* riders drew up; as they approached you could see how the long levers at either side of the bird's head pressed at the base of its mouth when the reins were pulled. The birds shook their heads and made low fluting sounds of resentment when their masters reined them in. The nomad's mount cocked its head at Jeremy and looked at him speculatively, rather in the way a robin did at a nice juicy worm; since its eye level was eight feet in the air, he didn't find that reassuring.

"*Eeeeat?*" it said, in a voice like a giant parrot crossed with an operatic soprano. "*Feeeed?*"

"Shut up!" the nomad said in his guttural dialect, and bashed it over the head with the flexible tapering steel rod that was his equivalent of a riding crop.

"*Owww!* Good bird, good bird! *Owww!* Foooood, master," it replied. "*Hungry*, master."

The nomad struck it again, and it hunched its head down and fell silent, giving an impression that it was sulking as it rocked slightly from foot to foot making an *oww-oww-oww* sound. The same beady eye stayed trained on Jeremy; he found its stare distracting, given its announced intentions. So were the great hooked beaks only a few yards away, and the six-inch claws on the yellow-scaled feet that flexed as the birds thoughtfully clutched at the soil.

The nomad chief reversed his lance and ceremoniously stabbed the blade into the bare desert dirt, a sign of peaceful intentions. Jeremy thought the effect was spoiled by the jewel-decorated skull on the high pommel of his saddle. Then he unbuttoned the face cover of his headdress and let it fall to one side. That was alarming in itself; the creature had reddish brown skin like cured leather, and no nose—simply two slits that showed a feathery white lining when they flared and snorted out twin jets of dust. His eyes were huge and pink, without any white, and two small tusks showed over his upper lip.

The type was adapted to the Deep Beyond. And one of the *Traveler*'s crew had been a hybrid between this and the standard Martian variety; it made you wonder about *somebody's* tastes, or exactly how that had happened . . . which was an image he really didn't want in his head, come to think of it.

The Martian beside him swung up the visor of his helmet. That was a shock as well, because of how closely he resembled Teyud, down to the yellow eyes and hair the color of raw bronze. His face showed a great scabbed-over graze on one side, too, and slightly puffed lips. The sort of injuries you'd get if you survived the crash of a landship at speed.

She looked at him sharply, then unfastened and shook back the sleeves of her robe, holding up her arms so that the long swirling red-and-black patterns that ran from the inner side of her wrists to the elbow joints were visible. The man did the same, and the marks were identical—even a little more vivid.

"Faran sa-Yaji, Independent Contractor of Coercive Violence in Wai-Zang-Ekk," the man said. "I require your life in fulfillment of my contractual obligations, and for reasons of personal satisfaction."

Teyud looked at him with one thin brow arched. "For *money*, Faran sa-Yaji? The Thoughtful Grace do not sell themselves for a bowl of *to'a*. *Sh'u Maz* forbids."

The man smiled slowly; when he spoke his Demotic had the same crisp, staccato accent as hers.

"*Sh'u Maz* has become no more than a metaphor, while a bowl of *to'a* is life to hungry offspring. And you are more than even the whole pot. Also, my pair-bonded partner and four of my immediate Lineage were killed when your technically brilliant counterstroke destroyed our landships."

"We were bred as the sword of the Tollamune emperors. I unite their Lineage with that of the Thoughtful Grace."

"It is debatable how much my immediate Lineage owes the Kings Beneath the Mountain—they who dismissed my ancestors for lack of resources to feed them. In any case you are the product of genomic theft, rather than a purebred or authorized cross, as has become commonly known recently. You would be flattered at the resources on offer for your person—or, alternatively, simply for your head, Deyak sa-Vowin."

That's right, Teyud's an assumed name, he thought; it was oddly disconcerting. *I'll keep thinking of her as Teyud. That's the person I got to know.*

"Ah. Alternative open contracts, then?"

"Several, from several parties. The offer for your living presence or your ova is the larger, but I foresee unpredictable complications even if you were safely delivered captive."

"You flatter me once more," Teyud replied.

Jeremy pushed aside bafflement. *Someone wants her alive to use as a figurehead. And this jerk is saying he doesn't think that would work.*

The mercenary shrugged. "Even a puppet Tollamune would have influence . . . and might someday cease to become a puppet. I had some acquaintance with your mother, and if you resemble her in character as you do in form, you will pursue the perception of injuries with malignantly unreasonable persistence. You see the implications from my perspective."

"Logical," Teyud conceded. "But your analysis neglects an important input, Faran sa-Yaji."

He assumed the position of polite-interrogative, leaning forward slightly with both hands turned upward and fingers crooked; his ears signaled ironic doubt. Teyud went on calmly:

"I am also Deyak sa-Sajir-dassa-Tomond, and I am the closest in genetic consanguinity to the Ruby Throne. Hence, if you were to *assist* me . . ."

"But you are not acknowledged with a Vermillion Rescript,

swaying the Real World. Preventing this is the primary motivation for those whose contractor I am."

Teyud's tone was ironic. "Yet there is acknowledgment, and acknowledgment. There is acknowledgment by a sheet of writing material, and there is—"

She put her hands to the sides of her head. Her eyes closed; her features didn't grimace, but they went wooden as the strain showed, and after thirty seconds there were even a few beads of sweat on her forehead.

Suddenly cold white light flashed, but he could tell that it was somehow *inside* his head, as if ice water had been injected into the fibers of his nervous system, an echo of that moment of shuddering blankness when Teyud had first put on the Invisible Crown. For the briefest instant it *wasn't* invisible, and then it was again and that glimpse of silvery mesh and bloodred jewel was fading, like the memory of a dream on waking.

The nomad chief yelled in fear and flung a gloved hand up before his eyes; both *rakza* screeched like an predatory orchestra's woodwinds, showing thick purple tongues vibrating within their beaks, and reared back with their crests flaring in a threat display. From behind his back the crew of the *Traveler* raised a brief harsh shout:

"Tollamune! Tollamune!"

"Perhaps, Faran sa-Yaji," Teyud said, *"Sh'u Maz* shall become more than metaphorical once more."

The Thoughtful Grace mercenary went as rigid as Teyud, his face as blank despite the automatic skill that gentled his bird back into quivering stillness; the nomad chief's *rakza* continued to prance for several moments, and the dust drifted towards them along with the hot, dry stink of disturbed bird and the dusty white droppings it shed in its agitation.

"Ah," Farad sa-Yaji said. "That is indeed remarkable." A long pause. "It also increases the value of your head to a level metaphorically comparable to the top of the Mountain."

Teyud's slight smile was cruel; when she spoke, it was to the silent nomad.

"You saw, wasteland dweller."

"I saw," he grunted, red-brown eyes wide. "We remember from the very long. We fear. We fear very much always."

"Then listen, and believe: If you attack me or mine here, your Lineage will die, to the seventh degree. So it is sworn by That Which Compels."

Faran sa-Yajir shot the nomad a quick glance, and his hand brushed his dart pistol. The inhuman visage of the chieftain wasn't designed for showing emotion; Jeremy couldn't tell if the tooth-baring grimace was anger or frustration or fear or amusement. The only question it definitely settled was that the nomads were designed to be meat eaters.

"I hear," he said, reaching out to touch the grounded lance. "We will attack neither you nor him who paid us. Not in this place, not this year."

Farad almost snarled with frustration; then his face smoothed, and he adopted a posture of rueful acknowledgment.

"*Atanj?*" Teyud asked.

"Excessively cerebral, in the present context," Farad said. He gestured at the desolation that surrounded them. "I also confess to a degree of personal resentment."

"I concede there is neither soothing music, nor good incense or stimulating chilled essence to maximize the satisfaction of the Game of Life," Teyud said. "Furthermore, the professional and the personal can never be entirely disassociated."

"Let death and the sword settle it, then."

Uh-oh, Jeremy thought, as Teyud slowly nodded.

The nomad war party and the crew of the *Traveler* each formed a half of the circle around the flat patch of desert that had been agreed upon as the field of death. The four standard Martians who'd accompanied Faran sa-Yajir stood in a group around him; they looked ordinary enough, if you were referencing by a group who looked as though they'd started playing with knives at an unpleasantly early age and had been beaten up recently. He was giving them final instructions, speaking too quietly for observers to do more than watch his lips move.

They don't look happy. Well, if he loses, they're alone with the no-

mads . . . that wouldn't make me happy, either. I bleed for the bastards;
I won't say from where.

It was an hour past noon, and the temperature was up to about
fifty. Both the duellists had shed their outer robes to reveal loose,
soft trousers and jackets of cloth colored a light-absorbing matte
black; the coats lapped over like a karate *gi*, and were held closed by
a sash, Teyud's crimson, Faran's dark blue. Both of them tucked
their daggers into the backs of the sashes and took their sheathed
swords in their left hands.

"You're going to beat this guy, correct?" Jeremy whispered,
standing behind Teyud and to her right.

He offered the canteen, and she took a slight sip and returned
it. Without looking around, she replied:

"That is, as you said, a *toss-up*. Faran sa-Yajir is slightly older
than myself and probably equally skilled."

Then she turned her head, and met his eyes; hers held an odd
warmth. "If I lose, shoot him."

"I would—but you're not going to lose."

"This is an irrational statement implying an unlikely ability to
anticipate event and randomness, but still oddly comforting," she
said.

Then her head turned back, and he could see her body drop
into complete focus; not tight or tense, but every nerve and tendon
aware, the way a cat could see with its fur. She took three paces forward and went down on her right knee. Her hand went over and
across, resting on the hilt of her sword beneath the elaborate guard.
Faran sa-Yajir did the same, and his motions had an equal, daunting
grace.

There was a moment of thick silence, broken only by the low
ghosting of the wind and the wistfully hopeful *Eeeat? Killll? Eeeat?*
from a couple of the nomads' mounts. Half a mile away, a dust devil
towered into the sky like a bloodred tornado faded to ghost-thinness.
The sky above was absolutely blue, looking as if it would bleed if you
cut it, and the small sun was alone in it save for a few distant dots that
were flying creatures; there was no sign of the airship they'd seen earlier. Pink dust drifted across the circle for a moment, outlining the
two motionless figures.

"*Kill!*" Baid tu-Or said.

Ting!

The swords touched, slithered, rasped apart before the flung scabbards struck the ground. Jeremy's breath caught; Teyud was bleeding from a neat slice below one eye. The razor steel had kissed the skin just enough to part it, and a slow red trickle dripped down her cheek, like a tear. It stopped as they circled, eyes cool and intent.

Ting! Clang-tang!

Jeremy's eyes went wide. Faran had tried envelopment in low line, usually suicide against a good opponent. He'd nearly brought it off, though; Teyud had saved herself only with a lightning whirl and disengage.

Damn, he's good. They both are. She's doing better now than she ever did when we fenced, and it's just barely enough.

Their feet scrunched on the sand, and steel rang on steel; the deadly fascination of it gripped him, almost as strong as his fear—swordplay on this level was impossible to follow unless you were an initiate yourself. Faran made a double attack—stepping in with a feint, and then disengaging for the lunge. Jeremy would have tried for a stop-hit on the sword arm there, but that was a fencer's reflex, not a duellist's; Teyud had been right to use a simple parry. It was one of those things that was possible to see only in retrospect; he briefly wondered how she'd known it was a trap.

He'd noticed how Teyud had an astonishing ability to sense where the points were by feel alone while they sparred. She did; unfortunately, it seemed that Faran did, too. Possibly it was a Thoughtful Grace thing.

They were motionless again, nothing but the controlled rise and fall of their chests showing they were alive. Then Faran was moving, a running attack *en flèche*. Teyud parried and riposted in the same motion, the speed so great it wasn't even a blur, looking like a short smooth tap-and-strike instead.

Jeremy felt himself making a mooing sound of eagerness, willing the long blade into flesh, then groaned in disappointment as Faran parried in prime while still extended; almost impossible, but he did it, knocking her blade out of line, then lunged with a cutover.

He went rigid; that *was* impossible, but now it was impossible to dodge or block. Yet the blade only scored across Teyud's left shoulder, as she dove *under* the attack, throwing herself down and forward with one hand on the ground.

Passata sotto! he thought exultantly. *I showed her that!*

Faran's sword froze. He looked down slowly, to where Teyud's blade transfixed him from just above the navel to just below the ribs to the right of his spine. His face was gray with shock, but showed no pain as he crumpled back off the steel. The black jacket and the sash held back the gout of blood for an instant; then it came, and he crumpled, bleeding also from the corner of his mouth. The sword must have nicked his lung as well.

He sank backward slowly as Teyud came back to her feet, blood running down her left arm. Then he rallied for an instant, and sank down on one knee.

"Supremacy," he gasped, bowing his head over a fist pressed into the sand. "Rule well. Give *Sh'u Maz* to the Real World once more."

Then he collapsed; the crew of the *Traveler* set up a cry of *"Tollamune!"*

The nomads raised an odd hissing clatter through their nasal slits that seemed to be their equivalent of applause, and waved their arms in the air with the hands flopping limply. Faran's ex-employees simply looked at each other, shrugged, slung their dart rifles over their shoulders, and headed for the lines where the *rakza* were picketed.

Teyud swayed slightly; Jeremy started forward, as did Baid tu-Or with the medical kit.

It was the nomads' mounts that gave warning. They all looked up at once, crouching backward and whipping their heads from side to side with their crests erect in a spray of red-bronze feathers. Their fluting screeches were machine-loud, terror and rage combined.

"Paiteng!" one of the nomads shouted, and drew his bow to shoot an arrow upward.

A javelin punched into his chest and he flopped over backward, clawing at the ground and the shaft in his ribs. Teyud dove at Jeremy's knees and he went over backward himself, landing on the sand with a thud that on Earth would have knocked him breathless;

here it was just emphatic, but he grimaced as some of her blood spattered into his face. His eyes were blurred with shock as something huge flashed over them.

Then he saw what it was. *Paiteng*—shaped like an osprey, but with a body the size of a lion, feathers lemon yellow save for the black crest along its skull and a blue breast and belly, wings broader than an executive jet's, and a mad, lime green gaze. And strapped into a saddle between its wings, a man in tight-fitting black, a goggled mask across his face and a dart rifle in his hands.

The *paiteng*'s feet had been extended to grab at Teyud. She'd dodged just in time, and one giant claw closed on Baid tu-Or's head instead. Then the wings beat like a roc's in some tale of the Arabian Nights, and it was lifting skyward in a cloud of dust.

The little engineer's body stood upright for an instant by some trick of forces, blood fountaining from the stump of her neck. Then it flopped forward; the bird released the head and it bounced a dozen paces. Another beat of the massive wings and the *paiteng* was soaring upward in a blast of wind. Jeremy felt himself frozen in disbelief; there were more than a dozen of the flying predators up there, wheeling—eleven of them with riders, and two with empty saddles. The nomads and the landship's crew were scrambling for weapons, some already shooting upward. The four who'd come with Faran were already mounted, riding at full tilt.

A pair of the birds swooped to attack. The dart rifles of their riders spat, and one by one the fleeing mercenaries toppled to the sand, bouncing and landing limp as sacks. The *rakza* continued in a head-out race, their great feet flashing, and the *paiteng* wheeled around again.

Teyud hissed between her teeth, her right hand clutching at her slashed left shoulder. That broke Jeremy's paralysis; he scrambled three paces, caught the discarded medicine chest and brought it back to her in a slithering rush.

"Get my harness and robe," she said, reaching inside.

A bandage crawled across the wound and bonded to her skin, holding the lips of the cut closed; she swallowed three egglike things from another tray and cracked a fourth between her teeth, sucking at the liquid within. The gray of shock and blood loss retreated from her face. He handed her the equipment and she scrambled into it; he helped her tuck her left arm through the sleeve, and then she thrust it into her belt for want of a sling.

The robe was armor as well as clothing; it would stop most dart pistol needles, as well as some from the heavier rifles. It wouldn't do anything against a sword or spear or knife, though. He began to catch her up and lift her toward the *Traveler*, but she shook her head.

"No," she said. "They will—"

Something fell upon the landship from one of the paiteng riders, tumbling as it did. When it hit the deck, fire burst forth, orange and red; it spread with unnatural speed, doubly unnatural in this thin low-oxygen atmosphere. A dozen more packets of the same flame-stuff struck, and in seconds the ship was ablaze from prow to stern.

A bird screeched as a shot from one of the ship's crew struck it, then fell from the sky, wings fluttering, landing upside down and crushing its rider beneath it as it thrashed briefly in the death-fit. More javelins and darts rained down in response, and only one at-tacker was struck. Terran guns would have had trouble with those fast-moving targets; most of them were out of range of the nomads' bows, and hard targets for the low-velocity dart rifles. Teyud's lion-colored eyes were darting back and forth, lucid despite the pain of her wound; she straightened as the stimulants took hold.

"There is something wrong here," she said. "They are using javelins only on the nomads. And the ones struck by their darts are not convulsing."

One of the crewfolk lay limp nearby. She ran over to him, put her pistol down and felt his neck.

"Unconscious!" she said. "They are using stun darts, not lethals."

She repeated it in a great shout. The *Traveler*'s crew had been edging out into the open as they were forced away by the bellowing pyre of the landship. For a moment Jeremy's archaeologist's con-science was glad that the artifacts from Rema-Dza were packed in fireproof trunks; they might be buried but they wouldn't be burned. The crewfolk stood more boldly and took careful aim; knowing that the enemy couldn't or wouldn't kill you, and that you *could* kill them, helped in the boldness department.

The nomads had noticed that the airborne attackers *were* trying to kill them. The surviving ones very sensibly leapt into the saddles of their *rakza* and scattered like beads of water hitting a waxed floor. That left Teyud, Jeremy, and eight standing members of the *Traveler's* crew stranded next to the burning landship.

"This is not going well," Teyud rasped.

"*Tell* me," Jeremy snarled.

"I did."

He ignored the miscommunication and snatched up the dart rifle of an unconscious crewman. The simple post-and-aperture sight was easy to use, but it just didn't have enough *range*.

They're going to dart us all asleep, then land and take Teyud with them. And since they'll then be able to tell who is who, they'll probably cut everyone else's throats. Or just leave them for the scavengers.

"These are the ones who want to capture you, right?" he said to Teyud.

She was squinting skyward. "That is the highest probability," she said. "But I do not know the intentions of the airship."

"*Airship?*" Jeremy said—his voice was almost a squeak.

"The one we saw earlier. It has returned at very high altitude, and I think it is dropping parachutists."

He couldn't see them, but he didn't have her eagle sight; he also wasn't sure whether that was a good thing or not. Teyud had the same look of frowning concentration as before, and he knew she'd go down to death with exactly the same expression, still calculating the optimum course of action.

The *paiteng* riders saw the airship as well. They reacted instantly. Most of them started circling upward, their mounts clawing for altitude. Three came swooping down in long, shallow dives. The lead bird headed straight for Teyud; Jeremy fired at it, but he wasn't sure whether it was his dart or one from her pistol that struck. The savage glory of the *paiteng* turned in an instant to tumbling ruin, striking fifty yards away in a cloud of dust and a shower of great feathers and a crackling of bones.

The next two came on regardless, looming suddenly out of the dust. They were flying wingtip to wingtip at a hundred feet, the slow vast *pom-pom-pom* beat of the giant wings driving them along very fast indeed. Something hung between them—a net slung below a cable, and one end of that clutched in each great set of claws. Things were *sticking* to the net, a yard-long feather . . .

Jeremy's eyes widened. He reacted without thought, and *leapt*. The jump put him twenty yards ahead of Teyud, and for a moment twenty feet up; the fine-mesh net came rushing at him like God's flyswatter.

Darkness.

CHAPTER NINE

Encyclopedia Britannica, 20th edition
University of Chicago Press, 1998

MARS: Dvor Il-Adazar

Olympus Mons is the largest known volcano in the solar system. The Italian astronomer Schiaparelli first identified it in 1879 as a probable mountain often surrounded by orthographically induced cloud cover. It is a perfect cone, like Mauna Loa or Fuji, but enormously larger; the base of the mountain is no less than 400 miles across, giving it a surface area similar to that of the American state of Missouri, and a length greater than the entire Himalayan range. A rampart of cliffs some three to four thousand feet high and impressively sheer surrounds the entire base of the mountain and marks it off from the Plains of Tharsis.

No less impressive is the height that Mons Olympus reaches; nearly 64,000 feet above the northern-hemisphere sea level, and 60,000 above the surrounding Plain of Tharsis—approximately three times the height of Mt. Everest on Earth or two and a half times that of Ad'cha on Venus.

Even on so dry a planet, a mountain of this bulk has profound climatic effects, enhanced by the presence of four other volcanoes of comparable if somewhat lesser size, located within a few hundred miles. Frequently wreathed in cloud or surrounded by ground fog, certain altitudes on Mons Olympus are the wettest areas on Mars, experiencing as much as thirty or forty inches of rainfall per annum—although one should bear in mind the length of the Martian year. The light, porous volcanic rock absorbs most of the rainfall, which in prehistoric times emerged as springs, seepage swamps, and rivers in the surrounding lowlands.

The presence of water, timber, and relatively abundant animal life attracted early settlement after the introduction of hominids to Mars by the ancients in approximately 200,000 BCE; the area may in fact have been the site of the first introductions and the hub from which intelligent life spread over the planet. Mons Olympus and the surrounding plains were definitely the scene of the earliest plant and animal domestication on Mars, circa 40,000 BCE, and the location of the extremely obscure pre-Imperial Martian civilizations.

After several Dark Age interludes known only through the equivalent of myth, the "modern" Martian culture developed as a series of city-states spaced around Olympus Mons and the nearby volcanoes in approximately 36,000 BCE.

The city of Dvor Il-Adazar—the City That Is A Mountain—emerged as an early center of learning and trade on the northwestern (and most humid) edge of the volcanic mass. Its rulers, the progenitors of the Crimson Dynasty, conquered widely about and engaged in equally impressive engineering feats that culminated in the construction of the Grand Canal, which encircles the entire mass of the mountain and channels its waters into the productive farmland of the Tharsis plains. Building on this base, they had unified the planet's habitable zones by 34,000 BCE, the traditional date of the ascension of Timrud sa-Enntar, the First Emperor, and created a brilliant culture which raised the characteristic Martian biotechnology to impressive heights and established the classical canons of art, philosophy, and literature.

With the fall of the unified planetary empire of the Kings Beneath the Mountain and the slow deterioration of the global climate . . .

Dvor Il-Adazar, the city carved from the barrier cliffs of Mons Olympus and tunneled deep into its bulk, has no real analogue upon Earth. It is incomparably older than any Terran city, yet it has been continuously inhabited and is still the largest and richest of the modern Martian city-states—almost as if Uruk in Sumer existed today—and occupied a role similar to Singapore or New York combined with that of Oxford, Boston, Rome, Lhasa, and Mecca. The striking carved-stone terraces that fall from the mountainside toward the Grand Canal are only the most obvious part of this great artifact. Forty thousand years of building and tunneling have turned much of Olympus Mons into a complex of tunnels, halls, reservoirs, river systems, and underground fungus farms heated by geothermal waters, much now lost and unknown even to the inhabitants. Whole ecologies, natural and artificial, exist within them.

Few Terrans have more than the most superficial knowledge of its immensity, and its rulers, who claim the heritage of the Crimson Dynasty, allow contact only on their own terms.

Mars, the Deep Beyond
Tharsis Plain, west of Dvor Il-Adazar
May 23, 2000 AD

Teyud leapt desperately as the net with Jeremy's limp form entangled in its meshes swept by overhead, despite the sickening jab of pain from her wounded shoulder. The tip of her sword nicked one thread, and then the *Paiteng* were soaring upward, trading speed for height and flogging at the air with their wings in beautifully synchronized unison.

She rammed the sword into the sand point-first and snatched at her pistol . . . and then lowered it. There had been a moment when she might have hit one of the great birds of prey with a dart, but then both would strike the ground—and Jeremy would be turned into a bag of crushed flesh and splintered bone.

I cannot fire, she thought. *Odd. I cannot pursue any course of action which results in his death, even if survival dictates it. My degree of emotional commitment is greater than I believed.*

Instead she slapped the pistol back into its holster and watched the *Paiteng*-mounted raiders ascend in a spiral until they were tiny dots headed east. Then she organized the four crewmembers still on their feet to drag the unconscious ones away from the raging pyre that the *Traveler* had become, treat the wounded, and lay out the dead.

"Regret," she murmured, placing Baid tu-Or's head next to the body; there was a look of enormous surprise on her face. "You fulfilled your obligations in exemplary fashion; I would have taken great pleasure in rewarding you."

By then, the party from the airship was visible; their rectangular parachutes opened little more than a thousand feet above, and they landed in a neat skirmish line. Any resistance would be futile; there were more than a score of them. Her eyes still went a little wider at the sheer snap with which they deployed . . . and at the black combat armor beneath their reddish brown–blotched robes. Their leader pushed up the visor of his helmet as he approached.

"I profess amiable greetings, Deyak sa-Vowin sa-Sajir-dassa-Tomond," he said, and gave the salute to a civilian superior.

His eyes swept the battlefield, took in Faran's body and the manner of his passing, and his posture of formal-respect changed to one of professional-appreciation.

"I am Notaj sa-Soj, Commander of the Sword of the Crimson Dynasty, operating out of Dvor Il-Adazar, and tasked with bringing you to your father."

"I reciprocate your greetings, Notaj sa-Soj," she said, searching his face.

The kinship of the Thoughtful Grace was there, of course. But there was something else as well . . .

"I was not acquainted with my mother," she said slowly. "But you, I think, show evidence of close genetic relationship."

The man made a gesture of acknowledgment. "Vowin was my brother's offspring, and her mother was my first cousin," he said, and smiled. "This mission is both a professional and a personal-lineage one."

Wondering, her eyes searched his face, and then she nodded.

"This is a most satisfying meeting," she said. "I have been isolated from my lineage for a very large proportion of my lifespan."

They advanced and touched hands, knuckle to knuckle, the intimate greeting of close kin.

"I am sent by the Supremacy to bring you home," he went on. "Your father thinks this urgent."

"I am acknowledged?" she said, raising a brow.

"Yes," Notaj said.

He made a beckoning gesture. One of his Coercives came forward with a ventilated carrying-box; its color was dark blood red, with the Imperial helix sigil on its side. Despite herself, Teyud felt a prickle of awe. When Notaj opened the case, a bird-form used for recording secure messages hopped out onto his hand; it was of the same color, its sightless eyes yellow. It bent and touched its tongue to his hand, then to Teyud's as she advanced it. It blinked once, twice, and again as the organ recognized the Tollamune genome and activated the recorded message.

Then it spoke. There was a raucous undernote to it, but the voice was one she recognized from her earliest youth. It was an old voice, tired, but firm . . . and with an overtone of command that made skin tingle along spine and scalp:

"I, Tollamune Emperor Sajir sa-Tomond, the Two Hundredth and Twenty-Fifth of the Kings Beneath the Mountain, acknowledge the recipient to be my offspring: Deyak sa-Vowin sa-Sajir-dassa-Tomond. She is the closest genomic heir to the Ruby Throne, and my Designated Successor. Let *Sh'u Maz* be restored through her."

A pause, and the voice took on a slight gentleness. "And I acknowledge that Vowin sa-Soj was my chosen consort, who with my knowledge and consent and through voluntary intromissive reproductive union became gravid with the individual now known as Deyak sa-Vowin sa-Sajir-dassa-Tomond. Permission for offspring was previous and general rather than specific."

A slight gasp went up from the listeners at the last sentence; Teyud felt her eyes widen slightly. That was an unprecedented honor, even for an Imperial consort!

"Return to me, Deyak sa-Vowin. I will set you beside me and share all the heritage that is yours as well as mine. Let us together restore Sh'u Maz."

The Thoughtful Grace commander and his subordinates took knee for a moment and bent their heads; Teyud gently returned the message-bird to its carrier.

Notaj looked at her, a smile in his yellow eyes. He touched a tube fastened to the belt of his harness.

"And acknowledged also in a Vermillion Rescript—"

"Swaying the Real World," Teyud said quietly. "But I have acknowledgment from another source, Commander of the Sword of the Dynasty. Another, and more authoritative."

His brows rose slightly. She went on, "You know where I have been?"

"Working for the *vaz-Terranan* . . . the other faction of them . . . searching ruins," he said, clearly puzzled. "This was why we were delayed, besides the storm. We knew only the general direction of your search. Odd that the Terrans wish to root about among desolation."

"Not so odd as one might think," Teyud said grimly. "We found some things of great value in the lost cities. Some are in the hold."

She gestured behind her to the roaring flames whose warmth she could feel on the back of her head.

"But one, the most numinously significant, remains with *me*."

Teyud locked eyes with the other Thoughtful Grace. His went wider and wider, first as the implications of the archaic phrase sank in, then as communication occurred on a level neither of them had felt before. His olive-tan skin blanched, and he took a half step backward.

Then he took knee with his right fist pressed to the sand as well.

"Tollamune!" he cried, and his troops echoed it. Another cry: *"Sh'u Maz!"*

When he rose, joy and fear struggled for mastery behind the impassive mask of his face; she could *feel* it, as if a communications ganglion were engaged with both their brain stems.

"It becomes even more imperative that you be brought before the Supremacy immediately, given that *that* piece is on the board of the Game of Life once more," he said. His eyes flicked to the remains of the landship's crew. "What of these?"

"Your craft has ample cargo capacity?"

"Yes. She was designed as a transport, not a warcraft proper, though highly modified."

"They come with us. They have rendered me good service, and

they shall have reward—even if it is only enough *tokmar* to kill themselves agreeably."

He nodded, and she could feel his approval. "Your father would respond so." Grimly, he added, "Not all of the Crimson Dynasty have understood that loyalty must be reciprocal if Sustained Harmony is to truly reign."

"But I am not merely of the Crimson Dynasty's genome," she said. "I am also Thoughtful Grace. And that is something *we* have always understood well."

He assumed a stance of respectful urgency. "Then we must return you to Dvor Il-Adazar and your father. This is the maximum priority, and may be difficult to accomplish with the necessary degree of security."

"No," she said softly; her gaze turned to the east. "There is another priority. Fortunately, it takes us in the same direction."

I am coming for you, Jeremy, she thought. *If you live. And if not . . .*

Notaj was not a man who was easily alarmed. He still took a step backward when he saw her face.

Jesus, I'm cold!

That was Jeremy's first conscious thought as he awoke from dreams of smothering with a plastic bag around his head. Then he realized something *was* covering his face, and tried to tear it away. That brought another realization; his hands were tied together in front of him . . . and he was moving, a rushing motion that combined with an up-and-down surge. It was a bit like riding a horse, but the way it would feel in a dream where you floated along with the hooves just touching the wildflowers.

He blinked gummy eyes open; they were covered by his goggles. They didn't prevent him from looking downward, and the sight of what was on his lower face sent him into a jerking frenzy for a moment. It was a translucent bag the size of a football, swelling and shrinking, and it had tentacles wrapped around his head and jaw and neck.

A sharp pressure brought him steady again. *I know what that is. It's a Martian oxygen-mask, one that has halitosis. And I'm riding on a goddamned bird!*

He was strapped into a high saddle that cradled him fore and aft, with his hands chained by something like organic handcuffs or a leathery worm, run through a ring on the saddle's horn. The great wings rose and fell on either side with a long, slow booming sound, feathers longer than his legs splaying out at either tip; then they stopped, and the *Paiteng* went into a long glide. He could see its eye shifting back to look him over, then shifting forward again. He took a quick look to his left and right and saw a dozen others, stretching out to the edge of sight on either side, black-suited riders wearing masks like his own. He looked down . . .

Eeeek! he thought. *Good thing I'm not afraid of heights . . . much.*

They were at least six thousand feet up. That didn't sound like much, when you'd flown between planets, but you flew between planets in a metal shell, seeing nothing but a starry blackness through video screens and pushed along by hydrogen heated by a gaseous-fission reactor. Even an Earth-to-Orbit or the shuttle down to Kennedy Base was little more than sitting in a crash-couch and being squashed by high G's.

Here he was really *flying* in a way his gut had no trouble understanding, and on a bird, at that. The ochre landscape of the Deep Beyond crawled by below, and there was nothing between him and it but air. He could feel the great muscles of the *Paiteng* swelling and flexing between his knees, and even with his face covered it was numb in the rush of the frigid air.

With that he shook off his shock enough to be conscious of just how much he hurt; he must have been knocked out by the net striking him. That meant at least a very mild concussion, which was no joke at the best of times, and despite the best efforts of the animate air-compressor plastered to his mouth and nose, he was probably breathing less oxygen than was healthy. And the air was dry; the whole of his mouth and sinuses and throat felt like tissue paper that had been left outside in the sun, and there were the beginnings of a savage headache between his eyes, along with a tinge of nausea.

He coughed, and the facemask swelled resentfully and increased the pressure of the air flowing into his face.

Okay, Okay, I'll let you do your job, he thought at it.

Another of the riders coasted closer, twenty feet up, a move that required agility by both the *Paiteng* to keep their wings from collid-ing. Jeremy stared back at the dark-goggled eyes; it was impossible to see features past those and the grotesque organic lump that kept him and the other rider alive at these heights, but he could sense a cold hostility.

Uh-oh, he thought. *I wonder why they kept me alive? They must have stopped to transfer me to a spare bird. Do they think I've got hostage value with Teyud?*

A disturbing thought struck him: *And do I? Or will she just write me off as an interesting perversion? It was all pretty intense, but quick, and she isn't really a human being . . . No, Goddammit, she'll try to get me out of this! I've just got to keep my eyes open and think.*

The sun was sinking down the horizon behind them, and the far horizon was turning purple-rose; that meant they'd been flying for hours. It got colder as the sun sank and the stars came out; the vast desert below shone with hoarfrost for a while, as if it were scat-tered with diamonds, and despite the pain in his head and the gen-eral misery in his abused body, his breath caught at the beauty of it. Other *Paiteng* soared to either side, vast falcon shapes against the stars, their wings moving occasionally as they flapped to gain height, then straightening to soar.

He dozed, woke, dozed, woke, tried to ignore the clawing of thirst that grew to a torture like hot pokers down the throat. Then light showed ahead; the night was ending, and the sun was rising in the east. They seemed to be flying over ocean . . . and then his sluggish brain realized it was clouds.

No, fog. It's ground fog. But you only get that around places like—

Something stood against the sun. Something so large that his mind refused to register the shape for long minutes. It was the white cone of Olympus Mons, just barely visible rising over the horizon. A mountain nearly 70,000 feet high, 400 miles across, so vast that it could be seen only from high in the air. There were glaciers on its lower slopes, but the upper ice was carbon dioxide, not water.

The line of sunlight rolling out of the east broke over it, and over the silver sea of mist around the base; and then the mountain itself vanished as they grew closer, hidden by its own bulk and the curvature of the planet. The mist shredded into patches, and through it he could see that the Deep Beyond was behind them.

A canal far broader than Zar-tu-Kan's curled like an artificial Mississippi, vanishing beyond sight to north and south, a vast, shining snake under its glassine roof. Through that clearness, he could see the tiny dots of barges and passenger craft, almost the only place on Mars where they were used.

The Grand Canal, he thought. *All the way around the base of the Mountain.*

It extended through a landscape covered in swirling, orderly patterns of ochre-olive-green with only occasional patches of atmosphere plant. The rest was orchards of fruits and fields of tubers and the fodder that grazing beasts ate, and the glittering plantations where spars and axles and gears grew on plants that secreted crystal and monofilament metal. Domed mansions stood here and there, and towns, and roadways of tough reddish vegetation down which landships sped.

His first sight of the City That Is A Mountain left him numb, if that wasn't just the cold. It was too big to take in; mile upon mile of the four-thousand-foot cliff at the Mountain's edge sculpted into towers and domes, avenues and colonnades, terraces and gardens that were shouts of color and trees impossibly tall and slender, even fountains and artificial waterfalls—an incredible extravagance on this world. In the center, where the cliffs had swerved out into the lowlands like the prow of a ship, was one impossible spire that ran from base to summit, a mile of stone crimson as blood, shaped like a frozen tendril of fire, the Tower of Harmonic Unity. The Tollamune emperors had commanded its shaping when they united and ruled a world, in the days long before earthmen first put words to clay, or built anything grander than a thatched hut.

The air was dense with traffic now; slender-winged gliders, tethered balloons, airships of every size, riders on the backs of *Paiteng*. The score in the party that had taken Jeremy captive grouped themselves into a column of twos and swerved off northward from the Tower of Harmonic Unity in disciplined unison. They passed over the streets of the city, its gardens and its courts, until they came to an amphitheaterlike building a thousand feet across and circled above it. The glassine dome that covered it split in the center and slid back to either side, revealing a shaft in the rose-colored volcanic rock that seemed to descend to infinity.

"Ohhhhhhhh shit!"

Jeremy found he had the breath to scream as the first pair of *Paiteng* riders commanded their mounts to fold their wings and plummet like arrows. The column followed them, two by two—and he couldn't even cover his eyes with his hands as his mount wheeled and stooped in its turn.

I can't even get the gumption up to close my eyes! his mind gibbered at him.

The whole formation turned downward like a giant spiraling corkscrew, or a tornado's cone-shape—but one made of golden feathers. Acceleration pinned him back against the high cantle of the saddle, and the darkness of the tunnel went by with a rushing impetus that made his eyes water even behind the goggles. He screamed into the living oxygen mask, regardless of its fretful tightening.

Light grew in a circle below him, growing with speed that was even more terrifying than the original plunge, until he saw it was the end of the shaft and an exit into some vast, dimly lit space. A *boom . . . boom . . . boom* sounded, over and over again.

Then his own *Paiteng* was through, and its wings flashed open like lightning; and like lightning it was followed by the sound of a thundercrack *BOOM!* as air compressed and exploded beneath them. The saddle punished him again as the great bird killed its speed like an osprey ending its stoop, and then they were gliding along above the stone surface of a great cavern. It towered away on either side, a huge bubble in the fabric of the volcano; the birds flared their wings forward and landed, hopping to shed the last of their momentum. Jeremy waited, humiliatingly conscious that his full bladder had gotten the best of him.

Two of the black-clad Martians came and unstrapped him, pulling him out of the saddle; on Earth the drop from the shoulders of the bird would have been a bit of a challenge, since its head rested ten feet above the ground, but even in his weakened state it wasn't too bad here. Attendants led the bird off with the others; they flapped up onto giant perches that ran around the interior of the chamber, over sand trays that caught their droppings . . . and evidently recycled them, from the disturbing ripples that went through the fine dust. *De'ming* pushed a cart around, throwing the

Paiteng gobbets of unidentifiable meat; they grabbed them out of the air, caroling pleasure. A few simply stuck their heads beneath a wing and slept.

One of the Martians peeled the oxygen mask off Jeremy's face and threw it into a bin, where it crawled into a cell-like container and stuck its mouth into the feed line.

"Water," he croaked, after several tries. Then as the Martian simply looked at him: "Water. I'm of the *vaz-Terranan*. We come from the Wet World. We need more than you do. Water, or I'll die."

The other nodded. "We went to all the trouble of getting him; best not to let him die, yet."

Jesus, I wish he hadn't added that. "Yet" is an ugly word.

The other wrinkled her nose. "He is already very wet; why does he waste liquid so?" she said, but grudgingly held her flask to his lips.

He sucked at it—it was faintly salty, the way Martians preferred water, and there was a rank undertaste, and it was the most delicious thing he'd ever tasted in his life. Some of it went up his nose, but he didn't even pause to cough; he could feel his abused tissues soaking it up and coming back to life, like wilted buffalo grass in a dry year back home. When the hand tried to withdraw it, he bit down with savage strength to suck the last drops out.

The impact of the water on his empty stomach almost made him throw up, but he mastered the impulse, and after a few seconds it gave him the strength to stumble along rather than be dragged as his blinding headache receded a bit. The two who frog-marched him along were standard Martians; they were about his height, but normally he could have picked them both up and cracked them together like eggs. Teyud was the only Martian he'd ever touched who didn't convey that feeling of fragility. But right now, a squad of medium-sized kittens could have handled him easily; not to mention the other rider following along behind with a dart pistol aimed at his buttocks. It *probably* had nonlethals in its magazine.

So an attempt to escape wouldn't be really practical right now even if he was in tip-top shape. He concentrated on getting his wits back instead.

The huge chamber might have started as a natural bubble in the rock; hands had shaped it into a perfect hemisphere of maroon-colored stone polished to a high gloss that reflected rows of glow-globes, until it was like a great aquarium filled with diluted blood. There were about a hundred of the *Paiteng* there, including some so small that they must be juveniles; others were being flown in circuits around the perimeter of the chamber, or put through maneuvers—probably some sort of training or drill. There was room for many more of the riding birds, hundreds, possibly a thousand, but most of the perches were bare, and the sand pits beneath them swept and empty. The place had a faint ammonia stink, but much less than he would have expected.

One large tunnel with fretwork gates led out of the chamber; it was big enough for the birds to fly in, single file, and he suspected it cut through to the surface of the mountain city. Other exits were smaller, though still usually with generously high ceilings; Martian buildings were the first ones he'd ever been in that didn't make him feel that six foot six was somehow too tall.

The escort party took him down one of those exits, then into a room with something like an adjustable recliner in it, and enough glow-globes to make its smooth white ceramic surfaces shine brightly. A Martian woman in a white robe and headdress waited there; shelves and cabinets held instruments of ceramic and steel and living tissue that squirmed or just lay twitching slightly; there were colored anatomical diagrams hung from the walls, and several of the bound-at-the-top Martian books as well as the inevitable *atanj* set on a desk that was made from a single block of polished hematite.

It might have been a dentist's office, or a doctor's . . . or a torture chamber. He dug in his heels a bit, but the three *Paiteng* fliers lifted him into the chair, stripped off his clothes, and strapped him down, with his head in a clamp. The white-robed Martian came and looked at him; she had a reflector attached to her forehead with a headband and a thin furry-feathery thing coiled around her neck.

That was a *little* reassuring; the creature was the Martian equivalent of a stethoscope. But not very reassuring, since nobody here had ever come up with an equivalent of the Hippocratic Oath. If you wanted to torture someone here, you just hired a neurologist, or commissioned your own G.P. if you were feeling cheap.

"You are agitated, in anticipation of pain, damage, or death.

This worry is premature as yet. I am to examine and, if necessary, treat you. There will be little pain."

"May I have some more water?" he asked.

She ran a tube into his mouth. "Do not attempt to rehydrate with excessive speed," she said. "As so often happens, desire may outrun capacity."

Then she began *doing* things. Even the normal doctor-style prodding and poking was harder to take when he couldn't move his head; the rest of the examination involved things that wiggled and felt slimy and waxy, and they were applied in ways that were . . .

Intrusive, he thought, gritting his teeth. *That's really sort of intrusive.*

Occasionally the Martian doctor muttered something under her breath; he caught technicalities about temperature and blood pressure, and an occasional exclamation of "interesting!"

Another presence came into the room. A face leaned over him briefly; a Martian man—or so he thought, it was hard to be certain sometimes if you didn't have time to look for telltale signs like the Adam's apple. The face was not quite the standard form; the eyes were even larger, the chin more pointed, and the bone structure a little less frail. This one's silken, raven black hair was held by a set of jade-and-gold pins tipped with tourmalines, and his fingers were each capped with metal fretwork cups like elongated thimbles. Jeremy had never seen a Martian quite so pale, though. It was impossible to estimate the other's age, except that he wasn't extremely ancient.

The gaze was wholly impersonal, the face immobile even by Martian standards. After a second, it withdrew; he felt a few contacts, as if those thimble-finger-covers had been gently prodded into him here and there. The doctor and the newcomer spoke, but he had trouble following it. Besides their voices being soft and low-pitched by his standards, they spoke an archaic dialect of Demotic; he supposed it was the same one that colored Teyud's voice, but much stronger. If he hadn't had some acquaintance with the High Speech, he wouldn't have been able to follow it at all.

"With a *Terran*?" the aristocratic face grimaced. "Why not intercourse with something more comely, such as a nomad from the Deep Beyond? Or one of their *rakza*."

Another of those metallic pokes, and he went on, "It has hair over huge sections of its body, like a *vash*."

A *vash* was the little kangaroo-ratlike jumper, one of the few mammals to be very successful on Mars, if you didn't count the hominids. And if you considered being a fast-breeding snack at the bottom of the carnivorous food-chain to be success.

The doctor replied, "I am not qualified to speak to that person's tastes in erotic entertainment, but the evidence of parareproductive intromission in the recent past is plain. There are traces—secretions, hairs and skin flakes—on the Terran's reproductive organ and adjacent areas, traces specifically of an individual who evidences Thoughtful Grace ancestry mixed with the Imperial strain. The traces are from a female. I have never seen a sample of the Tollamune genome even approximately as pure, but the gene markers are very clear even to a cursory examination."

The disdainful face leaned over him. "It is highly probable you speak the Real World's language, Terran subsapient?"

"My sentiments of affectionate respect for you are also unbounded," Jeremy replied.

"Do not express insolence. Fear me instead," the man said.

He flicked a wrist, and something long and thin uncoiled from it. The animal looked like a snake covered in very fine feathers with a spikelike beak, and it buried that in his chest with one quick vicious stab.

Fire ran out from it. Jeremy could feel the flame following the tracery of his veins, until it seemed to be penetrating down to his capillaries, hair-thin traceries of intolerable heat. His body convulsed against the bonds, hard enough to draw blood from the padded straps. The pain was too great for a scream; he could only grunt. A few seconds later, and an eternity, he blacked out.

When he came to, the pain was gone; nothing lingered but an itching around the little wound. The blackness must have been over quickly, because the doctor was still speaking with an aggrieved note in her voice.

"I cannot be responsible if the subject dies," she warned. "It has already been stressed and dehydrated and, as far as I can tell, is somewhat debilitated. Also, its metabolism is not identical to that of our species, and there may be atypical and unpredictable reactions to even such moderate excruciation."

Moderate! Jesus!

"I note your concerns and will take them into consideration," the man said. He leaned over Jeremy again. "Do you fear me, Terran?"

"Yes," he replied shortly.

It was the truth, anyway. He *never* wanted to feel that again!

"You were in the company of one calling herself Teyud za-Zhalt during the past month, commencing in Zar-tu-Kan?"

"Yes."

"You apparently sprang into the path of a capture net aimed at her. Why was this?"

"To save her."

The Martian flicked his wrist again; the pain-thing reared upright and hissed.

"It is obvious that I seek your motivations. Do not try my patience with evasive verbalisms again. I have expended much patience over the last few decades and my supply grows thin. I desire to know—metaphorical mode—if you are a Consort, an Initiator, a Boycott, or simply a first-line Brute in this game."

"I . . ." He paused, feeling his way through the nuances of the language as if it were scattered with pits full of vipers; and he'd never spent much time on *atanj*, either. "I feel a considerable emotional commitment to Teyud za-Zhalt; a pair-bonding."

"Is this sentiment reciprocated? Will she alter her aims and behavior to prevent your death or excruciation?"

Oh, I really don't like the sound of excruciation. *It sounds almost as bad as* yet.

"I am not sure," he said at last. "She has explicitly confirmed it, and I strongly suspect that she is sincere, but I am uncertain as to the extent and degree of her commitment. I cannot accurately predict her behavior in the hypothetical case you postulate."

"Still, this promises some profit from an otherwise futile expedition," the man said. His head turned to the doctor. "I feel less revengeful spite toward my operatives than I at first anticipated. What is the likelihood of a successful infestation?"

"With the control parasite?" the doctor said.

She frowned absently as Jeremy jerked involuntarily against his bonds. Something sharp touched him on one arm, and he relaxed—felt all conscious control of his muscles vanish, in fact.

"Yes. Infestation for excruciation and death would be counterproductive at this point, although I admit it would to a high degree of probability be amusing and novel."

Errkkk! he thought.

"Subtle differences in neurochemistry and immune-system response make the probability of complete success no better than one in three," the doctor said. "Such is the record of the Imperial physician's work with the *vaz-Terranan* of the base here—failures being defined as ranging from severe loss of neurological function to death, continuing with new subjects even with extensive experimental adjustment. I have less experience and my probability of success would be lower, particularly on a first attempt. Still, it would be an interesting exercise."

Errrkkk!

"No, the risk of degrading the hostage value of the Terran is too great. This analysis is in annoying contrast with my expectations."

"It remains accurate, nonetheless."

"At times I wonder why I tolerate you, Daiyar sa-Trowak," the man said.

"My estimation is that the difficulty of finding another as talented and otherwise suitable as I restrains your annoyance below levels of malice lethal to me; also, that you appreciate that if I were easily intimidated, the reliability of my estimates would be compromised by a tendency to tell you what you wished to hear."

"True; it is rarely wise to succumb to irritation. Keep the Terran restrained, but restore it to health as rapidly as possible. Also, be cautious; they are extremely strong and often irrationally aggressive."

For the first time a little emotion came into Doctor Daiyar's voice; a cool eagerness. "I have never had an opportunity to study a Terran's physiology in detail before. The available written sources are frustratingly incomplete."

"Be cautious; also, do not damage the specimen. My patience with the displeasing elements in our relationship does not extend to that degree, despite your generally high degree of utility from my perspective. You are categorically instructed to do no dissection or other destructive testing, as yet."

I absolutely hate that word "yet", Jeremy thought. There was another prick on his arm, and consciousness contracted to a dot and went out.

CHAPTER TEN

Encyclopedia Britannica, 20th edition
University of Chicago Press, 1998

MARS: Political Forms

When studying Martian political history, we are confronted with a unique difficulty; there is only one living tradition, one political history, one political culture, that of the Crimson Dynasty and its derivatives. The reign of the Kings Beneath the Mountain continued for so long that it became effectively coterminous with the history of Martian civilization, and in practice no memory of previous eras remained. It is roughly as if the pharaohs of Egypt's First Dynasty had ruled the entire Earth until a few centuries ago.

Hence it is almost impossible to deduce what features are due to the multimillennial reformatting of Mars by the Tollamune Emperors of Dvor Il-Adazar, wiping out any previous diversity of outlook, and which are due to the subtle but definite natural and genetically engineered physical-psychological differences between *homo sapiens sapiens* and *homo sapiens martensis*.

In theory, and to a large degree in practice, the Tollamune Emperors were absolute rulers whose pronouncements were law and who had no institutional check on their own authority besides their "recognition of proper procedure," to translate literally the Demotic term also often rendered as "virtuous rule." They ruled through a bureaucratic structure that also monopolized the higher grades of *tembst*, the biological technology that formed and still forms the basis of civilized Martian life. And they directed the huge public works that made that civilization possible, and whose loss has reduced the population of Mars to a fraction of its level during the Imperial era.

Their official ideology—*Sh'u Maz*, roughly translatable as "Sustained Harmony"—bears some resemblance to Zhu Xi's neo-Confucian synthesis, but it lacks the transcendentalist elements and is rigorously centered on "this world," expressing more modest aspirations. Despite this, it does contain lofty ethical elements; the most remarkable thing about it is that most of the Tollamunes seem to have followed it in practice as well as theory. It contains only one mystical element, the presumption that all past Emperors were "present" to advise the current holder of the Ruby Throne.

Hence the predominant tenor of Martian political life, even after the breakup of the planetary state, has been characterized as one of "low-pressure despotism." While often ruthless, no known Martian rulers have been tyrant-monsters of the stamp of Wang Anshi, Timur-i-Leng, Francia, Mao, Hitler, or Stalin. Conversely, Martian history also shows few of the resistance heroes or "social bandits" of the stripe of Robin Hood or Hereward the Wake, or the many exemplars in Chinese history, and vanishingly few martyrs of any sort. The extreme cultural significance given to the continuation of the Lineage may also account for this. Alternatively, the alleged greater realism of Martian psychology may be a factor.

Mars, the Deep Beyond
On board the *Useful Burdens* above Tharsis
May 23, 2000 AD

"Who strives to frustrate the will of the Tollamune Emperor?" Teyud said, looking down at the *atanj* board.

As worded in the High Speech, it carried an inappropriate overtone. As Jeremy would have put it, she'd asked who the Bad Guys were. She moved a Brute to the central apex, a conventional opening.

The transport that Notaj had brought from Dvor Il-Adazar was of moderate size, but the captain's cabin was comfortable in an austere fashion; she sat on a cushion between walls of laced fabric printed with leaf patterns in pale blue and green, and ate fresh strips of *rooz* meat with crisp piquant chopped *faqau* and an excellent *narwak* paste of musky pungency for dipping. The air was thin enough at this altitude to be slightly bothersome, but she countered it by taking deeper breaths. That was sufficient if no great physical effort was necessary.

Notaj touched his finger to the Despot on his side of the game; it was the dark set, and so that piece could also be called the *Usurper.* Though, of course, a successful Usurper became Despot in all truth . . . and not only in the Game of Life.

From the outside of the hull came occasional thumping and scraping sounds. The crew were working there in oxygen masks, replacing the *Useful Burdens*' paint scheme with another that would suggest an origin in a mercantile firm of the *Wai Zang* towns. It was a necessary delay, but . . .

Her hand clenched a little as her mind reverted to Jeremy; she saw his impossible, grotesquely charming grin at some whimsical joke . . . and thought of his possible excruciation or death. Then she pushed the thought aside with an effort of trained will, forcing her breathing and heartbeat to calmness. So often, feedback from body to mind was as important as the reverse.

If he has been taken alive, he will be kept alive to use against me; possibilities for action will present themselves. If not, not.

Instead she focused on the passing desolation below the flier, where the line of a dead canal glinted as it stretched through unpeopled wilderness. It was obviously imperative that she favorably impress Notaj; visible fretting over an erotic relationship, and with a Terran at that, would not do so. Thoughtful Grace prided themselves on their self-control and discipline.

Sustained Harmony, she told herself. *Duty to* Sh'u Maz *and the Lineage, the Dynasty. Yet perhaps the* vaz-Terranan *have corrupted me in part. I become convinced there is also a duty to individuals for their own sweet sake. Though I overcome all resistance and reign as many centuries as did the First Emperor, it would be . . . deeply unsatisfying . . . if you were not there, Jeremy.*

"Three parties seek to thwart your father," Notaj said, making his first move. "It is a multiplayer game. First is a faction of the Imperial bureaucracy alarmed at the prospect of the Supremacy forcing them to engage once more in the lapsed functions attached to their offices. These, to a high degree of probability, are those who sought to kill you through their hired irregular Coercives."

The term he used carried overtones of "pirate". The two ships Faran hired had probably been pirates, or at least rather dubious freelancers.

Notaj continued, "They are prepared to wait until the Supremacy's natural life span ends, but the prospect of a young and vigorous heir continuing these policies arouses their extreme distaste, the more so as it frustrates long-held expectations."

Teyud nodded. "And since my acknowledgment is not yet official, they may seek to kill me and claim that they merely execute lawful punishment on the product of genomic treason. They will at all costs seek to prevent me coming into the public presence of the Supremacy."

"Correct. Then there is Prince Heltaw sa-Veynau, an Imperial Kinsman of great resources and a one-sixteenth degree of relationship to the dynastic genome. And runner-up in the last Mountain Tournament."

"He does *not* wish me to die?" Teyud said, raising a brow. "Strange, since he would be in a strong position to claim the Ruby Throne if my father were to fall without issue. But one would expect subtlety in a player of that level."

"His calculations extend beyond the Throne to merging his lineage with the Tollamune genome. An offspring of yours and his would be in an unassailable position, and he has ample time to socialize it through to adulthood with a parental bonding."

"And hence I must be preserved for the necessary reproduction."

"Your ova or a reproductive sump would do, but that would introduce a higher degree of uncertainty; the *tembst* is not faultless."

"Clarify his position," Teyud said.

"In the last decade he has been required to reside at court," No-taj said; that meant *not trusted out of sight*. "He occupies the Palace of Restful Contemplation in the northeastern quadrant, and possesses extensive estates in personality and as lineage head. Specifically, financial instruments, farmland, structural plantations, and water rights from the Grand Canal, and more near Long Aywandis, and manufacturing shops with the appropriate *De'ming*, skilled employees, and managers."

Aywandis was the nearest of the other great volcanoes, never a city-state as wealthy as Dvor Il-Adazar, but rich enough by any other standard thanks to the water it reaped from the air. It was a typical asset profile for a prince.

"He retains the maximum permitted number of Coercives, and they are of high quality and well equipped; most are of lineages long associated with his, rather than independent contractors. And he owns *Paiteng*-breeding properties and training specialists. Hence I consider his involvement in the attack on your landship, particularly given the nonlethal emphasis, to be of a probability approaching unity."

Teyud nodded thoughtfully. "You have maps of his properties here?"

He silently handed her a folder bound with vermillion tape; she undid it and began flipping up the pages, imprinting them on her memory.

"And the third party?" she asked, as she worked.

"The Terran."

"Of the, ah, Eastbloc?" she said doubtfully; he'd used the singular-individual form of the definite article.

"No. *They* are less of an independent factor now than when you were conceived; subtle but energetic and successful measures have been taken to contain their autonomy. I speak of Franziskus Binkis. His relationship with your father is complex and ambiguous, with elements of both mutual aid and rivalry."

He lowered his voice, and leaned forward in the position of clandestine-confidences: "He arrived in a most extraordinary manner, in the Shrine . . ."

Mars, City of Dvor Il-Adazar (Olympus Mons)
Pits beneath the Palace of Restful Contemplation
May 25, 2000 AD.

Captivity is boring beyond belief, Jeremy Wainman thought. *I'm going crazy in here!*

In the adventure fiction he'd read as a child—which nearly everyone of his generation on a Mars-and-Venus-besotted Earth had read—there had been plenty of heroes and heroines locked in various dungeons. The heroes escaped, and the various princesses, girlfriends, and sidekicks waited patiently offstage while the hero went through exciting adventures to rescue him, her, or it.

Yeah, except I'm beginning to suspect I *am the fucking love-interest who patiently waits,* he thought. *I don't even get a nice, dramatic revolving prison at the South Pole with the vicious daughter of the priest-kings waving a dagger at me just before the door cuts off the view that would keep you-know-who from going insane, at least, but I've got nobody to talk to at all!*

Though to be fair—at the moment he wasn't feeling inclined to be fair to the people who'd locked him in here, but long training made him look at things from other viewpoints—Martians were a lot less vulnerable to sensory deprivation than earthlings. Their minds didn't become disorganized as easily, they didn't experience that minutes-stretch-into-hours thing, and at seventh and last they could drop into hibernation or semihibernation and just doze long periods away. They wouldn't enjoy being locked up alone indefinitely, but it wouldn't be the sort of mind-destroying ordeal it would be for him, either.

They can put the thumb up the bum and mind in neutral, as the Brits say, he thought; he'd worked a dig in England once, near Amesbury, and he'd heard the landlord at the Treadmill use the expression. *But I'm not a Martian. I can't turn myself off, no matter how much I want to.*

Even Doctor Daiyar's brief daily visits had become something to treasure, despite her lack of bedside manner. He'd mentioned that, and she'd given him the hairy eyeball and noted that she was not a pediatric specialist. Adults here considered the need for that sort of reassurance childish.

At least the cell they'd locked him in wasn't altogether cramped; it was a piece of tunnel twelve feet long driven into dark brown rock, three-quarters of a circle in profile, with the bottom fourth cut off by the floor. A bench in the stone at one end held a pallet and, after some complaint, they'd given him a sleeping fur that let him keep from shivering. A hole in one corner served for waste disposal, though not as well as it would for a local. Terran wastes were wetter and more abundant, and it smelled a little even with the heavy ceramic plug in place. Another hole halfway up the rear wall over the sleeping bench served for ventilation; it was about the size of his head and covered with a grill—no convenient duct-work sized for crawling here!

The door was a circle that rolled into and out of a slot by the en-trance, and it had a little swinging gate through which they fed him the equivalent of bread and water—a mush of *asu*-groats laced with dried grubs, and a cupful of the mineral-tasting liquid that came out of the taps here. It was too salty but if you could forget you were eating instant mashed potatoes with dehydrated maggots, the food was tolerable—fuel, if not a pleasure.

Jeremy tried not to chew too much; the fact that he was so hun-gry helped. He wasn't getting enough to eat or drink, particularly considering that the temperature was in the forties, but he wouldn't die of it anytime soon. They'd given him back his long johns and outdoor robes, too. He suspected that if the doctor who examined him hadn't issued special instructions they'd have just ignored him. From the records he'd read, Martian jailers usually withheld food and water, forcing prisoners in long-term containment to hibernate to avoid starving to death. They were a lot less likely to cause trouble that way and it was cheaper besides.

"Goddamn their fucking superefficient metabolisms, too," Je-remy said, pacing the eight strides to the door and back again. "*I'm* not the product of two hundred thousand years of famine and chilblains."

Memories were beginning to haunt him. Memories of Teyud were too painful to dwell on, but memories of lying in a hammock on a beach in Hawaii sipping a drink full of fruit and topped by a little umbrella were also pretty tormenting. Not to mention the rich, meaty taste of a burger at Bobcats' Bite, the little grill off I-25 just north of Santa Fe, which had the best hamburgers in New Mexico. And that homemade potato salad . . .

"Or just having a book to read or a movie to watch!"

At least he wasn't in the dark. There was a patch of clear material in the center of the ceiling that gave off a diffuse glow for about half the day; he suspected it was some sort of fiber-optic light-distribution system, linked to receptors on the surface above. That would be typical Imperial plan-for-the-infinite-future *tembst*, expensive to install but requiring less maintenance than a glow-globe system; once it was installed you could just leave it for millennia. Unless you had an earthquake, all you'd need to do would be to make sure that the upper end didn't get covered over, and you could shut it off by putting a lid on it. So far they hadn't done that, so he could tell he'd been in here four days.

Subjectively it felt like a *lot* longer.

He kicked the door—not hard enough to hurt, though it was tempting. That didn't even make any sound, beyond the light scuffing of his boot hitting the synthetic stone. It felt as if he'd kicked one of the cell's walls, or the side of the Mountain. There was no sound from outside except when the little pivoting gate in the door was opened to reveal the day's cup and plate, which had to be returned in precisely twenty minutes. Nothing to look at except the identical walls and ceiling and floor . . .

No, he thought, with a bit of a chill. *Not quite identical.*

He went down on his knees and looked at the floor. There were hair-thin cracks outlining rectangular plates; the walls and ceiling were solid rock, excavated by the usual enzyme-and-gnawing-critter methods and then polished smooth, but the floor was sections of extruded-digested stone laid down as a pavement.

He put his cheek to the cold smooth surface and looked. Yes, there was a worn path from the door to the sleeping platform and back . . . just barely perceptible but there.

The floor was laid as a wearing surface, so it could be replaced, he thought. *Mother of God, how long has it been here?*

He shivered. It was a couple of hours until feeding time, and he simply could not sleep anymore right now, despite being chilly and miserable. He began an exercise routine to keep in shape instead, although he resented the calories it burned; leaping back and forth from one end of the cell to the other, and standing on his hands and doing back flips back onto his feet, one-finger-and-thumb pushups, and fencing moves complete with stretches.

A slight sound came from behind him. A clicking, chittering sound. He whirled, jumping involuntarily with his head just brushing the light-fixture in the ceiling. Nothing . . .

Or is that a little movement behind the ventilator grill?

That was intriguing. He stood stock-still and stared, letting his eyes go out of focus very slightly to improve his peripheral vision. Yes, there *was* something moving there! After a moment it moved again, and he caught a momentary glimpse of two beady glowing eyes.

"Rats!" he said, smiling and relaxing. "Hey, I could tame you guys and teach you tricks."

Although that meant he'd be here for a Chateau d'If length of stay, and that was another depressing thought. Despite that, he slowly inched nearer and nearer. When he was close enough he stepped up on the bench-ledge and extended a hand very slowly toward the grill.

"Easy, little fellahs, I'm not going to—"

Click! Jaws clamped on the grill.

"Shit!"

Jeremy jerked his hand back convulsively, swayed on the edge of the bench for a moment, then steadied. The animal behind the grill was about the size of a rat and he thought it was a mammal of some sort, as the body was covered with fur, not the feathers more common on Mars. But it had naked jaws with spade-shaped overlapping teeth, and a black-and-red nose above them that worked avidly as it took his scent. Paws reached through the grillwork and groped for him; the digits had black claws on their ends, but apart from that they were unpleasantly fingerlike. There was even a stubby thumb—not fully opposable, but nearly so.

"I don't think you're trying to shake hands, eh, are you, you little son of a whore?" Jeremy said, with a grunt of loathing. "I know what that means. It means, *That's food, lemme at it!*"

He pulled off one of his boots to beat the thing back through the grill—and if he hadn't already tested that it was unbreakable, he'd have been cautious about that. The ratlike beast retreated, but only after it had been whacked a couple of times. Then it squealed, a sound like *uisouisouiso*, and it was joined by others from further back in the ventilator shaft. There was a hint of squirming movement there, as if bodies crawled over each other and naked tails lashed.

Jeremy threw himself down on the bench, looking up at the grillwork and shuddering slightly, a thin film of sweat drying rapidly on his face and making him shiver a little. The thought of those *things* looking down at him while he slept wasn't exactly calming, but there wasn't much alternative. If he tried to block the shaft they'd probably just eat whatever he used, or take it away to line their nests somewhere in the pits.

"For that matter, they probably have some weird ecological function. Or the Martians used *tembst* to make them," he muttered to himself. "Icky I *said*, and icky I *meant*."

Then something else occurred to him. *Wait a minute . . . this city was here before the Cro-Magnons started giving Neandertals a hard time in Europe, probably complete with dungeons. That's plenty of time for a new species to evolve just to fit the niche of the smaller ventilation shafts. Including hands to open latches and fiddle with doors.*

Just to be sure, he checked again that the grill over the ventilation duct was solid, not detachable somehow. It was solidly bonded into the rock of the wall.

Then his eyes went to the waste pipe. The opening was funnel-shaped, with the actual chute about the same width as the ventilation shaft . . . or possibly exactly the same diameter; that would be typical. And they hadn't left him with a close-fitting cone-shaped plug to block it just to improve the cell's atmosphere.

He went over and pulled the plug up by the handle molded into the upper surface, and looked at the bottom closely. He hadn't done so before, which wasn't surprising considering where it went. But the area was suspiciously clean, at that.

Besides a thin film of mold, there were hundreds of scratches in the bottom of the plug. As if something with small, sharp claws on its fingers had pushed and scratched and worried at it, trying to get it to move. So it could get at the food beyond.

He replaced it with a shudder, retreating to the sleeping bench with his feet up on it.

"I really, really have to be careful to use the stopper every time I'm finished with the john," he said to the air. "Because the consequences of forgetting and then going to sleep don't bear thinking about."

Then he stiffened. *I have to squat to use the damned thing!*

After a long moment he said aloud, "I'm *so* not going to complain anymore about how the diet here is too low in fiber."

Mars, approaching Dvor Il-Adazar
On board the *Useful Burdens*,
May 26, 2000 AD

"Traffic thickens, commander," the helmswoman said.

It had been a long time since Teyud had been aboard an Imperial warcraft, even a transport, in terms of her personal life span; not since she fled the Mountain, and that one had been damaged, several of the crew dying. This ship was very old—you could see that the frame had been regrown in patches, crystal paler than the rest in the looping girders and circular braces.

Yet the smooth efficiency of the operation was a pleasure to behold, a dream of *Sh'u Maz* in living reality rather than dusty records. The scent was clean, too, only the healthy flesh and tissue of well-cared-for machinery and an efficient waste system.

"Course twenty-two, neutral buoyancy at seven thousand," Notaj said. "Ahead half."

The ship turned northeast along the curving edge of the cliffs and away from the central city, and she could feel an infinitesimal lightness as it descended; behind and above, the auxiliary engines wheezed as they worked the pumps, compressing the hydrogen. Valving it was an emergency measure, and would attract attention.

Below her, the lands around the Grand Canal unrolled, mellow beauty and ancient wealth; before her was the huge, shield-boss bulk of the Mountain, the long home of her Lineage . . .

Of both my lineages, she thought. *I must remember both the genomes that have shaped me. And the environment and other individuals who have activated that potential. It is not enough to restore that which fell; for it would fall again. A new synthesis must be made, if Harmony is to be truly Sustained.*

"We avoid the main concourses?" she asked, as the five-thousand-foot spire of the Tower slid away from the flier's course and fell behind.

"Yes. While an isolated area is more vulnerable to direct attack, yet in congested lanes an accident is too probable. A direct attack will attract attention and may reveal who is responsible. It is a calculated risk; an oblique move to enfilade rather than overwhelm the board. We are to dock near a country palace the Supremacy favors when he seeks solitude and quiet."

She appreciated the ironic ear-flip that stressed the word and adopted a posture of wondering innocence. The guardsman almost smiled in response. The engines gasped and wheezed as the propellers drove the airship onward. She stood quietly, her hands in the sleeves of her robe, watching the terraces and domes and towers of Dvor Il-Adazar diminish and the natural cliff face reassert itself. Long before then, only an occasional structure showed the signs of living occupancy. The last sections to be built were usually the first to be abandoned as water levels fell and population shrank.

Then a speaker on the roof of the control gondola opened its mouth, repeating the words spoken into the ear at the other end of the neural ganglion:

"*Paiteng* approach! From the north at ten thousand feet, accelerating. Hostile action, probability unity; attack formation."

"He dares!" Notaj said, surprised.

"A straightforward subtlety," Teyud observed dryly. "The quality of play in the Mountain Tournament is not what it was."

Notaj nodded, grimly amused, and barked: "Lethal Conflict Stations!"

Feet sounded throughout the transport as the crew dashed to their posts. It had been modified, and was no longer quite the peaceful cargo-hauler it appeared from without. A crew member threw open a hatch in the center of the control gondola's floor, and lowered an openwork turret with a heavy darter mounted below the gunner's chair. The gunner slipped into the saddle, strapped herself in, and worked the control yoke. The long barrel of the weapon rose and fell, and the whole contrivance hummed in a three-hundred-sixty-degree circle as the clawed feet of the motor pushed it around. Others would be deploying, another like this further aft, three on the port and starboard, and two atop the hull.

The main helmsman looked up. Thoughtful Grace obeyed intelligently, not in blind *De'ming*-like submission, and the whole crew was of that breed.

"He dares at the appropriate tactical juncture, Superior. The engines are fatigued; we cannot outmaneuver the *Paiteng* riders. If we seek altitude or distance, we present other vulnerabilities."

"Even so, he must feel that some factor protects him from personal retaliation," Notaj said. "We must protect the Designated Successor and . . . that which she bears."

The crew all gave slight, decisive nods. Notaj bent and put his face into a masklike depression in the control dais; she could see tendrils that frayed out into filaments too thin for visibility to settle on his temples. That would connect his vision centers with eyes scattered the length and breadth of the *Useful Burdens*. The eyes were budded from stock originally taken from birds of prey, and had considerable distance-viewing ability.

"Half the *Paiteng* are carrying foot-burdens rather than riders," he said; the intelligent beasts could be trained to attack targets themselves. "Perhaps incendiaries."

Teyud put her fingers to her temples. The wave of frustration was more than she could bear. *She* could only wait, a passenger of her own fate, even though she bore the greatest of the Tollamune treasures. A *push* with her will was like a shove against an open door that left her windmilling in vast emptiness that threatened to swallow her mind. Then . . .

"They do feel such protection," she said. "Not personally; their principal does, and has conveyed this. But they will attack with enzymic loads, not incendiaries. Nonlethals, structural reduction agents. They still aspire to my capture."

"You are certain, Superior?" Notaj said, rising from the viewer.

In return, she simply looked at him. He nodded, absently wiped the little patches of clotting blood from his temples with his thumbs, and began to issue orders as he absently licked them clean. Teyud strapped on a parachute; the rest of the crew did also, those who weren't already wearing one. Enzymes were more of a precision weapon than fire; you could tailor what they were supposed to dissolve. In some cases that was skin and flesh—or just part of it, for example the eyeballs—but in this case she *knew* that it would be aimed at the hull.

The Invisible Crown *did* do certain things, and some of them didn't require her to know how to use it, only to believe the data welled up out of some new pit attached to her mind. The fact *felt* true. When it was That Which Compels telling her something it felt *heavy*, as if it weighed more than an ordinary conviction. That was imprecise, but it was as close as she could come to expressing the sensation, even to herself. They intended to capture her, or at least part of her.

Of course, dissolving the fabric of a flier around you could also be lethal, if it was seven thousand feet above the surface. Hence the parachute . . . though even a severely battered corpse usually had harvestable ova if you moved quickly, while a burned one probably would not.

"Come about, set course north, drop ballast and increase angle of attack to maximum," Notaj said, ordering the ship to rise to meet the challenge. "All engines ahead full. Obtain neutral buoyancy at ten thousand feet."

Ballast sand rumbled as it spilled out of the tanks along the keel. Teyud made herself useful by extracting oxygen masks from the storage cells and handing them out; the one she applied to her face slid home with waxy strength, beginning to swell and shrink as it pumped pressurized air into her lungs. The landscape swung beneath them, and the nose of the *Useful Burden* tilted upward as the control fins at the rear of the teardrop-shaped hull bit the air. She took her binoculars out and applied them as well, enduring the double sting.

When she did, she blinked in surprise. They were far more responsive than she had ever experienced before, requiring no conscious control. Now she could see the *Paiteng* approaching, a full fifty of them, growing from dots to shapes as the great pinions beat the air.

We will not reach their altitude in time, she thought. *They were too high.*

And they were using that advantage, each file of four making a swift, banking turn and then folding their wings, making themselves into missiles aimed at the airship. Spheres were clutched in their claws.

Ptank!

The sound came faintly, from the forward weapons blister on the top of the airship, directly over the control gondola. A growl of satisfaction went through the control crew as two of the *Paiteng* dodged, tilting to either side—Thoughtful Grace were a fierce breed. The flatulent swamp-gas reek of burnt methane drifted down from the upper hull, the smell of battle.

Ptank! Ptank! Ptank!

More heavy darts snapped out, as fast as the guns could recharge their gas-bladders. A great yellow shape turned from a thing of deadly grace into a tumbling ruin in the sky, whirling as it fell, centrifugal force spreading its limp wings outward. Feathers and a spray of blood surrounded it. Heavy darters didn't just poison; they had enough kinetic energy to smash through bodies. The rider slashed his saddle-harness with a dagger and dove free; a few moments later, a rectangular parachute blossomed above, and he steered it away from the action.

Another fell, and another . . . and cheers from the darter positions told of enemy casualties not visible from the gondola.

I am more apprehensive than in any combat I have ever experienced! Teyud knew, astonished. She took a moment to control breathing and heartbeat. *This is unprofessional! You are a Coercive; this is your function!*

After a moment's thought, she realized why her mouth had gone dry and her heart started to hammer.

This is not an ordinary exercise in coercive violence. I have more at stake here than my own safety. Many others depend on my survival—in fact, the Real World and Sh'u Maz itself. The burden of responsibility is great, and my subconscious realizes this.

A lizardlike hiss ran through the fabric of the *Useful Burdens*, and then a thump. Fractionally later the speaking tube reported:

"Hit amidships, upper hull." A slight pause. "Enzymic load, well-tailored. The outer hull fabric is dissolving."

"Damage control teams! Counteragents to the upper gasbags!" Notaj snapped.

Before he could countermand, Teyud leapt to the ladder and raced upward into the vast dimness of the hull. Her left arm was still sore and weak, but it was better than inactivity. Or than her thoughts . . .

Jeremy, how does event and randomness and the malice of our enemies deal with you? Are you well, closest of commitments?

Jeremy Wainman sat upright. It was early morning; the intake for the light conduit must be facing west, for that was the dimmest part of the day. It was four hours until he was due to be fed; he stretched and yawned, pulling the sleeping fur around his shoulders for warmth.

Astonishingly, the revolving hatchway in the center of the door opened. It stopped halfway, and he began to jump forward until a muffled voice said sharply:

"Stand back! Destructive agents will be applied. The vapors may be injurious if excessively inhaled."

His heart thumped. *Someone* was trying to bust him out. The problem was that he couldn't tell who; he couldn't even tell if it was a woman or a man, given the rather androgynous way Martian voices sounded. It might be someone who wanted to rescue him or just another bunch of enemies who wanted a hold over Teyud. In fact, the latter was a lot more likely.

The area around the door's central lock began to hiss. A few seconds later acrid green smoke billowed from it, looking almost black in the dim light. Jeremy retreated further, standing up on the sleeping bench and pulling part of the wide sleeve of his robe over his mouth. It smelled rather strongly of not-too-clean Jeremy Wainman, since he hadn't had the chance to wash or change it in quite some time, but it was better than the choking acid-and-metal smell of the vapor. He coughed as a whiff of it got past the fabric. The cloth was incredibly tough and hardwearing, comfortable, warm even in Martian weather, and the russet and green colors were handsome. It stopped low-velocity projectiles about as well as DuPont's stuff did back on Earth. But as far as he knew it didn't have any special power to filter toxic vapors.

"*Owww!*"

Something had grabbed a tuft of his hair right above the robe's high collar and pulled *hard*. He jerked his head forward, swearing, and looked behind him. One of the rat-things was sitting just behind the grille that closed the ventilation shaft, holding the bars with one hand and stuffing a tuft of brown Terran hair into its mouth with the other, giving every sign of enjoyment. Teeth shaped like miniature spades chopped happily, and its long sticky tongue caught floating wisps and flicked them back between its jaws.

"*Shit!*"

The whatever-it-was reached out for him with clawed fingers and a squeal that probably meant *Tasty-yum-yum! More, more!*

He couldn't even hit it—getting his hand into range was just what it wanted, and if he stopped to take a boot off it would be gone before he could strike. The little bastards learned fast. More of the green vapor poured out of the cell door. Luckily zombie-rats—which was what he'd privately christened the things—weren't all that came out of the shaft; a cool, dry waft came from it, and fairly steadily. As long as he kept his head close to it, if just far enough away to be out of the thing's reach, he could breathe.

Then there was a *shunk* sound. After an instant he realized that it was the locking bar in the cell door withdrawing. An instant after that, someone pushed the door aside into the slot in the wall that held it. The green vapor billowed out into the corridor. A robed figure stood there, face hidden by a smooth mask of brown ceramic, dart pistol in hand. Another two figures robed in black lay motionless on the floor. As the air cleared, the Martian with the pistol unhooked the mask.

Jeremy felt his mind boggle. It was Daiyar, the doctor who'd examined him . . . and sounded so enthusiastic about dissecting him, too.

"Come quickly," she said. "I am an agent of the Supremacy and the Crimson Dynasty; this piece of Prince Heltaw's has predefected. The Tollamune will be interested in what you have to say of his offspring."

Oh, Christ, Jeremy thought, pulling up his jaw. *I just get involved with this really great woman, and already I have to go meet her dad?*

The reservoir of neutralizing agent bumped awkwardly against Teyud's side as she crawled through the space between the gas cells and the outer hull. The fine mist she sprayed settled on the ragged edges of gaps and rents; she could see the pale blue-pink of the sky through them, and feel the steady chill beat of the high-altitude air.

A *Paiteng* flashed by outside, a brief glimpse of gold-and-blue ferocity, and the dart rifle of its rider snapped. The projectile thumped into the gas-cell beside her, and there was a brief hiss. Then the material humped up around the puncture, turning semiliquid for a moment and then sealing. It had probably been a nonlethal dart, although a rifle's projectiles could do serious harm even without their load. And slipping backward off the cell and crashing down into the hull would produce trauma as well.

She went back to work, grimly conscious that the damage-control teams were not going to be able to seal enough of the hull.

The calculated risk did not eventuate as we hoped, she thought. *Although the other faction probably had an airship ready to "accidentally" explode too close to us, as a failsafe if their first attempt failed. Even the randomness of the dice is patterned in the Game of Life.*

The fireproofing anticatalyst did fail sometimes; and you could find a pilot willing to undertake a suicide mission. There were drugs, mind-control parasites, and leverage on the individual's lineage.

Another hiss, this one much louder. A little farther along droplets of attack enzymes had spattered through onto the gas-cell. A hole appeared; it grew wider as she watched. When she sprayed the neutralizing agent on it, the rate of growth slowed, but it did not stop. A look around showed more such spots, and too few crewfolk to control them.

With a shrug, she shed the harness that controlled tank and hose and let them drop—the chance of their doing important harm was negligible. Then she crawled down to one of the curved ladders that ran around the lower support rings of the hull, and from there down to the gondola.

"The attack will succeed in disabling this craft shortly," she said.

Notaj had his face in the view mask again. He made a gesture of acquiescence before disengaging; there was less blood this time, as he used the recommended slow procedure and gave the neural link time to secrete a clotting compound.

"I express reluctant agreement. This is unfortunate," he said. "The *Useful Burdens* has been a valuable resource, in this and a number of previous missions. I have been comfortable utilizing it and will regret its destruction."

A *Paiteng* dove toward the nose of the airship, then twisted in midair to flip and dive. As it did, it released the globe in its claws, and swept by beneath with a thunderclap *boom . . . boom* of giant wings as it maneuvered. The heavy *ptank . . . ptank* of the darter turret in the floor of the control gondola followed it, and there was a shout: *"Exultant triumph! Destruction of the target!"*

Or in Jeremy's language . . . yeee-ha! Teyud thought. *Imprecise but evocative.*

That meant the bird had been struck, although only after the damage was done. The globe followed its expertly launched trajectory, smashing on the gondola's prow just below the forward control post. A broad swatch of the tough transparent material went opaque immediately, as the liquid began to eat inward.

"Bridge crew, with me," Notaj said. "Inaugurate self-destruct sequence."

Then, into an ear for broadcast throughout the *Useful Burdens*, he ordered: "Crew, prepare to abandon ship. Rendezvous Alpha-seven. You have striven earnestly to accomplish your mission; a commander could desire no better personnel. May event and randomness favor you." A long breath. "Abandon ship!"

The hatches at the sides of the control gondola fell away as their emergency release levers were tripped. Despite the fact that she was retreating from a lost battle, Teyud leapt through the opening into the cold thin air with a burst of savage exultation.

She was going to Jeremy . . . and toward those who attempted to defy the Tollamune line.

CHAPTER ELEVEN

Encyclopedia Britannica, 20th Edition
University of Chicago Press, 1998

MARS: Development of Weapons Technology

Weapons technology on Mars has long been in a state of relative stasis, like most other *tembst*. This is partially attributable to the prolonged contraction of population and economic activity in the post-Imperial period; the surplus for large wars and indeed for intensive scientific research does not exist. Furthermore, the general attitude is that optimum solutions to most *tembst*-related problems were discovered long ago and that further effort is a waste of time. Martian culture lacks the concept of progress. Rather, it views the present as a long declension from the glories of the High Imperial period. And the Crimson Dynasty at its height had a global police force, at most a gendarmerie rather than an army; its equipment reflected this orientation.

Yet even during the period of conflict that followed the breakup of the planetary empire—what Martian historiography refers to as the Age of Dissonance—there is little evidence of an arms race, de-spite seemingly strong incentives as provinces and fragments of provinces broke free of control from the center and fought each other for dwindling resources and critical territory.

Another factor is the inherent limitations of Martian biological technology. While subtle and often very effective, *tembst* tends to lack the raw power of Earth's post–Industrial Revolution approach to technology. It arose on a planet without fossil fuels or uranium, where basic energy sources were limited to those that could be har-vested from plants—that is, from life, and life on Mars is sparser than that on Earth or Venus. Hence use of *tembst* always required careful cost-consciousness and intensive conservation and recy-cling; the necessity for this has been so self-evident that it has never been seriously disputed. Biological energy used for machines or weapons always competed directly with food for the population.

Explosives are known, but are often rather feeble because of the high cost of manufacture; the primary weapons are based on toxins delivered by relatively low-velocity projectiles propelled by methane-air combustion, and an assortment of lethal or dam-aging fungi, enzymes, and incendiary devices. These are often very deadly, but effective defenses or countermeasures also exist. It follows that hand-to-hand fighting with bladed weapons has re-mained a major factor in most combat.

Yet Martian civilization could probably have invented more powerful weapons if motivated to do so. The extremely rationalist approach to conflict of all recorded Martian cultures seems to be the ultimate reason more resources are not devoted to this end. Martians fight wars, but they have never had anything analogous to crusades, jihads, or the industrialized "total war" of the twenti-eth century on Earth.

Martians will fight, and fight with vicious ingenuity and deter-mination as long as they see a probable advantage to doing so; when the balance of power is clearly demonstrated, they will then negoti-ate and make peace with little lasting residue of hostility. This re-sembles some patterns in Terran history—the "cabinet warfare" of Enlightenment-era Europe, the formalized condottiere warfare of the Italian Renaissance, or the period of the Warring States in China before the rise of Chin—but is more uniform and thoroughgoing, and appears more "natural" to the Martian mind. Similarly, there is a universal reluctance to fight in ways that damage the prizes for which the struggle takes place.

In this context, the lack of competitive innovation in weapons technology makes considerable sense. Martians engage in conflict for limited aims; innovation would increase the overall costs of the system without in the long term giving any one party a decisive advantage. This calculation is similar to that which prevented all parties in World War Two from using poison gas, and which has to date prevented widespread use of nuclear weapons on Earth, but such unspoken bargains appear to be more natural to Martians than to their Terran cousins.

Mars, City of Dvor Il-Adazar (Olympus Mons)
Pits beneath the Palace of Restful Contemplation
May 25, 2000 AD

Jeremy paused to strip the harness and weapons from one of the unconscious—he hoped they were just unconscious—guards in the corridor. That gave him a pistol with clips of darts and syringes of gun-food, sword, dagger, and personal items—iron-ration biscuits that tasted and felt like the metal, a small flask of water, and Martian grooming gear. He tossed the pouch containing the latter; it wouldn't help him shave and he was damned if he was going to clear out ear wax by letting a miniature beetle *eat* it in situ.

Besides, a brief thumb test showed the dagger *was* sharp enough to shave with. This Prince Heltaw evidently got his personal troops *good* equipment.

While he was busy, Doctor Daiyar put a small ceramic canister on the tunnel floor, gave the top a very careful twist, and stepped back. He didn't want to know what it did, and followed her silently when she turned and started trotting down the corridor.

After a few minutes the doors to the cells were retracted, their organic locks long removed or dead; a thin film of fine dust coated the floor, making him cough as their feet stirred it into a dry mist. They were probably the first to come this way for a very long time. About the same time, the glow-globes stopped—or rather, became inert and dark.

"Wait up!" Jeremy yelped. "I can't see!"

Something was pushed into his hand . . . or was placed against it and *grabbed* his hand; he made himself stop his first impulse, which was to beat it off against the stone wall. It *squirmed*. Gritting his teeth, he applied it to his face. Four tentacles wrapped themselves around his head and shook hands behind it; he could feel them knotting together and then smoothing out. Waxy, flexible flesh covered his eyes; then a greenish light seemed to appear, and it coalesced into the face of Doctor Daiyar, who had a similar device on *her* face.

Fortunately, it wasn't one of the ones that plugged into your nerves; he wasn't even sure if those would work with a Terran and he didn't want to experiment. It just showed things on the equivalent of a viewscreen. From the glowing, mottled appearance of his surroundings, he suspected that he was seeing heat, an infrared view. In Martian terms it was cheap and nasty, inferior modern *tembst* rather than the subtle power of the ancient Imperial variety.

I don't care, he thought, and said aloud, "Thank you."

Actually I said "I express polite appreciation for your assistance," he thought. *But it comes to about the same thing.*

The doctor shrugged. "You would be hard to guide if you were effectively blind," she said. "And I anticipate rewards of extreme generosity for your safe delivery. Bringing you to the other edge of the board for doubling will decide the outcome of this round of the Game of Life."

"Why did you wait four . . . no, five now . . . days," Jeremy asked, "if you were going to spring me anyway?"

"Releasing you was contingent on the random occurrence of favorable conditions. Most of Heltaw sa-Veynau's Coercives have been drawn off to some other endeavor, and the rest were distracted," Doctor Daiyar said. "Thus risk was reduced to a reasonable level, calculated against the possible result. I could then seize an opportunity to poison a number of the remaining guards, and then shoot the last two before they became aware of my lethal treachery."

"Oh," Jeremy said.

Well, you asked. It is like atanj *and that's a game where you have to keep in mind that any piece may change sides at any moment.*

The doctor-spy went on, "When the periodic all-is-in-order signal is not given, more of my employer's Coercives will appear, deduce my actions, and pursue us."

As they spoke, she took a right turn, then a left, and then more in bewildering sequence. The tunnels mostly joined at right angles, but sometimes in angled Y-forks; he got the feeling that they'd originally been based on natural fissures or volcanic tubes, and such things didn't form exactly the same way on Mars as they did on Earth. The floor coverings were more deeply worn here than they had been in the cell he'd occupied, or the corridor outside it nearer the *Paiteng* base. Given the dust, that probably meant they'd been abandoned when maintenance costs exceeded some curve of use. Occasionally they came through a hall or chamber, ranging from living-room-size to one about the same dimension's as the interior of St. Paul's in Rome.

"Where are we heading, and how the hell are they going to follow us?" Jeremy asked.

There was relief in his voice; but he was never going to be entirely easy about walking under a darkened ceiling below a Martian city again. Not after Rema-Dza.

"We will attempt to reach the deep levels. There are tunnels there that give ready access to areas occupied by the Imperial Coercives. And they will follow us with—"

The word she used meant roughly "sniffers," implying scent-hunting domestic canids.

"That was why I left the scent-bomb in the corridor; I have several more. But they will delay pursuit, not completely frustrate it."

Jeremy remembered the weird dog-thing at the entrance to the central dome in Zar-tu-Kan and shivered. A bloodhound that could talk wasn't pleasant to contemplate.

"How long will it take?"

"Assuming we survive and overcome all obstacles with dispatch, seven days."

"*Yikes!*" he said. "Wait a minute—pursuit isn't an obstacle."

"No. However, the pits, even the abandoned sections, are far from uninhabited. This is Dvor Il-Adazar. The water resources are large and life is correspondingly abundant."

Yikes! he thought; he was afraid if he said it aloud this time, it would come out something more like "yelp!" Or even *"help!"* Rema-Dza had been bad enough, and it was in the Deep Beyond.

"Feral engines?" he said, clearing his throat.

"Those, and others. That is why the tunnels are not blocked beyond the detention center."

"How so?"

"It was assumed that no rational captive would attempt to escape, given the alternatives."

They came to a spiral staircase, winding down around a central pillar.

"Ah, a swift means of descent. Follow me."

The doctor hopped onto the balustrade. It was polished and smooth; she vanished around the corner with a *sssss* of robes on stone.

The Terran hesitated for a long moment. *Those, and others*, he thought, looking into the pit of darkness below. He remembered a theory some of the paleontologists at Kennedy Base had expressed, that the first protohumans introduced on Mars a couple of hundred thousand years ago had spent a good long while as cavern dwellers right around here before coming up and conquering the surface.

Then: "Oh, what the hell," Jeremy said, grinning. "Here goes!"

He jumped up, hooking a boot over the rail below himself for braking if he had to, drew his dart pistol, settled his sword, and kicked himself into motion. Speed built, and he was accelerating in a descending whirl until the cold air rushed into his face like the wind in the mountains of home, and friction caused the seat of his pants to heat up despite the insulation of the robe's tough fabric. His hair fluttered, and the long sleeves peeled back up his forearms.

"Yeee-ha!"

Mars, over Dvor Il-Adazar (Mons Olympus)
Altitude 11,000 feet
May 26, 2000 AD

The air was no thinner outside the *Useful Burdens*, but it seemed so, and it was colder; the oxygen mask labored to compress air for Teyud. She spread her limbs to stop the natural tumble, and the horizon stopped flipping from land to sky and stabilized. She was on her back when it did, and she could see the long, finned teardrop of the airship silhouetted against the aching blue of the sky, like a thistle-ball shedding seeds in a breeze as the crew abandoned her. The binoculars focused with their new, unnerving speed; she could even see the faces of the individuals as they planed away from the vessel. *Paiteng* wheeled about it, the riderless ones plunged away sharply at command-whistles from their mounted handlers.

Then her vision darkened for a moment as two million cubic feet of hydrogen exploded and the binoculars shielded against the glare. All of the crew were far enough away to escape, as were most of the *Paiteng* with riders, but two were caught as the frame of the burning flier plummeted to the ground. Behind the oxygen mask Teyud's lips parted in amusement; they must have been very surprised . . . very briefly. The rest of the riders turned in disciplined pairs and began stooping downward, splitting up to follow the crew; those scattered in turn, body-surfing through the air to make their pursuers' task as difficult as possible. All of them would delay triggering their parachutes until the last possible moment, that they might spend as little time as possible dangling slowly and to make the attackers' task of identifying Teyud as difficult as they could.

Teyud rolled facedown, selected a spot below—an abandoned terrace below a mansion, between two peaks shaped into half-*dhwar* faces—and turned her body into a knife, head down and arms at her side. That position presented the least resistance to the air, and the ground swelled with alarming speed. Two *Paiteng* suddenly dove past her, braking with a boom of wings and matching her speed at fifty yards to either side—well beyond practical pistol range at this height. The riders turned the blank black-goggled shapes of their faces toward her, studying her . . . and then signing *Confirmation: target* to each other.

She prepared to dodge a strike by a *Paiteng*'s claws, but the pair of riders were too skilled, their birds too highly trained, for crude tactics like that. One of them unstrapped himself and launched his body into the air toward her, swimming in the swift-moving onrush with minimal flicks, like a fish in water. The other unslung his dart rifle and angled his mount in closer. The riderless bird spiraled below them, matching the speed of their fall and ready for the rider to steer her unconscious body to its saddle. It couldn't support two for long, but landing wouldn't be much of a problem.

They were halfway to the ground. Teyud pulled the oxygen mask from her face and tossed it aside to flail its tentacles as it vanished in the wind. The rifle spat, and the dart banged painfully into her gut—the rider was a *good* shot. Robe cloth wouldn't always keep out a rifle dart, but this time it did. Teyud let herself go completely limp; even let the pistol whip away from her relaxing fingers. Now she fell instead of steering herself, limbs flailing akimbo, the world spinning around her once more.

The dismounted rider swooped in—he had only seconds to act, now—hands reaching out for her, ready to accept a bad thump to achieve his goal.

Thump.

Teyud forced herself not to grunt; there was a sharp pain in her partially healed shoulder. Then they were spinning around the axis of their meeting, and the man was struggling with arms and legs to stabilize her. Teyud waited until he had. His mouth was a compressed line of fierce concentration; then her own left hand shot out and grabbed him by a chest-strap, and the other came up with the long curved knife.

He was very fast; she could *feel* his determination, somehow. He managed to get a wrist on hers; and then something made him let go, thrashing to escape. That killed him; the blade punched through his body suit and up into the heart and lungs. She released him to fall straight down and snatched at the toggle of her parachute. It would be extremely close . . .

Thump.

The shock of the fabric scoop's impact on the air made her teeth click together and her vertebrae gave a series of clicking sounds; some distant corner of her mind outside the diamond focus of concentration reflected that the orthopedic effect would be beneficial. The ground came up and hit the soles of her boots a bare minimum of time later; if she hadn't had the strong bones and tendons of the Thoughtful Grace—and the Tollamunes—she would have been injured and rendered helpless, if not dead. As it was, the rolling impact left her breathless for an instant.

She hit the quick-release catch of the parachute and rolled erect. The cloth billowed out of the way, to reveal the dead rider's *Paiteng* swooping toward her. She could *feel* it, too, with that same massive certainty, feel the killing rage and grief in the small, fierce mind at the death of the one to whom it had bonded as a chick, like a raw wound rubbed with salt. It flipped out of its swoop and flared wings like the shadow of falling night, coming at her with huge claws outstretched in a trajectory that would scoop her up like a *vash* . . . and break half the bones in her body at the *massive* impact.

It was screaming as it came, its own hunting-shriek commingled with a half-intelligible wail of *dieeeee!*

Her hand flashed to the hilt of her sword. But something else moved within her, too, a ferocity that matched the bird's. It went *through* her, out into the bird's body, like the point of her out-stretched sword. She felt the *Paiteng* die, every nerve in its body flaring into overload and its mind flickering out like a pinched wick; the final stoop turned into a tumble that struck the soil of the dead garden and fountained it toward her like spray from a projectile weapon.

That Which Compels, she thought; and then the weight struck her, and there was nothing.

Mars, City of Dvor Il-Adazar (Olympus Mons)
Pits beneath the Palace of Restful Contemplation
May 27, 2000 AD

"Don't you have any lights?" Jeremy grumbled a day after his balustrade ride, tired of the green-glowing infrared view.

Everything was so uniformly cold down here that his viewers was less useful, too, barely giving an outline. He stumbled again on an irregularity in the tunnel floor and cursed.

He did that in English. "Consanguineously mated male off-spring of a domestic canid" just wasn't very satisfying when he stubbed his toe. Neither was "excrement!" or "feces!" And shout-ing "I feel extreme annoyance" didn't do it for him at all, when you came right down to it. Swearing in a language without taboos was *hard*.

And she *did* have lights; he could see half a dozen glow-sticks clipped to her harness, and there were some in the equipment haversack on his.

"In fact, why don't we *use* a light?"

Doctor Daiyar turned to look at him. "I do not wish to absolutely confirm that nourishment is available to the entire local ecology," she said, which was savage sarcasm, in Demotic. The epithet "you unfit-to-survive individual of subnormal intellect" was unmistakably implied.

Stupid me, Jeremy thought, forcing his teeth not to chatter. *I asked the same question in that tunnel back in Rema-Dza.*

The tunnel they were in was quite different from those on the higher levels, save for the roughly twenty-foot diameter that it shared with most of them. It was crooked, for one thing, wandering along like a natural fumarole, which it probably was. The walls were roughly shaped, either by chisel-like tools or chisel-like teeth. And for almost the first time since he'd left the shores of the Great Northern Sea where Kennedy Base sat, the air felt damp.

They'd gotten down to the edge of the great, lens-shaped aquifer that underlay Olympus Mons, or at least to one of the fracture zones that wicked down moisture from the upper slopes to feed it. This might have been a collection channel when the water table was higher.

The floor and walls glistened in spots with moisture or slush-crystals, and it was blotched by some pale, lichenous growth. Doctor Daiyar carefully avoided brushing against those, and so did he after her sharp warning, "*Infective!*"

The air had a dank, moldy smell as well. Doctor Daiyar seemed apprehensive.

No, she looks scared shitless, Jeremy thought. *In an undemonstrative Martian way. I'm beginning to think Teyud is this planet's equivalent of a passionate, emotional Sicilian.*

They both had sword and pistol in hand. Daiyar stopped and cocked one large, mobile ear. It was as silent as a tomb—Jeremy pushed away the image with an effort—or at least very quiet, except for the novelty of the sound of water dripping somewhere.

Daiyar stopped short. Jeremy felt a waft of warm—or warmer, at least—air on his face. It felt good, after having been cold for days. The last time he'd actually felt *warm*, he'd been in bed with Teyud, on board the *Intrepid Traveler*. And even she had cold feet. He remembered the way she'd twine them with his and compare him to a heating element with a longing that made his eyes prickle for a second.

When Daiyar resumed her steady pacing, he asked, "I take it that warmer air isn't a good sign?"

"Geothermal heat," she said. "It and the associated chemicals sustain fungi and algae which are at the base of subterranean food chains. Exercise extreme caution. Predatory fungi will be present, and perhaps rodents of unusual size. Use this on exposed flesh, and wear your mask."

Errrkkk! he thought. *Those rodents back in the cell were bad enough; I really don't want to meet any that are bigger.*

He smeared on the ointment she offered; it was thin and had an astringent smell, and made his skin feel leathery somehow, as if all his pores had been filled with wax. The mask was a triangle of ceramic, like the bottom half of a hockey goalie's. You breathed through its pores, and it made each breath a little harder—you had to suck—which he found made his heart pound harder, until he ran through a few Zen exercises. He'd never been zazen, exactly, but his home state was lousy with them, or at least the northern part was, and the techniques were helpful. The beating of blood in his temples receded.

Then her ears swiveled again; she turned and they pointed forward at full extension. "We are pursued," she said. "That was the chase-call of a sniffer. We must move faster—yet still cautiously. *They* are moving very rapidly indeed."

Between the devil and the deep blue sea, he thought.

He remembered the thought an hour later, when they came into the chamber. It was huge; just how big he couldn't tell, because the view through his goggles faded off into hints of twisting heat. Where the geology was suitable, Mars' lower gravity meant it could have cavern complexes bigger than anything on Earth. The part nearest him had *puddles*. Shimmering mist covered them, turning into patches of low fog here and there; spires and stalagmites rose out of it in brutal inverted exclamation points.

"No, not puddles," he said to himself, watching one patch of water a hundred feet or more across; there was a distinct smooth ripple for a moment, as if something long and sinuous was gliding beneath the surface. "It has pools. Deep, interconnected pools. Linked to very large underground lakes or rivers."

Irregular pathways of comparatively dry ground twisted off into the same indistinct distance, ridged and rough with irregularities and boulders. Luckily the surface was gritty beneath his boot-soles, a bit like strong pumice.

He thought that the goggles must be failing him and put up a hand to remove them until he realized what the headache-inducing shimmer was; many of the pools were hot, hot enough to send tendrils of mist up into the air. It had gotten much warmer, but this area was uncomfortably hot, especially as it was downright humid as well. Smooth, glittering discolorations near the water hinted at mineral rime, and *shapes* stood all about. Some looked like elongated versions of Terran mushrooms; others, growing on spires and outcroppings of rock, looked like shelf fungi. One type looked remarkably like a heap of cow intestines, which he recognized because he'd visited his mother's brother's ranch fairly often as a kid.

The goggles conveyed only hints of color; most appeared gray-white, but some had what he thought must be savage bands and whorls and spots of pink and dark purple. And some of them were— very slowly—turning in his direction. He heard the drip of water loudly now, and ripples and gurgles, and a dry, feathery, creaking sound. And, yes, very faintly a musical belling, echoing through endless spaces in the huge sponge of stone.

It sounded like a group of very hungry silver trumpets.

The horns of Elfland, he thought, picturing again the starved, skeletal elegance of the Sniffer in Zar-tu-Kan. *But the Dogs of Fangs-In-Your-Ass, if they catch up to us.*

"Most of the fungi are not very motile," Daiyar said tightly; he suspected that the words were as much for herself as for him. "Follow me closely. Do not stop if at all possible. A collective frenzy will result if we are immobile for any length of time. This is—metaphorical mode—very much like a game of *atanj* with time-limited moves."

She started off at a brisk walk, turning and twisting to keep the two of them as far as possible from either the thicker growths or the edge of the pools. Jeremy followed precisely in her footsteps. A tall, bulbous, spotted thing about fifty yards away creaked alarmingly, then burst with a loud dry pop. A cloud of white mist drifted in his direction.

Daiyar whirled and took an aerosol-like container from her harness and twisted it. Another mist poured out from it, and intercepted the cloud of spores—or at least all the ones he could see. Jeremy fought not to hold his breath as they walked on; more and more of the pods back there were bursting.

"You are perspiring. Cease at once," Daiyar said, her voice muffled by the mask that covered nose and mouth. "The wild spores are most dangerous in mucus membranes but they can sometimes germinate on any damp surface and sweat tends to remove the protective ointment. Then the filaments of their roots can dig deeper into the pores and spread with explosive speed as they consume tissue."

"Oh, I'll do my level best not to perspire, despite the clammy heat and the terror," Jeremy said hollowly, with a brief, horrific flash of the way Sally Yamashita had died. He fought down an insane urge to giggle—the doctor probably believed he *could* stop sweating on command. "You bet, no sweat."

The Deep Beyond was looking more and more attractive. At least lethal fungi came there only if someone brought them in.

They walked on toward a clearer patch of flattish rock with only a single massive triangular piece of lava sticking out of it, like a deformed, acne-ridden troll's nose twenty feet high that trickled smoke from cracks around its base. A shimmering greenish light seemed to hang over it, and Daiyar stopped, looking backward and forward. Her ears twitched.

"What is it?" he asked.

"The heat indicates high-metabolism life forms," she said.

It did. The first few skittered out of the fissures in the base of the rock as he watched. One made a beeline for his boot, and he stamped in reflex. What he could see when he raised his foot was just like the zombie-rats that had plagued him in the prison cell, the ones he was beginning to remember with nostalgia.

Except that this one was about the size of his thumb, or a large cockroach.

"Rodents of unusual size!" Daiyar said, a frantic overtone in her voice. "Quickly! There will be thousands in a few moments!"

Unusual size? Jeremy thought—or some part of his mind gibbered. *I thought that meant unusually* large *size! Damn Demotic and damn its precision!*

They began to spring forward to get around the nose-shaped protuberance. Jeremy caught a flash of motion out of the corner of his eye and threw himself down with a yell; Daiyar did the same an instant later. Something flashed by over his head, a creature like a huge manta ray, right down to the lashing tail that sang through the air where his head had been like a steel whip. When he jumped back up—soaring five feet into the air as he did—the base of the triangular rock was already black and heaving with a mat of the rodents; the whole thing started to boil toward him.

"Surrender!" a voice boomed, as if magnified by a megaphone, echoing off the walls and roof and stony spires of the great chamber.

He turned. A dozen Sniffers were at the entrance to the cavern, gabbling and rising on their hind legs to point in his direction, then dropping back to stand with long red tongues lolling over thin jaws lined with gripping teeth designed to catch and immobilize. Their baying and babbling subsided at a harsh command from one of the ten guards behind; all of them were mounted on fat-tired, self-propelled unicycles, the only things with the speed and capacity to handle rough footing to catch them so fast. The riders had dart rifles and the round helmets with pivoting eyestalks he'd first seen in Zar-tu-Kan, the kind that plugged into your optic nerve.

You *needed* eyes in the back of your head in a place like this.

"Drop your weapons and surrender!" the voice boomed again.

Jeremy had gotten much better at interpreting the musical but low-affect Martian voices. This one sounded distinctly frazzled.

Daiyar had frozen, except for her head, which whipped back and forth between the approaching horde of miniature zombie-rats, the darkness above where mantas made ready to stoop, and the fields of sporulating fungi they'd passed though. Jeremy made the same calculation, and acted: He scooped up the doctor's elongated form, slight and with a hollow-boned lightness. Then he ran at the troll's nose, and *leapt.*

One of the manta-things passed him on the way up, the long, barbed whip of its tail barely missing him. He landed halfway up the rocky height, scrabbled for footing, crouched, and leapt again. This time he came down on a small, four-foot-square, patch at the top. He was close enough to the far edge that he had to squat frantically and push himself backward to avoid toppling down the far side. It was reassuringly solid, though, so they needn't fear anything crawling out of the rock to get at them.

One of the manta-things dove at them. As it did, Jeremy saw bones and the half-dissolved bodies of zombie-rats and dozen other things stuck to the glutinous surface of its underside. It passed inches over their heads, and he managed to shoot it with the dart pistol he still gripped in one hand. It jerked in midair and circled downward, still with trembling waves moving across a surface that looked like custard or jelly close to. It settled on the rock floor, with hundreds of the rodents underneath it; they all gave a galvanic jerk that heaved the manta up like a blanket with a bunch of puppies underneath.

Then it grew still, although the edges rippled as if it was trying to throw itself back into the air or crawl away. More of the zombie-rats rushed in and began nibbling at its fringes; those that skittered out on top of it stopped and began to sink into it . . . or at least the first wave of them did. Jeremy restrained an impulse to shoot at it again as his pistol gave a pip of readiness.

"They are not wholly animal tissue," Daiyar wheezed as she stood up. "Most of its mass is a symbiotic motile fungus. Hence, the neurotoxin is less effective."

"Oh, great—*shit!*" Jeremy yelled, throwing himself down again and slashing with his sword as he fell backward.

That met a lashing tail as another flying thing whipped by; the blow to his wrist was like striking a moving baulk of teak, but the severed tip fell to the rock beside him. Daiyar scraped it off the edge to the surface below with her sword, and the rodents scattered back, leaving a clear space about it. They covered the fallen manta in a heaving mantle three or four deep by now, but enough were left over to send columns climbing up the rock face. They came on like ants.

The pursuing Coercives came on, too, leaning forward and racing their unicycles along the path the fugitives had followed, tilting and banking with crazed skill. One failed and crashed sideways into a pile of the cow-gut-looking fungus; it closed over him like a spring-loaded trap, with a wet plop sound. Another shot as something started to haul itself out of a pool, and whatever-it-was collapsed back into it with a froth of limbs or tentacles that churned the water to foam. More of the mantas sailed down from the roof; looking up, he saw one detach itself from where it hung by something that looked like a snail's foot. The organ sank back into its body as it uncurled its wings and swooped.

"Go!" Jeremy said to Daiyar. "They won't kill me! *Get me help from the Emperor!*"

He picked the doctor up by the back of her harness and tossed her down, on the far side of the prominence, the one that faced the round black mouths of tunnels leading out of here. He didn't have time to see how she was doing; he had to spend a few moments stamping and kicking as the miniature zombie-rats tried to swarm over the edge. Once or twice he crushed them with the flat of his sword or the barrel of his pistol as they climbed up the fabric of his trousers, hitting himself hard enough to give his bones bruises

"*I should have brought a fucking bullwhip and called myself Oklahoma Jones!*" he screamed as he danced and slapped, on the edge of hysteria. "*Goddamn the Lost City and all its fucking secrets! I should have stayed home and watched the video feed!*"

A dart rifle round whistled past his ear. A manta dived again, missing him, banking and landing on one of the Coercives and encasing him like hot shrink-wrap.

"*Mother!*"

CHAPTER TWELVE

Encyclopedia Britannica, 20th edition
University of Chicago Press, 1998

MARS: Family Structures and Gender Roles

The differences between Terran and Martian family structures are profound, and derive from both Martian history and the differences in the biology of reproduction in the two species.

Although like Terrans, Martians remain sexually active year-round from puberty on, Martian females do not share our continuous fertility. Research indicates that the ancestral stock from which modern *h. sapiens martensis* descends had an estrus cycle like most mammals, whether preserved from previous periods or re-evolved in the Martian environment. The bioengineered sub-sapients known as *De'ming* maintain such a cycle, becoming fertile twice in the Martian year, or approximately once per Earth year.

The standard variety of Martian humanoid, however, has a reproductive pattern unique among primates: females must consciously activate the reproductive organs. This ability appears at puberty, and doing so produces a period of heightened libido. It requires some training, but the ability itself is genetically programmed; learning it is analogous to an infant learning to walk or talk. Speculations on the origins of this phenomenon have tended to attribute it either to early biological engineering, or to evolutionary pressure in an environment where an unplanned pregnancy would often be disastrously risky to both mother and child.

Another relevant biological trait is the longer Martian life span, approximately twice the human norm, with lives of one hundred fifty to two hundred years not uncommon, and several decades more far from unknown; anti-agathic drugs may double this, if taken consistently from adulthood. (These life span figures do not take into account possible periods of hibernation; see *hibernation, Martian*.) Since Martians achieve sexual maturity only slightly more slowly than Terrans, and since they experience no equivalent of menopause—as with the male, fertility among Martian females simply declines gradually after middle age—the potential breeding span of a Martian female typically exceeds a century and may extend over two or three hundred years, particularly among high-status individuals with access to anti-agathic treatment.

Combined with low levels of mortality from infectious disease from very early times, and the fact that total fertility rates have rarely exceeded two or three per female, this drastically reduces the proportion of her life span a Martian female need spend either pregnant, lactating, or caring for infants. In most preindustrial societies on Earth this period exceeds seventy-five percent of a statistically typical woman's adult life; on Mars it has rarely exceeded ten percent, and is often less. Furthermore, all pregnancies are conscious choices, not unscheduled accidents.

Hence for Martian females reproduction is an episode in their lives, rather than the major part of it; it is an important episode, to be sure, and parental feelings of obligation are very strong. Most Martians also grow up without nonadult brothers or sisters; and the proportion of children in a Martian population is radically lower than in a Terran one, even at comparable levels of lifetime fertility. Effectively, for psychological purposes, every child is an only child and children grow up in an overwhelmingly adult world.

It is probably these factors that make Martian "marriage"—to the extent the term is applicable at all—more explicitly contractual than that in most Terran societies, and universally term-limited rather than indefinite. Reproduction is seen as a means of perpetuating lineages, or making alliances between them; usually the considerations are partly based on the economic resources each party will devote to the child, partly on eugenic concerns, and partly on the pledge of continued cooperation between the "merged" bloodlines. Typically, reproductive partnership agreements are drawn up to specify the number of offspring, and the length of time and precise nature of the resources each party will devote to it.

While the present-day Martian culture, as did its Imperial-era predecessor, possesses a concept of romantic love, this notion is much more detached from reproduction than in any Terran society. Long-term personal relationships and partnerships and erotic bonds may involve reproduction, but more often do not.

This pattern, and its biological underpinnings, together with the lower level of sexual dimorphism among Martians, probably account for the fact that no known Martian society has ever segregated the genders or emphasized divergent gender roles to the extent common on Earth. Total or near-total equality of the sexes is the rule; even in folklore, there is no memory of a time when this was not so.

Mars, Dvor Il-Adazar
Abandoned sections and pits, Northwest Quadrant
May 27, 2000 AD

Cell division is occurring very rapidly, Teyud thought. *Full function should be restored soon.*

The dream was an unusual one. She could see the cells splitting and the fluids of her body streaming around them, carrying away waste; vivid colors of red and white and brownish green, and somehow the senses of feel and taste were involved as well—salty and acrid. Stem cells of various sorts rushing to spawn and repair damaged and crushed tissue, white blood cells efficiently combating infectious agents from the soil, antibodies wrapping around them and transporting them away to the lymphatic disposal system, new red blood cells engorged with oxygen and nutrients arriving and being supplemented from the stores in her marrow.

All of it was as plain as looking through a magnifying device during her childhood, with one of her tutors sharing the neural link to the instrument and giving her a running commentary. Yet the whole was immensely amplified, and as she had the thought, her disembodied point of view stepped back, until she had a momentary sense of her whole body—not as an object, but as an infinitely complex *process,* a series of interactions and feedback cycles that made of it a complete universe moving on its own world-track through time, yet intimately linked with the world outside. And the rapid on-off-on flashing of her nervous system, the delicate holographic structures of memory . . .

Teyud blinked her eyes and knew that she was awake, smelling the scents of dry earth and warm stone and blood. She felt wonderful—something that was in itself surprising; it wasn't the first time she'd awoken after being knocked unconscious, when it was normal to have severe headaches and nausea and general pain for some time. Now the only unusual thing was her lack of motivation to rise. She brought her hand to her face and found that the binoculars had crawled away; something told her that they were neatly contained in their canister.

Could this be the euphoria and sense of patterned delusions said to precede death? she thought curiously. *Of course, such reports are necessarily from those who do* not *die. And I have not seen a narrow tunnel of light leading to the proverbial concourse of those to whom I owe money or other favors.*

Something like a tent arched over her head; she could see bits of sunlight through its golden mass. It stank, as well, a smell she remembered . . .

That is the wing of the Paiteng *that I killed . . . compelled to die, rather, with the Invisible Crown. I wonder if I can do that again? If so, I truly have the powers of a Despot on the board of the Game of Life!*

She probed at her own mind with her will, as if it were her tongue touching a newly sprouting tooth, trying to find the points where the ancient device melded with her own self. There was a slight soreness there, like an abstract abrasion, an ideational wound on the surface of her inner being.

Do not do it often, she thought. *There is a potentially lethal strain involved; to strike so is to weaken oneself. Like the Game of Life indeed! Yet the Invisible Crown definitely seems stronger and more active here in the Mountain.*

The feeling of lassitude diminished, and she turned and crawled out from under the beast's wing. That led her past its head; the fierce raptor beak was open, with the purple tongue lying in the dust, and the bright green of the eye faded and glazed. She nodded soberly to it. A thousand feet or so overhead, a score of its nestmates still circled; as she watched, a harsh cry drifted down the air and they formed into a circle, cruising lower in a descending spiral.

"Supremacy!" Notaj said. "To cover! Here!"

His parachute was still fluttering, draped over a stone wall carved in the likeness of a reedbed, the ancient, delicate tracery broken in spots but still solid and twelve feet high. She had been unconscious for a brief period, then.

Odd. My wound feels much better, she thought as she dashed to his side and crouched behind the protective bulwark that some ancient noble had commissioned to adorn his estate.

She worked her left shoulder, and felt only a slight sting and pull where the sword of Faran sa-Yajir had scored the muscle between shoulder blade and neck. Thoughtful Grace healed quickly, and Tollamunes with yet greater efficiency, but that was still startling.

"Are you injured?" Notaj said.

"Not at all. Somewhat repaired, in fact. I find the Invisible Crown increases the efficiency of my physiology to a marked degree."

He nodded, awe in his eyes. "We had best seek shelter."

"This way," she said, pointing eastward and upslope.

They had landed in what had been the walled and terraced outer gardens of a large structure halfway up the cliffs of the Mountain—perhaps a series of apartments, or more likely a palace. Nothing remained of the plantings but the shattered ends of glassine irrigation pipes; that and the brownish red color of the soil, which now bore a rich but wild knee-high growth of atmosphere plant. The building lay above them, rising in three stepped blocks carved from the fabric of the Mountain, cut with balconies and broad windows, columns and whimsical carvings of sinuous vines and trees.

Downslope was sheer cliff, dropping in veils of frozen lava to the inhabited plains beside the Grand Canal two thousand feet lower and miles distant.

Notaj nodded and whistled sharply. A dozen of the *Useful Burden*'s crew had survived the fall and the passage through the gauntlet of the *Paiteng* riders. Several were too badly hurt to move—slashes, or broken bones. Quick first-aid was given, but it would be safe to leave them here. Coercives did not harm each other's wounded, in the usual course of things; in fact, they generally would do what they could to help—you might be on the receiving end all too easily the next time. That would hold true even between Imperial Thoughtful Grace and the retainers of Prince Heltaw sa-Veynau; the custom was very ancient.

Whenever the buildings had been abandoned, the departure had been orderly—the exterior doors were all locked. But they had been built before the end of the long peace, and where a modern structure would have shown only blank stone for twenty feet at least, here there were broad, sliding portals of glassine set in runways. Teyud felt an irrational pang as one of Notaj's crew wrecked the lock with a brief spray of enzyme, as if the indignant prince or lineage head might return, and demand why *Sh'u Maz* had been violated through so wanton a destruction of another's property.

Within was a broad entrance hall walled in intricate patterns of ceramic tile, a marble staircase leading upward and a tunnel extending back into the depths of the Mountain; the air had a slightly musty stillness that meant the ventilation ducts had been blocked as well, to prevent vermin from entering the abandoned structure. Channels also extended upward, funneling sunlight through their glassine conduits and giving a diffuse glow to the colors of the murals on either side. Notaj looked at her.

"Shall I command a rear guard to give you more time to break contact, Supremacy?"

Teyud shook her head. Her eyes glazed slightly as she looked within. The bright, hot minds of the *Paiteng* were mirrored there, and the fear and aggression-anger of their riders. It was as if she *contained* her surroundings somehow. And could affect them, within limits, like an *atanj* player moving pieces—although, as in the Game, the pieces could show wills of their own.

Indeed, with the Invisible Crown one can hold and sway the world. Could I kill them all?

The temptation was like teetering on the edge of a cliff. There was more vehemence in the way she shook her head than strictly necessary.

"No," she said. "They will not follow on foot; they are discouraged by their losses and resent the orders that produced them. They will not exceed their instructions, and so will guard this place and send notice to the Prince."

Several of the ex-crew of the airship snorted quietly, and assumed postures that subtly hinted of scorn as they walked. Thoughtful Grace would have been more aggressive.

"Although," Notaj observed judiciously, "it would be irrational for them to pursue us too closely. We *are* Thoughtful Grace and highly trained as combat generalists, while they are not. They are specialists in *Paiteng* operations. In air combat they showed to advantage, with commendable determination and skill; in confined spaces or underground, it would be too likely that we would turn on them and kill them all without difficulty."

Teyud nodded absently. Something was trembling on the brink of her awareness. The Mountain hovered in her mind's eye, not an abstract concept but somehow a representation that was the whole monstrous *thing*, as well as the modifications that humanity had made in it, from the first terrified bands crouched in a cave to the latest shaft driven or blocked.

The knowledge itched at her, and it felt dangerous—as if a single misstep would break a barrier and flood her mind with more than it could contain and crush her consciousness into oblivion.

To extract what I need . . . and there is something more. Something is watching, even now. My father might know what this implies and what should be done; I do not.

"This way," she said.

She turned into a side corridor and pushed open a set of doors of frosted crystal etched with patterns of stylized songbirds in flight— an ancient form of musical notation still taught around Dvor Il- Adazar. She hummed the tune to herself and felt her brows rise in surprise; it was one her primary nurse had sung to her as an infant. How had the words gone?

> A *long journey*
> *Long journey into night*
> *Long journey into day*
> *Rest well, tiny one*
> *Rest and grow strong . . .*

She stepped through the doorway and looked into the suite of rooms as they hurried through; it had been a nursery, she saw, with murals of pretty gardens and children playing with pets and toys. One made her smile slightly; it depicted two humanized migratory fowl with white heads, yellow beaks, and blue robes supposedly playing *atanj*, one erupting in sputtering fury as it lost its Despot. There was a suite for the nurse, and a few cubicles for *De'ming*, and a bed for the children, its circular frame still hanging on coated orilachrium chains from the ceiling, though the bedding had long since perished of hunger and decay.

This had been a palace; the interior was too rich in rare, shaped stone, worked glass, and fine tiles to be anything else, even in the prosperous days of the High Imperial period. Probably all the infants of the staff as well as the proprietor's lineage had played here— interaction with others of their own age was supposed to help their psychosocial development. Teyud had never had more than a few brief meetings with other children before her own adulthood. Hers was the more typical pattern, particularly in recent millennia, even in view of the peculiar necessities of keeping her existence secret in an Imperial palace where there were more spies than courtiers—if that distinction had any meaning.

How strange it must be to have not just companions but siblings of one's own age, as Jeremy did. From his description, it seemed very agreeable, and certainly his personality is extremely pleasant. On the other hand . . . how could his parents do anything but socialize their offspring, with virtually no gap in age between them? If done at proper intervals, the previous one is fully adult and may even contribute resources to the task.

It was very puzzling; someday when she had leisure, she must make a study of the *vaz-Terranan*. Ideally one would do that before plunging into a pair bonding with one of them.

The vaz-Terranan are headlong and heedless, and it seems to be contagious. Although many say that of the Thoughtful Grace . . .

She smiled to herself as they left the long-silent nursery. Notaj glanced over at her; she could feel that he was puzzled, and impressed, that she was so pleasantly at ease despite battle and pursuit. They came to a pair of doors cast in bronze—far more expensive than crystal—and shaped like a section of a cylinder. They were worked in bas-reliefs that showed a formal procession traveling from right to left; a prince borne in splendor, attendants with feather fans, Coercives in strange, antique gear, *De'ming* servitors carrying trays of piled fruits. It was covered in a coat of glassine, and as bright as the day it had come from the foundry. The only thing that could have affected it was photons.

"We shall descend through this disused elevator," she said. "The shaft descends to the pits below the palace, and there are old water distribution channels now dry—or rather not flooded—that connect southward to the city proper."

Notaj was impressed again. "This is information derived from That Which Compels?" he asked. "I would have suspected it, but . . ."

"Yes," Teyud said. "If you find this alarming, I must add that it is even more so from my perspective. The Invisible Crown seems to contain a great deal of data—and continuously updated data, at that."

He briefly adopted a posture of consolation, with a slight exaggeration to show that it was in the ironic mode. She inclined her head, agreeing with his humor. She was the first Tollamune to find the ancient artifact in more than six thousand years, so she really didn't have grounds for complaint.

Nevertheless, it is alarming to have one's mind altered so. And the changes are accelerating. I am far from certain that this is entirely a positive development in the long term.

While the brief exchange went on, two of Notaj's followers had inserted the thin ends of pry-bars into the middle of the elevator's doors. Two more tallied on to the outer ends, and then they all heaved in unison. There was a screech as the long-disused bearings beneath the heavy metal portals ground into motion, and they slid back. Pieces of glassine pattered down to the marble. The air would begin to attack the bronze now, turning it green and then eating it away with corruption over the course of centuries. So did time gnaw at the Crimson Dynasty's work, turning *Sh'u Maz* to the chaos that entropy wrought.

For an instant, the thought brought a pang of wistful sadness, like a pressure beneath her breastbone. She pushed it sternly away.

I am seeing a side of Dvor Il-Adazar I never witnessed while I lived within it, she thought. *Though of course I mostly saw the more remote areas of the Imperial centrum.*

One of Notaj's detachment tossed a fragment into the black maw of the elevator shaft. They all cocked their ears forward and mentally counted time until they heard the faint sound of it striking the bottom.

"Eight hundred feet," Teyud said. "Nothing has blocked the shaft. And no sand infilling from below."

The others looked at her. She shrugged. "I have been in the Deep Beyond and the dead cities for some time," she said.

They nodded and returned to readying a line, clipping together the bandoliers of fine, strong cord they all wore on their battle harness. A vision flashed into her mind: Dvor Il-Adazar, but with the Grand Canal shattered and empty, and the fine pink sand drifting against the barrier cliffs as it did over Rema-Dza.

That shall not occur, she thought firmly, as the first of the Imperial Coercives slid downward out of sight. *Sh'u Maz* shall *be restored, shall indeed be extended to a previously undreamed-of extent. The recovery of the Invisible Crown is an indication of this.*

Teyud snapped a stop-ring onto the line, one that would squeeze the cord when she tightened her hand on it, and stepped off into the darkness.

"Your report is remarkable," Sajir sa-Tomond said. "It contains elements both encouraging, dismaying, and astonishing."

Doctor Daiyar had taken knee with a courtier's smooth grace; now she rose, adopted a brief posture of professional acknowledgment to the Imperial Physician, and returned to respectful attendance, hands folded inside the sleeves of her hastily donned green and gold robe. They were meeting on a flange-balcony of the Tower of Harmonic Unity; a glassine cover bonded to the edges and the wall of the Tower behind kept it pleasantly warm, and the view from the four-thousand-foot height over the multicolored majesty of Dvor Il-Adazar was unmatched.

Squads of *Paiteng* riders coasted by, the Sword of the Dynasty on patrol. One flew close and banked as he watched, the great wings flashing across nearly the full width of the enclosure; the blue undersurfaces melded with the horizon, as if a piece of sky had become solid. The shadow slid over his face, like a brush of feathers made of darkness.

The Tollamune considered Daiyar, blinked, and made a motion. The Thoughtful Grace guards hesitated a fraction of a second, and then one of them slid forward with a stool. That was a very great honor in a public audience—an acknowledgment of great service to the Dynasty. Though, to be sure, this gathering was "public" only in the most technical sense.

"I respectfully disagree with the compliment done me," Daiyar said, her voice dour as she sat; she was also visibly exhausted. "If I had *succeeded* in bringing the *vaz-Terranan* to the Supremacy, then the piece would be doubled and the Prince's attempts to defy the Tollamune will would be at an end. As it is—"

"As it is, you have provided me with very valuable data, and placed me in a better position to favorably resolve this situation. The game is not over until the Despot is toppled . . . or the Usurper."

He paused for a moment, enjoying the tinkling sound of water circulating in the nautilus-shaped fountain, and the scent of the blossoms that nodded around it. A foot-long bird whose plumage was a rainbow of blue and red and green and black drank from it, then walked across the jade and marble floor to nudge him sharply in the calf with its hooked, nut-cracking beak.

"*Food*," it sang on a plaintive, rising note. "*Food. Food.*"

He flipped a triangular nut with a thick brown shell to it from a shimmering bowl beside his table. The bird caught it, cracked the shell, ate the oily meat within and then scratched itself vigorously behind one ear, chortling with enjoyment and muttering:

"*Yummie, yummie, yummie.*"

Then it began to sing quietly, an ancient tune with a cadence that blended with the tumbling water; and as it sang, it danced, wings and tail and head making a complex harmony with the music. A *De'ming* stepped forward silently, swept up the shell, and returned to her endless waiting.

The bird serves a purpose beyond the aesthetic, Sajir told himself. *It reminds me that political supremacy is a literalized metaphor, rather than an aspect of the natural order itself. To the bird, I am merely a source of nourishment and a familiar presence, so evoking an unselfconscious affection. Any shopkeeper or technician could have a similar relationship with one of its breed. Yet if I were to die, it would grieve and search for me.*

"What is your estimation of the Terran, this Jeremy Wainman?" Sajir went on aloud, his pronunciation considerably closer to the phonetic pattern of English than Daiyar's.

"There are fascinating differences in metabolism. In terms of gross anatomy, less is obvious, but one notes—"

"I did not request discourse on the nature of the species, with which I am somewhat familiar, but an evaluation of the individual," Sajir said gently.

Daiyar adopted an apologetic stance, head slightly down and hands open with the fingers curled.

"Highly intelligent, Supremacy; not merely in the abstract, but in terms of rapid adaptation to fluid circumstances. Surprisingly well informed concerning the past of the Real World, though with amusing gaps. Capable of great determination. Rather demonstrative—I understand this is typical of the Wet Worlders—though somewhat naïve, and oddly charming in a rather innocent manner. This contrasts with extreme physical strength and prowess, comparable in overall terms to that of a Thoughtful Grace, though differing in detail."

"Ah. And my offspring, you say, has formed an erotic and companionate pair-bonding with this Terran."

Sajir brought his hands together beneath his chin, back-to-back with the digits touching: data have been registered, but their extraordinary nature resists assimilation.

Or, as the vaz-Terranan would put it: "No, really?"

Daiyar adopted a stance that implied the existential inexplicability at the core of existence and amplified: "He would not be my

choice of an erotic partner, even in the short term. The physical differences are . . . startling to some extent."

She shuddered delicately and went on, "Yet I believe his statements to that effect to be sincere. I am not altogether sure whether
he accurately represents the sentiments of . . . your offspring. Their
relationship might be merely experimental on her part—an adulthood spent as an itinerant contractual Coercive is not likely to lead
to fine discrimination in such matters."

"Intriguing. Most intriguing."

Judging from the report, I think the Terran's statements are *accurate.
Odd. One would expect Deyak—Teyud, as she calls herself now—to be emphatically negative in her sentiments toward the* vaz-Terranan. *Of course,
those were a different* faction *of the* vaz-Terranan, *but how many would
make such a distinction? This shows that she has unusual flexibility of
mind, and is unswayed by preconceptions.*

"I suspect that Deyak will bend her earnest endeavors to making the seizure of Jeremy Wainman an action which Prince Heltaw
regrets. Her mother was also inclined to pursue revenge."

"Revenge is, after all, Supremacy, one of life's pleasures. Apart
from near-ideal recreational coitus, there are few elementary satis-
factions more keen; though I grant that victory in a hard-fought ses-
sion of the Game of Life approaches it."

"To be sure. Yet Vowin was often unreasonable in its pursuit
and her childhood indicated that Deyak has inherited this trait."

"I anticipate stressful experiences for Jeremy Wainman if he
falls under the control of Heltaw sa-Veynau again," Daiyar said,
with a tinge of regret.

"True. Prince Heltaw is a man given to impulsive judgment
when subject to frustration . . . which indicates a possible course of
action."

He moved a finger, and a clerk slid forward. "Draw up a rescript, requiring the listed individuals to make immediate Apology
and Reparation. This to be individual only."

He heard a very slight sigh of satisfaction from Adwa sa-Soj. She
had been advising such an action ever since her sibling Notaj had
left on his mission . . . and *he* had been advising it for some time.

*As he put it, the bureaucracy has grown over the machinery of the state
as does the shell of a sessile-stage canal shrimp, leaving it frozen to the*

ground, unable to do anything but wave its buttocks in the air. Yet one does not necessarily produce good sculpture with a blunt and heavy instrument . . . or even a fine sword.

"An excellent order, Supremacy," she said. "It was time that nest of venomous invertebrates was sterilized."

"The deaths I have decreed will not cleanse it. You Thoughtful Grace are too confident in the utility of hammer blows. It will merely throw the covertly hostile portions of the bureaucracy into confusion for a crucial period of time, and preoccupy them with their internal quarrels. That, however, will be sufficient."

She nodded, unconsciously touching the hilt of her sword.

Ah, he thought. *If only that sharp simplicity were as useful as you think! Will my offspring's share of the Thoughtful Grace genome incline her to that outlook? I have communed with many of my predecessors who expressed rueful regret for a too-ready resort to blades. Of course, there are also several who regret most bitterly their excessive trust in their own subtlety. At times a blade thrust through the eye will negate the most cunning brain and the most intricate plotting.*

"Go personally," he said. "Witness the deaths, and publicize them. Answer no queries, except to specify that this is the Tollamune will."

He went on to the clerk, "And a Rescript, for general publication, listing the information contained in the one which Notaj sa-Soj bore."

The second in command of the Sword leaned close. "Naming Deyak sa-Sajir Designated Successor, Supremacy? That will force his hand."

"Just so, Adwa sa-Soj. But I wish to force it *emphatically*. Let the Rescript name her as co-occupant of the Ruby Throne; there is precedent for a dual rule, particularly where a reigning Emperor wished to establish the succession beyond doubt."

The Thoughtful Grace blinked, considered, then slowly smiled. "You seek to press him to precipitate action, anticipating gross errors of judgment on his part?"

"Just so. He is a man of some cunning and skill, but far less prescient when he acts in haste. In conjunction with demanding Apology of half my ministers, it will engender sentiments of the most desperate haste."

Jeremy Wainman hadn't known you could *really* scream until your throat was raw. He thought he tasted blood from his lungs and throat, not just his lips and tongue; the pain of the creature's beak itself faded rapidly, but that just made it possible for him to grasp how absolutely wretchedly awful he felt all over the rest of himself.

"I am severely annoyed, man of the Wet World," Prince Heltaw sa-Veynau said, and flicked the pain-serpent back so that it coiled around his forearm.

The weirdest part of it all was that it was *true*. The Martian bigwig didn't seem to be beside himself with fury, or like a sadist getting his rocks off. He merely looked *annoyed*, like someone who had a dog shit on his front doorstep and then stepped in it.

Trying to stand erect was too much effort, although slumping forward against the chains that held his arms above his head hurt just as much. There were six reddish wounds on his chest, and when the last of them were made he'd thought his heart would tear loose from the cavity that held it. Blood drooled down from his bitten lips, and other wastes made a hard stink in the sterile atmosphere of the clinic. Despite the humiliation, Jeremy was glad of that. Martians had much better sphincter control than Terrans; Jeremy's wetting himself had probably convinced the Prince that he was going too far and stood in danger of killing his hostage.

"I am even more severely annoyed with Doctor Daiyar," Heltaw said. "In the event of her capture, I shall begin as I have with you, then progress to all the time-tested techniques, combined with several innovations that have occurred to me."

He turned to one of his black-clad Coercives. "Is the recording adequate?"

"It is clear, Superior," the man said.

He tapped the drab reddish bird—it looked like a monochrome cockatoo with extra-large nostrils—on the head. It opened its beak and screamed in Jeremy's voice, with occasional babbling and pleading mixed in, all of it in English. He'd retained enough control to keep to a language Heltaw wouldn't know.

The household trooper tapped the bird again and it cut off.

"Food?" it said hopefully, fluttering its wings, and he tossed it something from a belt-pouch.

Heltaw looked again at the copy of the Vermillion Rescript lying on Daiyar's desk.

"Make copies, and append the following message: 'Deyak sa-Sajir-dassa-Tomond, I acknowledge your accession. Nevertheless, the Terran will be subjected to further and lethal excruciation unless you consent to immediate and intensive negotiation over our political differences, and do so prior to consultation with your father. Location of negotiations is to be as follows . . .' "

The man bowed his head, hazel eyes impassive behind the slit in his headdress. "I anticipate no positive result from such negotiations, Superior," he said. "The Supremacy has checkmated us. Flight, or perhaps unconditional submission to spare your lineage, at least?"

"Negotiations are not my actual intent. I plan decisive and situation-reversing treachery."

"Ah!" the man said, sounding pleased. "Yes, for such stakes, the inconvenience of damage to one's reputation for reliability in the future would be worthwhile. A reputation can be rebuilt over time; dissolution is proverbially final."

Jeremy raised his eyes and glared at Heltaw with dull hatred. *Can I provoke him into killing me?* he thought. Half regretfully he concluded, *No. He's just too damned cold-blooded . . . but he's not smart enough to sucker Teyud!*

Heltaw looked at him again. "And see to the Terran. At present, it is of some importance. I anticipate with some pleasure an alteration in this circumstance."

A gesture of contempt, like a man flicking something from his fingers. "The half-breed is evidently poorly socialized, remaining attached to its toys."

My girlfriend is so *going to kick your ass*, Jeremy thought.

CHAPTER THIRTEEN

Encyclopedia Britannica, 20th Edition
University of Chicago Press, 1998

MARS: Martian Psychology

In discussing Martian psychology, it is crucial but extremely difficult to distinguish between the cultural and the biological. This is far more so than is the case on Earth; we have thousands of separate cultures, and Mars only one; we share a common genetic heritage with all other Earth-humans, but there are definite if subtle differences in "human nature" between *h. sapiens sapiens* and *h. sapiens martensis*. We can build on the common features that cut across the grain of cultural differences; on Mars, with its monoculture, they reinforce each other. Is the detached, ironic positivism that characterizes Martians a matter of genes or of memes, their learned equivalents? Is their preoccupation with intellectual puzzles and chesslike games? Martians themselves find the question troubling, now that they have a separate species—closely related, but distinct—as a basis of comparison.

Mars, Dvor Il-Adazar
Abandoned sections and pits, Northwest Quadrant,
May 27, 2000 AD

"We have lost only two personnel," Notaj sa-Soj said, looking around as he raised the glow-stick. "That is an extremely moderate casualty rate for a rapid transit of such difficult passages. I grant that we are not yet in the Tower of Harmonic Unity, but we approach the endgame."

Teyud nodded, frowning slightly. It was true that they hadn't suffered unduly, especially when they'd had to cross several large caverns in the geothermal zone—the heat and chemicals added to the water made for a life-rich environment. Now they stood at the base of a great, semicircular staircase. It was plain stonemelt but glistening with trapped crystals fed to the beasts that had digested and regurgitated it so long ago; this had been a landing stage for barges using the water-distribution system when the aquifer was higher.

Two tunnels gave off on either side of the stairs at the lower level; another opened at the top, twenty feet high and twice that across. The *thing* in her head told her that it was a main artery, driving straight south toward the inhabited center of the city.

She frowned again. Normally she was quite at home in underground passages—any city on the Real World had them in plenty. Now there was a sense of oppression in the air, as if something terrible approached.

Perhaps it is the Invisible Crown once again, she thought.

Something fluttered in the portal at the head of the stairs. A dozen dart rifles were raised; it was a message-recorder bird, but such had been used as carriers for assassination before.

"No," Teyud said. "Let it live."

She held out her arm, and she felt a strong clench of claws through the leather of her glove as the bird settled on her wrist. It whistled and cocked an eye at her; she breathed on it, and it opened and closed its beak meditatively. Its eyes rolled up in its head for an instant and then it croaked:

"Identifed: Deyak sa-Sajir-dassa-Tomond, current Designated Successor and co-Emperor as of receipt of rescript on date—"

Notaj's eyebrows shot up as it specified place and time. Teyud heard herself make a slight sound of surprise; the Thoughtful Grace and his command all made a field-obeisance, pushing the right hand down with its palm to the floor and bending a knee. The bird continued its message.

"Communication from: Genomic Prince Heltaw sa-Veynau. Content: Part one, recorded excruciation of *vaz-Terranan* individual Jeremy Wainman."

Teyud's face might have been stone as she listened to the screams. And the English words "Don't! It's a trap! Don't!"

Notaj and the other Thoughtful Grace listened impassively, an ear folding back here and there when the volume rose too high—it was a messenger bird of the first quality, with an impressive tonal range and large lung capacity for its size.

"Content: Part two, verbal message from Genomic Prince Heltaw sa-Veynau."

The grating, impersonal voice of the bird itself shifted. Now it spoke a smoothly melodious court dialect, archaic Demotic strongly flavored with the High Speech.

"Deyak sa-Sajir-dassa-Tomond, I acknowledge your accession. Nevertheless—"

There was another message appended to the end of it, an Imperial proclamation in her father's voice raising her to the status of co-Emperor, and another announcing the apology of a very, very long list of senior personnel. Then the bird shook itself, groomed a few feathers, and looked at her hopefully: "Food?"

Notaj held out his arm; the recorder hopped over to his wrist and accepted a ration biscuit.

"Blah!" it said, but steadily devoured the hard-baked mix of starch, fruit, and nuts.

"Elevating you to the position of co-Emperor is a move of considerable cunning," Notaj said, absently stroking the recorder's crest with a finger. "It has driven Heltaw to the last extremity of foolishness. You have only to reach the Tower of Harmonic Unity, and he will have no alternative but to make Apology in the hope that his lineage will be spared."

"Blah!" the recorder mumbled again, dropping crumbs on the ancient pavement, then launched itself into the air and headed back to its nest.

"Or he may rebel," Teyud said, watching it go.

"That would be equally foolish," Notaj said. "His own Coercives would be unlikely to support such a move for long . . . perhaps some of them, those of long-affiliated lineages, but the remainder would defect."

Teyud smiled crookedly. "If my father were in a similar position, would you or any of your lineage defect?"

"No," Notaj said. "But we were socialized as Imperial retainers, and we are of the Thoughtful Grace. His are neither."

"Do not underestimate the potential of long affiliation to a dominant lineage," she said. "Particularly in an isolated area such as Heltaw's main holdings on the slopes below Aywandis."

Jeremy had told her of wars on Terra where hundreds of thousands, millions, had thrown themselves into certain destruction, even accepting compulsory enrollment as the Terran equivalent of Coercives.

Entire populations behaving in the manner of the most committed partisans of a lineage, she thought with wonder. *The Real World does not function so, and this is a positive factor. Civilization here would have destroyed itself many times over if rulers could order such waste without mass defection.*

"Also, he may flee to Aywandis and raise his rebellion there, where many are accustomed to his immediate rule," she said. "Regrettably, secessionism has succeeded all too often in recent millennia. This would prompt many either to support him or to remain neutral and not withdraw their contributions, lest they be caught on the losing side."

Notaj inclined his head. "A possibility. Imperial control of Aywandis is not as secure as it might be, though better than it was earlier in the current Supremacy's reign. As soon as you are safely returned to the Tower, we must take precautions—perhaps the dispatch of troops, and the publication of documents laying out the circumstances."

"We will not be returning immediately to the Tower," Teyud said. "A diversion to the location specified by Prince Heltaw is necessary before my return to my father."

Notaj's face went blank with surprise. "That would be a less than optimal strategy!" he said. "Heltaw can recoup his position only by somehow gaining possession of you. We must at all costs prevent this."

"Nevertheless, it is the course we will follow. Dispatch one of your personnel as a messenger with the recording; the rest will follow me."

"You are taking such risks for a *Terran?*" Notaj said; he was scandalized, and several of his followers looked at each other doubtfully.

"Am I now invested with the Tollamune authority, or not?" she said. Then she quirked her lips. "I am Despot on this board, Commander of the Sword of the Dynasty."

That depends on whether one speaks of strict accord with the regulations, or political reality, she thought.

Thoughtful Grace were loyal, yes, but it was an *independent* loyalty. They would follow what they thought to be the best interests of the Crimson Dynasty; obedience to the actual desires of an incumbent did not always take precedence. And an untried, unknown incumbent who had established no personal aura of respect and command . . .

"With respect, Supremacy—" he began.

"Obey!" she said, cutting him off and using the absolute-imperative tense. Then more gently: "This individual will be my Consort."

The world seemed to twist slightly, as if it were behind a crystal screen and the two were moving in opposite directions. Sight split along fracture lines; pain twinged in her skull, lancing to the stem of her brain. There was a sense of the irrevocable in her mind, like watching the fall of boulders when a glacier melted away from the side of the Mountain.

Notaj's face was wooden as he inclined his head and clasped hands inside the sleeves of his robe.

"I obey, Supremacy."

That Which Compels, Teyud thought with a shiver. *I am apprehensive. Such power will grow on one, like a* tokmar *sniffer's habit. Though simply to possess the Ruby Throne is power enough.*

Chinta sa-Rokis sighed as she saw the row of Thoughtful Grace in the crimson-edged black armor of the Sword of the Dynasty spread across the loading bay where her personal airship was docked. Her own Coercives looked at each other and then at her; their commander gave a very slight shake of the head. Several of the Imperial troopers carried short stubby launchers for fungus grenades. That was a statement of the seriousness of their intent; so were the recording birds and eyes on their tripods.

Hopeless, then? Chinta thought, and asked by arching her brows and tilting her head slightly to one side.

Her commander of Coercives spread his hands slightly in apology and reply.

But I was never inclined to direct violence in any case. It would be futile and vulgar to play at being a general at this terminal point.

The sun-dappled stretch of marble between her and the circular docking collar normally would be occupied by the deferential captain of the *Gracious Leisure*, perhaps with servants carrying trays of spiced juvenile canal shrimp or sweet blossom-paste on little pastries . . .

Suddenly the movement of sunlight on stone had an unbearable poignancy, a memory of delights so intense as to be visceral; she remembered the first time she had been brought here by her parents, fifty years ago, as young as her own daughter was now, full of the excitement of the treat and the promised travel to their country house. Even the memory of her emotions at that time was sharper than most of her life since—a bright, primary color next to muted, faded pastels. Not even the raw salt of fear could be as intense.

The entire crew of the airship was there now, kneeling in rows under the muzzles of the dart rifles. A slight, sulfurous smell of charged guns supplanted the usual scent of resin-bud incense. Ahead of the Imperial Coercives stood a high officer, the mandibles and faceted eyes of her lowered visor no more expressionless than the eyes of her subordinates above their fiber-bound ceramic battle masks. The hand resting on the hilt of her sword tapped fingers once, twice.

You have time, that said. *But not a great deal.*

"No need to roll the dice to see how this move will eventuate," Chinta murmured to herself. "A great pity."

The *De'ming* carrying her daughter whimpered and clutched the silent infant to her. The Supervisor of Planetary Water Control looked behind her at her household, and those of her confederates.

There was fear among those of lower status; terror lest the Imperial troops be given orders to make a clean sweep. The other High Ministers sighed as she had and adopted postures of resignation, with heads bent and hands held palm-down by their waists.

Chinta clasped hands to wrists within the sleeves of her taupe-and-gold traveling robe and strode forward. At the proper distance from the Thoughtful Grace officer she took a half-knee, as one must before the Emperor's personal messenger at such a time.

The soldier raised her visor and returned the courtesy with a crossing of wrists: *With regret, I am bound by the Tollamune Will, as by bonds of adamant.*

A polite fiction; she could tell from the hard yellow eyes that this was not a reluctant obedience. There was always that edge of intelligent savagery in the Thoughtful Grace, a swift directness like a swooping *Paiteng*—they were a sharp-edged tool that only the Ruby Throne could wield safely, and would be a terror worse still without its restraint. Nevertheless, it was better to die in the presence of courtesy and ancient ritual than by brusque violence; one's last moments should have some dignity.

"I am High Minister Chinta sa-Rokis, of the Ministry of Hydraulic Works, by rank Supervisor of Planetary Water Supplies."

"I am Adwa sa-Soj, Second Prime Coercive of the Sword of the Crimson Dynasty, currently commanding the Household Troop."

"You show punctilious courtesy, according to the precepts of *Sh'u Maz*, Adwa sa-Soj, as might be expected of a Thoughtful Grace of high rank and good lineage."

"Your own deportment, Chinta sa-Rokis, is also a model of Sustained Harmony—in your response to current circumstances, at least."

"The terms of the Vermillion Rescript, swaying the Real World?" she asked.

"Unconditional Apology is required from the following," the officer said, and read the names.

There will be many promotions, Chinta thought mordantly.

"You, High Minister, in recognition of your long service to the Dynasty and the record of your lineage, are, as you see, at the head of the list."

I am the most dangerous and the most likely to successfully flee beyond the current boundaries of the Crimson Dynasty's control, she thought. *Still, recognition of one's importance is always soothing to the ego.*

"There is no supplementary direction to extirpate the lineages?" she inquired in a tone of polite interest. "Not even to the first degree?"

"No. Infants will be required to reside at court for socialization, but at adulthood a reasonable share of the personal properties will be restored and they will be allowed to perpetuate your lines."

"*Tollamune!*" Chinta said in a crisp ringing tone, taking knee, and the others echoed her. "The Emperor is both firm and magnanimously free of personal spite."

"This is both an essential courtesy and, in the main, objectively true; at the risk of seeming to admonish, I state—hypothetical-conditional tense—that event and randomness would in all probability have fallen out more favorably from your perspective if you had kept this fact firmly in mind at all times. Consider the length of the Supremacy's reign."

"I concede that my previous analysis is discredited by event and randomness. From a personal viewpoint, however, this has now become largely irrelevant and I am disinclined to prolonged meditation."

The other ministers walked forward and knelt beside her. The chief Coercives of their households gathered and looked a question at the Thoughtful Grace commander, who nodded permission.

"I acknowledge that your Coercives have not defected," she said. "Nor have they withheld knowledge of an approach by any under my command from their employer."

Another formality, to assist their career prospects. They most certainly would *have defected if I were foolish enough to order a battle, nor would any rational being have blamed them. This fight was lost when our assassin failed. Against the entropy embodied in randomness, there is no victory.*

Aloud, Chinta said, "They have fulfilled their contractual obligations, save for the Last Assistance."

A faint sound came from behind her: the whisper of the steel-and-ceramic casing of a pistol being drawn from a holster. A slight pip came an instant later, a sign that the pressure gauge was showing sufficient methane, and then a *snick-click* as nonlethals were substituted for the usual neurotoxin. A shot into the base of the brain would be quick enough for practical purposes, and would leave her gracefully limp rather than convulsing and spraying the surroundings.

The Coercives of her colleagues made similar preparations. Two more of her own household troops knelt before her to either side, spreading an absorbent towel; it was always in readiness, but usually simply a matter of ceremony . . .

I have lived all but a few moments of my seventy years in the Real World by ceremony, she thought. *It is appropriate that I terminate my world-line in a congruent fashion.*

"I make Apology without Condition to the Ruby Throne. I express my final gratitude and praise to the Emperor for his mercy," she said firmly, drawing the small sharp knife from her sleeve. "Tollamune! Tollamune! Tollamune!"

The edge was kept sharp enough to part a hair drifting downward, and the steel had a slight blood etching; this was not the first time her lineage had made a miscalculation, though few as serious as hers. She set it under the corner of her jaw and drew it down diagonally with a single hard stroke.

There was an instant of intense stinging pain, hot and cold at the same time, and the world vanished.

The Thoughtful Grace shrank back a little from Sajir sa-Tomond's anger. The recorder they had intercepted for him on its journey back to the Palace of Restful Repose fluffed its feathers and hid its head under a wing—memories of cases when the bearer of bad tidings suffered for it having been imprinted on its genes. Then the Tollamune Emperor contained himself with an effort that brought a blue tinge to his ancient lips and a frown to the face of the Imperial Physician.

"I am disappointed!" he said in emphatic mode, leaning back in his chair. "This chain of events is unfortunate in the extreme!"

All the chair's efforts could not massage the tension out of the muscles of his back; he ignored it as he might have the siren call of sleep when alertness was essential. *De'ming* made small humming sounds of distress as the interrupted meal disrupted the smooth progression of the courses, and the physician frowned again. Sajir's appetite had been irregular of late, another sign of stress. Suddenly the sweet-musky scent of the incense and the way it blended with the iodine odor of the chilled soup was nauseating.

There was a ritual to an Imperial meal, even an informal one here in the presence chamber of his personal rooms. The others who had been given the privilege of eating with him stood and took two steps backward from the pearl-inlaid surface, hands in sleeves and faces toward him. Sajir saw, and forced himself to relax, drawing several long deep breaths and feeling his forebrain take command of the hormones. And the deep patterns of the limbic system at the base of his brain, where the club-wielding ape still snarled beneath the most cultured of beings, and the reptile brain below that.

We are not beasts to be commanded by instinct, he thought. *My body readies itself for fight or flight, but neither is appropriate here. I must* think, *not react. Mindless, hasty reaction is the role in which I have cast Prince Heltaw in this round of the Game of Life.* Sh'u Maz!

"Prince Heltaw will *not* sacrifice his hostage; this is a mere bluff," he said meditatively. "To do so would be to lose his last piece."

He took up another wedge of fluffy bread and dipped it in the *nakaw* and nibbled, despite the way it turned to dust in his mouth and caused the threatened closing of his throat. The others sat once more. Several of them were young Thoughtful Grace; it was his habit to invite junior officers of the Sword of the Dynasty to such occasions on a rotating basis, for several purposes. Despite every-thing, he inwardly smiled slightly to see them eat once more with speed and voracity, trying to finish before he lost his temper again. The food of the Imperial table was quite different from that com-monly served in barracks.

The momentary amusement washed away in an ocean of sorrow: *If she dies, it will be as if I have lost Vowin again. I do not think I could* endure that a second time. Even the Imperial role in Sh'u Maz *recognizes that there are limits to what one individual can sacrifice for duty.*

Daiyar cleared her throat in the long-standing signal that meant reluctant-contradiction.

"Supremacy, he will order a lethal excruciation of the Terran if your offspring refuses to meet with him."

Sajir looked at her. She went on, "He will calculate that no amount of acquiescence will be sufficient to spare his lineage in the event of Deyak sa-Sajir's effective accession to the Ruby Throne.

In part this is a projection of his own most likely course of action, were he in her position, and in part a rational extrapolation from the known personality traits of Teyud's . . . Deyak's . . . parents. Thus, he will take revenge before ending his own life. At that point, there would be nothing to lose."

"All or nothing," Sajir murmured. *The problem with that is the likelihood of receiving nothing,* he thought.

"Bring me the Terran, Franziskus Binkis," he said. "And mobilize a battalion, with appropriate transport. Transport for myself as well. Heltaw did not specify a meeting within his own demesne. He is not yet so powerful that he can prevent a Tollamune making transit through Dvor Il-Adazar. Pieces may yet be doubled, to his detriment."

CHAPTER FOURTEEN

Encyclopedia Britannica, 20th Edition
University of Chicago Press, 1998

MARS: History of Contacts

The strategies of the U.S. and Eastbloc missions to Mars have been mirror images of those adopted on Venus. Whereas on Venus the United States landed its probes close to Kartahown, the only large city on the planet, the USASF base on Mars was established on the shores of the Northern Sea, far from any civilized Martian settlement, and made its first contact with the provincial city of Zar-tu-Kan. In turn, the Eastbloc mission was placed close to the curious Petra-like capital of Dvor Il-Adazar, once the center of the Crimson Dynasty's planetary empire, and still the largest and wealthiest of the Martian city-states.

This choice may have derived from a serious underestimation of the power and subtlety of the culture based there.

Mars, Dvor Il-Adazar
Palace of Restful Contemplation
May 27, 2000 AD

Jeremy Wainman almost missed the pain. "Emphasis on the *almost*," he murmured to himself.

They'd put him back in his old cell. *Very Martian*, he thought. *I escaped because someone outside busted me out. So they take precautions against that, and otherwise just stick me back in the same jar. Terrans would have put me in a different cell, or added all sorts of new locks, whether it made sense or not. But if there's no problem, they don't try to fix it. Very . . . sensible.*

They hadn't bothered to feed him, either. Whatever they were planning would be over and done with by the time he really began to weaken with hunger, so why waste food and water and effort?

Also very Martian; I wouldn't have believed that being compulsively sensible *can be so goddamned* annoying. *If it weren't for Teyud . . . and Bad tu-Or, God rest her . . . and Doctor Daiyar and a couple of others . . . I could become sorta prejudiced about them. Poor Sally—I can understand how she felt.*

At least they'd restored the personal kit he'd come with, so he had depilatory cream and wipes to clean with. Looking and smelling a little less like a monkey fresh out of the jungle couldn't hurt, and certainly improved his morale. He paced while he thought; the same set of beady eyes stared hungrily at him from behind the ventilator grille, and the same clawed hand occasionally reached hopefully at his face.

What's Teyud doing? Where is she now? Is she all right, Goddammit?

The door opened. Three of Heltaw's Coercives stood there, two with their pistols leveled; one held a pair of manacles, flexing and writhing in his fingers.

"Extend your hands," the one with the manacles said. "Cause no additional difficulty, or excruciation will be administered. Haste is essential and the irritation born of frustration is rife."

Which boils down to: Don't fuck with me, it ain't the time. But I like the sound of it, a little, anyway. Prince Heltaw's in a hurry. That means things can't all be going his way.

He held out his hands; the Martian flicked the . . . whatever it was . . . and it wrapped around his wrists in an instant double loop, tightening until the bare, suedelike surface was just short of being uncomfortable. He had a strong suspicion that if he tried to wrench his wrists loose, it would clamp down harder, and the glinting, wirelike intrusions in its surface would probably make it a stone bitch to cut.

Well, he thought snidely, *even tying people up with worms can work if you've got forty thousand years to get everything* just so.

They hustled him out of the cell, down the corridor and into the great, hemispherical chamber where the *Paiteng* riders had their lair. He blinked in surprise when they entered; it was empty of people and of every adult riding bird, and there was a litter of gear and papers—very unusual for Martians, who tended to be finicky about neatness unless they were in a tearing hurry. Then they turned along a colonnade flanked by arches, and into an elevator. Despite the fear gripping him, he found himself distracted for an instant by the interior—the crystal walls were shaped like the feathers of a *Paiteng*'s wings, so that you stood as if embraced by them. The effect was striking, even if recent events had made him a little jaundiced about the giant creatures.

The room the doors opened onto was almost as large as the *Paiteng* stables below. *Would you call it a courtyard?* Jeremy thought.

It was open to the sky above, at least visually, though covered by a high arched dome of glassine; within it was a broad shallow bowl chiseled—or gnawed and dissolved—from the reddish native rock, and shaped into concentric rings of terraces. Those bore gardens, tall lacy trees and banks of plants in stone urns or trays, and pavilions ringed by slender columns of jasper and chalcedony. Those might be open or closed off for privacy's sake by an ornamental stone carved into the consistency of lacy fretwork. The strong, almost medicinal perfume of Martian flowers was in the air, and the faint musky-spicy smell of incense.

People thronged the terraces; they weren't crowded, but as close to it as it came on Mars, many of them leaning on the balustrades whose uprights were carved in the likeness of predatory *dhwar* with their wings outstretched, making an endless series of arches. It was quiet, much quieter than it would have been with a Terran crowd of the same size, despite a fair number of children being held up so they could see; just a murmur running like the wind through leaves. And it was *warm*, which was also something he hadn't often experienced on this icebox of a planet.

Then his mouth quirked as he realized that it was only about sixty degrees Fahrenheit—his standards had changed. He was still sweating a little in his longjohns and desert wear and robe. It was moist, as well; an artificial waterfall ran down the opposite side of the bowl, flanked by broad staircases and sprouting upward in a fountain at each level. His sinuses and nose drank in the vapor gratefully and greedily, and he could feel the constant slight ache there start to abate. He'd gotten so used to it that it was the fading that attracted his attention.

"Well, that's extravagance," Jeremy muttered in his own language.

He fell silent when one of the guards prodded him with the narrow muzzle of her dart pistol.

Well, it is, he thought resentfully. *It's like having a bunch of diamond-and-emerald mechanical birds in the trees in your garden, even if it's recycled. It's like the sort of thing the French court did at Versailles before the Revolution. Look at the way the kids are being shown the rare sight of actual running water in the open air . . . though I suppose the dome counts as a kind of cover.*

The center of the bowl-like courtyard dropped sheer for twenty feet, down to an octagonal platform of white marble, cut into squares by strips of jet. It was surrounded by a water moat . . .

Jesus, that's an atanj *board! But it's huge! And where are the . . . uh-oh.*

The Game of Life was occasionally played with living pieces, particularly here in Dvor Il-Adazar, where archaic habits lingered on; he didn't think that any Terran had ever seen it done, certainly nobody from Kennedy Base. Each of the eight sides of the board had an arched stairway leading up to the surface level, gossamer-light structures like spun silver, built so that they could be retracted. They were the "Despot's Road," the way for the master player to access the surface below. Two of them were extended now, one on the eastern side and one on the western.

I don't know what's going on here, but I certainly don't like it.

On the side of the wall opposite the stairs-and-waterfall arrangement was a tall gate, wrought in curling black iron and polished bronze in the shape of lilylike flowers. That showed how old this place was; it had been built during the Lilly Period. A prickle of awe touched his spine. *Atanj* matches had taken their bloody course here when his ancestors were cracking hand-axes out of flint and each other's heads with the result. However many times everything had been renewed, it was a place that had seen crowds like this during the Great Tranquility.

The gates swung open. A flock of ruby-colored birds with blue crests and golden rings on their claws flew through, their long tails following them like foaming curls of plumed silk and their six-foot wings stroking the air in an intricate dance. They cried out, their high musical voices chiming in eerie silvery unison with an effect like echoes from wind chimes:

"Genomic Prince Heltaw sa-Veynau, Proprietor of Aywandis! Through inheritance and ability in the possession of one eighth of the Tollamune genome as a cross on the purest Imperial Administrator breeding, and holder of vast economic resources! Let persons of inferior genetic standing and lesser possessions show due deference!"

There was a long rustle as the crowd adopted social-deference postures; he could hear a child's voice in the sudden hush, asking as his mother tried to shush him:

"Who is that person, mother, and why does he have so many birds talking about him?"

A hundred Coercives came through on unicycles, leaning into the curves as they wove around the perimeter of the *atanj* court. Their blue-trimmed black armor glistened, but it was entirely functional as well. Behind them followed what looked like an oblong brass tray ten feet by five, with a dozen feet on either side, shaped much like a dog's but nearly as large as a tiger's, on the ends of short digitigrade legs that grew from the bottom of the machine. They padded forward with an evenness that left the metal surface moving as smoothly as if it were floating in a bath of oil. On it stood Prince Heltaw, dressed for travel—or war—in a short-sleeved robe that came to his calves, practical dark jacket, trousers, and boots, with only a few platinum ornaments on his harness.

The haughty face was calm, and his long, raven hair was caught back in a fighting bun at the nape of his neck. The tray came to a halt beside Jeremy, and Heltaw flicked out his left hand. A long, thin line looped through the air toward the earthman, swift as the crack of a bullwhip. Jeremy started to dodge, but the pistol prodded him again, and it wasn't the pain-snake after all. Instead, something like the manacles settled around his neck and tightened; it had prickles on the inside, and his skin itched the way it would after pressing too hard with a razor when you shaved—just a hint of rawness and pain. And there was a weird undertone to it, growing as he noticed it, as if he were suddenly not seeing, but *feeling* himself doubled, as if his body had been copied and another of him was a few feet away.

"Step onto the traveling platform, man of the Wet World," Heltaw said.

Jeremy did; there was no give or rocking at all, and it felt like stepping onto a solid ingot; the thing around his neck seemed to contract in perfect unison with his movements, remaining in a taut thumb-thick line between his neck and the Martian's wrist before vanishing up his sleeve.

He noted as he stepped up that the front part of the platform had two eyes tucked underneath it, on stalks that let them see backward as well as to the front, and a foot-long mouth. Luckily, it seemed to be toothless; fangs would have made him more nervous.

"I shall inform your ignorance: This organism linking us is the Dead Man's Worm, connected to my nervous system and now to yours. Should I die, it will instantly crush your throat, at the same time injecting a slow-acting but absolutely lethal neurotoxin for which there is no remedy. This will result in a lethal excruciation, the discomfort of which will make all my previous efforts to that end seem—metaphorical mode—to have been pleasurable caresses. Should I feel pain, you will share it, redoubled."

Heltaw tapped his left heel down on his own right toe. Jeremy suppressed a yelp; there had been a sharp stab right in his big toe, exactly as if someone had stamped on it . . . hard.

"It is now in your interest to hope most earnestly for my physical well-being. Do you comprehend your position?"

"Yes. I'm standing next to a maniac," Jeremy said, trying for the dry tone he thought Teyud would use.

Instead it came out as a croak from a dry throat, but it was the best he could do. Heltaw gave him a glare, but didn't do anything.

Right. He can't excruciate me directly either. This must be a two-way link. He can only hurt me by hurting himself.

Heltaw signaled to the platform with a slight whistle; it turned in place and headed down to the *atanj* board, stepping confidently down the slender bridge. The prince took the position with his back to the west; that was the Usurper end, and a frank statement of self-confidence. At once he stepped down from the traveling device, and Jeremy hopped off as well. The platform turned and trotted back up, laying itself down and training its eyestalks on its master, a pink tongue hanging slightly over its broad lips.

They waited. Jeremy found himself trying not to swallow, because doing so pressed his Adam's apple more against the *thing* around his neck.

The acoustics here were fantastic. He could hear the voices of people in the crowd almost as if they were beside him, the shifting rustle of a robe, a chuckle, a clink as a globe of essence was set in the matching depression in the top of a balustrade, and he suspected that the reverse was true as well.

At least nobody's selling hot dogs and beer, he thought sourly. *"Watch the soppy Terran get it where the domestic egg-layer got it in the esophagus!"*

Then the gates opened again. His heart thundered at the sight of the tall, striding elegance he saw before him, and a pair of yellow eyes met his. Then she nodded very slightly and put her foot on the crystal bridge.

Teyud took in the situation as she walked down the staircase, keeping her hands carefully away from the hilt of her sword and the butt of her pistol.

A pity, she thought. *Heltaw is not altogether lost in hubristic self-regard and consequent arrogant dismissal of possibly negative randomness. But then, if he were, my father would have killed him before this date. Either that, or had no need to kill him.*

The Dead Man's Worm had been developed precisely for this sort of contest . . . what had Jeremy called it? Yes: a Mexican standoff. Even if she were quick enough to slash it before Heltaw could command it to administer its agonizing death, it would do so in the spasm before it died itself, which would leave her with no alternative but to kill Jeremy to spare him excruciation. Her eyes probed his anxiously, but despite gauntness he seemed to be fully functional. He was so gentle and empathetic that you tended to underestimate his core of toughness.

Odd that he should care for me so deeply, she thought. *From his perspective, it must be—metaphorical mode—similar to mating with a* Paiteng.

And through the Invisible Crown, his emotions blazed even more brightly than the chill of Heltaw's malice and throttled rage, a hundred times more than the vast but detached and diffuse interest of the crowd, few of whom really cared who prevailed here. The intensity of the Terran's focus on her made her feel a little abashed; he had forgotten all apprehension for his own safety or the prospect of unbearable pain, and was concerned only for her.

I am committed to this pair-bonding, even though the gaps between us are very large and our time of acquaintance so very short, but can I equal his intensity? she thought. *On balance, do I even* wish *to do so?*

A moment's thought as she glanced within herself; the Crown seemed to make that easier as well, as if she could examine her own emotions from a spectator's perspective.

Fascinating. I do wish *to match them. All the more imperative to bring this matter to a satisfactory conclusion for me, and a deeply distressing one for my remote cousin from Aywandis.*

The staircase retracted smoothly behind her. She clasped her hands and inclined her head fractionally, the greeting of equals. It would not do to anger Heltaw, and he seemed abnormally sensitive to matters of status. Of course, this *was* Dvor Il-Adazar, where such concerns were savored like fine essences, and considered as essential to life as water.

And if I triumph in this game, I must endure this metaphorically flatulence-ridden atmosphere for—possibly—centuries. Like gravity, irony is a force which suffuses the universe with its power.

"In accordance with your communication, I have come to discuss our antagonistic interests," she said.

"You were accompanied by a unit of Thoughtful Grace enrolled in the Sword of the Dynasty?"

She adopted a posture of slight regret. "It was necessary to direct them otherwise, before their conviction that I was making a serious blunder could overcome their reluctance to compel me. They were ready to make Apology afterward."

"Thoughtful Grace are given to immoderate passions and to swiftly decisive action in their pursuit," the Prince said. "In my opinion, the Dynasty allows them entirely too much autonomy in the interpretation of their instructions. Your order was to a high degree of probability a necessary move if we are to conduct our negotiations unhindered."

She ignored his own household Coercives who ringed the rim of the floor around the great sunken *atanj* board, though they were close enough for very good shooting to kill her and spare him. There was something else the Prince was contemplating . . . but she found that the Crown required much more effort to tap the thoughts of someone with Tollamune genes. That was logical; otherwise usurpation would have been impossible in ancient times, which from the chronicles was obviously not the case.

He must control me, or at least my heredity. If I am dead, he becomes once again the nearest heir, although my father may not let that influence him; if I am under his control, the likelihood of the Emperor acceding to his desires is still greater. Controlling my genome combined with my death is an intermediate position, not as satisfactory but better than merely killing me.

"I presume that you will now release the Terran?" she said aloud. "Since I have complied with your wishes."

Heltaw raised one eyebrow. "Please, let us not delay. To survive, I must ascend the Ruby Throne."

Teyud kept her hands in her sleeves, and her body loose and ready to respond instantly. The Imperial Administrator lineages could be physically formidable, and this specimen had been crossed with the Tollamune four generations back; that made him even more dangerous. And she would have to be strictly on the defensive.

"Kill him!" Jeremy cut in, and suddenly lunged backward, dragging his captor off balance.

Heltaw's eyes darted sideways in surprise. Teyud was surprised as well—the move was nonsensical—but reacted instantly nonetheless. The Prince's free hand flashed up and caught her by the wrist as she lunged, but her strength was greater; her dagger pricked him under the angle of the jaw. Jeremy gave a little gasp and clapped his hands to his throat, blood welled between them.

"You cannot kill me without killing your paramour," Heltaw pointed out, breathless and still off balance. "I confront your Despot."

"It is my estimation that you will kill him in any case," Teyud said.

Something, something . . . he feels insufficient fear and far too much hope . . .

"Therefore release the Dead Man's Worm without harm to him. If you do so, I pledge the Tollamune Oath that you and your lineage will not be excruciated or executed or required to make apology."

"Very well," Heltaw said, face like something cast from glassine as he concentrated.

The noose slumped from around Jeremy's neck; he tore the slackening creature free and threw it into the moat around the *atanj* board. Something thrashed in the water as it attacked and ate.

Teyud opened her mouth to speak. Instead she half shrieked, half grunted at the stabbing pain at the base of her head, like a hot needle rammed home into her spine over and over again. Volition fell away; her body staggered, then rose erect again, but as if it were under the control of someone else . . . which was more or less the case.

Heltaw straightened and adjusted his harness and weapons. When he spoke it was in a clear carrying tone.

"I have treacherously violated the implicit terms of my negotiated meeting with Deyak sa-Sajir-dassa-Tomond, in order to secure her compliance through the implantation of a mind-control parasite," he said.

There was a rising murmur of dissatisfaction from the gathered crowd. Heltaw adopted a pose of rueful acknowledgment, tinged with regretful firmness, and continued: "This is in no way a change of policy on my part; I recognize that even the most powerful of individuals must generally maintain his pledged word, even when it is seriously inconvenient in the short term. However, the negative and positive incentives before me were such that I accept the damage to my reputation for probity. If I achieve my goals, I shall make restitution, and as earnest of this: I shall not kill her *vaz-Terranan* paramour at this time, though it is now within my power to do so."

"Oh, shit," Jeremy said quietly.

An unearthly wail came from the amphitheater's gateway, followed by words.

"Tollamune! Tollamune! Tollamune!" a voice cried. "The King Beneath the Mountain comes! Let all align their behavior with his will! Let none harbor thoughts of disloyalty to the Crimson King! *Sh'u Maz!* He who maintains the Harmony of the Real World comes! Show deference!"

There was a manifold rustle of cloth as the crowd, including Heltaw, took knee. Only Teyud stood, lost in the vastness of her skull, looking through eyes like inverted telescopes. Another wave of needles seemed to penetrate the base of her skull, as the creature drove its tendrils into the structure of the brain itself, probing for the higher centers of cognition.

"Abandon all anticipation that I will merely accede to your wishes, Prince Heltaw," Sajir said. "The probability of refusal approaches unity."

The Tollamune Emperor made a small *tsk* sound at the sight of his daughter standing like something carved from a block of wood. Reports indicated that infestation with the control parasite was excruciation of unparalleled intensity.

That was, if not deserved, only to be expected. What had happened to her was obvious; the Thoughtful Grace *were* too headlong, and they *did* depend too much on the straightforward blade. She had probably been alert for all ordinary treachery, ready to meet or parry outright violence. Of course, she had also had the disadvantage of being away from court intrigue and faction most of her adult life. That would have dulled her instincts.

"It would seem that I command the significant pieces," Heltaw replied, with a spare gesture.

Sajir raised a brow. "The *vaz-Terranan?* They are useful at times, true, but I have one of my own."

He indicated Binkis with a slight flick of one ear. The Terran was staring at the rigid form of the Emperor's offspring; there was something disturbing in his fixed gaze. But then, Binkis had always been disturbing. It might be simple madness . . . or could he perhaps sense the Invisible Crown? Data did suggest that persons once touched by the ancient devices remained somehow in contact, as if their worldlines were thereafter entangled. What had Binkis said once . . .

I also see in my mind devices that are not machines at all but relations, *contiguities of time and space as complex as the dance of neurons in a brain and as abstract as a mathematical theorem.*

It was severely annoying to have to operate thus on hints and ambiguities. Not unfamiliar, but annoying.

"Supremacy, you seek to irritate me beyond bearing and thus affect my judgment," Heltaw replied. "I concede that this stratagem has irritated me, but the truth is still plain: The decisive piece on this board is your heir."

"But the heir is only of value while it exists," Sajir said. "Since you cannot destroy, you cannot control absolutely."

"Draw your knife and kill the Terran," Heltaw said to Deyak.

Teyud, Sajir thought.

He cocked his head, watching with interest as her hand went jerkily to her harness and began to draw the blade. Her arm trembled, as if something invisible were forcing it to move against every straining sinew. It was tempting to wait a little, and let the complication of Jeremy Wainman be removed before he proceded.

No, Sajir thought. *I had best intervene. Simplification does not serve my purposes. And I would greatly have appreciated the play of events if someone had intervened on behalf of Vowin.*

"Agreed, you have a *degree* of control," he said to his opponent.

"Cease!" Heltaw said to Teyud. To the Emperor: "Control of the only possible heir of sufficient genomic resemblance."

"On the other hand, I have overwhelming physical force, and may—simply by adjusting my own attitudes and priorities—decide that confounding your ambitions is a task more crucial than anything which happens after my death," Sajir pointed out with cool good humor. "I ruled without an heir for a very long time and presumably would be content to do so again. You, on the other hand, have no fallback position."

Prince Heltaw was far too experienced to show his surprise by any physical movement; Sajir thought he detected a slight flux in the pupils of his eyes.

"Stalemate?" he said.

"Not necessarily. You may return my offspring, and retire to your estates in Aywandis. I will pledge to take no action against you or your lineage as long as you remain passive. This would leave you free to act after my span comes to a close."

"Unacceptable. The loss of prestige would diminish my support to a fatal degree. Nor will I likely have an opportunity to infest the heir again; once infested, twice reluctant to approach."

"Or we could wage war. I can kill you here, but you would take my heir with you . . . and your lineage, I understand, fled by fast *Paiteng* some time ago. They would undoubtedly rally your supporters in Aywandis."

"Supremacy, grant me more tactical *nous* than Chinta sa-Rokis, who thought only of preserving the status quo. *Of course,* my lineage fled. Together with most of my personal Coercives."

Sajir conceded the point with an inclination of the head. "There is little point in destroying infrastructure and killing valuable personnel when the outcome may be settled more economically. Therefore let us use the traditional method of adjudication: the Game of Life. We are already standing on an *atanj* board, after all."

Prince Heltaw adopted a posture of respectful agreement, with ironic exaggeration. "There is extensive precedent for such a course. If your playing in the Game of Life is as passive as your technique in the nonmetaphorical form, then I have little to fear."

"You would be prudent to consider the fact that I have reigned for two hundred years of the Real World. And that I have achieved a nearly maximum life span, while thousands of contemporaries and competitors have not. Perhaps a certain degree of watchful passivity is prudent, where a more headlong approach is contra-survival."

"Your survival is due largely to the fact that you had no close heir," Heltaw pointed out. "Others could afford to wait."

Sajir sa-Tomond smiled slightly. "In point of fact, I *do* have a close heir, particularly considering the past interactions of the Tollamune and Thoughtful Grace genomes. *She* has all the necessary markers to control the Devices."

"An heir whom I now control, as I have demonstrated!"

The ancient face smiled thinly in reply; an ancient wickedness seeming to glow from within for a moment, casting the network of wrinkles into contrast. His voice was imperturbable as it continued, "Yet this, in fact, guarantees my victory. Even if you were to topple me, and sit upon the Ruby Throne—metaphorically, because a linkage would, in fact, kill you—you could hope to hold it only by a genetic merger with my heir. To do otherwise would alienate far too many, beginning with all the Thoughtful Grace lineages, who now have a genetic stake in the matter as well. Thus, my lineage would prevail, with you as merely an episode."

"But this would not constitute victory from the viewpoint of your personal continuity of consciousness."

"Which entropy will sever soon; I freely concede that against *that* opponent, I am overmatched at last. I in turn concede that there would be a deep personal satisfaction in witnessing your demise; yet even if the reverse is true, in a fundamental sense I cannot leave this board defeated, even if my remains are carried from it."

His smile showed teeth. "As the *vaz-Terranan* say, 'Heads I win, tails you lose.' Let the pieces assume their positions."

Heltaw's voice was smoothly cruel. "Deyak sa-Sajir, assume the square of the Chief Coercive. The *vaz-Terranan* shall be Consort."

The earthman they'd called Binkis circled outside the squares of the *atanj* board.

It couldn't *be the one who'd disappeared on Venus twelve years ago, could it? He was supposed to be dead . . . he and his wife died in that cave when the ancient whatever-they-were blew up . . .*

Behind Jeremy, he spoke softly, in English, which probably nobody here spoke except the Emperor. "Among its other attributes, the device that the woman found operates to magnify the will," he said.

"You're *Binkis*?" Jeremy blurted. "Look—"

"I am the Yellow Jester, here in the Court of the Crimson King," the man said cryptically. "There is no time for explanations. The Crown strengthens the will but the parasite subverts exactly that. Strong stimulus *might* make it possible to use the one against the other. Throw double or nothing, *Yanki*. So must I. Administer the strongest stimulus you can."

Jeremy wanted to turn and babble questions, but the dance of death and treachery was beginning across the stone squares of the *atanj* board. Steel flickered and bodies fell; when Teyud fought, it was with the leopard fluency he'd seen before, and her voice was crisp when she called orders to the Coercive pieces. That was a *bad* sign; the filthy thing in her head must be getting a better grip.

The ancient, seamed face of the Tollamune Emperor was impassive as he directed his pieces, a symbolic representation of his actual life's work . . . the Game of Life. He spoke, and an unarmed courtier with a bag of symbolic *valuata* stepped toward Jeremy—a Clandestine Subversionist couldn't take other pieces outright, but it could slide past barriers of Brutes and Coercives as though invisible.

"Usurper's Consort, you are offered extensive properties to defect," he said in a Court accent thick enough to cut, with his voice shaking slightly—he had a good deal riding on this game too. "In return for your information, your personal lineage will be preserved."

Decision welled in Jeremy's mind. *Double or nothing.*

"I accept and will defect!" he said clearly.

Prince Heltaw turned, the trained calm of his face cracking. The defection of a Consort was an important move in *atanj*; it closed off a whole chunk of the board to him. *Now* he was angry, not just annoyed; incredulously angry. The *vaz-Terranan* worm had turned . . .

"Chief Coercive! Coerce the defecting Consort!" he half screamed. "Administer lethal force to deter others!"

Ooops, Jeremy thought. *Her father waited until she could access this square before he moved the Clandestine. Guess he was thinking along the same lines. C'mon, bladder and bowels, don't disgrace me now.*

His guts *did* feel liquid, as those yellow eyes turned coldly on him, and the long blade turned toward him. The half near the hilt still shone, but there was a liquid coat of red on the forward twenty inches. A drop splashed on the marble below as she advanced, feet turned in a perfect Martian fencer's stance.

"Jeremy," she said, as she approached.

It was a soft murmur, dreamy and warm like a whisper on a pillow, an utter contrast to the bleak killer's mask it came from.

"Teyud," he said, his voice husky with fear and with something else. He spread his arms. "I'm not going to fight you."

"Jeremy . . ."

Then she lunged, blurring-swift, and the shock of the steel in his flesh was like a needle of ice. He sank slowly to his knees, look-ing incredulously at the sword through his shoulder. She fell back from the lunge and into stance, pulling the blade free—and then it *really* began to hurt. Not as bad as Heltaw's pain-snake, but more real and less virtual; his body knew he'd actually been damaged now, and that his life might pour out. He stifled a scream and clutched at the wound with one hand.

"Teyud, it's okay," he whispered, his eyes locked on hers. "I know it isn't you doing it. I love you. Remember me."

She lunged again, fluid and swift; the blade pricked his chest just left of his breastbone. It barely dimpled the robe, but the needle point still pierced his skin, and he could feel another trickle of blood starting, this one running down his chest. Teyud's face was as calm as ever, but she was *sweating*, beads of moisture rolling down into her eyes from her brow, and he could see the faintest trembling.

Jeremy kept silent, eyes still meeting eyes. Behind her Prince Heltaw nearly left his Despot's square and stopped himself only an instant before he forfeited the game. Instead he pursed his lips and whistled, a coded modulation.

Teyud screamed. The steel bit a little deeper into Jeremy's chest muscles, and he could feel it quiver with the tension in her hand. From behind the Emperor's square another whistle rose. Teyud screamed again, and blood was running down her face as well, from her nose and eyes and ears; he could smell the rank salt-and-copper smell of it, stronger than his own.

Then she stumbled back, her face working in a grimace that was half agony and half a feral determination like a wolverine in a trap. Something was *wrong* with her, or with Jeremy's eyes; she seemed to shimmer as he watched, a silvery nimbus that crackled on a level too low for vision to catch. The sword dropped from her hand, but it seemed to *drift* downward, the flexing bow as it struck the stone and sprang back visible as an undulation in the metal. Teyud was screaming continuously now, raw animal sounds. Her hands went to her head, and she stumbled in a circle howling like a wolf.

God, I've killed her, Jeremy thought numbly. *It's cutting up her brain inside, I've killed her.*

The knowledge that he would die with her didn't seem to help, but he knew that the thought of living wasn't something he could bear.

She fell to her knees, but it was as if she were moving in a different time frame than everyone else. The whole complex dance of the game had ceased, and the great-eyed Martian faces weren't locked or inscrutable for once. Only the Emperor himself seemed calm. When Teyud spoke, the words rolled inhumanly deep and slow.

"*That . . . Which . . . Compels!*"

There *was* something wrong with the way she looked; it was like staring at a photographic negative with the colors reversed, but also like staring into the heart of a sun. The Invisible Crown wasn't invisible any more, and the glowing hum that came from it made every cell in his body ache. When she stood, a wave of silver light washed out in a blast wave like an explosion; it didn't strike him, but he fell backward helplessly anyway.

It isn't light. I'm not really seeing it with my eyes at all. That's just how my brain's interpreting it because I don't . . . know . . . how . . .

She screamed again, and flung her hands upward. The column of light around her began to swirl. Prince Heltaw looked up from the surface of the *atanj* square and screamed in counterpoint. He drew his dagger and began plunging it into his own chest, over and over again, long after he should have been dead.

Another shriek, but there seemed to be modulation in it now. A second column of light surrounded Franziskus Binkis; it whirled *inward*, into the substance of him. Jeremy stared with his mouth gaping, and . . .

He's smiling. He's smiling, and it's dissolving him.

"*Jadviga,*" the man said.

Blackness.

Teyud's mind felt like a vast raw wound. Thought was excruciation beyond bearing; she stumbled and shook her head. Something fell away from her neck with a wet *thock* on the smooth marble.

Her father lay on his back in the Despot's square. His face was smoother now; she saw the Imperial physician shaking his head in bewilderment.

"Come!" she said.

The word seemed to tear its way through her larynx; it sounded barely human, but he obeyed; the Thoughtful Grace stayed around their Emperor's body, heads bowed in grief.

The physician reached toward her. "Attend . . . *him*," she said. "Quickly!"

CHAPTER FIFTEEN

Encyclopedia Britannica, 20th Edition
University of Chicago Press, 1998

THE ANCIENTS: Purpose and the Lords of Creation

As the twentieth century draws to a close, humanity is confronted with an existential crisis, as the implications of what our astronomers and astronauts have discovered over the last two generations sinks in.

That we are not the only planet with intelligent life has been strongly suspected since the late nineteenth century, and obvious since the mid-twentieth. That life is common among the stars is now also obvious, and we have no reason to doubt that such life is intelligent, too. The truly troubling feature of the universe that we have discovered is this: Our solar system itself has been extensively reshaped by intelligent design, for at least the last two hundred million years. We inhabit not so much a world as an *artifact*.

We have dubbed those responsible the ancients, but other than one enigmatic artifact and the awesome power indicated by their accomplishments, we know virtually nothing of them, not even whether they still exist.

We now know that Mars and Venus were sterile until terraformed and seeded with earthly life. We cannot *prove* that Earth itself was not turned into a life-bearing globe by the same ancients; all we can be reasonably sure of was that if they did so, they did it at a much earlier period. The same is true of our wider stellar neighborhood; we cannot tell whether the life-bearing worlds we have detected are "natural" or not, or indeed whether the evolution of the universe itself is "natural" in the sense of being the product of the blind operation of natural law. And the enigmatic objects observed farther in toward the galactic core—the near-invisible stellar-sized constructs detectable only by their emission of waste heat—pose questions even more troubling.

All we can say with any confidence about the ancients is that they possessed powers beyond our comprehension, in their nature if not their effects. What was their purpose? The general opinion among those in the scientific community, that they represent some gigantic ongoing experiment in the development and interactions of life, is plausible—but it may be simply a professional deformation, a projection of our own motives onto the alien other.

There are two possible responses to the universe in which we find ourselves. The first is despair that we are simply the laboratory rats of minds as far beyond our comprehension as that of a human is beyond a rat. The other is exhilaration in the knowledge that intelligence can transcend itself, and eventually wring from the fabric of reality powers equivalent to those mythology attributed to gods, and that we ourselves may become the Lords of Creation.

Mars, Dvor Il-Adazar
Hall of Received Submission
June 21, 2000 AD

"You sure you want to go through with this?"

"I just wish I had Sally here to be Best Person," Jeremy said.

Robert Holmegard and Dolores were in Earth-style diplomatic garb, white tie and tails and long black dress respectively, with only the discreet earphones at all out of place. Jeremy wore a robe of shimmering moth-silk that had been woven when Charlemagne was crowned. It looked almost plain compared to some of the others in the vast arched hall below the Ruby Throne. The scale of the building should have made the Throne look insignificant; somehow it didn't. The rows of gorgeously clad dignitaries stretched back into the distance, leaving the central isle clear, lit more brightly by the glass-fiber circles in the uppermost arch.

Banners hung in the shadows above on either side—the banners of kingdoms thirty thousand years dead; the murals portrayed their lords kneeling in submission before Timrud sa-Enntar.

From their niches in the walls, man-high birds like living jewels sang of glory in a language long dead even on Mars. The ranks of armored Thoughtful Grace below them might have been carved themselves, save for the watchful golden eyes. Incense scented like cloves and cinnamon smoked into the air, like a soothing fire along the nerves.

"Washington is ripshit," Holmegard said quietly. "You're going to be in deep, deep trouble if you ever go home again."

"I *am* home," Jeremy said, and felt the same ridiculous grin trying to break through on his face.

He suppressed it; wouldn't do to grimace like a monkey, not in public.

I've been keeping straight-faced all through the ceremonies, he thought. *This is the end of it. Well, except for all the other ceremonies, which will be a pain in the ass, but it's worth it.*

"And if you think Washington's ripshit, think about how Beijing's feeling. All their people *are* going home, the entire base."

He nodded slightly to the glum-faced rank of Eastbloc diplomats. They were probably still adjusting to the fact that they'd been parasite-ridden puppets for years, something they'd realized only after the vile things had been removed . . . and he was very glad that Teyud had ordered the entire stock destroyed and the records of how to make them trashed and lethal excruciation decreed for anyone who tried to re-create them. A lot of the Martians had thought the decree unreasonable and hasty . . .

And I just don't care, he thought happily.

"Yes," Dolores said. "But their toys are staying."

Which was the reason the Despot of Zar-tu-Kan was here to

offer submission, as well as many others—that, and the presence of the Invisible Crown. One good thing about the Martian reasonableness that could be so annoying was that when they saw the game was up they shrugged and made the best of it.

"We'll have a much better friend in a Mars that's united and on the way up again," Jeremy said firmly. "Just remember to bargain in good faith from now on. The bad guys didn't, and look what it got them."

The heraldic birds stooped from their perches in an aerial dance and cried out, in voices melodious but stunningly loud even in a space that dwarfed St. Paul's:

"Take knee before the Emperor who holds and sways the Real World! The Tollamune comes! Bearer of That Which Compels! Wearer of the Invisible Crown of the Crimson Dynasty! The King Beneath the Mountain! The Crimson King! The Lord of earth and sky! Ruler of all who live! *Take knee and bow your heads to the Tollamune will!"*

A vast rustling followed as the last echoes died and the multitude knelt. All but the Holmegards; they were, after all, the representatives of the Republic, and just bowed or curtsied.

Jeremy took knee with the rest. *What's good enough for the rest of the folks is good enough for you, old son,* he thought, looking down at the white marble set with semiprecious stones in High Tongue glyphs that recorded glories vanished before the ice came down from the north on Earth. *Besides, you get a special role.*

Up the living carpet of red fur that covered the pathway came the *pad-pad-pad* of many feet. The platform on which Teyud stood was platinum, burnished and set with intricate patterns in ruby and gold; the birds circled above it in a spiral that reached up into the light-haze along the arch of the roof far above, singing "Tollamune! Tollamune! Tollamune!"

Jeremy's throat went dry as the platform halted. Teyud stood like an image; then her right hand came out, palm uppermost, the only motion save for the imperceptible rise and fall of her chest beneath the crimson robe.

He came to his feet gracefully—and, Jesus, but this would be a time to trip over the hem of the robe! He stepped up onto the platform and laid his hand on hers; she closed her fingers around it and the platform paced its stately way up the strip of red.

It sank to the ground before the Ruby Throne; there was a recess in the stone, so that it sank flush with the pavement. There was another chair, much more ornate than the monumental plainness of the Ruby Throne but smaller and three steps down on the dais. Jeremy stopped before it and turned; he kept his eyes firmly above the heads below. Having that many eyes staring at you—and knowing how many were alive with envy and/or hatred—was a bit disconcerting.

"The bitterness of thrones" was a saying around here. He suspected there were similar ones back on Earth.

Teyud stood for a moment facing the throng. "*Teyud* shall rule," she said clearly, proclaiming her throne-name.

A vast murmur went through the throng. That was the first time any Tollamune had used it; a strong signal that precedent wasn't going to dominate *this* Emperor's reign.

A great rippling chant replied, Martian voices beneath the birds: "Tollamune! Tollamune! Tollamune!"

Then she sat and leaned backward. Jeremy licked his lips, waited the prescribed thirty seconds—the protocol-masters had casually informed him it would kill him if he didn't—and did the same. He didn't like the prospect of contact with another Martian nerve-interface machine-animal, but there wasn't any choice. And Teyud had to do it, too; you couldn't really *be* Emperor unless the devices accepted you.

At first there was simply a sting in the back of his neck. Then he was . . .

Here and not here. This is amazing. *I can see and feel and smell just like always, and I could disengage and stand up if I had to, but . . .*

It was as if he had an extra set of eyes—thousands of them, in fact. Seeing thousands of *worlds*, created ones . . . while the one he usually lived in was immobile, like a freeze-frame.

The face of Sajir sa-Tomond smiled at him as he strolled up to the garden bench where Jeremy sat beside Teyud. The woman on his arm had a look of her; perhaps a little harsher and more eaglelike, but she was smiling, with a small bird sitting on one finger and preening itself. And Sajir was young, his sleek slim body clad only in a soft kilt. The gardens of a younger Mars spread about them, with a view over a balustrade down to a lake.

"I feel to a degree as if I were taking another's credit," Teyud's father said. "My own personal memories only run to a few moments before I left the Tower to rescue you from the consequences of your haste."

Teyud nodded. "I will share those memories, Father," she said. "Though they were somewhat disorganized." A smile quirked her lips. "One might say my mind was not my own just then."

The dead Emperor laughed with the living. "And Mother," Teyud added to the woman.

"Strange to meet one's offspring so long after one's death," the woman said, and lifted her hand; the bird flew off, whistling. "But . . . Sajir says the *vaz-Terranan* have a saying: 'Better late than never.'"

To Jeremy: "It is even stranger to realize that you are merely memories yourself, fellow consort. Enjoy even the least pleasant aspects of your real existence! But the company here is good, and the environment as pleasant as we can imagine . . . exactly as pleasant."

Jeremy nodded. *I am seriously weirded out,* he thought.

The people in front of him didn't exist, really. They *thought* they existed, and they had all the subjective *experience* of being alive; but all they really were was, as she'd said, memories—stored in the vast protein computers that were part of the Ruby Throne. One day he'd be nothing but memories here himself—or he'd be immortal, depending on whether you thought a perfect copy of something *was* the something or wasn't. He supposed it depended on the soul and that sort of thing. Most Emperors apparently died in communion with the Throne, and didn't experience any discontinuity; they went unconscious there and "woke up" here, wherever here really was . . .

Too complicated for a country boy from New Mexico, he decided. *Jesus, though, what a way to do research! The whole of Martian history is stored in here—and I can get it from the Emperors who made it happen, and their consorts!*

Sajir nodded to Teyud. "You are the working member of our lineage now," he said. "We can advise you—all but a few who are somewhat sullen—but my first warning is that *tokmar* itself is by comparison a benign addiction. The world in which you must operate is the *Real* World. This secondary one that we . . . figments . . . inhabit is more appealing in many ways because it responds to our will; but it *is* secondary, and derivative."

"I comprehend the temptation," Teyud said gravely. "But I have far too much interesting work before me to feel any desire to linger overlong through despair or boredom. I will . . . visit."

"Excellent," Sajir said. "And now we must proceed to the integration. It has been a very long time since that could be done with full efficiency, since the Invisible Crown was lost."

A brow raised. "And never before with a *vaz-Terranan* as consort."

Both his brows went up. "Oh, remarkable!" he breathed.

Jeremy started to his feet. If that meant anything here; he could tell his body was simply sitting, on the consort's throne back in the Hall of Received Submission. The gardens around him were suddenly . . . *gone*. Instead he stood in a gray nothing, with a gray surface under his feet which seemed to be *crawling* somehow, as if each individual nano-scale piece of it were blinking in and out of existence. Teyud's mother and father were gone, but she was beside him, and—

"Binkis!" she said.

The Lithuanian, or his facsimile, looked back at her. "No," he said. "Binkis and his conjugal partner are elsewhere. They have been of assistance, within their limitations, and will be given a more satisfactory environment. This is the most suitable interface for communication with you, and I have tapped and duplicated its data-storage and integration facilities; it should serve for this one occasion."

"One occasion?" Teyud said sharply.

"The contamination is severe enough as it is. The primary supervisory pattern has been fully reactivated by the anomalous data. Contact with the True Source is overdue by—" a hesitation, and the bony face tilted a little, like a bird, or possibly a machine—"three thousand Martian solar periods. Six thousand of Earth's."

"You're that thing that was on Venus," Jeremy said slowly.

Teyud gestured impatiently; he'd told her that story. "No," she said. "That was not a sentient entity, judging from the description. This apparently is."

Errrkkk! Jeremy thought. *I suppose she's used to the thought of artificial entities—all her ancestors and their main squeezes are just that, after all. Seriously icky and weird, though.*

The Binkis-interface nodded. "That was a subroutine of lower capacity. Primary storage was on Mars, with its greater geological stability.

I"—he indicated his "body"—"am located beneath the Mountain, with a heat-tap as my primary energy source."

"Are *you* a sentient entity?" Teyud asked, curiously.

And I feel like gibbering, Jeremy thought. *Jesus, don't I have enough on my plate already?*

"That is a matter which the semantics of this language, or the others your two species have created, are inadequate to address."

The Binkis-interface smiled stiffly. "To simplify: I was created to oversee a program of . . . the nearest analogue is *studies*. But I was intended to be under closer supervision. Again, there are semantic difficulties and what I have said is seriously misleading. Suffice it to say I must now make a decision at the very limits of my permitted autonomy."

There was a long pause. At last Teyud spoke: "And your decision is?"

"Given the degree of intraplanetary interaction, I will proceed to the next stage."

"Next stage of *what?*" Jeremy blurted out.

"That was strange," Jeremy said several hours later, in the Imperial private quarters.

"Private" was a matter of definition. He'd insisted that the *De'ming* servants usually on hand to pour drinks and fetch things be sent out; Teyud hadn't seen the point, but hadn't argued, either. Now she looked down at him, braced with her forearms on his chest. There *were* advantages to the lower gravity . . .

The great bed rocked slowly, hung from the ceiling by its chains; the furs and silks were pushed down to the foot, and a flask of essence stood on a pillar of crystal by the sideboard. The light was low, starlight and moonlight collected by receptors at the summit of the Tower and channeled to this chamber. Music sounded in the background, soft and languorous.

Teyud leaned down and kissed him on the nose. "Slightly strange, but I am becoming used to it," she said. "And to think that only a few months ago, I had nothing to look forward to but ennui."

Then she tickled him. Martians didn't get ticklish, and she found it fascinating. Things went on from there; when they'd settled down again, he said, "No, what happened in the throne room."

"Yes, but speculation is futile without further—"

The door sang, breaking in on the birds and silencing them. They looked at each other in surprise; *nobody* was going to interrupt what amounted to the Emperor's wedding night without a very, very good reason. They sighed together, rolled out of the bed and threw on robes. Teyud made a step toward her weapons belt and then left it; with the Invisible Crown, it wasn't really necessary, not here.

The door rolled open. Notaj sa-Soj stood there, his face pale beneath its natural olive. Even more surprisingly, Robert Holmegard was there, too.

"Supremacy," the guards' commander said. "A strange phenomenon has . . . appeared. In Tharsis."

"That's not the half of what's happened off Bermuda," the ambassador said. "And allowing for the lag in transmission time between here and Earth, at *exactly* the same moment. And on Venus, too. Your Majesty, we'd like an explanation."

Teyud's brow went up; she gestured, and the lights brightened. Even then, Jeremy blushed a little; the tousled state of the bed was rather obvious. The Tollamune Emperor brushed through into the presence room that lay beyond the bedchamber.

"Best you had explain first," she said. Then she smiled. "I told my father that I was unlikely to be bored. It appears I was more correct than I anticipated."

Mars, Dvor Il-Adazar
Moon-World, Initial Base
July 19, 2000 AD

"Well, that's impressive," Jeremy said.

The Tollamune Emperor simply nodded. *If this does not impress, then the mind observing it is immune to the sensation. Mine is fully engaged with sentiments of awe and wonder.*

From the airship they could see the outline of the Gate simply by the cloud that resulted instantly when denser, warmer, moister air pushed through into the thin cold atmosphere of Tharsis. That was magnificent enough, with the setting sun turning it ruddy and gold, an arch three miles high and six across at surface level, as if a giant invisible oval had been pushed down into the ground to its midpoint. From the other, eastern side it was an impervious blankness. From the west . . . things came through. Came through from somewhere absolutely else.

"Things such as that river," she murmured.

Though it did not fill the entire gate, it was still vast, bigger than the Grand Canal at its greatest extent and of considerably greater flow—Jeremy had compared it to the Amazon. Already at Teyud's command thousands were at work channeling the torrent that poured through, De'ming and laborers and turtle-shaped earthmoving machines puffing and grunting a thousand feet below. There was a long stretch—five hundred miles—before the course of the land would take it into the Great Northern Sea. Her mind whirled at the thought of the life the superb, low-mineral water could bring to that stretch of the Deep Beyond, when properly canalized.

Though perhaps my mind is merely showing its parochial limits, she thought, and her hand crept into Jeremy's.

He linked his fingers with hers. "Shall we?" he said.

"At the appointed time . . . ah, yes."

An airship came through the fogbank; it was the *Questing Dhwar,* a fast scout of the Imperial fleet.

"All . . . clear . . ." she read, as a signal lamp flickered from its bow.   "No . . . new . . . hazards . . . encountered . . . fascinating . . . phenomenon . . . in . . . excessive . . . abundance . . ."

She felt bitter envy for a moment that Notaj had been first to visit, but it was illogical and politically impossible for the reigning Tollamune to take irresponsible risks. She was stretching the boundaries of the permissible by taking herself and the consort through now, weeks later.

"The savants are having a field day with the life forms coming through," Jeremy said. He cocked an eyebrow. "Nothing dangerous so far, and much that is quite compatible. I particularly liked those fish, done in *asu*-batter."

She took a deep breath, savoring the ozone and lubricant smells of the control gondola. And the fish *had* been delicious, even if Jeremy insisted on calling them "silent immature canids" for some reason.

"Forward," she said.

The crew were Thoughtful Grace of the Household; despite their palpable excitement, they kept to a disciplined sequence of essential comments as the *Tollamune Rebirth* turned and headed into the stiff headwind coming out of the . . . artifact. The engines panted, but this hull and power system were derived from a warcraft designed to operate during storms, and the airspeed indicator writhed to show a ground speed of more than fifty miles an hour. Clouds closed in, and she could see veritable beads of water appearing on the windows. Teyud had seen actual rain once or twice, on the slopes of the Mountain, but it still seemed unnatural.

Then everything lurched. "Valve ballast!" Adwa sa-Soj said crisply. "Maintain neutral buoyancy!"

Sand rumbled out into the air from the keel. Not too much, for though the pull of this place was heavier than that of the Real World, the denser air also improved the efficiency of the hydrogen tanks. *Paiteng* flew well here, too.

"The air of another world," she said softly.

Everything felt heavier; a little more than ten percent heavier, no great matter for a Thoughtful Grace, and tolerable for a standard form.

Perhaps we will use tembst *to adjust colonists*, she thought. *Or perhaps it will not be worth the trouble.*

Below her, the river shone in the light of a sun smaller that that of the Real World and with a slightly greenish tinge to its yellow. That was not the only light in the sky; there were two moons, far larger than those she'd been born under, and also a great banded giant that covered a third of the sky, yellow and white and more . . . and this new world revolved around *it*, not the primary.

As they turned and rose, she could see the vast stretch of mud where the natural course of the river had been; from six thousand feet, it ran glistening to a sea on the edge of sight. On either side were lush forests of unfamiliar, olive green trees, some hundreds of feet tall; beyond natural levees rolled parkland, covered with a low-growing stuff whose reddish-green tint was the only homelike thing about them. Far and far in the distance was a line of dreamlike white, mountains far lower than the Mountain but large enough for year-round snows. The precise seasonal rhythms here were as yet unknown, and they would be complex. The gas giant gave off a significant quantity of heat itself and calculations were still under way as to the precise orbits involved.

"Open to the environment," she ordered.

The alien air rolled in as the armored glassine was cranked up; it was full of an unexpected freshness, like a garden under a dome, but wilder and sweeter and utterly free of the slight tang of dust that had been the backdrop of her life. It was as warm as equatorial high summer, and the dampness was almost uncomfortable. One would have to dress more lightly here; it would even be comfortable to go naked save for utility harness, as in a sealed environment.

"Our crops and domestic animals will probably require modification," she said. "Of course, local material will also be useful."

As they swung over the open ground a group of hexapodal creatures panicked at the flier's shadow and thundered away; she blinked in surprise, her nicating membrane sliding over her eyes as she estimated their numbers.

"Greater than a million. This is an abundant biosphere," she said. "Odd. I cannot even describe their social unit; we have not named them yet. *Owkimi?*"

That meant literally "a group of beasts characterized by six limbs." Not particularly poetic, but accurate.

"This vista resembles some tales of the most ancient times, when the first sentients emerged to name the life they encountered for the first time. It is as if I now inhabit a literalized metaphor."

"Yeah, *owkimi* is finicky enough for Demotic," he said. "It all reminds me of reconstructions of the Great Plains back home. Though the buffalo didn't have six legs and four eyes and spikes on the ends of their tails and slate gray skins with cream-colored stomachs."

"Yes, we are definitely not dealing with an introduced flora and fauna," she said thoughtfully. "Although the basic biochemistry suggests that there were indeed linkages, if at a more remote period. There will be surprises."

"You say 'surprises' as if it that were a bad thing," Jeremy chuckled . . . in English.

After a moment she nodded. In Demotic, a surprise *was* a bad thing unless you specified otherwise; the unexpected was usually negative and often lethal. There were advantages to knowing another language, in the way it gave you multiple perspectives and promoted self-questioning of your world-view. Not *all* of the surprises here would be bad, not on a world that teamed with life and did not die.

And now the Real World also has alternatives.

The savants said that it would be a very long time before pressure equalized on both sides of the gate—a planetary atmosphere was a most massive object. The effects on the Real World would be far greater than those on the new planet . . . which reminded her that they must establish a name for it.

New World? That would be appropriate, though it posed the difficulty of an infinite-regression series: Would you name the next accessible planet Newer New World, and then Still Newer New World?

"Hear the Tollamune will!" she said. "This planet shall be known as *Vow'da!*"

A pleased murmur went through the crew, and then a brief cry of "Tollamune!"

The name played off her mother's Thoughtful Grace title—Vowin also derived from the root for "swift"—and the literal meaning was Moon-World, which was objectively appropriate.

Three more airships were lashed down to the ground by the campsite atop the bluffs, a little way from the rows of temporary shelters and lines of tethered *rakza* and *Paiteng* and the beginnings of permanent structures as machines burrowed and ate and transformed; the skeletal form of a temporary docking tower was already rising there, made from the huge trunks of the lowland trees. A few cargoes of those had already been floated through the gate; timber merchants from Dvor Il-Adazar to Zar-tu-Kan were going into quiet frenzies at the prospective accumulation of *valuata*.

"And this is not the only gate upon this planet," she said meditatively.

"At least one other; I wonder where the hell that one goes? Wasn't *that* a surprise. Maybe Earth didn't get the best of it after all. *Theirs* just leads to the inside of a habitable sphere. Claustrophobic, if you ask me."

"A very *large* sphere," she pointed out.

"What's a thousand billion times the surface area of Earth?" he said.

"A very *large* sphere," she said.

"Well, yes, but it's the *principle* of the thing."

She thought about that for a moment and then squeezed his hand. "I believe your sense of humor will distort my mind, over time," she said.

"Good," he replied. A sly look. "I wonder what parareproductive coitus would be like upon this—"

"Vow'da."

"Yes, Vow'da."

"I do not think my added weight will discommode you even amidst vigorous intromission," she said solemnly. "But we must make the experiment. A course of experiments, rather. The matter is worthy of serious and earnest study from all possible angles of approach."

A signal lamp flashed from the ground as the *Tollamune Rebirth* came nearer and began to slant down through the air. Ground crew waited there, as did the contingent of the Sword of the Dynasty and the rest of the pioneers as well. Teyud read the message.

"Notaj sa-Soj . . . Commanding . . . Base One . . . I . . . express . . . obedience . . . to . . . the . . . Dynasty . . . and . . . note . . . that . . . the . . . hexapodal . . . animals . . . are . . . exceptionally . . . tasty . . . when . . . roasted . . . with . . . a . . . crust . . . of . . . *narwak* . . . several . . . are . . . in . . . preparation . . . suggest . . . you . . . dock . . . soon. Ah, Notaj maintains his pose of whimsical irreverence."

"A man after my own heart," Jeremy said.

Teyud turned toward him and smiled again, touching him lightly on the cheek.

"This echoes my sentiments, but I direct them toward you," she said.

They kissed as the *Tollamune Rebirth* was drawn downward to the soil of the new world.